MacDonald's Choice

John Little

© 2019 John Little

© Photographs 2019 John Little

All rights reserved

No part of this publication may be reproduced, stored in a retrieval system, stored in a database and/or published in any form or by any means, electronic, mechanical, photocopying, recording or otherwise, without the prior written permission of the publisher.

ISBN 9781692477073
MacDonald's Choice

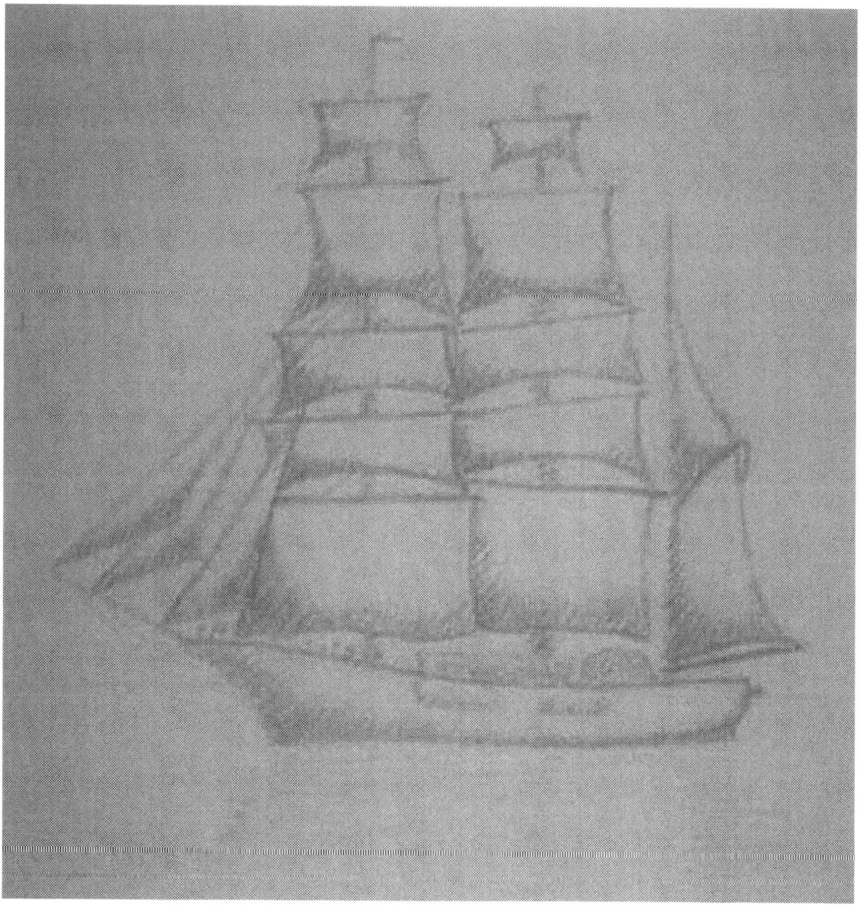

To my wife Ruth

Preface

In the history of the sea there are many incidents and stories that excite admiration and often disbelief because of the sheer scale of the heroism and fortitude involved in them. Among these tales are a very few which tell of people undertaking extraordinarily long voyages across open ocean in vessels that are little more than rowing boats, perhaps with a sail to use if the wind is favourable. For people to pit themselves against the great oceans, to battle wind and weather and to brave all that a furious nature can hurl at them, is something that even today makes heroes of the men and women who undertake such things. The names of Francis Chichester and Alec Rose rang round the world not so long ago for their single-handed voyages around the globe, whilst more recently Chay Blyth became famous for doing it non-stop by going westwards. Robin Knox-Johnson had already done so by going eastwards; Blyth already had national and international fame when he and John Ridgeway rowed across the Atlantic in 1966. These were all voyages made with ample provisions, good communications and the best equipment available, but they brought honours and celebration to the people who achieved them, and rightly so. In our own time, Ellen MacArthur broke the world record for the fastest circumnavigation of the globe by a sailing boat in 2005 and international and national plaudits flowed in. The people who do these things could almost be seen as heroes by design.

A century ago feats of endurance at sea were often involuntary, though not necessarily; Joshua Slocum in 1895 was the first person ever to sail around the world single-handed, but again he did it by design and was equipped for the purpose. There were, however, other great voyages that were involuntary and the one that stands out above all the rest is the journey of Captain William Bligh and his men who were cast adrift from *HMS Bounty* in 1789. Nineteen men, crammed into a twenty-three foot boat with minimal food and water sailed and rowed 3,500 nautical miles to safety. It was a feat of seamanship and endurance that inspired awe when people learned of it. Even when public opinion turned against Bligh for his perceived cruelty that caused the Bounty's crew to mutiny, grudging respect was given to the astonishing feat of seamanship that accompanied his return home.

Ernest Shackleton took an adapted open boat, the James Caird from Elephant Island to South Georgia in 1916, a distance of 800 miles in a desperate bid to get help for his stranded crew. He was successful in his aim, and he and his boat crew became national heroes, respected and honoured. There are doubtless many others, such as Willem Bontekoe's open boat voyage from Java to Batavia in 1618, but it may well be that some have slipped from history, quietly unnoticed, and that they deserve another look. One such is the subject of this book. It would be wrong to place a spoiler here, but there is no harm in stating that this story is based on real events and on real people. In some cases I have invented background detail for them, and as with all historical novels, I have put dialogue into their mouths that they may never have said. On the other hand, all my characters existed, and in some cases the words they speak are direct quotations. It is necessary to take liberties with thoughts and words in order to breathe life into their actions, but I hope that what I have done sounds at least plausible. The historical detail is all real and verifiable and indeed may be found on the internet and in online newspapers from the time.

I wish to thank my wife, Ruth, and David Banks of Beechville, Nova Scotia, for proofing the book; a painstaking and vital task, the first stage in publishing. My cousin Gordon Little has drawn a very evocative picture of a barque as a frontispiece which I am grateful for. I would also like to thank my beta readers Kate Roxburgh, Gerard Keegan, Eunice Small, Betty Telford, Irene Martin and Rebecca Ruth Hebda, for their comments and help in ironing out any absurdities or anomalies. I am very grateful to Linda Gowans on the Isle of Lewis for translating MacDonald's Gaelic for me. Special thanks must go to the descendants of Thomas Morgan and John Crone who have read this work and also commented helpfully, and to Maggi Gibson, who put me in touch with Captain Lattimore's family. Robin Cameron who is related to Captain Lattimore provided invaluable help and useful detail for which I am very grateful. I acknowledge with thanks the use of the British Newspaper Archive, because although I have not quoted their material, without it I could not have written the book. This is a revised version of my original novel, because Gus MacDonald from the Isle of Lewis drew my attention to material that I did not know existed until after original publication. I am grateful to him for referring me to *The Gaelic Vikings* by James Shaw Grant, which was invaluable in providing detail, which has given my novel a better measure of authenticity and I acknowledge that and am thankful for it.

Finally, in the last fifty years there has been some small mention of what happened on Palmyra Atoll in 1888 in a few local newspapers in Cumbria. The version of events that was published was so inaccurate as to mislead several families and a whole community and this was a regrettable thing. The version of those same events that is set forth in this book is fiction; but I have to observe that it remains a far more accurate retelling of what happened to the survivors of the *Henry James* than anything set out in those newspapers. It is my hope that the reader not only enjoys the story, but marvels at the strength, determination and endurance of the people who did the things described in it.

                                John Little, January 2020

Chapter 1

The Barque

Donald MacDonald, first mate of the iron barque *Henry James*, might be excused for his thoughts being absent from his ship, but he was not on duty, so it did not matter that much. He knew the captain was hosting dinner to the passengers aft in the small dining saloon, but he was excused attendance from the task of keeping them entertained because he was to relieve the second mate, John Crone, at 10.00pm when the first watch began. To him it was a blessing because he was not a man fond of gatherings. It must not be thought that he was any sort of misanthrope, because he was not, but he liked to pick and choose his company. To a small group of friends he could be ebullient, good humoured and eloquent, but in a group of strangers he was always the man who stood silently listening and saying nothing. If confronted with a crowd, or if there was any hint of having to speak in front of any audience, he was tongue-tied and quite unable to think straight. People generally thought him a dour man of few words, and his somewhat lugubrious face, clean-shaven and hiding nothing, seemed to confirm this in their minds, but they did not know him. His true nature revealed itself only to a select few, or to his aunt when he was at home, which was where he wished to be at this very moment. He was the son of the headmaster of a small village school at Bayble on the Isle of Lewis, though his family originally came from Bernera and he had been born in Stornoway. It was not often that he felt a pang of homesickness, a most inconvenient thing in a deep-sea mariner, but here, on the far side of the world, he missed his Aunt Margaret. Donald's parents were both dead by the time he was seventeen years old and his aunt supplied the place of a mother to both himself and his brother John who was the ship's carpenter on the *Henry James*. Her house was the only home they had and they were the nearest things to sons that she had. It was whilst living with her that MacDonald had acquired his seagoing skills, working the hard life of a herring boat fisherman. It was she who had encouraged him to apply himself to his books and work for his mate's ticket, so that he could rise in his profession. When he and John had set out to go on the deep sea merchant ships that wandered the oceans of the world, it was she who waved them off with both tears and pride. Accordingly they had evolved a small custom when either of them departed for sea. Margaret would grasp each of them by the ear and in a voice that masked her sorrow at parting, she would make them promise something,

'Just remember, Donald and John. There is one golden rule, and only one. Do not do anything foolish and so get home safe to Lewis.'

Then she would pretend to skelp their lugs, which would make them laugh, for she was a tiny woman and they great hulking men, then she would turn and walk away back to her two-up, two down wee house without looking back. He knew well that she walked away quickly so as not to upset them by the sight of the tears in her eyes.

It was Aunt Margaret to whom MacDonald was writing at this particular moment at his desk in the stuffy cabin he occupied in the deckhouse midships on the barque. MacDonald had always been something of a lone wolf without the need of a house or a settled existence, his home for years being where he dumped his ditty-bag in sailor's homes, seamen's missions, cheap hotels, forecastles, or junior officers' cabins all over the globe. Still, he was a man and sometimes found it in himself to envy those who had a more settled and domestic existence. He had discovered in himself a liking for children that had always been there, though dormant, and occasionally tried to think of himself as a husband and father at some undefined point in the future, though it seemed a remote possibility and something unlikely to happen to him. He was one of those men to whom small children warmed, sensing in him a strong store of humour and fun, though really what they could sense was that he would protect them. There were some little girls on this boat who made him feel particularly protective and one of them who made him smile. She was a small American personage called Laura Mary Hastings and for this trip she had elected him as her special friend and had quite melted his heart. He felt that he must produce a piece of carving for her as a remembrance and so had been whittling a piece of driftwood into the form of a rabbit, which he thought she would delight in. A bubbling and effervescent child, quite his opposite, she had nonetheless drawn him out in a way that he had not thought possible and he found that he actually liked telling stories. If he ever had children they would benefit from this realization and discovery of a new talent, but the chief beneficiary was himself, because in the discovery that she liked him, MacDonald found that he liked himself more than he was accustomed to do.

MacDonald's great problem was that he was one of those men who carried a heavy weight of inadequacy round their necks like the figurative albatross. Although he was an excellent seaman and clearly officer material, he had been involved in several shipwrecks during his career to date. The idea had formed in his head after the fourth time that he was some sort of Jonah. Linked to this soon came the thought that he was somehow unworthy to command, for if he was going to be a focus for disaster, he did not wish the responsibility of being in charge. Feelings of unworthiness tend to spill over into other areas of life and MacDonald did not like himself very much. That children sensed in him something that was of worth, in turn made him feel something of the same.

The letter he was writing to his aunt could not be posted for another 3,000 miles or so when they reached San Francisco. There was little point in posting it in Honolulu because it would probably go home around the bottom of South America, which was the route the *Henry James* would take after touching at California. Such a letter might not arrive in Glasgow until shortly before his own arrival home, but from San Francisco it would cross the North American continent in days on a train and go on to Britain in a fast mail steamship. Aunt Margaret would know that he and his brother were safe. Listening to the occasional laughter which drifted down to him from the dining saloon under the poop, he reflected that the captain's dinner seemed to be going along with a deal of good humour. There was another reason why MacDonald never wished to be a captain. He was not a sociable man, inclined to be solitary and would be far too shy to act the host at any formal dinner table. For the moment there were a few hours until he went on watch so he settled back on his bunk, a light above him on a projecting sconce, and began to read some more chapters on practical navigation.

In the day cabin Captain Ralph Lattimore gave an inward sigh of contentment as his steward cleared away his plate and those of his passengers sitting round the table. The heat of the tropical night did nothing to detract from the taste of one of the best plum duffs with rum sauce that he had ever sat down to. Leaning back in his chair he felt in quite an expansive mood and good humour. Through the open windows of the great cabin whose doors lay open behind him, a relatively cool breeze kept the atmosphere in the saloon, rather larger than MacDonald's cabin, nicely warm, which was a relief from the oppressive heat of the day. As the *Henry James* glided at eight knots through the waters of the Pacific 400 miles north of the Equator, Lattimore, like MacDonald, sometimes felt himself thinking of the rain and the wind back home, but in his mind it was blowing through Larne, and a longing for its coolness would come on him. This he dismissed as soon as he became conscious of it, for he had chosen his profession with care in order to satisfy his wanderlust. He was a member of a family who had been stone-masons for several generations; he did not have to go to sea when a young man, but had chosen not to follow the family trade. This would be the third time that he had taken the *Henry James* around the world on the clipper route since he had watched her being launched six years previously, in 1882, and he had no intention of settling down just yet. It was now 10 April 1888; he was halfway through this voyage, which had gone very smoothly, and he was a satisfied man.

'Coffee in thirty minutes if you please Thomas.'

'Aye Captain,' replied the steward. 'Will you be wanting brandy sir?'

'Reverend, Mr Hastings, can I tempt you to a glass of Cognac?'

Down at the bottom of the table, the Reverend William Taylor smiled through his large dark beard, shot through with grey. Lattimore's own beard was short, neat and trimmed, but Taylor's was long and bushy to his chest; the captain thought it a bit too showy in a priest, but perhaps it might impress those whom the Reverend attempted to convert. It was, after all, a rather apostolic feature though Lattimore suspected it hid a small chin. The Reverend also wore a pair of pince-nez spectacles on a black lanyard, an aid to sight that Lattimore was not fond of. His own glasses were firmly in his breast pocket as he was still shy of using them since giving into necessity six months previously. Being long-sighted was not much of a handicap to him during the working day, but in his work with charts and documents he had little choice now but to use them.

'That's the sort of temptation I can live with Mr Lattimore and I know that Frederick can as well. Perhaps when the children have withdrawn?'

His wife, a matronly lady with greying dark hair in her late fifties, was prompt in taking the hint.

'Come along Dorothea,' she said to the younger woman sitting opposite her. 'Let's leave these gentlemen to smoke and drink spirits and speak of manly things.' Here her eyes twinkled in a slightly teasing manner, 'But we shall be back William, for I wish to have some coffee also.'

Two little girls also stood up from the bench they were squeezed onto and, ushered by their mother and grandmother, made their way into the small cabin adjacent to the saloon where their two smaller sisters were already asleep. On voyages without passengers this would be the accommodation for one man, the Second Mate, but he was bunking in the deck cabin midships, along with the First Mate and the Steward. They accepted this as a necessary evil because the *Henry James* had to pay her way as she nosed round the world. Each adult passenger had paid £10 for their berth from Samoa and £5 for each child. This represented a healthy profit for the North British Shipping Company and paid their wages, so they accepted their temporary exile with good grace. If there were no passengers past San Francisco, then they would resume their places.

The Bosun's whistle was heard up on deck, and the pattering of feet, which caused Lattimore to pull out his watch and look at the time.

'What is it, Captain,' asked Frederick Hastings. 'No trouble I hope?'

Lattimore glanced at him, an anxious looking man with wispy ginger hair and carefully brushed mutton chop sideburns which he evidently endeavoured to cultivate like plants. The thought crossed his mind that Hastings had a right to look worried with four children to provide for and another on the way; missionary work was reputed not to pay very well.

'No sir; no trouble at all. Five bells; that's six-thirty to you. Second dog watch men are just going on duty.'

'I'm never quite sure of these "dog watches" Captain, though I'm told it's to do with the evening and Sirius the dog-star becoming visible.'

'Well that's true, Mr Hastings, but the dog watch is divided into first and second because a crew has to eat by watches, starting at four-thirty.'

'When does the watch end?'

'Eight bells sir; ten o'clock, when the first watch begins.'

'I'm afraid it's all rather complicated and I do not think I shall ever understand it.'

'Then it's as well you don't have to, sir. It's enough to know that Mr Crone is on duty now until ten when Mr MacDonald takes over until 4.30am. The way I see it is that we all have our allotted tasks in life and a man cannot expect to be master of them all. Why, look at me; I'm as god-fearing as the next man, but I could not do what you do. It simply isn't in me.'

'Who is on duty at 4.30 in the morning Captain? That's a very early hour to start work.'

'It is to be sure and I echo the sentiment, because it happens to be me. Thomas will waken me at four with coffee, good and hot, and I take over the ship half an hour later whilst you all slumber on as long as you please.'

Lattimore looked round the table with a smile that was returned. He was fortunate in his passengers this trip for they seemed a well-humoured family, though he had some slight reservations about the Reverend who appeared to be a rather bossy paterfamilias, very strict with his grandchildren. There was a pause; Bruno the captain's Newfoundland, lifted his head from his basket in the corner as Thomas Morgan came in with a tray and decanters, then relaxed as he saw who it was.

'Your pardon gentlemen,' said Lattimore. 'I offered you brandy, but that was more convention on my part. As an Ulsterman I have to say that I prefer a good glass of whisky, so if you'd rather; it's Irish I have to say, which I find superior to Scotch, though I do admit to a certain bias.'

Lattimore was not sure that he liked Taylor, though this was nothing to do with religion and far more to do with his tendency to instruct all around him, but perhaps this went with being a preacher. However, whatever face the Reverend might show to the rest of the world he had thus far been amiable enough to the captain of his vessel so he offered him some of his prized whisky. Many men of the cloth eschewed liquor and made a badge of their own abstinence to use as a signal of virtue. Taylor did not; the first time Lattimore had asked him the Reverend had made it clear that Jesus had liked a drink and so too did he. For him it was all about self control and resisting the temptation of too much; alcohol was sent by God as a pleasure and as a temptation and it was up to men how they used it, a view that Lattimore found refreshing. If Jesus had turned water into wine for people's enjoyment then that was quite good enough for the Reverend Taylor, and for Lattimore this ameliorated his reservations somewhat.

'Brandy for me please,' said Mr Hastings.

'I'll try the whisky.'

'Bravo Reverend; I think you'll find that's a good choice, for it is a fine one and especially with one of these.'

Lattimore took a cigar from a box proffered by the steward and lit it at the hanging lamp, an action followed by both Taylor and Hastings. When the steward had retreated Hastings resumed his interrogations.

'Captain. You said that you could not do what I do, but I think you could. You're a man who is accustomed to giving orders. Do you not command and men do as you say? I imagine that you would have no problems at all in speaking to a congregation.'

'In general, Mr Hastings, I understand what you are saying and it is true that I have no trouble in speaking to groups of people and giving orders. That's why I am a captain. But you see it's a question of what to say. I could not stand in front of a crowd of heathen as you do and preach the word of God to bring them to Christianity. I would not know what to say or where to begin. Each to his own I think.'

The Reverend Taylor smiled, 'I think that is wise Captain. I've heard it said that any man can preach if the spirit of the Lord comes upon him, but between us I have to confess that I have heard some rather dire ones in my time. I won't be asking you to preach a sermon if you won't be asking me to navigate your vessel. I'd have her on the rocks in no time at all!'

'Now there you have a bargain sir, for I would not wish to see her in such straits.'

'I should think not; she is your home is she not?'

'She is when I am at work, sir. I have lived on board her for most of the last four years now since she was launched and many of my worldly goods are in that cabin behind me.'

'Have you no other place on land to call your home? No wife or family?'

'I have a wife sir, Agnes, back home in Larne and a house right by the water there, called Waterloo Cottage. It's a good home for a sea captain. We've been married eight years. As to family, I come from a large one with a legion of brothers and sisters. Why even the bosun on this ship is a cousin of mine.'

'Will you settle down in Larne one day? Does your wife not miss you being away so often?'

'I imagine that I will if I am spared, and yes she does miss me while I am away, but of course she knew what I was when she married me. Long absences are part and parcel of a seafarer's life and Larne is a busy port. Agnes knew what she was doing and anyway she has accompanied me on several voyages.'

'Have you any children captain?'

'No sir, but I hope that we will eventually, if Providence allows.'

'You are a fatalist, Captain.'

'I think you are right. Perhaps it has something to do with being from the North of Ireland, for there is a strong feeling there amongst people of my persuasion that what will be, will be.'

'Have you any other family, Captain? I see that you must have friends aplenty, from the ring you wear, but are there many relations?'

'Some Mr Hastings; I have a brother, William, who lives in Auckland, where he works as a stone mason. I saw him there on my last voyage and he appears to be doing well, though trade in his line is slow. As to my ring, it was presented to me when first I joined the Freemasons, as is natural for a seagoing man to do. I did not attend many of their meetings; my profession does not allow for it. I have few close associations in the craft, but I do go to meetings whenever I can. There is often a lodge to visit in any port that I call into.'

'It has not been of much actual service to you then, being a member I mean?'

'No. I cannot say that it has, at least up to this moment. I joined because I was invited to; most of the seafaring men in my circle of acquaintance were members anyway and it was just the thing to do, but not because of any hard held convictions or hopes. When I decided to follow a seagoing career, it was the natural thing to do.'

'You said you have a brother in New Zealand. Why did you not call there on this voyage?'

'Because my owners had already arranged a cargo by cable in Newcastle, New South Wales. We take the most direct route, calling at Samoa for fresh water, supplies and passengers if there are any.'

'Do you normally carry coal Captain?'

'This ship will carry anything that we can, Mr Hastings. I sailed from Maryport, Cumberland, with a cargo of railway lines to Bowen and then in ballast round to Newcastle, where I took on 1,600 tons of coal for Balfour, Guthrie and Co. of San Francisco, departing on 26 February for Samoa.'

'Which is most convenient to us for going home after our inspection tour of mission schools.'

'Quite so Reverend; very fortuitous. I'm glad that we are more than halfway home on our circumnavigation, though I found Samoa fascinating.'

'As do I. That was the second time I have called there and I find the islanders very hospitable to passing ships.'

'They are generally that to everyone, but if you were a German then you might not have found them so helpful.'

'Why so, sir?'

'You'll have noticed that the German company there has considerable interests.'

'Indeed, though I did not have any cause to go into their holdings.'

'Perhaps it is as well. The company employees tend to have a rather high handed attitude towards the Samoans and would dearly love to take over the whole.'

'I take it that Britain and the United States both oppose that?'

'Indeed they do, and they back the opposing side to the Germans for that reason in the civil war.'

'I have to say Reverend that although I heard that there was a civil war in Samoa, I saw no signs of it.'

'You wouldn't. Inside the municipal area most of the population is white and the Samoans do not intrude. They do not wish to give any of the powers sufficient outrage as would cause them to intervene. Such a thing might mean the end of their sovereignty and they are well aware of that.'

'But you went traveling into the interior, sir. Did you not feel in any danger in the middle of a civil conflict?'

Taylor smiled, 'Good Lord, Captain; not at all; Samoans are almost uniformly good Methodists, though some other denominations have made inroads. A pastor like myself is immune from harm in that line. Not a hand would be lifted against me; if anyone did so then he would be an outcast. They may support different candidates to be their King but on matters of religion they are punctilious. Besides, they are not hostile to foreigners, rather the reverse; the arrogance of the Germans they do not like, but neither do we. Generally, they are glad to see us and to talk to us.'

'Even gladder of the trade, I should think. On a previous voyage I called at Pitcairn Island and it's a pity we did not call there this time. It's a curious thing that we sailed from Maryport when we left England and it would have been fitting to call at Pitcairn.'

'Why so?'

'Well, that's the neighbourhood where Fletcher Christian, the Bounty mutineer, came from. Still a well-known and respected family in the district.'

'Now that is interesting. I imagine that he has gone down as the black sheep of their family.'

'I think he has, though there is a touch of romance beginning to be attached to the story.'

'That's a large amount of coal you mentioned though, Captain. This vessel is very heavily laden.'

'She is, Mr Hastings, though well within margins of safety up to the Plimsoll mark. We sail slowly, but we sail steadily. Ah, here are the ladies returned. Alexander!'

The cabin boy, hovering by the door of the steward's pantry immediately came to Lattimore's elbow.

'Tell Mr Morgan that we'll have the coffee now.'

Isabelle Taylor and her daughter reseated themselves as the fragrant smell of freshly brewed coffee scented the air, mixed with the fumes of burning spirits from the stove in the pantry.

'Tell me, Captain, does the ship weigh more than the cargo or vice versa?'

'In this case, Reverend, the weight of the cargo vastly outweighs the weight of the ship. The *Henry James* weighs in at 964 tons.'

'I would not have thought she was strong enough to carry such a weight of coal.'

'If we were a wooden ship then you would probably be right, for we would need a lot of bulky timbers to reinforce her sides and bottom, but as we are an iron barque she is very strong for a lot less weight. The use of iron has changed the face of ship building this last twenty years and this design, you may take it from me, is the last word in cargo sailing ships.'

'How so?'

'The hull is lighter and she can carry more cargo than a wooden ship. The top hamper is also lighter for all the permanent rigging is steel wire and the masts steel tubing; and the sail layout of two masts square rigged and one fore and aft means she needs far less crew than an old square rigged vessel. Oh, you be assured gentlemen that the *Henry James* is as fine a vessel as may be found afloat.'

'Would you not rather command a steamship, Captain?'

'Not I; those kettles depend on supply of coal. That costs a lot of money, but the wind is free and that is good for commerce.'

Thomas Morgan now came back to serve the coffee.

'Mr Crone begs to inform you, sir, that it is sunset.'

Lattimore again looked at his watch.

'Four minutes to seven. It's a clear night and a smooth sea; if you ladies and gentlemen would care to take a turn on deck later I daresay you would find the sky much to your liking; it's very pleasant. Thank you, Thomas; would you take Bruno out now please? It's time he had a walk around.'

The Newfoundland dog cocked an ear as he heard the familiar word and headed out of the door without delay. There might be rats that needed his immediate attention. Dorothea Hastings, whom the captain thought a wan looking lady from too much child bearing, now asked a question.

'Captain Lattimore; what was the name of that island we saw in the distance just before sunset?'

'That was Palmyra Atoll, ma'am.'

'These little islands look so inviting; it's a pity we could not land there just to have a look at them; it would be so romantic.'

Captain Lattimore looked dubious and pursed his lips with a wry expression.

'You don't think so Captain?'

'No ma'am, I do not. As I said before, this is my third voyage through these waters and I've heard things about that island that I do not like. It is not inhabited for a start.'

'I can see that it would not be so interesting without people, but what else have you heard?'

'Since we are safely past it, Mrs Hastings, I can tell you that there is a very strange tale associated with Palmyra Atoll and it goes back about seventy years.'

'I'll start by saying that it was discovered by Captain Fanning, the American navigator who ran his ship onto it one night in 1802. Thankfully he managed to get off the reef and repair his ship, but since his vessel was called the Palmyra, he named the island after it. Unfortunately, although he recorded it in his log, he neglected to mark it on the chart until later when he noted its approximate position.'

'Oh, I love a good tale of the sea,' said Mrs Taylor. 'Please Captain; do tell us more about it. A strange tale you say?'

'It goes back to 1818 if I remember rightly, when Spain was still bankrupt after the French wars; they were squeezing everything they could from their South American colonies and especially from Peru. Apparently the demands from Madrid made the colonial governor strain every nerve to gather all the gold and silver he could from old Inca graves and tombs and from mines. The treasure was placed on a ship called the Esperanza and she sailed for Spain.'

'Esperanza. That means "hope" does it not?'

'Yes ma'am; it does; but in this case any hope was dashed, because some pirates had got wind of the news and they were waiting for the treasure ship.'

'Oh my!'

'Indeed; apparently the pirates attacked the Esperanza, took the ship and sailed off with her after killing the crew who would not join them.'

'And they sailed to Palmyra!'

'No ma'am; they were attacked in turn themselves by another pirate crew who slew them all, burned the Esperanza, and made off across the Pacific with their ill gotten gains. Unfortunately for them they ran straight into Palmyra one night and wrecked their ship beyond repair. They were able to offload the treasure and supplies and set up camp on the island where they remained awaiting a ship to pass, for eighteen months.'

The Reverend Taylor leaned forward now, his attention evidently caught.

'And did a ship come? Were they rescued?'

'No Reverend; a ship did not come, and they were not rescued. So after eighteen months on the island, supplies were running low and they decided that they must leave. They built two stout rafts and provisioned them with all they had left, and set off to find their way to the nearest land, having first buried their treasure on a small island just offshore.'

'Ah; so they could come back later with a ship to get it!'

'Exactly so Mrs Hastings.'

'And did they ever return?'

'Wait a minute,' interjected Mr Hastings. 'How do you know all this? How do we know this is just not some old yarn of the sea?'

Lattimore smiled thinly, 'Because of the rafts, sir. One of the rafts disappeared, never to be heard of or seen ever again. What happened to it no man knows; or at least no-one who wishes to make himself known. But the second raft, ah now, that is a different story.'

'Well, what happened to it man?'

'It was sighted by a whaling ship, adrift in the north Pacific and of course they went to investigate it. On board were two dead men and one who they thought was dead, but who turned out to be alive on closer investigation. He was desperately ill with pneumonia, but told his story before he died. The legend is well known along the Pacific seaboard of the United States and through the islands.'

'What was this man called? What was his name?'

'James Hine or Hines ma'am, a Cumbrian name I am told, but how he came to be a Pacific pirate I do not know.'

'Has anyone ever found this treasure? Or looked for it?' asked Dorothea Hastings.

'That I do not know. To sail a ship to Palmyra to look for treasure would be an expensive and perhaps a fruitless undertaking, so to the best of my knowledge no-one has ever looked.'

'But if all you have to do is go there and dig it up, then why not?'

Lattimore smiled, 'Ma'am that sounds very easy, but an island is a big place and there will be more than one offshore island at Palmyra. Where would you look? It might take years. It would be as difficult as trying to find Drake's silver reef.'

'What was that?'

'When Drake was circumnavigating the world, his ship stuck on a reef in the Spice Islands. She was full of treasure and the reef was just below the water. To float her off he ordered that all heavy items be thrown overboard; the ballast, the cannon, the water; all to no avail. Then he ordered the silver to be thrown over; thousands of pounds worth of it. They had just started to throw the gold when the ship came free. Although he beached his ship for repairs, there was no hope of recovering the silver because in those days they had no diving equipment. It's still there. Riches beyond avarice.'

'How fascinating! Would it not be wonderful to find it!'

'It would indeed, ma'am, but with so much sea and so many reefs it would be difficult to know where to begin. I know that there have been people who have looked for it but no-one to my knowledge has ever found it.'

'Oh Captain, it seems so very formal to call us "ma'am". We have been on this ship some days now and I feel I know you well enough to call you by your name. Ralph is it not?'

'It is Mrs Taylor, but I do not pronounce it in the way you did; the old Northern Irish way is my preference.'

'Ah, so you do not prefer it as it is spelt but as "Rafe". Why do some people say Ralph, I wonder, and others pronounce it as Rafe?'

'I think some of the reason is to do with Gilbert and Sullivan.'

'You mean Ralph Rackstraw! Oh, I loved "*HMS Pinafore*". He is pronounced as Rafe.'

'Yes indeed,' interjected Mr Hastings. 'It was as popular in the States as it was in Britain.'

'So I understand, sir,' said Lattimore. 'But for me it just added to the confusion with so many people trying to call me "Ralph". That's a new pronunciation of the name and I've nothing against it for those who want to be Ralph, but I've been Rafe all my life and I think I must stay with it.'

'But you can still call me Isabelle.'

'I do confess ma'am that I find it difficult to call my passengers by their given names; it seems somehow disrespectful. Imagine calling a man with the bearing and dignity of Reverend Taylor "William". Why he's a Reverend and that fits him like a glove.'

'Well I call him William all the time.'

'Yes ma'am, but you are married to him.'

Lattimore liked to maintain the social forms when engaged in business. Carrying passengers was business, and in the same way that there was a line between himself and his officers, a similar demarcation existed between him and his passengers. He was comfortable with this relationship and his sensibilities were a little jarred by Isabelle Taylor's attempt to storm through it.

Reverend Taylor was smiling, as he had divined Lattimore's thoughts.

'Whatever else, Captain, I am in no doubt that you tell a very good yarn. I am comfortable with both Reverend for me, and Captain for you. Now you are up early, I think you said?'

'Before 4.30am, sir, for the morning watch.'

'Then I would think it selfish to keep you at table any longer. My dears, the captain needs his sleep. Let us to our prayers and bed.'

So saying, Reverend and Mrs Taylor, and Frederick and Dorothea Hastings said their goodnights and went to their cabins. Ralph Lattimore sat for a few minutes thinking. The conversation had been free flowing and easy, but although he had enjoyed the evening as a whole, he had the feeling that under different circumstances the Reverend Taylor's bonhomie and ebullience could so easily turn into something not quite so affable. There was something about his manner that hinted at his being a dominating, if not a domineering character, who liked to get his own way. Certainly his wife pried too much for the captain's liking, but he did not blame Taylor for that. One thing he felt sure of, and it was that his instinct told him that the preacher was not a man to cross. Still, he would in all likelihood never see him again when the voyage was over, so he shrugged, then drained his whisky before going to the great cabin and into his own cot. He did not go on deck; good men were on watch and there was nothing but deep water between the *Henry James* and the Pacific coast of the United States 3,000 miles ahead.

Chapter 2

Nothing on the Chart

John Crone stood forward of the wheel at the rear of the well deck looking into the darkness of the Pacific night. Out there were no lights, no other ships and indeed no land, only thousands of miles of, apparently, empty ocean. Steering the ship was able seaman Bill Crosby, a good and reliable man, a quiet Nova Scotian with an accent part Canadian, part Scots. They did not need to see where they were going and indeed could not, as the forward part of the ship was a raised forecastle where the crew bunked. In between was the deck cabin where the mate and himself had their temporary quarters, but it did not signify. All that mattered was the compass in its binnacle illuminated by a storm-proof lantern, and a good hand could keep the ship on course quite safely; his own presence was barely necessary and especially on a night such as this. The wind was gentle and the ship sailed along as in a dream on a sea that was virtually smooth. Crone thought that life could hardly be better because he had worked hard to be here and was enjoying his first long voyage, which he did not intend to be his last. He was twenty-two years old and had not long since gained his Second Mate's licence; he continued to read and to learn his craft and in due course wished to acquire his Mate's certificate, then his Master's certificate to become Captain Crone, but not quite yet. For the moment he wanted to see the world, to sail in different vessels and widen his experience.

If this sounds too sober a position for someone of his years, then it must be said that he did not articulate what he thought as any sort of plan. Young men often do not and Crone took life as it came and enjoyed it, loving new things, meeting people, conversation and above all the sea, which he was in love with. There was, as yet, no gravity to him because he laughed a lot, told jokes, liked a good story and had very quickly earned himself a reputation as a convivial and indeed jolly companion. This made him popular with the crew and his fellow officers, but it was combined with openness and a sense of duty that looked to make him into a very fine seaman. He was born in Maryport, Cumberland, where his parents lived in Christian Street; his father was a master mariner and John expected to follow in his footsteps. That was why he was bound apprentice to the captain of a collier at the age of fourteen, sailing cargoes of coal from Cumberland, mostly to Belfast or to the Isle of Man. As he grew older he shipped in other colliers engaged with rough men in a rough trade. He was quite a short man, but powerfully built and well able to hold his own in such company. It was hard and dirty work, but a good university for seamen in which he had risen. At twenty-one when he had applied for his licence he had a whole sheaf of good references and recommendations and got the vital piece of paper with no difficulty at all.

What was necessary at this point was a blue water vessel outward bound on a long voyage as Crone had no intention of spending his life among the coal boats. He had heard many a story of far-off seas and remote islands and he thirsted to see such things, to smell them and to travel. Maryport was a very busy haven and the vessels there were not exclusively given over to coal. On 22 June 1887 the *Henry James* had arrived in the harbour carrying a cargo of floorboards from Arbroath, which were advertised for sale in the Maryport Advertiser. It was then that several of her crew left, having no wish to continue on her next voyage, because it would take her round the world and too far from their families, for too long. The *Henry James* required a Second Mate and John Crone, hearing of this, walked straight onboard and offered his services.

Captain Lattimore had accepted right away, since the two men had taken to each other. The truth was that Lattimore had seized on Crone as good company and more in tune with his own disposition than his First Officer. He viewed Donald MacDonald as an excellent seaman; he was also a fine person, but he was no conversationalist, being somewhat dour; he was not a laughing man. Lattimore had not seen the reality of MacDonald, not appreciated the tremendous strength of him.

Crone did not feel entirely that he was shipping out with strangers because among the new crewmen were three others from Maryport, all of whom he knew. Born and bred in the town, it would have been surprising if he did not and indeed had been to school at the same time as Thomas Morgan, the captain's steward. It was down to Morgan that the ship's cook, James Wilson, had got his position, and this pleased Crone because he had known Wilson for a long time, having shipped previously on two colliers with him.

Ordinary Seaman Samuel Young came with Crone wherever he went and followed him from ship to ship. They had met on Crone's first vessel and although the friendship was not a balanced one, Crone being the lead and far brighter, there was a degree of fidelity from Young that Crone accepted as fealty, and he knew that he would always see Young right. The four men liked each other, which was important and although Crone was their superior on board ship, they did not abuse their positions or act as his familiars; but they did see him as their leader.

The *Henry James* had sailed from Maryport on 27 July 1887 with its cargo of railway lines for Bowen in Queensland, and no passengers. From Bowen she had traveled round the Australian coast to Newcastle in New South Wales, to pick up a cargo of coal. The officers had got to know each other fairly well and the *Henry James* had become a happy and well-run ship. Crone had reason to be well satisfied with his chosen career, though he was rather put out with his ship's latest cargo of coal bound for San Francisco; he thought he had put coal carrying behind him, but a seaman had to accept whatever freight paid his wages so he was philosophical about it.

Up the mast in the lookout's platform was Patrick Burns a very experienced and older able seaman, but he did not have much to do because down at sea level all was pitch black. Above was a different story though as the sky was studded with a million stars which Burns never tired of looking at; there was no moon. Up on his perch the stars the only things Burns could see apart from the binnacle light and the glow from the cabins aft where the captain and the passengers made ready for bed. These three men held the ship and all aboard her, safe in their hands; at any time they could call out the entire crew if necessary, but on such a night as this there would be no need, unless there were a sudden change in the weather.

'Good evening Mr Crone.'

'And a very good evening to you also, Mr MacDonald. You're a little early I think?'

'Aye, well it's rather hot in my cabin, so I thought I'd come up a little early to catch the night breeze. You'll not mind, I think?'

Crone did not mind; he liked MacDonald although they were very different characters to each other. The chief mate did not say a lot, but when he did his words were considered and worth listening to. Each of them had accents that were quite marked, Crone's being fairly broad West Cumbrian and MacDonald's being the soft and precise lilt of the Western Isles, so they had to listen carefully to each other. Conversation required some concentration at times. There was something he could say to MacDonald tonight though.

'I see that young Miss Hastings has taken a shine to you.'

MacDonald smiled broadly, 'Oh she's a lovely wee thing and if she has then I've a tenderness towards her too.'

The young lady in question, Laura Mary Hastings, was a mere nine years old. Many children would have found MacDonald forbidding with his long face and somewhat gloomy manner; not so Miss Laura. Two days out of Samoa whilst walking on deck with her mother she had spied MacDonald seated on a hatch cover smoking a pipe and had made a beeline for him. She had climbed up onto the hatch and straightaway reached up and removed his cap, setting it on her own curls with a loud giggle. He was not used to little girls, and dealing with one of Laura's age was novel to him. Her laughing child beauty had taken his heart by storm and the 'bonnie wee bairn' had cemented their friendship by showing a partiality that made her seek him out whenever they were both on deck. He sat happily with her and displayed a loquaciousness that many people would have not thought him capable of; he told her stories.

'That story that you were telling her today; did you make it up?'

'The Selkies? No, I did not. The legends of the seal-folk go back hundreds of years in the islands where I was born.'

'Up in Lewis?'

'Oh yes.'

'And these people live under the sea but can come up on land and take off their seal-skin and live as humans?'

'There are numerous tales of such things. My own mother used to tell me them when I was a wean at her knee.'

'That one you told her about the man who married one and locked her skin up in a chest so she could not return to the sea; did your mother tell you that?'

'Yes she did.'

'I liked the ending of that one.'

'So did the bairn; but there is a justice to it, for the husband was cruel to her and when he dressed up to go to a Christmas party she found the chest key in his day clothes, put on her skin and went back to the sea.'

'I would not have thought you would have approved of that Mr MacDonald, for I know you are a believer.'

'I do not approve in the general run of things, of wives leaving their husbands, it is true, but Selkies are not Christian people. The rules they live by would be different to ours.'

'You've given it some thought I see; do you believe in them?'

MacDonald did not answer straightaway, but mulled the question over with a puzzled expression then answered slowly.

'Well I'm not at all sure Mr Crone. They do say that there is no smoke without fire and, as I said, there are tales of Selkies throughout the Isles, aye and round to Orkney, Shetland and Caithness where they called them the Finfolk. I think it would be arrogant in me to dismiss such things, because there is much in this world and doubtless in the next, of which I know nothing. Now what is the time?'

'Ten o'clock, Mr MacDonald.'

'I thought it might be. Thank you Mr Crone; please ring the bell; I relieve you.'

Crone smiled, reached over and took hold of the lanyard attached to the clapper of the ships bell, and rang it eight times. From somewhere forward Bruno barked several times. Immediately two men came to relieve the lookout and the steersman, but before the changeover was complete a voice came from above.

'Deck there!'

It was MacDonald, now on duty, who answered.

'Hello; is all well?'

Patrick Burns' answer was almost non-committal, but caused some consternation.

'I think I can hear waves breaking, sir.'

'Where away?'

'Dead ahead, sir.'

MacDonald looked at Crone, 'It cannot be so; there is no land here. Are we on course?'

'We are. We've steered ruler straight past Palmyra; there's nothing out here.'

'Nothing marked on the chart, Mr Crone. Ahoy lookout!'

'Yes sir?'

'Can you still hear it?'

'Yes sir, and louder now.'

'We will not hear it down here I think. Mr Crone, I am going forward to the bows; would you mind staying here a few minutes?'

'Not at all, but he's said that he thinks he can hear waves breaking.'

'Not definite enough to alter course; but if he really can hear waves then it's already too late.'

MacDonald strode forward, but he was right. No sooner had he reached the bows than he heard the waves swashing and a thrill of fear hit him as he realized that there must be a reef dead ahead, though he could see nothing except a vague white froth not far in front of the ship. All he could do was yell at the top of his voice.

'All hands! All hands! Hard to port now Mr Crone! All hands!'

There was nothing to be done. The *Henry James*, gliding along through smooth water crashed straight into sharp coral rocks and rode up onto them with a screeching of tearing metal as the reef opened up her bottom as keenly as a can opener. The men on deck were thrown off their feet, whilst Patrick Burns up in his lookout post was catapulted forward, bruising his ribs on the guardrail that surrounded him, but which now saved his life from a great fall. From all over the ship came hoarse cries of alarm, and from the cabins the screams of the children, rudely awakened by falling from their bunks onto the floor. The ones affected most immediately were the ordinary seamen in the forecastle. The *Henry James* was low in the water and the first they knew of trouble was when the ship rode up onto a fang of coral so sharp that it pierced the deck of their accommodation with a huge gash and water spouted in on the men, many of whom were fast asleep. Worse than that, with the heat of the night, many were sleeping naked and ran in panic out of the door with nothing more on them than what they came into the world with. They poured onto the deck where all was dark and milled about yelling questions in confusion. Strangely there was no falling of masts or spars, or any falling rigging. The steel wires held the masts firmly in place and the mizzen and bowsprit sails remained set; so they became MacDonald's first duty, for he was the first to recover his wits.

'Mr Crone, take four men and get those jibs down and the foresail. Bosun, see to the spankers. The rest of you man the hand pumps while I see to the firing up of the steam pump. We have hit a reef I believe, and I fear our bottom is torn open.'

'Aye sir!' Crone ordered the yelling group to be quiet and the habit of obedience made them silent. The ship had been sailing under shortened sail, it being night, and it did not take long; the crew knew the ropes of the ship even in the dark. The clanking of the hand pump began and the gush of water was soon heard splashing into the sea.

'Have you sounded the well, Mr MacDonald?'

MacDonald turned to see Lattimore clad only in a nightshirt with no shoes.

'No sir, not yet.'

'Do it please, and report back immediately.'

MacDonald shouted for the ship's carpenter whose duty this was and together they went amidships and drew up the metal sounding pole. There was twelve feet of water in the ship already, so he returned to where Lattimore waited.

'Shall I start the steam pump sir?'

'No Mr MacDonald; there is little time and we must use it as best we can. If that amount of water has entered in such a short time the ship is lost and the pump will not keep pace, especially given the time it will take to get steam up.'

In answer to MacDonald's querying look he continued, 'It's an iron ship Mr Mate with over 1,600 tons of coal onboard. She's not going to sink; at least not yet. She's stuck fast on whatever she has hit; a reef you say. If she were not we'd be heading for the bottom like a stone right now. My first consideration has to be the lives of the crew and the passengers, because if she slips off the reef she will go down fast. I'll have the pinnace and the launch in the water immediately, if you please.'

'And the jolly-boat, sir?'

'Not yet I think. We shall need it presently though. Meanwhile, all except those I select must abandon ship; now Mr MacDonald.'

'Aye sir!' MacDonald hurried off to obey his orders.

A bearded figure appeared at his side and the light of the lanthorn showed a very worried face.

'Captain, what shall we do? Are we shipwrecked?'

'We are Reverend. You must get your wife and the rest of your family into the ship's launch immediately, and I do mean right now. Do not lose an instant sir!'

Momentarily Lattimore found it in himself to marvel at how calm he felt. He had often wondered what it might be like if he were wrecked, but up until this moment it had all been hypothetical. Now that it had happened he felt almost detached from it and watched as his own body did its job. He felt no fear at all because there were things to be done. The same could not be said for everyone; that would be too much to expect, because human beings respond to rude shock in individual ways. Order had been restored among the crew because they had jobs to do, and were doing them with a frantic fear that the ship was going to slide under the waves at any minute. It was obvious that the rear end of the *Henry James* was sinking, and as the weight of water inside her increased, so the front drove down more onto the sharp fang she was impaled on. The door of the forecastle was open and water could be seen pouring up from below.

A frightened female figure clad in a nightdress appeared beside Reverend Taylor. Behind her, Mrs Taylor shepherded her four granddaughters, all clad in nightgowns and all crying and wailing with fear.

'Captain, there is water on the floor of our cabin and a flood coming from under the door of yours. What does it mean? Are we sinking?'

'We are Mrs Hastings, and I want all the passengers off the ship now. Do not stop for anything, but into the launch as soon as she floats, all of you. No, do not go below, but straight into the boat. Yes gentlemen; that includes you; you can bear a hand at the oars.'

This last remark was addressed to Mr Carter and Mr James who were traveling steerage in a small cabin next to the crew's quarters.

'Captain, there are our belongings to consider. I shall return to our cabins to bring out whatever I may be able to.'

Lattimore looked at the speaker and fixed him with a basilisk stare.

'Reverend, I have instructed you to enter the lifeboats for the very good reason that I believe we must abandon ship now. By that I mean this very moment. If you disobey me then I cannot answer for your life. Please do as I ask; there is nothing in your cabins that may be weighed in the balance against not drowning.'

When he was under stress Lattimore's strong Ulster accent gave a force and impetus to his words that were formidable. Taylor hesitated a moment and seemed about to retort or protest, but thought better of it, swallowed, and followed his family to a position by the rail to await the launch which was being swung out at that very moment. Lattimore was able to continue dealing with the ship, free from further distraction from that quarter.

'Mr Crone, pick four able seamen and take charge of the launch. You will attach a rope to the stern and lie off until dawn when we may be in a better position to see what can be done. Mr MacDonald, please tell off some good men to begin to gather some stores and place them in the jolly-boat.'

He added softly, 'If she goes Mr Mate, she will go fast. We may not have much time. Get those boats out quickly.'

Several rats appeared on the well deck, which Lattimore knew to be a bad sign; to the Newfoundland dog they were a job to be done and he rushed about efficiently dispatching each that he could find, but in perfect silence. The passengers were too preoccupied with their own peril to notice him, but rats indicated that below the cargo area was flooding fast. Hoarse shouts and screams from the ladies accompanied the next development as air pressure from the rising water suddenly blew off the aft cover with a loud bang. The hatch remained attached on one side and flapped over violently onto the deck where it splintered. Lattimore stared at it for a moment.

'Thank God no-one was standing there. Mr MacDonald - carry on.'

Leaving his officers to carry out their instructions Lattimore returned aft and looked at the door of his cabin. Sure enough there was water coming underneath it. Pursing his lips, he lowered the handle to open it. It swung outwards and a flood of water threw the door open, throwing him backwards and banging his arm painfully; the water was over three feet deep by the door. The rear of the ship had sunk very quickly while the front was held on the reef. He could see into his cabin by the dim yellow light of the oil lamp above his bed, still not submerged. Towards the stern windows the water was already four feet deep; there was not much time as she was settling fast at the stern, dragged down by the immense weight of her cargo, whilst the bows remained wedged on what was almost certainly a reef. Lattimore waded to his desk, thankfully in the middle of the room, and the incoming sea was only just below the top of it. He quickly packed a sextant and the box containing the ship's chronometers into a leather bag, which he took from a shelf. The charts were open on the top of the desk and still dry; quickly he rolled them up and tucked them under his arm. Hastily he took his book of navigational tables from a shelf and added it to his load. He hoped to get to his clothes, but they were under water near the windows, and as he thought about diving for them, the ship gave a lurch; his time was running out. His eye fell on a large sheath knife, which lay on a shelf, so he placed that also in the bag. His spectacles were still in the breast pocket of his jacket, now swirling round somewhere in the deeper water near the cabin windows. Momentarily, he thought again of diving in to try to find them, but a groaning noise from somewhere deep within the hull dissuaded him. He gave a swift glance around to see if there was anything else that was both useful and within reach, but there was nothing. Then he left, thinking that he must close the door behind him, but dismissed the thought as absurd. As he passed the binnacle on his return journey he stopped and undid the nuts holding it closed, lifted the ship's compass out from its gimbals and carefully placed that into the bag. Going over to the ship's rail, he saw that in the short time he had been at his cabin, water had begun to wash over the well deck. Crone had the launch, but to get the passengers away from the water he was embarking them over the rear of the poop, which was a few feet higher. He called to Crone who was helping a weeping Mrs Taylor into the boat.

'Mr Crone; I think we may need these. Look after them well.'

He had been unable to close the bag, but handed it to Crone who could see the contents, along with the roll of charts he had managed to save.

'Yes, sir. I also have my own sextant, Captain.'

Two crewmen passed the little girls down into the launch and still they wept.

'Steady on Miss; you'll be safe in the boat.' This did not reassure them at all.

'Are we all going to drown Mama?' was a question from seven year old Estella, but genuine inquiry though it was, it was enough to set Laura, Ada and Nancy wailing. Soon, with nothing but what they wore, all the passengers were in the launch and Crone and two crewmen with the assistance of the steerage passengers, both young fit men, trailed aft and sat attached to the ship by a long rope. They could be seen from the *Henry James*, the light of a single lanthorn illuminating the occupants.

Looking forward, Lattimore saw that MacDonald's team had lowered the sails and the second boat, the pinnace, was standing off to the rear. As with Crone's boat, she was tethered to the ship by a line. To his dismay he noted that some of the men were stark naked as they had been sleeping unclothed because of the heat. Their quarters had flooded so quickly they had fled with nothing. The ship now appeared to have stopped sinking, at least for the moment, hung up as she was, but Lattimore did not wish to take any chances.

'Mr MacDonald, get your men into the pinnace for now, except for Anderson, Crosby, Donnell and Shearer. They will crew the jolly boat when we have provisioned her. Oh and take Bruno too. We would not want him to drown now, would we boy?'

He rubbed the dog's head affectionately and encouraged him to jump into the boat, which MacDonald brought round to the ship's rail where the deck was now level with the sea. Quickly the boat crew scrambled over the rail into the boat.

'Do you not wish me to stay and help, Captain?'

'No Mr Mate, I want an experienced officer in the boats. The only land near to us is Palmyra; it's at least a thousand miles to anywhere else. If anything happens to me I want to know that the passengers and crew can be taken to safety.'

'Aye sir.'

Lattimore relented, on seeing MacDonald's crestfallen face.

'It begins to get light just after 5.30. We'll be able to do something more then, but not while it's as black as your hat. There's no point in putting people in more danger than necessary.'

'Is there danger, sir?'

'In this situation? I don't think so, unless she slips off the reef, but you know and I know that she's finished. We must salvage what we can to help our own survival. Lay off and try to get some of the hands to sleep. It's going to be a long day tomorrow.'

Eighty yards to the stern of the ship Crone and MacDonald lashed their boats together firmly and looked out across the darkness to where the only light now showed Lattimore on the roof of the poop deck with his four helpers.

'What is the Captain doing, sir?'

'Gathering supplies and piling all he can find into the jolly boat. Even if we land on Palmyra and find it a deserted place we should at least feed well until we're discovered. I doubt he'll get much; he can only gain access to the passenger cabins, the steward's pantry and the deckhouse, and probably not them for long.'

'And what do we do now Mr MacDonald?'

'We do as ordered, Mr Crone. It will be a very long day tomorrow. I shall stand watch for three hours with two men on oars. Everybody else needs to try to sleep.'

'Sleep?' retorted Mrs Taylor. 'The children are frightened half to death, the ship has been wrecked and we are afloat in a lifeboat in the middle of nowhere and you tell us to try to sleep? How do you propose we do that exactly?'

'Madam, this is not what you might call a lifeboat. It is a launch, the largest of the boats we carry. She is clinker built and very strong, a sea-going vessel, so you may set your mind at ease, for you are quite safe. If you look forward you will see that she is partly decked over. If you and the children crawl into there, it may be quite cosy and you must try to rest. Tomorrow will be arduous.'

Turning to the other people, MacDonald, a halo of assuredness around him, continued, 'Reverend Taylor, Mr Hastings we may need you also tomorrow for we will be rowing. The wind is against us for Palmyra, which is the nearest land.'

'Palmyra!'

'Yes Mrs Hastings. What of it?'

'The Captain told us things about Palmyra...'

'I am sure that the Captain was entertaining you Madam. I am certain that you will be glad to get dry land under your feet by the end of the day and it will not matter what it is called. Now please will you get some rest if you can, except Dordey and Young who will stand watch with me.'

On opposite sides of the two boats the Ordinary Seamen he had named manned oars, which they needed to use occasionally to prevent the slight breeze from drifting them down back towards the ship. Right across MacDonald's view men, women and children lay or leaned in some very awkward positions and closed their eyes. Before long there was silence as some dozed and some even slept, though fitfully. It was the end of their day after all and they were tired. Although they were shipwrecked, MacDonald's air of confidence and being in charge, made them feel safe. The Mate's apparent nonchalance was not entirely assumed either. He had been wrecked before, as had several of the crew. It was a hazard of the job and you dealt with it if it happened. This businesslike approach radiated professional competence and did much to take the fear out of the situation. In the yellow light of the lanthorn beside him MacDonald saw someone small clambering over towards him from the other boat and he smiled as Laura Hastings sat close beside him and snuggled up so he put his left arm round her, his right resting on the tiller. This was not to give her warmth but for comfort, the night being still quite hot.

'Are you alright, my wean?'

'Yes.'

'Well then you go to sleep. There is nothing to worry about and you are safe now. I'll wake you if anything happens.'

Silence fell over the two boats, leaving only the watchful MacDonald and the two crewmen alone with their thoughts; even the dog had curled up in the bows and had gone to sleep. On the poop deck of the *Henry James*, by about half past two in the morning Lattimore and his four men had piled all they could onto the poop by the jollyboat which, although the smallest of the ship's boats, could still hold a large load of provisions, blankets, clothes and all kinds of stores.

'Men, that's enough to last us for weeks if not more, but we will wait for first light until we lower her and I shall get some more hands to help load. All we can do now is wait; try to get some ease and I shall watch.'

'Sir; wake me up in an hour and I will take over the watch. We need you rested as well.'

'Thank you Anderson; I appreciate that and accept your offer.'

The barque had stopped sinking; the bow was out of water and the rear of the poop deck was about eighteen inches above it, the great cabin being wholly submerged. As his men settled down to rest, Lattimore sat with his back to the rail and waited. Much had happened in a very short time and he had lost his ship with most of his possessions. But all was not bad; no one had died, they had provisions to last a long time and land was not too far off in a smooth sea and a light, though contrary breeze. The only real problem now was the dark and that would change in a very few hours. When they could see properly he would set about fulfilling his immediate task; getting his passengers and crew safely onto dry land at Palmyra Atoll.

Chapter 3

A Rolling Swell

Lattimore watched for an hour as his companions lay down on the poop and his time was uneventful. Just after 3.30am he woke Anderson, who had managed to get some sleep, and the Able Seaman took over the watch. However, the captain did not get the period of dozing that he had hoped for. Despite the dangers of the situation he was in, he was extremely tired having been awake for well over twenty hours. Having settled down with his back to the taffrail he closed his eyes and allowed himself to drift almost to the edge of consciousness, but did not quite go to sleep. He was jolted back to full wakefulness as water flooded through the hawsehole beside him and soaked the backside of his nightshirt. Quickly getting to his feet he took hold of a lanthorn and held it over the taffrail to look at the sea; it was no longer calm.

'Wake up you men; we may have to leave quickly.'

'Are we sinking, Captain?'

'No I do not think so, but if the waves rise then we may be washed away.'

'Is it the tide, sir?'

'I doubt it; I believe the swell has increased and because she no longer floats rollers are beginning to pass over the ship. It may get worse.'

'What must we do sir?'

'We wait Anderson, if we can wait. It's pitch black still away from the lanthorns. There are rocks hereabouts and I do not wish to launch the jollyboat until it is daylight. For the moment get some of these stores into the boat before they get soaked.'

'Aye sir.'

44

A hail came from out of the darkness and Lattimore strained to look towards the faint yellow gleam, which indicated the presence of one of the boats.

'Captain Lattimore!'

'Mr MacDonald; I hear you. Do you have a problem?'

'Not immediate sir, but we are in danger of being carried down towards you.'

'What do you wish to do?'

'I think it would be prudent to release the boats from the ship, sir, and stand off further out. We are having to row constantly to maintain distance.'

'I agree Mr MacDonald. We shall let the ropes go from this end and you must reel them in. They may be of use. I take it that you wish to unlink the boats too?'

'Already done, sir. They ride better singly in this swell. Do you need assistance, sir?'

'Not unless the situation worsens considerably. If it does then we shall launch the jolly boat, but do not hazard your boats near these rocks in the darkness Mr MacDonald.'

'Aye sir!'

It was indisputable as the minutes went by that the swell of the ocean was increasing markedly, which in some ways was strange because there was not a lot of wind. The cause was not apparent, but the large amounts of water could have been moving because of a storm a hundred miles away or because of some underground seismic activity. It really was not relevant, though its result was, because although the superstructure of the *Henry James* was still above sea level, soon anyone on board her would be swept away by rising waves. They could climb the masts of course, but that would mean abandoning the boat and all the stores. The boats rose over the huge slow rolling masses of water with ease, though by now the passengers were all awake and suffering with the motion of the sea. Several were sick, but the launch and the pinnace were in the hands of skilled seamen so there was no immediate danger for them.

On board the *Henry James* Lattimore quickly surmised that the danger was increasing by the minute. Looking towards the bows he could see by the light of the lanthorns that the water was now surging between the poop and the forecastle with great force. He wondered how long it would be before the strong bolts, which held the deckhouse in place would give way. Before long the waves would be high enough to come over the taffrail and they would inevitably be swept away.

'Men, we have no choice. The boat must be launched now.'

'Shall we carry on loading her, sir?'

'No; that will make her too heavy; with what is in her already she'll be hard enough to shift.'

'Why not just cut the ropes, sir? She's only a couple of feet above the water already.'

'Because Crosby, if one goes first we will end up with a tipped up boat; we must lower her, so stand by on those handles. We shall load the rest of the supplies when she floats.'

The *Henry James* was not an old ship and Lattimore was a conscientious and professional captain so the manila ropes on the two small davits hanging over the rear of the ship were fairly new and the pulleys had been kept well greased. When two men on each handle took the strain they were not really sufficient to hold the weight of the jolly boat, but they contrived to maintain some control as they turned the screw mechanism that lowered the boat slowly to the water. There she floated easily enough, though the pressure of the waves kept pushing her against the stern, which was protected by two rope fenders fore and aft. Two of the seamen got down into her whilst Lattimore and the other two began to pass down boxes of supplies. They did not need to be told about load distribution and as each box came down it was stowed in such a way as to keep the boat even in the water. She also became a lot heavier as tins of food and crates of dry-goods, clothes, tools and all kinds of useful objects were passed down into her. With five men in her she would be well laden, but seaworthy enough to make for Palmyra Island where they would be adequately equipped to survive.

The best intentions of mice and men do not always play out as they might wish, for as they worked the swell of the ocean rose more and more, and as the weight of the boat increased, the pressure with which she was forced against the ship also mounted. The rope fenders that protected her sides could only shield against a certain level of impact. If the pressure pushing the fragile boat against the ship increased more, then there was a danger that one side of it could simply cave in. Lattimore saw to his alarm that the side of the jolly boat bent like a bow every time she contacted the *Henry James*.

'Run her round to the side with her bows to the waves; look sharp now for she cannot take much more of this.'

The men needed no convincing and set to work immediately. In the darkness the struggle was a hard one, but their manoeuvre was initially successful. The boat was tethered to the side of the ship by a bowline and rode protected by its fenders, swinging gently against the poop on which they stood. The two men on board her climbed back onto the poop. Lattimore moved to the rail of the poop, looked forward and caught his breath. The large waves coming from the rear were sweeping past the vessel to break on the reef ahead, but the well deck of the ship was a swirling foaming mass of back eddies and whirlpools. If the jolly boat was untethered and got sucked in to that area it would be smashed to pieces against the deckhouse and the mast.

'Man the boat, Captain?'

'Look over here Donnell.'

'Good God, sir!   If we get swept in there it would be the end of us all. What must we do?'

'We shall try calming it. There's a cask of oil in the boat. Hand it back up here and we shall pour it all out. If it has any effect then we shall take our chance.'

With hope high in his mind Lattimore watched as the oil was poured onto the water in the well deck area, only to feel a keen disappointment, as there was no discernible effect. For a moment he stared non-plussed, then turned to find his four men awaiting further instructions. By now the water was breaking over the poop, swirling round their feet and it would not be long before the waves would make a clean break across the whole length of the ship. The only saving mercy was that the sky had turned grey and to his surprise Lattimore found that he could see the horizon; it was Civil Twilight. He wished that he knew what time it was, but his watch was below his feet in the flooded cabin, as were his reading glasses. He regretted those, for although he could see perfectly well for most things, he could not read or see detail without them.

'The only thing for it is to go. However, if we attempt it from here we shall inevitably be pulled into the well deck area. There is nothing for it but to heave her back to the stern with her nose to the waves and try to row her away. Even that will be risky so I want a boat nearby.'

Lattimore looked over to where Crone's boat bobbed up and down in the swell, four men at the oars; he was closer to the ship than MacDonald at that moment.

'Mr Crone!' he yelled over at the Second Officer.

'Aye sir!'

'Move closer in and stand by if you please. We are coming off and may need help. But not too close Mr Crone.'

'Aye sir.'

Lattimore turned once more to his men.

'We need to haul the boat round to the stern and I think it's going to take all of you to do it.'

'Best we have a man in the boat too sir, to fend her off.'

'I agree Shearer, and that will be me.'

'But that's not the captain's job sir. Let one of us go instead.'

'You know as well as I do that the boat is a dangerous place to be.'

'It's that for sure, sir.'

'Which is exactly why I am not asking you to do it. It's my responsibility. No arguments so let's get on with it.'

The rise and fall of the jolly boat with the waves was by now considerable, but Lattimore was able to stand on the taffrail holding onto a stay from the mizzen mast and jump into the jolly boat as it rose beneath him; that was the simple part. Taking hold of an oar he fended the boat away from the ship as the men on the *Henry James* hauled on the rope to heave her back round to the stern. It all went well until the difficult manoeuvre of placing the boat so that her stern was against the ship and her bows facing the waves. The front end of the jolly boat was caught by the pressure of a huge roller and turned broadside onto the waves. To Lattimore's horror water swamped the boat and heeled her over; then to crown his anguish the rope holding her to the ship snapped and his men fell back on the deck in disorder. The sudden jerk caused the jolly boat to reel in the water and Lattimore was thrown into the sea. He could not swim. The boat, caught by the waves was swept away and into the well-deck area. There, under the eyes of the appalled sailors clinging onto the poop, it smashed to pieces against the deckhouse and all the stores on board her disappeared into a welter of furious water.

Lattimore sank a short distance, but it was now quite light and his initial reactions were those of most people when they fall into water. If it is not cold enough to shock them, their first instinct is to solve the problem; he did this by holding his breath and flailing his arms and legs in a rough imitation of what he knew swimmers did. It had the desired effect and he broke the surface, gasping like a fish slapping the water and attempting to stay afloat.

It did not work of course, and he went down again weighed by his soaked and voluminous nightshirt. He held his breath again, but salt water got up his nose and down his throat so he opened his eyes, which also stung. By more flailing he again managed to break surface. This time, however, he was choking and gagging as his airways reacted to the fluid invasion. Then he sank a third time.

John Crone had watched the events of the last few minutes with mounting disbelief from his place in the rear of the launch some 100 yards out from the ship. When the captain had fallen into the water Mrs Hastings had screamed, whilst Reverend Taylor had expressed the hope that Lattimore could swim.

'I'd be surprised if he could sir; most sailors cannot. Pull men; I want us closer in.'

'What are you doing, Mr Crone?'

Mrs Hastings was looking at Crone, who was fastening the long rope that had been used to tether the boat to the ship around his waist.

'I'm going to get the captain, Madam.'

Turning to the men on the oars, he gave instructions.

'McClements; you are in charge. Close up on the poop and get our fellows off there. Reverend, may I ask you and the other passengers to haul me back in when I have the captain?'

'You are not going into that sea, man? You'll drown.'

'I most certainly am; and I will not!'

As the launch closed in on the poop Crone stood up, dived into the sea and headed straight for where Lattimore's arms waved impotently as he sank again.

Crone swam like a dolphin and ten powerful strokes took him to where the captain had just disappeared. Grabbing beneath the water he found his hand entangled in Lattimore's hair, so, gripping it, he heaved him up and his head broke water again. Shifting his position he put his arm around Lattimore's chest and shouted at him roughly.

'Now stop threshing about or you'll drown us both!'

To his great relief Lattimore stopped his frantic struggling and began to gasp in a rather alarming manner; he had evidently taken on a lot of water. Crone turned his head towards the launch and shouted, 'Haul away!' and the willing hands on the boat began to pull him towards safety as he held Lattimore's head above water. As they pulled him towards the launch Able Seaman McClements maneuvered it so that the four men on the poop were able to jump down into her. The captain was barely conscious of what was happening; the process of half-drowning is weakening to those who go through it and he wheezed as he struggled to get air into his lungs, at the same time as he tried to cough out water. Reverend Taylor was surprisingly strong and it was he who first grabbed Lattimore and began to haul him in, ably assisted by Mr Carter from steerage, and by William Lancaster, the stowaway.

'Loosen his collar and set him face down,' commanded the Reverend. 'It'll help get the water out of him.'

They laid Lattimore over one of the seats, bent in the middle and he coughed and spluttered, retching for breath, panting and sobbing the air into his lungs. Crone in the meantime had been pulled back into the boat and sat calmly wringing out his shirt. For modesty's sake he did not perform the same office to his trousers, as there were ladies present.

'Lay us alongside Mr MacDonald's boat,' Crone commanded the oarsmen. 'I think we need to talk.'

'Mr Crone.'

Lattimore managed to turn himself round and sat in the bottom of the boat looking at the Second Mate.

'Have you the men off the poop?'

'Aye sir, safe and well.'

'Mr Crone I owe you my life; thank you. Thank you so much John Crone; give me your hand.'

Taking Crone's hand Lattimore shook it firmly. 'Thank you John; I am your friend for life.'

'Aye sir,' said Crone with a grin, 'but also my commanding officer. Orders, sir?'

He knew well what the orders would be.

'Palmyra Mr Crone, and with all speed possible. I've lost all our supplies, but let us get these good people safe to land and then worry about that.'

'You did not lose them sir; it's the way of the sea. I saw the whole thing. The sea took them and God knows that there was nothing more you could have done that would have prevented it.'

'That's a very phlegmatic view in a young man, Mr Crone.'

'I have no doubt that it is, Reverend, but I've been sailing since I was a child and my father and grandfather before me. What you get is no more than my own thoughts.'

'I can see that. Is there anything I can do to help?'

'There is, sir. See to the captain, for he is exhausted; some spirits might help and there's some whisky in that locker. Above all pray for our deliverance. It's between thirty and forty miles to land and against the wind. We shall need all the help we can get. Mr MacDonald, did you hear the order?'

'I did, Mr Crone. I'll lead and you must keep close company with us. Use six men and change them every half hour. Be sparing with both water and food for we are in God's hands now; anything can happen. All hands to take a turn, officers included.'

'Aye sir; that goes without saying.'

Crone took an oar and set it in the rowlocks.

'Ready; give way together; pull!'

'By "All Hands" I take him to mean all the men, Mr Crone?'

'No Reverend; he meant all the crew.'

'Well for my part I wish to take a turn. Our lives are at stake too; I'm sure I speak for the rest of the men. I will pull at an oar Mr Crone and will accept no demur.'

A chorus of approval greeted this forceful declaration.

'I've rowed before,' declared the young American, Mr Carter. 'I was in my college team.'

'It's a bit different to rowing on a lake sir, but I have no objections to saving the energy of the crew; we have a long way to go. If the captain is happy about it then I'd be glad if the gentlemen took a turn, but I warn you that it will probably mean blisters.'

'When I consider blisters,' rumbled Reverend Taylor, 'I judge them preferable to the alternative.'

'Which is, sir?'

'Being lost at sea with an exhausted crew and possibly dying, when I could have lent a hand in my own salvation.'

'I will readily concede, sir, that you know a lot more about salvation than I do. You may have this oar in thirty minutes and glad of your help.'

'How long to the island do you think?'

It was Lattimore who answered.

'The wind is against us, but it's light. The sea is against us too, but we are making way through it. At this rate if all goes well we should reach the island this evening.'

'At what hour?' asked Mr Hastings.

'That is hard to say, but I should think between six and seven o'clock.'

'But it will get dark around 6.30 will it not? It's seven o'clock now. That's only three miles an hour; can we not go faster?'

'It will indeed get dark at that time, so we must hope to arrive when there is sufficient daylight to land. As to going faster, that can only happen if the wind backs, which may well happen. We are in the hands of Providence in that regard.'

'Amen!'

'Indeed, sir. Mr Crone, where did you learn to swim?'

'In the River Ellen near Maryport, sir; my father taught me.'

'I'm glad he did.'

'So am I sir; it's been useful on a couple of occasions.'

'Now Mr Crone, you said a curious thing earlier. You said that most sailors cannot swim.'

'That's right Mrs Taylor.'

'I find that odd. I would have thought that it would have been one of the first things that men who sail on the sea would learn; such a thing could save their lives at times like this.'

'I do agree ma'am and so did my family, but there's another argument you see and I can see both points of view.'

'What other view could there possibly be against having such a vital skill?'

'Take a look around you ma'am. What do you see?'

'Why the ocean, as far as I can see.'

'Exactly; far, far from land and out of sight of ships. If a man is in the water and there is no rescue, what does it profit him to swim? It is also why so many sailors wear gold earrings.'

'I don't understand.'

'If you can swim ma'am, all you do is prolong the agony and stave off the inevitable, preserving hope where there is no hope. Imagine the anguish of mind, the realization, the despair, the panic; and in the end you die. It's better in the minds of many sailing men that the end should come quickly.'

'Oh. I can see that now, but is it not a bit like suicide? To deliberately ignore that which might save your life? And what have earrings got to do with it?'

'It could be seen that way I suppose, but I take a more charitable view which is that it's an acceptance of the will of

God. If your time has come, then there's not a lot that a sailor man can do about it. Which is correct from a religious viewpoint I am happy to leave to the Reverend. As to the earrings they are gold so if a man is washed up on a foreign shore there is enough about him to pay for a decent burial. To many men death is not worse than ending up in a pauper's grave.'

'Well my dear,' said Reverend Taylor 'Mr Crone has to row and I imagine that it is hard to both talk and row at the same time, so let us leave him in peace; philosophy can come later. What do you say, Captain?'

There came no reply. Lattimore, twenty-four hours without sleep and exhausted by what he had gone through, was unconscious to the world, drying out in the warmth of the morning sun, occasionally emitting a small snore.

On the pinnace MacDonald was steering and on the face of it was very calm.

'Are you not worried at all, Mr MacDonald?'

'The speaker was the bosun, William Ferguson with whom MacDonald was on good terms, for each man respected the professionalism of the other. Ferguson was a prime seaman who aspired to have his master's ticket one day but for the moment had accepted the post of bosun on the *Henry James* as Captain Lattimore was his cousin. This could have created some tensions in the chain of command were it not for the fact that the cousins were not particularly close and Ferguson was quite happy to take orders from a male relation. He was not a large man, but wiry with long arms and a bullet head which could have given him a natural air of aggression, but it was tempered by a brown moustache that he thought looked military, but in fact gave him a slightly doleful appearance.

'Not at all Mr Ferguson; not at all,' replied MacDonald.

'Why would you not be?'

MacDonald looked at the bosun, and then spoke loud enough for all the men in his boat to hear.

'Man and boy I have been going down to the sea for over fifteen years and I have been wrecked before. We have escaped with our lives and though we have nothing but what is in this boat, there is a good sea and land within our grasp. Those who use the sea must expect something like this as part of their work so you will not find me cursing fate because of it. We must accept it as what it is. No-one has died so let us be thankful for this mercy and work our way towards Palmyra Island.'

Here he broke off and felt in the pocket of his trousers, fishing out a well used pipe, which he stuck between his teeth, sucking on it.

'I would guess that no-one on this boat has any dry matches about them? Mine are soaked.'

Looking around and seeing shaking heads, he continued, 'Ach weel I see that I shall not be having a smoke until we get to the island, so pull away my lads for the sooner we get there, the happier I shall be.'

To dispel any remaining doubts about the positive nature of his thoughts he looked around and addressed the sail-maker.

'Mr Campbell; I have heard you in your workshop many a time singing away at your labours. In my opinion, sir, you have a fine voice and can hold a tune well. Give us a song to pull along to and help the time go better.'

'Aye, sir. Thank you for the compliment; I do have a voice and a song you shall have.'

So he commenced a well-known shanty, the chorus of which was joined in by all:

"I've got a coat and a nobby, nobby coat
I've got a coat a-seen a lot of rough weather
For the sides are near wore out and the back is flying about

*And the lining's looking out for better weather
Here's to the grog, boys, the jolly, jolly grog
Here's to the rum and tobacco
I've a-spent all my tin with the lassies drinking gin
And to cross the briny ocean I must wander."*

As the crew sang, MacDonald found time to reflect on their situation and thought that it could be worse. The most important thing in his mind was that he would be able to obey his aunt's strict instruction and a mental picture of her face formed in his head.

'Get home safe to Lewis.'

'Aye; I will. I'll always make it safe home,' Was his emphatic, though unspoken response.

The boat fairly flew across the waves and eventually MacDonald had to admonish the men at the oars to go steady as they did not wish to leave Mr Crone's boat behind. Three hours of hard pulling took them nine miles towards their goal by his reckoning, but the rowers were getting tired; it was a long time since they had eaten their last meal and the supply of food and drink on the boats was sparse. Another and far more serious problem was manifesting itself. Most of the men had no shirts and a few of them no clothes at all. The tropical sun was doing its work and MacDonald could see that the searing rays were turning men scarlet, in some cases all over. There was no place to put them either except under the covered front end which was too small for all affected. To gain them some respite he took to telling two men at a time to shelter under it for 30 minutes at a time; unlike Lattimore he had kept his watch. These poor souls, he thought, were going to be very badly burned and in a lot of pain before too long. The strain of men rowing for miles who had not had a meal for many hours was another worry to him, and he prayed for a change in the wind which he felt in his skin, could not be far off. When the change in the weather came, it came quickly, suddenly and was noticed first of all in the other boat.

'Mr Crone; that is a most curious cloud formation, is it not?'

'It is Mrs Hastings,' replied Crone who had been looking at the tall cloud that had appeared over the horizon with a black line underneath it. 'It's a squall and I fear we are going to get rather wet.'

'What is a squall please?'

'It's a sudden and very quick increase in wind speed, ma'am. It comes with rain and sometimes thunder. They can come with a change of wind direction which can be a good or a bad thing.'

'Is this a good one?'

'Only time will tell us that, ma'am. You men, stand by with the bailers.'

Anticipating that they were all going to get a soaking, the people in the boats continued to row, but tropical squalls are fickle things. This particular disturbance in the weather was such a one, and it became apparent that it was going to pass them by, but on the west; the direction they were heading. It was MacDonald, an experienced blue-water man, who became aware of what was really happening first.

'You men; get that mast shipped. I want that sail up now.'

Then he called back to Crone; 'Mr Crone, I believe that the wind will be with us very shortly. You know what to do.'

'Aye sir,' shouted back Crone, waking up Lattimore in the process. MacDonald was right in his surmise. The wind stilled as the squall passed to their front, then backed to blow south easterly. Both the pinnace and the launch now positively raced over the sea towards Palmyra.

'It may not last very long, but we must be doing at least twenty knots and maybe more,' said Lattimore. 'A fine brisk wind.'

The condition of the people in the boat grew perilous during the day and MacDonald feared that some might perish of sunstroke. In the expectation of getting to land quickly he was free with the water supplies, but the skin of many men was turning a vivid red and under these conditions they would be crucified in their own boats if their ordeal went on for much longer. The wind lasted enough to blow them twenty nautical miles or so on their way and by the time it died down they were within sight of Palmyra Atoll some five or six miles away. With the calm and in the lee of the island the swell of the waves also subsided which made rowing much easier. Lowering their sails and unshipping their masts the boats approached the island steadily, only to find that they could not reach it because the way was blocked by a coral reef. Inside the reef was a shallow lagoon perhaps a mile wide, temptingly calm and with white beaches and green palm trees tantalizingly close. The boats drew near to each other.

'We must try to find a way through the reef Mr MacDonald,' called Lattimore over to the Mate. 'I know there must be one from stories I have heard of people being on the island. It will be dark soon. I think it would be safest to lay offshore until first light or we may come to grief in the dark.'

MacDonald heard this clearly enough but thought it foolishly over-cautious and decided that he had not 'heard' it. He looked across at Lattimore. Some distance away and gestured at his ears with a frown, indicating that the captain's words had not been clear enough. Turning to the men in his boat he told them to pull quickly away, parallel to the reef, which they did, some smiling broadly. Soon they really were out of clear earshot of the captain's boat, though they could hear incoherent shouting. Lattimore's boat followed, but they could not catch up to MacDonald.

MacDonald's boat led the way steering well clear of the sharp coral, heading round the island in a clockwise direction.

59

In the clear water numerous reef sharks could be seen, sleepy in the warm sunny shallows. Finding a way in was not easy and it took another three hours of rowing until they found a gap in the reef on the western side of Palmyra by a sandy island. They headed straight for land in front of them where they could see tall trees. The water in the lagoon was deep enough to float the boats, but as they got closer in towards the shore it became shallow and also evident that this was high tide. At this point of the lagoon, at low water they would be standing on a rock platform. Now the men got out of the boats, deeming it not deep enough for sharks, and began to pull them through the shallows towards a white beach, only the women and children staying on board. The sun went down at 6.35pm and they still had not reached the island so in the Nautical Twilight they continued to strain and pull until at exactly seven o'clock the nose of the pinnace touched the sand, followed shortly afterwards by the launch. The first foot to shore was canine as Bruno bounded out of the boat, splashed to the sand and ran straight into the trees bordering the beach barking excitedly; the humans were a little more restrained. It was exactly twelve hours since they had left the *Henry James*. There was no conferring about what should be done next; in the pitch black, some exhausted men climbed back into the boats, rejoining the women and children, draped themselves over the seats and went to sleep. Others simply flung themselves down onto the beach and did likewise. The one exception was the Reverend Taylor who went down on his knees with clasped hands.

'MOST blessed and glorious Lord God, who art of infinite goodness and mercy; we, thy poor creatures, whom thou hast made and preserved, holding our souls in life, and now rescuing us out of the jaws of death, humbly present ourselves again before thy Divine Majesty, to offer a sacrifice of praise and thanksgiving, for that thou heardst us when we called in

our trouble, and didst not cast out our prayer, which we made before thee in our great distress: even when we gave all for lost, our ship, our goods, our lives, then didst thou mercifully look upon us, and wonderfully command a deliverance; for which we, now being in safety, do give all praise and glory to thy Holy Name; through Jesus Christ our Lord. Amen.'

'Amen,' said Ralph Lattimore, and then he too fell asleep as if dead.

However, there was not much sleep for anyone that night, for a tropical storm hit the island; furious and lashing with rain, it blew up in the small hours causing the whole company to run into whatever shelter they could find in the tree-line until its rage had passed over. When it was done, once again all flopped exhausted onto the sand by the palms. If they had been offshore during this storm, waiting for dawn, they would have been swept away and perished within sight of the island.

Chapter 4

Palmyra

Ordinary seaman Charles Dordey awoke in the greyness before dawn the next morning with a loud yell, which in turn roused everyone to alarm. He was one of the men lying on the beach and had been fast asleep when a huge something had run over his legs. Waking immediately he had seen what looked like an enormous spider scurrying away towards the sea. The dog Bruno pursued it barking loudly, though keeping a cautious distance, until Lattimore called him back.

'Why that's good news anyway,' declared Mrs Taylor. 'That's a coconut crab such as they have in Samoa, and they are delicious for eating; there's no danger of starving if we have crab meat.'

'Is that so Madam?' declared Dordey. 'In that case I'll have that one for breakfast,' and made to go after the crab.

'Belay there!' said Lattimore. 'We may well eat that crab or another, but not raw. At the moment, Dordey, we have no fire and your crab may well rot before we are able to cook it.' Then he called to the rest of his company, now roused from sleep, 'As we are all awake you might as well gather round for breakfast; or what will pass as it.'

The survivors grouped themselves around the bow of the pinnace while MacDonald and Lattimore allowed them each a half of ship's hard tack biscuit and a measure of water from the emergency supplies in the lockers. The water container had to be passed round for each person to drain off, as there were not enough containers for everyone. It was a sparse meal and not very satisfying. They did not present an edifying spectacle. Most of the crew had been off watch and in their hammocks; some had no shirts or shoes, and one man was without trousers, clad only in his drawers; three were stark naked and suffering much from the sunburn they had received in the journey to the island. They had been exposed to the full fury of the sun for twelve hours. Some of the burns on their backs and shoulders were deep and angry looking and great blisters were appearing all over their bodies. The men who had no clothes could barely move, weeping for the pain of it and at their joints or wrinkles the epidermis opened and seeped clear lymph. There was nothing to treat them with either, and Lattimore thought they would be best out of the sun as soon as possible. Sooner or later there would be infection, pus and possibly blood poisoning and the burns needed to be tended with something. It was his duty, in the absence of a surgeon, to see to the medical needs of his crew, but he had nothing with which to do so. All the medical equipment had gone with the jolly boat and now lay at the bottom of the sea. The passengers were in similar case, the ladies and children being in night-dresses whilst Reverend Taylor looked like an old testament prophet, a flowing night-gown down to his ankles, tied round the middle with a piece of cord that he had found on the launch. Few of them had any headgear save MacDonald and Crone who had retained their cheese-cutter hats, and the tropical sun was making them wince also as it hit their skins, already inflamed from the previous day's exposure. Taylor, Hastings and their wives had not suffered as much because they all wore nightgowns, as did Lattimore, whilst the four little girls had abundant hair, which protected them well. They were as ragged a bunch of scarecrows as could be imagined and very badly equipped to face what was in front of them. Still they were on dry land and would not drown; Lattimore had decided to say nothing to MacDonald about his not following his instructions the previous evening. There was, he thought, no point. After a few minutes he addressed the group again.

'You men with no clothes and those with hardly any; you must go into the tree line out of the sun. There will be little of practical use that you can do and the best thing for you is to get into the shade. Go there now and await my orders.'

Eight seamen shambled into the dimness under the trees fringing the beach. Lattimore now addressed himself to the remaining members of his party.

'We now need to look round this area and find what is in the immediate vicinity. It's one of the few places to land, so logic says that if there is any human habitation, it may well be in this area. Please get yourselves into groups of four or five, let us go into the trees and see if we can find anything useful. By that I mean people, huts, fruit trees, berries, anything! If you find nothing then return here in one hour; if you find something then shout and we shall all come to you.'

'Are we likely to find any people here Captain?' enquired Frederick Hastings.

'I think not, sir. As far as I am aware the island is uninhabited; if there are people then we shall be fortunate unless they be castaways like ourselves.'

'No pirates Mr Lattimore?'

'No pirates Mrs Taylor; the tale I told you happened many years ago. I think we shall be quite safe in that respect.'

'Why then let us go and look to see what we shall find. I declare that I feel quite the intrepid explorer.'

Very delicately, for she was barefoot, she began to pad over towards the tall trees fringing the edge of what turned out to be tropical jungle. There she stopped and turned to her husband.

'William. This is absurd. If we go in there with our feet bare then they shall be cut to ribbons.'

'I agree my dear, but what do you suggest we do about it?'

'Each of us is walking about in a voluminous ankle length garment of good quality cloth. I should like to cut them short and make strips to bind feet with.'

'Would that not be rather immodest? I think we should keep them as they are.'

Mrs Taylor had been married to him for a long time, and though he might aspire to rule people's actions, she had set her red lines many years before and was very much her own woman.

'Oh fiddlesticks! I'd rather have bare legs than cut feet; or would you rather have me hobbling round with sore and infected feet. Just think of all those Polynesian women you have ever seen wandering around bare chested. Land sakes I'm not proposing to go that far, but let us show some sense. Some of those men are in the same case as ourselves as regards footwear. Needs must William and the Lord helps those who help themselves; and in our case, clothed in abundant cloth, it would be downright unchristian not to share what we have. Just think of St Martin sharing his cloak, then think you might do likewise.'

She called over to the nearest group of sailors,

'You men; yes you. Will you come over here please?'

The nearest group of sailors came over to hear what she had to say.

'Have any of you got your knives about you? I know that sailors carry good blades and I have need of one.'

Several of the men did indeed have their jackknives and readily offered them and she took the nearest.

'Thank you. Mr MacDonald is it not?'

'Yes ma'am; ship's carpenter.'

'Is it not rather confusing that you have the same name as the First Officer?'

'Oh no ma'am. He is Mr MacDonald, but I answer to plain "Mac" so there is no confusion. Also as you may have noticed, he has an air to him which I do not share, though he is my own brother.'

'He's your brother! Now I come to think of it there is a resemblance that I had not noticed. You mean that you laugh a lot and he does not. Well Mr Mac, you have bare feet. If you will tarry a few minutes I think we shall be able to help you. Children come here. And you also William - and yes Frederick too! Dorothea; come here too.'

Mrs Taylor was evidently what the Americans might have called 'a pioneer woman.' She was of strong mind and would not let the vicissitudes or accidents of life gain any advantage over her. If there was a challenge that she was required to overcome then she was game to give it a go. Telling all the men to avert their eyes and turn to face the sea, she slipped off her nightgown and hacked away at it with Mac's very sharp knife, removing a good part of its length, and also the sleeves. Then she put it back on and set about those worn by her husband, son in law, daughter and grandchildren. Within a short time each child and the four night-shirted adults were wearing what looked like Roman tunics to just below their knees, with very ragged edges, and Mrs Taylor was carving up the sleeves she had gathered into long strips. The first two she folded, and then took a thick leathery leaf from a nearby shrub. Placing the leaf under her foot she wound the material round and round binding it into place as a 'sole', tying a knot on top. When both feet were done she stood up.

'There! That's better than nothing. Now I feel that I can explore.'

Over the space of about half an hour her husband, Mr and Mrs Hastings and the children were similarly shod, using some but by no means all of the material made available. Handing over some strips of material to a grateful John MacDonald and some of the other shoeless men, she left them to do as she had done, and walked over to where some of the unclothed men were lying on the edge of the jungle under the trees. Seeing her coming, they were horrified for she was a Reverend's wife and they were naked; sailors they might be, but if they had not been scarlet from the sun then their blushes would have made them so. A couple of them appeared disorientated and were having difficulty staying upright, but the rest of the group were embarrassed beyond measure.

'Please ma'am. Mrs Taylor it's not decent to see us like this.'

'Stuff and nonsense! The indecency of it would be to leave you so; just look at the state of those burns.'

'But you're the Reverend's wife! T'aint right!'

'Nonsense! It makes it even more necessary that I come here and help you for if I did not then Our Lord would not be pleased with me.'

Seeing their puzzled looks she explained,

'I was a stranger and ye took me not in; naked and ye did not clothe me. Now stop being so foolish and take these lengths of material. Each of them is enough to make either a kilt or a loincloth. See? I have given you raiment so all is as it should be; as the Bible commands. I cannot protect you fully from the sun, but this will be of some help.'

That was different; if it was in the Bible then it was right, so each man took a piece of cloth and wrapped it round his waist, making it stay up, not without difficulty, by tucking it in round the waist like a towel.

'There. Does not that feel better? And do you not think it right?'

They did, and were profuse in their thanks. She was even able to give them some strips from the sleeves and to show them what she had done to protect her own feet.

Mrs Taylor was not alone in making the most of the clothing that she and her family had about their persons. Lattimore himself cut up his own nightshirt and made for himself a knee-length kilt wrapped round his middle, and some foot protectors, then handed the rest of the cloth to men who had nothing. It was unfortunate, as he well knew, that his upper protection against the sun was thus given away but there was little choice save to have the men walking about in a state of indecency and ill protected against nature. At least he had a choice of walking in the sun or under the trees; in the boat that option had not been available to those who had been badly burned. To an outsider now, he would have cut a very strange figure, rags wrapped round his feet, a crude kilt and a sheath knife stuck in the waist, his only other item of adornment being the gold ring on his left hand. He looked at this closely, wondering if he could make a fishhook out of it if the worst came to the worst. The compass and square engraved within its bezel twinkled in the sunlight and he decided that he did not really wish to do that. He might not have had much to do with the Freemasons since he joined, but it was a link to a civilized existence that he now yearned after with a keenness that surprised him. For the moment, the Robinson Crusoe of popular illustrations, if placed alongside Lattimore for comparison, would have looked the acme of civilization.

Further along the beach, John Crone, who had his shoes, was already well into the undergrowth. Once past the tall trees that bordered the beach he had entered a lush green world under a great canopy of leaves and found it quite dim, though it was humid and damp smelling. The undergrowth was easy to walk through, being composed of various types of fern, growing in a black damp soil that cushioned his feet as he walked. There were few stones and no plants with thorns or prickles. He was beginning to think it quite pleasant, so shady and out of the sun, when he heard a growling and a chomping noise. For a moment he froze, thinking he had come across a dangerous animal, but then he saw a dark shape on the other side of a bush nearby and recognized Bruno. He had caught a small red land crab and was eating it with some relish, having cracked it open with his teeth. It was apparent that he did not care for the hard bits of shell because there were several carapaces around that had been treated similarly; Bruno had learned that there was meat inside and bit and licked it out. Clearly the dog could fend for himself and was not going to starve.

'Good lad Bruno,' said Crone. 'Just don't try it on one of those big buggers for their claws would bite you in two.'

The dog paused momentarily to look at him and for one crazy moment Crone wondered if he had understood. Then he realized that he was being daft, dismissed the thought.

'Well, if you can eat land crabs then so can we. Well done, lad. I shall try mine boiled if you don't mind. If we can find something to boil them in.'

Donald MacDonald stood on the beach with able seaman Ned Tumelty, another western isles man, and had a most considering look on his face.

'Well Ned, you've seen as many fishing villages as I have. If you were to site a house in this bay and on this beach, where would you place it?'

Tumelty considered this for a few moments.

'I would want it well above high water of course; and away from the wind; so behind the trees, but not too far because I should need to fish. Water would be a consideration, but I do not see any. The prevailing wind here is the nor' east trades and the beach faces sou' west. I think that I would wish to be on the western side of the bay or my house would be facing into the waves coming through the gap in the reef all the time. I would prefer to launch my boat where it was calmer.'

'That was my thought too. Shall we?'

The two men set off along the beach without deviating into the forest at all.

Lattimore was still at the boats, this, for the moment, being the centre of operations. He had retained Thomas Morgan, his steward, and James Wilson the cook with him because he needed to talk to them privately.

'I think you can probably guess why I want to talk to you.'

'Aye sir,' replied Morgan. 'Food.'

'Correct,' said Lattimore. 'We are thirty souls on this island and we need to eat at least one good meal a day if we are to survive.'

'Jim and I have already been talking about it, sir, and we have a few ideas, but it depends on foraging. If people find stuff we reckon we can manage. We've already seen a few things that can be ate, but we'll need a fire, sir, and I don't think anyone's got matches.'

'Don't worry about that,' said Lattimore. 'We shall have fire, but tell me, what have you seen?'

'For a start, sir, there's those big coconut crabs. That's a fine meal for a lot of people, especially if you make it into a broth. They eat them in Samoa.'

'And I've seen peppergrass growing in the tree-line, sir,' interjected Wilson. 'And there's salt in the rocks near the shore.'

'Lots of coconuts as well, not forgetting seaweed, fish, shellfish and whatever else we find. That's just what we know about. There'll be other things when we come across them.'

'What is peppergrass?'

'It's what it says, sir. I take an interest in food as you might expect.'

'As a cook I should think it a natural thing.'

'Yes sir; well when we was in Samoa I tried the local food. Anyway, sir, they use peppergrass and I asked the cook what it was and he showed me. You can use it as a vegetable or as a seasoning; very useful flavouring it is, sir. I actually used it in a stew I served you the other night, sir.'

'The hot mutton stew?'

'Aye sir.'

'And a fine stew it was too. Oh well, if you are certain, please make further use of it.'

'So, as you can see, sir, provided we can find something to cook in, like a pot or similar, we should be able to get by.'

'You seem very confident about that Morgan. Why is that?'

'Bless you sir; we're from Maryport; we're Cumbrians.'

'I don't follow.'

'Folk can go through very hard times there, sir; wages are low and sometimes not enough to live on. If it's edible Cumbrians can cook it, don't you fret. It'll be a sort of burgoo, but without flour to thicken it because we ain't got any. There is only one problem though.'

'What's that Morgan?'

'Water sir.'

Morgan pronounced it 'watter' but he did not need to elaborate; his pithy delivery said more than a page of explanation.

'There does not seem to be a stream near here. We must find one.'

'Yes sir, but if there is none?'

'There has to be. I've heard of people surviving on this island and they could not have done it without water.'

'By your leave sir, it might take a long time to find it and thirty people take a lot of water. Jim's had an idea about that too.'

'What's your idea, Wilson?'

'It's been my observation that it rains a lot in tropical waters, sir.'

'You are proposing that we gather rain?'

'Yes sir; if we position some palm leaves to run like gutters down into our water butts we should be able to keep them topped up.'

'It's a good idea; I think you two should set about it now.'

'Aye sir.'

71

Lattimore reflected that a diet of burgoo, the sailor's staple diet, a stew into which anything could be thrown, would at least keep them alive, even if it did become rather monotonous.

By now MacDonald and Tumelty had reached the point on the beach where they thought a settlement might be and they entered the tree line. As they did so, a broad smile crossed Tumelty's face. In front of them were six huts. They were overgrown and surrounded by ferns; the roof of one of them had fallen in and red land crabs scuttled out of them as the men approached, but huts they were, and could be used for shelter. They were well built and of ships' timbers if MacDonald was any judge; and though they had been there some time they were clearly still sound.

'You've a loud voice Ned. Go and tell them.'

Tumelty moved back onto the sand, cupped his hands and roared, 'Ahoy!' back towards the boats. He repeated the call and figures began to appear out of the trees, moving towards him. MacDonald went to the huts and looked into the first one. Of all things that could possibly have been there, the most incongruous object that caught his eye was a round grindstone. How long it had been there could not be known. Scattered round the floor were some old square tins, quite empty, but his mind noted them as being useful. The other huts revealed more objects of potential use; in the corner of one, a rusty old harpoon leaned, covered in dust, but the real prize came in the third hut he visited. In the centre of it, under an aperture in the roof for letting out smoke, was a large old cast iron cauldron style cooking pot suspended from an iron tripod. A few smaller pans were scattered round the floor. Inside the big one was a black mess, evidently the remains of some meal, abandoned uneaten. Walking over to the next hut, he paused by a large tree where he could see that someone had been carving into the bark. The letters were mostly illegible, but his eye was caught by one name in particular that he traced over with his fingers -

'Iona'. Had some countryman of his been stranded here? The men of the western isles travelled the world, he knew, for salt water was in their blood and the urge to sail, out west to find the setting sun was strong in his own mind as he well knew. Had a man of the Hebrides been here before him and carved the name of the land he longed to see on this tree far from home? There was no way of knowing, but he wondered who it was, this wayfarer, maybe even kin to him, who had spent time in this strange place on the far side of the world from where he longed to return. How long had he spent here? Did he make it home? Dour he might have been, but that single word carved on the tree made MacDonald think of far away isles shrouded in mist, green and purple with heather, and sharp damp air which people breathed to speak the Gaelic. Homesickness was almost alien to him save when he thought of his family, but a pang touched his soul as he thought of fishing between Tarbert and Lochmaddy. Ah, he would do that again no doubt, but not today. This day was about how to survive, and he had no doubts that he would, and get home safe to Aunt Margaret.

It was not long before people began to arrive, including Lattimore. John Crone also walked into the space in front of the huts accompanied by the dog, bounding in front of him panting with excitement. It was plain that at least one being on the island liked living on the beach and by the sea.

'Are there any spiders in the huts?' asked Estella Hastings with all the fear of her young age.

'I should think there are a few Miss,' replied Hugh Shearer, one of the able seamen, 'but don't you worry about that. I'll soon see to them!'

Ducking down into one of the huts, Shearer looked round and found a few small spiders which he grabbed, cupping them in his hands, taking them outside and releasing them into a bush.

'Those are cane spiders, aren't they?' asked Reverend Taylor. 'Do they not bite you?'

'Well Reverend,' smiled Shearer, 'They try, but you see they don't succeed.'

He held out his hands for Taylor to look at and they were quite literally as hard as horn.

'I don't think they'll get through that, do you Padre?'

'I should think not!' marveled Taylor. 'That's as hard a hand as I ever saw.'

'Hard hauling on many ropes does that Padre. Spiders don't worry me, fangs or not.'

'Were these huts built by pirates?' asked Mrs Hastings, a slight note of anxiety in her voice.

'They might well have been,' replied Lattimore, surprised at such a level headed woman fearing such things, 'But whoever built them they are good huts and they will shelter us better than sleeping under a palm tree.'

He now asserted his authority.

'It's quite clear that this will be our base for now. Let us spend an hour or so clearing out these huts and making them fit for use, and then we must forage, if we are to eat more than bread and water. Anything useful that you find, please bring out into the space here, which I shall clear with Mr MacDonald, Sam Young and Charles Dordey.'

It was slightly more than an hour later when the space in front of the huts was cleared, the huts made suitable for use, fronds and ferns laid down in them for beds, and all useful objects placed in the open space. Several sailors swarmed up onto the roofs of the huts repairing the gaps in them with fresh palm leaves. In the open space were the grindstone, the harpoon, tin cans, the cauldron, a very rusty saw, an axe, an equally rusty large boathook and the remains of a machete that had been bent out of shape. There were even three tins containing an amount of paraffin, an old oil lamp that hung from a hook on the wall, and a few empty bottles. In addition to this Morgan and Wilson had brought up the water kegs from the boats along with their arrangements of palm leaves to catch water and channel it into the butts. Two parties of sailors had been detailed off to collect the boats and bring them round to the beach just below, so that they were within a couple of hundred yards of the huts.

Around midday a torrential rainstorm hit the island and soaked everything. The water butts overflowed and it became obvious that if this were a regular feature of the climate, as turned out to be the case, then shortage of water would not be a problem. As it turned out, this being the tropics, it rained every single day, and the supply of water was limited only by the number of receptacles available, which was not great. Nonetheless, in Lattimore's mind, it was an unpredictable source and until he found a supply of water he could rely on, his mind would not be completely at ease. Unfortunately the rain brought another problem that was to prove an incessant battle. Palmyra was home to an especially persistent and voracious form of leech. If anyone sat down or lay down to rest, even for a few minutes they very quickly acquired several of these creatures sucking at them. In disgust the men would tear them from their skins and throw them to the ground, squelching them flat with their feet, a process accompanied by much cursing and swearing. This was to prove to have some bad effects in a very short time.

Now that it was clear where the survivors would live there were two matters that needed immediate attention. He had divided them up once again into seven notional groups of four and sent them off to forage for food. The badly burned men would join their allotted group only when they were fit to do so, and in the beginning some of the groups consisted of only two people. The instruction was plain enough; each group was to come back with something to eat. It did not matter what it was so long as it was edible. Every person able to go hunting for food went, which in practice meant all but two. The only people remaining at the huts were the burn cases, Mrs Taylor and Lattimore and Thomas Morgan because they each had an important task to perform.

Mrs Taylor had approached Lattimore shortly after donating some of her spare cloth to the naked men and voiced her concern at their condition.

'Captain, I fear that the men who have been burned are in a more serious condition than may appear. I am not any kind of expert, but I have seen a few things in my lifetime; sunstroke is one of them and it is my opinion that several of your men are suffering from that.'

Lattimore looked at her consideringly.

'I have to say ma'am that it is a thing outside my experience and if you say so then I do share your concern. What has led you to this conclusion?'

'They all have headaches, they feel weak and some of them feel sick. There may be other signs but I do not know what they might be.'

'I'd be glad of any suggestions that you might make as to what we should do.'

'I think that I should stay here and do what I can Captain. It may not be much, but these poor men are in need of treatment and we must do out best with what we have.'

Mrs Taylor had procured a number of coconuts and had taken on the role of nurse, gathered the burn cases into one hut where they lay on palm leaves and grass. She had gently rubbed large amounts of coconut milk over their skins telling them that there was nothing like it for cases of burn. However, they must not go into the sun because if they did the oily milk would have a frying effect, which would make things worse, so they must stay indoors. They found it soothing and thanked her very much but there was little she could do for the severe pain that most of them were in. They all spent their day dropping into and out of sleep in a semi-comatose state, sleepy and dopey, apparently their body's way of dealing with their plight. A couple of them had their sight affected by the glare they had been exposed to, but Mrs Taylor assured them that this was temporary in her opinion and would improve if they kept out of the sun. The worst cases were those whose blisters had burst and their pain was most acute for deep sores appeared and wept all the time.

Everything was soaked when the rain came except the interior of the huts; the jungle floor was dank and steamy with tropical heat. Inside the huts though were a few sticks and fragments of leaves that were dry as dust. It was these that Lattimore and Morgan gathered now into a heap in the middle of the hut floor where fires had evidently been lit before. Taking his telescope out of its protective leather case, Lattimore unscrewed the large lens at the end and used it to focus the rays of the sun onto another small heap of dry material piled just outside the hut door. Soon it began to smoke and Morgan bent down as Lattimore held the glass steady on the leaves that it was burning. Softly, oh so gently, Morgan blew at the smoke, and the area around the bright spot began to glow. Suddenly a small flame flared up and Morgan fed it with more dry material that caught light. As it spread he added sticks and before long he had a large fire to which he could add wood. He carried a flaming brand into the hut and lit a small fire that could be protected against the rain; the smoke rose up and out of a hole in the apex of the roof. Even slightly damp wood would do the job, especially fallen timber from the woods chopped up with the rusty old axe.

Over the fire he hung the cauldron on its tripod, which he had taken down to the sea previously and scoured out with seawater and sand. In it was salt water.

'It needs to be well cleaned, sir,' he explained to Lattimore. 'If we do not boil it out first then our people may get stomach ailments. We shall boil this well, then tip it away. When we have done that it will be fit to use.'

When he judged that the cauldron was clean enough he tipped out the seawater and replaced it with fresh rainwater from their butts. To this he added salt, garnered from the shore where it crusted the rocks and threw in some of the peppergrass that grew in profusion near the huts. By this time the first of the foraging parties had returned. They carried six dead seabirds and were led by William Lancaster.

'Boobys and noddys; they have no fear of us and all you have to do is get close enough with a stick.'

'Well Lancaster, I'm glad to see them and I've no doubt our cook can make us something edible with them. Did you catch them?'

'I did Captain; three of them. I'm quite nippy on my feet.'

'Well done. Under the circumstances I think that wipes the slate between us. I can hardly prosecute a man who's provided me with a meal in the wilderness.'

Momentarily Lattimore's opinion of Lancaster soared and he thought that he might have misjudged the man. This thought was soon dashed.

'That's mighty big of you, Captain. I wasn't particularly looking for forgiveness, but I'm glad not to be facing any magistrates when we get out of here.'

Was it Lattimore's imagination, or did he detect a sneer in that remark? You could never tell with the stowaway, because a lot of what he said could have more than one meaning. Lancaster had been discovered hiding under the hatch of a cargo hold, shortly after leaving Australia. He was a man in his mid twenties who had been fined heavily for trespassing and poaching, or so he said. Lattimore wondered if it was something more serious, but took him at his word for want of any evidence to the contrary. The stowaway had apparently no prospects of any sort of life at home and had heard that the *Henry James* was heading, ultimately, to San Francisco. Having some recollection that California was a place for a man to make his fortune, he determined to stow away on board her. He had been intending to make his presence known for he was fed up with his lodgings. He had spread part of an old tarpaulin on top of the cargo of stacked coal bags, an uncomfortable bed, and had a knapsack with only half a loaf of bread and a bottle of water. It was Crone who had discovered him and ordered him out of his hidey-hole to face Lattimore in his cabin. The captain had slated him as a waster and a vagrant and warned him that he faced prosecution when they reached America. In the meantime Lancaster could damned well work his passage and if he worked hard enough Lattimore might just reconsider sending for the police. Lattimore was not sure what to make of the new addition to his complement. The stowaway was no ordinary working man; that much was clear from his cultivated vowels and evident education. He had the air about him of a gentleman fallen on hard times and Lattimore wondered what it was in his circumstances that had led such a man to stow away on a boat bound for San Francisco. He could have put him ashore at Samoa, but when they had completed the first part of the voyage Lancaster had worked hard in general labouring round the ship so Lattimore, finding him useful, had kept him on board, though still insisting on entering any mention of him in the log as 'stowaway.' His stowaway had told him after a few days at sea that actually he wished to go to California so Lattimore had allowed him to continue to work his passage without pay. Now it seemed that Lancaster had other useful talents as he held the dead birds aloft.

'I'll even pluck and gut the birds myself to seal the bargain.'

'No you won't!' said Wilson. 'I'm the cook here and there's an art to doing the job properly. I'll do it myself.'

Lancaster assented with a good grace as Lattimore thought, but the captain could not shake himself of a vague sense of dislike when he looked at him. He could not quite put his finger on why he felt this way about the man, and this acted on his sense of fairness, making him more determined to do well by him, even though he did not like him. If he were honest with himself he might have admitted that something indefinable about Lancaster made his skin crawl.

'Save the feathers Wilson; they may prove useful; oh, and Bruno might like the guts.'

Soon the other foraging parties returned with more seabirds, land crabs, peppergrass and coconuts. No-one had found any water, but almost as soon as they returned the heavens opened again. The water butts refilled rapidly and Lattimore was content, though still unhappy at the irregularity of supply. If it ran out and the rain did not come; the thought made him worry. During the rain everyone took shelter in the huts and encountered another problem; several people got up when the rain stopped and discovered that once again they had leeches clinging to them. Even Bruno had two. Lattimore's first instinct was to get a glowing stick from the fire to remove one on his leg, as he had read that flame or salt was the best way to detach them, but to his surprise, as he was about to apply it, Estella Hastings stopped him by placing a hand on his arm.

'Miss Hastings?'

He had not had much conversation with her, but had observed that she appeared to be a very self-assured girl whose manner took much after her grandfather.

'That's not a good way to do it Captain.'

'It isn't?'

'No. It's better with something flat.'

The Reverend Taylor laughed, 'We can learn from the young Captain, and in this case Estella is quite correct, as she knows from her own experience. We have leeches in California and many people use fire or salt to get them off. It's not the best way, for it can leave stuff behind under the skin that causes infections. Let me show you.'

He was right; a few of the crew who had torn the leeches away from their skins had developed infections where the mouth parts of the creatures had remained under the surface. Several of them looked poisoned and might need lancing. In the circumstances this would mean a heated jackknife and a lot of pain, something best avoided. In serious cases it could lead to blood poisoning and death.

Taking the flat lid of a tin he slid it flat along the captain's skin to the edge of the leech's narrow end and pressed slowly against it, releasing the sucker. Within a couple of seconds the leech relaxed its bite and detached. Keeping the lid flat so the leech could not re-attach, Taylor slid the lid to the other end and did the same, handing the leech to Lattimore. The captain looked at it in disgust and threw it to the floor where he squashed it to a bright red splodge.

'Guess that one won't be troubling you any more.'

'Thank you Reverend; I think it would be a good idea to show this to the rest of the company because infections are something we really do not want.'

'You're right, sir. We already have some infections arising from their ignorance. I shall make it my business to instruct them in the method.'

Taylor moved off with the intention of carrying out his purpose. His pleasure at being in command of the situation was obvious; the Reverend clearly liked to be in charge of things. This was very evident in his treatment of the children with whom he was, on the face of it, a benevolent grandfather, but he had no compunctions about making his point with the flat of his hand if he found them disobedient. Lattimore was not a man who approved of the old adage that if you spared the rod you spoiled the child, but the children were not his and he could not really comment on the matter.

Before too long Wilson and Morgan announced that the cauldron was ready, the meat was cooked and ready to eat.

'Hold hard you men.'

Lattimore looked at the grayish-green mixture in the cauldron.

'What is in here?'

'Well Captain it's booby, noddy, pepper grass, coconut and salt with a few clams that Burns found in a rock pool.'

'It smells like the jakes.'

'Well there's no denying Captain that seabirds do taste and smell a bit fishy when you cook them.'

'I see. Well kindly put some of the meat and juice into this coconut shell. We shall try it on Bruno before any of us eat it.'

People were hungry but saw the sense of the precaution, though the time until the portion cooled sufficiently to offer it to the dog seemed interminable. At long last it was at a temperature where a hungry canine would not decline it, and Lattimore called the Newfoundland over. Breath was not exactly bated, but the dog sniffed it, then without hesitation wolfed it down then wandered off and lay down in the shade. Still they waited and after another fifteen minutes Crone called Bruno to 'Come!' and the dog bounded over to him. However it smelled, the mixture was edible. Into a motley collection of mugs from the boat, coconut shells, tins and dry palm leaves the cooks ladled the meal. Despite the smell it was not unpleasant and evidently sustaining, being greasy and meaty. Lattimore made a mental note to get the sailors with knives to see if they could whittle some platters and spoons from local wood to make mealtimes easier in future.

'Well done you two men,' he said to Morgan and Wilson. 'I'm glad it did not poison my dog; I am quite fond of him.' To his surprise they shuffled about with slightly anxious expressions.

'Whatever is the matter? You have given us a meal where we had nothing.'

'It's not good enough sir.'

'Well it seems so to me. Why is it not?'

'There's no starch to it, sir. No bread, no potato; no nothing.'

'It will sustain us though; will it not?'

'Aye sir; it will for a time. But we'll get weaker, sir, and a lot thinner; some people might get ill.'

'I see. Well we have an amount of hard tack. Would it help to crumble it up into the broth?'

'It would that sir.'

'Then do so; but sparingly; it has to last.'

'There's something else sir.'

'What is it?

'Nobody brought in any fruit or berries, sir. There do not seem to be any at all.'

'Ah. You are thinking of scurvy?'

'Aye sir.'

'The peppergrass is an antiscorbutic I should think.'

'It's likely sir.'

'Then you must use it every meal since it's the only plant we know that is not poisonous. I'll explain why to the company.'

The last thing that Lattimore ordered that day was for a long thin palm tree that had fallen over to be dragged onto the beach below the camp. Trimming it with the old axe the sailors contrived to dig a hole in the sand at the edge of the trees. To the narrow end they attached a Union Jack that MacDonald fetched from a locker in the pinnace, then they raised it up into the hole and filled it in, wedging a cairn of rocks all around it to keep it upright. The bright flag streamed out in the wind, vivid against the dark green of the forest. Above the huts a plume of smoke streamed into the sky. Lattimore was no jingo but the flag was an unmistakable signal to any passing ship that there were people on Palmyra. With this done, food secured, and a palm bed to sleep on which may or may not keep the leeches away, he could go to bed content that there was some order to things, and that all was as it should be considering their circumstances.

Just then there came a piercing scream from the jungle behind the huts. Dropping everything, men ran from all sides to where Dorothea Hastings stood looking down at a human skeleton with an axe firmly embedded in its skull.

Chapter 5

Defensive Measures

John Crone stared at the skull lying in the bushes with a small axe sticking out of the top of it. Little wonder that Dorothea Hastings had screamed, for in the shade of ending day it looked quite sinister. It would be better, he thought, if ladies in her condition did not get such shocks as these, but it had certainly given her quite a turn. However, Mrs Taylor was made of sterner stuff, and was soon on the scene though her words to her daughter were not those that many women would have uttered.

'For Heaven's sake Dorothea, do pull yourself together. You've seen death before. What are you thinking of?'

'I'm sorry mother. It just took me by surprise in the shadows and I guess I was startled by it. It's a man isn't it?'

'Yes; you can always tell by the width of the hips. These are narrow, so it's a man.'

Crone could see why Dorothea Hastings had been scared. He had never seen a skeleton before, which was understandable for a man from West Cumberland in his early twenties. Death was something that was quickly tidied away into coffins before it began to smell, and ceremonialized over with wreaths, black armbands and veils. This skull grinned at the people who were gathering round, rather as if it was mocking them; almost, in his mind's eye it nodded its head, as if to say, 'Well if you had an axe in your head you'd look like me too.' It was undoubtedly a sinister looking scene.

'What is that?' asked Estella.

'Isabelle, I do not think that the children should be here. Why did you not keep them away?'

'Well,' replied his wife mildly, 'I might very well ask the same of you, William.'

'Is that a skelington?'

'Yes my dear, but the word is skeleton.'

'Oh let me see,' said Nancy pushing her way to the front, then stopping at the sight of the bones and sucking her thumb.

'Isabelle, I insist you remove the children now,' said Reverend Taylor.

'You may insist William, but it is of course educational for children to see such things. They may not be protected against them forever.'

'I hope you remember that when they have nightmares.'

'That being a reasonable objection, I shall take them to look for shellfish on the rocks which is far more interesting anyway, is it not Nancy?'

The little girl shook her head, but nonetheless followed her grandmother away from the grisly scene.

'Well I don't think there's any doubt as to how he met his end, poor devil, but who did it?'

'Pirates Frederick! I have no doubt of it. We could all be murdered!'

'Don't distress yourself my dear. In your condition you must stay calm.'

'Bother my condition. How can I stay calm with a murdered man just behind the huts?'

'He can't stay here for certain,' said Reverend Taylor. 'We must give him a Christian burial and I hope that will allay your fears Dottie.'

His use of what was evidently her family pet name, and the sheer confidence of her father's presence steadied her.

'You're right Father. I would feel better if this poor soul is given a proper funeral. I shall help you lay him out. These poor bones must not be buried willy-nilly, but set out in the form of the human being that he was.'

Around them many of the sailors nodded in agreement. Among the most superstitious of them having no proper grave was a terrible end for a sailor. It was right and fitting that this man should have the right words said over him by a real live Padre and that he be sent on his way in the correct manner. Returning to the huts, leaving the murdered bones for now, the party was met by Mrs Taylor who had set the young girls to their shellfish hunting.

'What were you doing out here on your own in the jungle at this time anyway?'

'Mother! You know what I was doing, surely.'

Lattimore knew and reacted accordingly.

'I beg your pardon ma'am. It is my fault. Tomorrow morning I shall order the digging of two pits with logs to be placed over them and screens of leaves constructed round them. It is something I should have thought of before and I do apologize.'

'Thank you Captain. It is something that we ladies would greatly appreciate, but I am sure that the gentlemen would think so too. I don't see that you are to blame though; there has been so much to think of since we arrived.'

'That's good of you Mrs Taylor, but I command here and I should have thought of such a basic thing earlier.'

'Perhaps you are too hard on yourself Captain,' mused Reverend Taylor. 'After all, we are no longer on the ship; do you actually command here now that we are on land?'

Lattimore's face set and he looked at the Reverend with a terrible eye, aware that the gaze of several seamen was upon him; the man had questioned his authority in front of his men. Unwitting it may be, but it was downright foolish, given the circumstances. His hold over these men was absolute on board ship, but there were some men among the crew that he did not know. What they might be capable of in conditions of starvation and thirst, was an unknown. One thing he was certain of; order had to be maintained and that meant that he must be seen as in charge, beyond question.

'I do sir. It is the law of the sea that in the case of shipwreck the captain stays in command until rescue is effected. My authority has the full force of law and may not be questioned; it extends to passengers as well and would be upheld in any court.'

Taylor was quite clearly taken aback by the force behind the words.

'Thank you for clearing that up Captain Lattimore. I knew that the captain on a ship has many powers, but I'm glad to know that it applies in this situation. It clarifies things to have a definite chain of command.'

He clearly had more to say, but Lattimore headed him off abruptly.

'It does sir. The captain may conduct services on board ship, marriages, burials, and is answerable only to God once the voyage has been set upon. He may punish even unto death should he see fit, and his authority is absolute. It's written into the ship's articles which every man aboard has signed.'

'That is as may be Captain, but I must insist that your strictures do not apply to me or to my family; indeed they do not apply to the other passengers at all. You do not command, and never have commanded, us.'

This was a direct challenge now, and Lattimore had to address it.

'May I ask why you take that position Reverend?'

'You may, Captain Lattimore. I was a passenger on your ship; a position I paid for and my contract with you was that you carry myself and my family from A to B. At no point did I place myself or any of mine under your command. If I met you in the street you would have no authority over me and even now you do not have an authority over me. I am the head of my family and they will obey me as is proper. You may request of me sir, but you may not command. I might add that this condition applies to the other passengers also. I may do as you wish sir, but from goodwill, not from compulsion.'

Lattimore forced a smile, though inwardly he was seething.

'I take your point about the passengers sir, but I am quite clear on the matter of the crew. They must obey; the matter is clear in law and I am certain of it. I am glad that you will comply with my requests for our mutual benefit, but as for the crew my requests are actually orders and must be obeyed.'

The captain's certainty evidently had an effect on the members of the crew who were listening. Some of them were men who had signed on for this voyage, and he knew the fractious and rebellious nature of some sailors when authority was questioned or unclear; the 'sea lawyer' was an object of dislike for most captains. Lattimore swallowed hard because his words were no more than a bold front. He was by no means certain that what he had said to Taylor was true for ship's articles were not specific about being stranded on desert islands, but if he wished to stay in charge and preserve order, then he needed to maintain the position. The crew had indeed all signed the articles, but some of them were illiterate and did not know what they had put their name to. One thing that Lattimore noticed while this conversation was taking place was the face of William Lancaster. The stowaway had listened to the exchange between Taylor and himself very attentively with a strange look on his face. It was a look of intelligent comprehension, but it had more in common with the expression of a fox approaching prey than of a moral man weighing up his position. Lancaster was not a member of the crew. He decided to give a more concrete and persuasive argument that would still any tongue that might have questioned further.

'There's also the question of pay, sir. All these men will continue to be paid until they reach a registered port where they may be discharged. Payment after that is at the discretion of the shipping company, so if they wish to be paid until they get back to Britain, they must obey orders.'

Again, he was far from sure on these points, but it had the desired effect. The sailors nearby drifted away back to their huts content that all was as it should be. There were apparently no malcontents and no thoughts of questioning his orders. For the moment at least, this was a relief to him for on the island and in his mind, there was a clear choice between order and chaos. In this situation he represented order, but if his group was to divide and split and cease cooperation, then chaos might ensue, to the detriment of all. Taylor had voiced the first division, the one between passengers and crew; there was nothing he could do about that, but he was determined that he would do all in his power to stop further dissension. Communal living required certain necessities and were in themselves a unifying factor, even those of a more basic nature.

Toilet facilities, Lattimore reflected, were an elementary consideration, because without such an arrangement and with thirty human beings relieving themselves all over the place, the vicinity would soon become very unhygienic, unless a more rational system were put into place. He really should have thought of it before and chided himself for not doing so. This was something solid that he could do, but for now he forced himself to smile and said to Taylor, 'There's nothing we can do for that fellow in the woods until morning. I think we should all get what rest we can. I hope, Reverend, that I can impose upon you to carry out the burial service? I fancy that you have rather more experience in that line than I have.'

This appeal to Taylor's expertise brought immediate reward and cooperation as the preacher smiled.

'I think you are right, Captain, though it is no imposition. I'd be pleased to do it.'

Back at the huts they now had no need to go to bed immediately, though it got dark very shortly after they reached their base. As well as the cooking fire, a larger fire had been built in the clearing outside the huts where people could sit and talk if they wished. As Lattimore moved to go and sit near the fire a figure detached its self from where the seamen sat chatting among themselves and came over to him; it was Patrick Burns, an older AB and one who commanded respect among his fellows.

'May I have a word please, Captain? In private if you please, sir.'

Lattimore moved over to the side of the open space, motioning Burns to follow him.

'What is it Burns?'

'I think I've got an explanation for the skeleton, sir, if you'd like to hear it.'

'Of course I would, but why the mystery?'

'I don't want to speak in front of the ladies or the children, sir, bearing in mind that Mrs Hastings is obviously worried by pirates and also bearing in mind her condition. Anyway, sir, several of us in the crew know the story of what happened here a few years back. It's common knowledge all around the Pacific seaboard Captain.'

'Forecastle gossip you mean?'

'No sir; it's more than that. You hear lots of stories knocking about the world as we do, but a lot of them are scuttlebutt. This one's real enough.'

'Better spit it out then.'

'Aye sir; it seems that a few years ago, 1870 in fact, there was a ship wrecked here by the name of the *Angel*. From what I heard most of the crew made it to shore.'

'Only eighteen years ago. And they were rescued?'

'No sir; a ship passing the island called in because they saw boats on the beach, but they were all dead.'

'Dead? What had they died of? Starvation? Thirst or disease?'

'None of that, sir, they'd all been murdered. Throats cut, heads bashed in. All that could be done was to gather up the bodies they found and bury them. They'd been dead just a few days by all accounts.'

'But who killed them?'

'That's just it, sir. Nobody knows. To this day the people who carried out this massacre have got away with it.'

'And somewhere near here is a mass grave.'

'That's about it, sir.'

'You did right coming to me Burns and very well to keep it from the ladies. I take it the crew know?'

'Oh aye sir; they've been talking about nowt else since the bones were found. I reckon the search party was in a hurry and missed that one and there may be some more.'

'But the officers don't know yet?'

'No sir, which is why I thought I'd better tell you.'

'Thank you; I think I'd better have a word with Mr MacDonald and Mr Crone.'

'Aye sir.'

Lattimore walked in search of the men he wished to speak to and his thoughts rained with his field of vision across the visible part of the island. Palmyra, or rather his perception of it, had changed since the discovery of the bones. The heavy warm damp of the tropical air with its earthy green smell had taken on a new quality. A morose and foreboding miasma seemed to hover over the island, as if it were haunted by some evil spirit of bad things.

Gathering the two officers with him, Lattimore walked down onto the beach and told them what Burns had related to him.

'That's a bit sobering, sir.'

'I agree John, and the men are worried about it as well.'

'I'm not surprised,' said MacDonald. 'To find ourselves at the scene of a massacre and not know why it happened or who did it. I'm worried myself.'

'It's a problem gentlemen. In fact it's more than that; it's a threat, because if it's happened once then it could happen again.'

'Then we must face it, sir.'

'But how Donald? We have no guns or swords and pistols with which to fight off an attack.'

'Nonetheless, Captain, the murders took place less than twenty years ago; they could have been committed by marauding savages, for there are plenty such still. We must be able to defend ourselves and those in our charge.'

'It could have been pirates,' said Crone.

'To me it does not matter who did it. I am a Scot and if someone attacks me then I will do as Scots do.'

'Fight back.'

'Aye sir.'

'We are much the same in Ireland, but what with?'

'We must arm ourselves, sir. With weapons that we can make.'

'What sort of weapons?'

'Clubs and pikes. We have an axe and the tin cans may be beaten into sharp enough heads to put on a pole.'

'I agree, sir,' said Crone. 'It's only plain common sense to have some means of defence other than the men's jack-knives. The men will understand why we are making them. Leave it to me, sir, and I'll make sure that every man has a pike within the next two days.'

'It seems to me that we ought to reinstate the watch system too, at least for a few men to act as sentries. The crew will see the necessity of it I think.'

'I should think so! No-one wants to be murdered in their sleep. This entire situation is a powerful persuasion that we must preserve order and obedience. It is very clear gentlemen; we either have order or we have chaos and we shall meet any threat far better if there is order.'

The two officers nodded their agreement.

'Very well Donald, please see to it that there are at least three men awake and armed during the night, officers included. I shall explain it to the passengers as a precaution in view of the condition of the skeleton, but I do not think we need to tell them the story of the *Angel*. They'll sleep better without that knowledge. Now Donald I'd like a word with you alone if you do not mind.'

'Aye sir,' replied MacDonald, a slight wondering tone in his voice, and he and Lattimore walked a small way down the beach on their own as Crone returned to the huts.

'I'm aware Mr MacDonald, that you have a great experience in small boats and I am almost ashamed to admit that I do not.'

'It's true sir; I have passed a lot of time in open boats in the western isles. I am well used to the handling of them.'

Lattimore did not beat about the bush, but turned to look MacDonald right in the face.

'I would like you to take the launch Mr MacDonald and go to fetch help. I have not the skills to do it; you have, and I am asking you to go and find a rescue party.'

MacDonald was taken completely aback and looked at him with astonishment.

Lattimore now produced the charts of the Pacific that he had rescued from the ship.

'If you see Mr MacDonald, it is about 1,300 miles in a direct course straight down the wind at this time of year. A man of your experience should be able to do it.'

'Show me the chart,' said MacDonald.

Lattimore rolled it open and MacDonald put his finger on it, jabbing in some indignation.

'There it is; Samoa. A speck in the ocean, and beyond it, thousands of miles of open water. If I run down the latitude as you suggest and find no land there, on which hand shall I look for the island? You are asking me to chance myself and a boat crew on something that will almost certainly lead to death in some form or other.'

Lattimore's cheeks burned with embarrassment and he could not answer.

'I do not know how you can find it in you to ask me to do such a thing. It's 1,300 miles across open water to Samoa. Anyone who makes the attempt is inviting almost certain death. If I even tried to do it, then any man who came with me would be condemned to die. I will not take that responsibility on my soul; no by God, I will not do it.'

The captain had not been expecting such a direct response from the usually compliant and taciturn MacDonald and he backtracked immediately.

'I am sorry Mr MacDonald. It was too much to ask. I should not have said it.'

'No. You should not. You have no right to ask such a thing. Some things a man may decide for himself, but to ask me to do something you are not able and certainly not willing to undertake yourself; well Captain it is a surprise to me. I would not have thought it of you. The answer is simple and it is no.'

MacDonald walked off in a temper, muttering 'Contemptible' under his breath.

Lattimore stared after him, his composure completely in pieces. He felt like weeping. He should not have asked, but he had felt impelled to do it for the sake of the people on the island, his responsibilities. Now he had sacrificed MacDonald's good opinion of him. Looking after his first mate he hoped that MacDonald would come to see why he had asked the question. Disconsolately he walked back towards the huts. He had no fears of MacDonald causing trouble, for he knew him as a man far too steady for such a thing, but the relationship between himself and the first mate was now soured, and perhaps for good.

Lattimore was right about the story of the massacre and it was of great use to him, because there is nothing like an outside threat to bring unity to a group of people. MacDonald relayed to the crew the news that the captain thought defensive measures were necessary, and they saw the sense of it. He told off two men to stand first watch with him and named their reliefs under Crone; the new regime was accepted without demur as a sensible precaution. As the rest of the camp bedded down, MacDonald sat on one side of the clearing as Michael O'Flaherty and Samuel Young, who were friends, settled down on the other and chatted in low voices. MacDonald, the line of rank between himself and where they sat, simply pulled out his pipe and lit it from the fire. He would have to ration himself with his smokes because his pouch was half empty and he had no way of getting any more. His conversation with Lattimore and the captain's suggestion had disturbed him profoundly and he felt the need of a good smoke.

'What does that taste like?'

She did not make him jump, but he was mildly surprised, because she was supposed to be asleep.

'Well now, Miss Laura why are you not in your bed my wee girl?'

'It's not really a bed, just leaves, and it's not very comfortable. I can't sleep. So what does it taste like?'

'It tastes of smoke.'

'That doesn't sound very nice. Smoke makes my eyes water when I go near the fire. Why do you suck it into your mouth?'

'Because this sort of smoke relaxes me and makes me think about things.'

'Is that why Daddy does it too?'

'I should think so.'

'Should I smoke too if it's good for you?'

'I do not think so; it's not a thing that little girls do.'

'Why not?'

'Well it is not considered ladylike.'

'What's ladylike?'

'Goodness, but you are full of questions, aren't you?'

'Isn't it good to ask questions?'

'It is good, but sometimes I do not have all the answers. Would you not prefer a story instead?'

'Yes please! For now I would. I like your stories.'

'And do you think that you would go back to sleep if I tell you a story?'

'I think so.'

'Promise?'

'Promise.'

'Then I shall tell you of Cuchulain.'

'Who was Cuchulain?'

'Well if you don't stop asking and start listening, then you may never know.'

'I'll listen.'

'Cuchulain was a great hero in days of old who fought many enemies with his mighty sword and was never beaten. His favourite weapon though was a spear called the Gae Bolg which always came back to his hand whenever he threw it.'

'That was clever.'

'Yes it was. Anyway, Cuchulain heard one day of a woman who was a great warrior also and who had never been beaten in a fight.'

'A lady fighting?' asked Laura, her eyes as big as saucers.

'To be sure,' said MacDonald. 'Why not? In those days ladies went into battle too.'

'I can't see Mummy fighting anyone.'

'Well I should hope not. Those days are long gone. Where was I?'

'A lady who was a great warrior.'

'Oh yes. Well Cuchulain was over in Ireland and he heard that this lady, whose name was Sgathaich, was running a school for warriors on the Isle of Skye, to teach them how to fight. He decided to go and see for himself what was going on.'

'Where is the Isle of Skye?'

'It's an island off Scotland and is not far from where I come from.'

'So did he go?'

'He did, but when he arrived he was treated just like anyone else, because everyone was a warrior; he didn't like that because he thought he was so famous that they should show him respect. To get noticed he challenged all of the students to fight him and he beat them all.'

'Did he kill them all?'

'Oh no, Miss Laura. I would not be telling you a story like that. No it was practice fighting and not one of them was as good as him. Anyway, Sgathaich saw this and thought that she would soon settle him. She told her daughter to go and put Cuchulain in his place.'

'And did she?'

'Oh no. She was better than the students, but Cuchulain beat her too. That made Sgathaich very angry indeed.'

'Did she go to fight him?'

'Oh yes. She took her sword and went at him and he attacked her and they fought for hours. Neither would give up.'

'But who won in the end?'

'Oh Sgathaich's daughter wanted them to stop because she thought they might kill each other or drop dead from being tired, so she prepared a delicious meal. They took no notice and carried right on fighting.'

'I wish we had one of those here right now!'

'Oh, so do I little maid, so do I. She must have prepared five or six meals, each better than the last, but they carried right on fighting day and night for three days. Finally, she cooked a whole roasted deer stuffed with hazelnuts and when the smell of it came to them they stopped fighting and stared at the food. Without a word they threw down their weapons and came to eat.'

'Oh Mr MacDonald, I could just do with some of that venison right now,' called over Michael O'Flaherty. 'That's a proper meal for an Irish hero, so it is!'

'That's as may be, but we have none here. But I'll echo your sentiments O'Flaherty. It would be welcome. Anyway you cannot be interrupting me. I have a tale to finish.'

'Were they friends now?'

'They were. As they were eating, with the gravy running down their chins.' MacDonald stopped to glower across the clearing where despairing moans came from the two seamen. 'They realized that they would never ever beat each other, so they made peace and shook hands. Realizing also that the other was a great warrior, they swore an oath that if ever the other needed help, they would come to their aid. To cap it all, they sealed their friendship because Cuchulain was so impressed by Sgathaich's daughter that he asked her to become his wife.'

'What was her name?'

'The daughter? She was called Uatach.'

'What a strange name.'

'Aye well, they all had strange names in those days. Now are you going to keep your promise? You've had your story.'

'All right Mr MacDonald. I'll go back to bed.'

So saying, she reluctantly dragged her feet back to towards the hut where she slept with her mother, sisters and grandmother.

'You tell a good story, Mr MacDonald. My mother used to tell me stories of Cuchulain when I was her age.'

'Ach well O'Flaherty, if I'm sure of anything in this life it is that I am not your mother. Now if you'll excuse me I am going to smoke my pipe.'

MacDonald puffed away at his briar, to all intents and purposes content with his lot, but in fact his mind was working furiously. The fate of the children troubled him and especially for his wee pet. It was bad enough that they were all stranded here on this island with no ground water and precious little food, but he looked ahead and saw them wasting away over the next few weeks. It was no place for women and children and a bad enough one for hardened sailors. For himself and for the adults he was not so concerned. If you were grownup and knocked about the world then in the course of a lifetime there were many perils to be faced. This was especially true of sailing men, but to innocent wee bairns, and little girls at that; somehow it did not seem fair that they should have to face this ordeal. All his protective instincts were roused at the thought of the children having to suffer privations and his having to watch them waste away, perhaps even die. The thought was to trouble him increasingly over the next couple of weeks, and the growing germ of an idea, however unwilling he might be to face it, that it lay in his power to do something about it. He was not sure if it contradicted his aunt's stern injunction that he was always to make sure he got home safe, and he would have to decide that matter, because the promise that he would was binding to him.

Breakfast the next morning was coconuts and water; the main meal of burgoo would come later. Reverend Taylor and Dorothea Hastings went back to the bush where the skeleton lay. With them they took two sailors and a pair of planks lashed together as a rough sort of stretcher. There they carefully began the process of laying out the bones in a semblance of order on the stretcher so that it at least looked like a human being and not a jumble of pieces that was to be buried. As they were doing this four men scraped and scratched at the sand by the edge of the forest to make a grave deep enough for respectful burial.

Lattimore had sent the rest of the survivors out in foraging groups, but instructed them to return by noon. The one exception was Patrick Burns, who was the best topmast hand in the crew. He had been appointed lookout and was up the highest tree near to the huts watching the ocean with Lattimore's telescope, hoping to see smoke or a sail in the distance. The tree he had climbed was declared by Reverend Taylor to be a fine example of *Pisonia grandis*, which species he had seen in both Samoa and Hawaii. It had broad leaves high up that shaded the forest floor like large umbrellas, so that all that grew in any profusion under them were large ferns and little else, which were easy, even pleasant, to walk among. The *Pisonias* appeared to like the coastal fringe, for further inland were coconut palms in profusion, which the sailors had no qualms at all about scampering up as if it were the mast of a ship. The tree, at the top of which was Burns, apparently comfortably ensconced on a kind of platform he had shaped, was about a hundred feet high and he could see for miles, though he did wear a broad hat that he had woven from palm leaves and coconut fibres which made him look very disreputable. Thus far he had seen nothing, but Lattimore kept the fire going outside the huts with a pile of green leaves beside it. If Burns saw anything, then whoever was on fire duty would send a plume of thick smoke into the air hoping to attract attention, but as Lattimore well knew, Palmyra was not on a shipping route that many ships used. In a spirit of optimism the fire was kept going all night by the men on watch, with dry wood and kept quite large; it could be seen for miles out at sea. The captain called it his beacon, but it was not just a signal to passing ships that he thought of; it was a beacon of hope, and hope preserved order.

The foraging parties had evidently gone further afield and onto rocks bordering the sea, for they came back with hatfuls of seabird eggs. They returned and delivered them to the cook who told them that if they could find some fish he could do a fine omelet that evening to go with the burgoo that was now their staple. It would make a good variation to the 'normal' diet, which would otherwise be a bit monotonous.

Far more serious was that a few of the men returned with nothing edible, but not empty handed. They carried with them bleached human bones that they had found in two other places, including a skull, on which were the unmistakable signs of violent death. Quite obviously they had been chased and killed as they fled.

'Captain, something awful has happened here,' said Dorothea Hastings, her eyes worried; to him, her need for reassurance was obvious.

'I agree, ma'am, and it has been so for the poor souls whose bones we are finding, but from the condition of them it happened a long time ago. I do not think we have anything to be unduly alarmed about. We shall bury them along with the man you found; and any others we may come across, but please regard what happened as being of the past. I do not think we are in any sort of danger at all.'

He was not very good at dissembling and he knew his words sounded hollow even as she fixed her worried eyes on him, but she said nothing, for which he was thankful.

It was time for the burial and the skeleton, with the newly discovered bones, could be laid to rest, and Lattimore reflected that it was a good idea. The more superstitious among his men might fear that the dead peoples' ghosts would walk if they were not buried in Christian fashion, and he did not need this night terror to stimulate their imaginations. It may have been just his fancy, but more than once he had found himself thinking that Palmyra had a strange and ominous atmosphere hanging over it and there was something menacing about that he could not quite see but was almost within his vision. When this thought surfaced, as it had occasionally since they landed, he dismissed it out of hand because Palmyra, of all places, seemed to have nothing against it as desert islands go. There were no four-legged animals, dangerous or otherwise, and so far he had seen no snakes. He had mentioned this to Reverend Taylor who had smiled.

'Yes indeed Captain. No snakes. This is common on many Pacific Islands, so it would not surprise me if there were none here either. It's a form of Paradise I think; Eden before the serpent.'

'No apples either though, Reverend.'

'True and I do allow that a nice apple would be very welcome right now.'

At this particular moment though, Taylor had other things on his mind than apples. The survivors all grouped round the grave into which the skeleton of the murdered man had been lowered on its stretcher. The other bones were now laid in alongside him. There was no shroud to wrap them in and although there was a carpenter, there were no tools, nails or cut timber from which to fashion a coffin. That did not matter; what mattered was the ceremony.

As Taylor began, they all bared their heads as he said, 'We brought nothing into this world and it is certain that we can carry nothing out. The Lord gave and the Lord hath taken away; blessed be the name of the Lord.'

'Amen.'

'Let us pray...'

Taylor led them through the Lord's Prayer and then spoke a brief homily on the unknown man's fate and expressed the hope that the gates of Heaven would be opened to him. Then he went into the actual burial service: 'Man that is born of a woman is of few days and full of trouble...' At the conclusion of the first part he invited the company to sing the hymn 'Why do we mourn departing friends?'

> *"Why do we mourn departing friends?*
> *Or shake at Death's alarms.*
> *'Tis but the voice that Jesus sends*
> *to call them to his arms &c."*

They sang surprisingly well, Lattimore thought, for people in their situation, the voices of the women rising in pleasant contrast to the bass growls of most of the men, though there were a couple of melodious tenors among them. By the time the final section of the service came, 'Earth to earth, dust to dust…' he sensed a mood change among the group. There was an edgy mood to them beforehand, nervousness, perhaps because of their situation, or maybe the unburied man, but the service, in some way restored normality to things. He, the captain, was authority. The church was here too, and things would be done properly; God was in his heaven and the civilized order of life was here on this island. The communal nature of the singing was a call that reminded all of home, of Sunday services, of the battle of good and evil in the world, and of civilized order. As somber an event as it was, the funeral ritual drew them together, suffering humanity facing ill in a hostile world. The only real pang of regret that Lattimore felt at this time was that he had alienated MacDonald and lost his respect by asking him to do something that he should not have. He knew it very well, but was conflicted because as captain it was something he had to suggest simply because it was an option. However, the option had been instantly ruled out; he hoped MacDonald would come to see why he had asked but knew that it would take time. When the service was over and a crude cross put over the grave, the castaways drifted off to continue their foraging, but Lattimore felt more secure. They had come together as a group, more united in the face of their misfortune, and he felt that he would sleep better that night.

Chapter 6

An Expedition

'The problem is clear,' said Lattimore. 'I have been along the shore for a mile and a half, looking in every nest I could see, and it is certain that there's not an egg left in any of them. This cannot continue.'

'But we like the omelets, sir. Without them it'll just be burgoo.'

'I do appreciate that Anderson. I remind you that we are all eating the same and it's what is keeping us alive, but if we keep taking eggs there will be no birds; then where should we be?'

There was some shuffling of feet among the crew members, but the sense of his words had weight.

'I'm afraid we have no option. I intend to see if we can send out foraging parties further onto the other islands, but until we do I believe we should not eat any more eggs from this immediate area. And when we find eggs further from here we should only take a few and very occasionally.'

'I go along with that Captain,' said William James, one of the steerage passengers. 'My folk farm for a living. It stands to reason that if you take all the eggs there will be no hatchlings and if there are none of those, then our meat supply will be gone unless we live entirely on crab.'

There were a few wry faces made at that thought. Coconut crab and land crab had featured a lot in the burgoo, which had been popular and tasty to start with, but it was very rich meat and the crew had come to link it with upset stomachs and diarrhea which had made an unwelcome appearance among about half of them.

'So there it is,' continued Lattimore. 'We do not know how long we are to remain here so let us go easier on the eggs. I also think we should look more to the sea. How many of you have been fishermen?'

Several hands went up.

'There are always a few fishermen in a crew. There are fish in that lagoon, and eels.'

'There's kelp too, sir, and that's edible. It's very good for you.'

'Well there you are Tumelty. You've expanded our diet already. What else is there?'

The suggestions came in; sea cucumber from the lagoon, eels, giant clams could all be obtained in water only knee deep and crystal clear.

'Shark meat too, sir.'

'Aye there is that, but they tend not to come close in I think; they do not like the shallows.'

'We could get them from the boats, sir.'

'Something we might try I think. But for the moment I'd be glad if you could put your mind to how to catch fish.'

Part of what had prompted Lattimore to give thought to the problem of food, was the plight of the children. Two weeks on the island had made a difference in the appearance of the adults who were beginning to look very pinched around the face and thin in the body. The children had also got thinner, but the unaccustomed diet gave them digestive problems, which had only just started to manifest in some of the adults. Laura Hastings in particular had suffered with very severe stomach cramps, so badly that they had driven her to lie weeping in her hut, not wanting to do anything. To some extent she had been revived when Lattimore opened some of the tinned mutton from the emergency supplies on the boats and given her a decent meal, but there was no doubting her distress. When it came to mealtimes she was very reluctant to eat the burgoo and had to be coaxed. Nancy and Estella ate their food, but neither could bear the appearance of some of the chunks that found their way into the pot and often left pieces uneaten. Ada was the only child who accepted everything she was given for she was older than the others and acted often in the role of little mother in looking after her siblings. Reverend Taylor in his usual manner, the stern grandfather, had instructed the girls to eat all that the Lord provided, and if they did not then he would punish their ingratitude. Such was his personality that his views on how children should be treated appeared to dominate over those of their father and mother who deferred to his opinions in all matters. Despite his slapping Nancy's bottom for throwing her food on the floor, declaring that it was disgusting, the younger children were still sometimes reluctant to eat some things. Mrs Taylor and their mother had spoken to the girls on several occasions, encouraging them to eat what was set before them, but had given up when Estella, willing enough, had swallowed a piece of sea snail and immediately been violently sick.

The captain was conscious that his passengers were used to fresh meat, unlike sailors who could quite happily subsist on hard tack, salted meat and burgoo for months provided they were also fed enough antiscorbutics such as lime juice or sauerkraut. In his more ruthless moments when thinking this through, he had thought of feeding Bruno to them, but this idea had fallen on several counts. Firstly, he was a very thin dog now and would not provide the adults with much of a meal. Secondly, if he fed fresh meat to the passengers and not to the crew, a line would be drawn where part of his company would be seen as 'favourites' and resented. Thirdly, he liked Bruno because the Newfoundland was his own dog, which had completed three voyages with him; the thought of eating him was abhorrent. The dog had shown that he was quite capable of fending for himself, but like other crew members he had his own bowl of burgoo every mealtime; he did not seem to mind the taste. The dog also had one great friend on the island whose objections to eating him would over-rule all others, and that was Laura Hastings herself who had taken to riding him and hugging him as a personal friend. Bruno was presently curled up in his favourite place, which was next to her in her hut. Bruno was safe.

The plight of the children was also much in the mind of Donald MacDonald who had gone off on his own down the beach to where a coral outcrop jutted out towards the sea. There he stood, eyes as grey as the Atlantic, looking out towards the horizon. Almost he seemed not to be there, but his gaze fixed on another horizon thousands of miles away, insulated from the immediate present and location by what he was thinking. After a while he sat down, his head bowed, his hands loosely in front of him, and evidently deep in thought; it was the travails of the young ones that dominated his thoughts now, and troubled him both day and night. So it was that John MacDonald came and found him.

'I ken what you're thinking Donald.'

'Ye do?'

'Aye, we're brothers remember; I ken how your mind works. I've been thinking the same.'

'Well you'd have to wouldn't you?'

'It would be a natural thing for men from our part of the world.'

MacDonald looked at his brother and paused a moment before replying with a ghost of a smile.

'Father had a friend on Bernera remember; with a boat.'

'A wild and windswept sort of place. I remember; it was Rory McKenzie.'

'Indeed; as it would be facing the Atlantic. He was a crofter in a small way.'

'On Bernera most people are.'

'Aye, but his croft was small and there was not a lot of grazing for his sheep.'

John MacDonald was quite used to this roundabout way of getting to things, for the way of the people of the Western Isles was one of careful consideration and explanation, not always direct, so he listened and asked questions. Donald would get to the pith of the matter when he was ready.

'As you know the men of Bernera have the right to graze sheep on Na h-Eileanan Flannach.'

'The Seven Hunters; I have been out there a couple of times.'

'Yes; what some folk call the Flannan Isles. They take sheep out there in open boats; aye and bring them back too.'

'It's not too far if you sail; it cannot be more than about twenty miles.'

'Indeed John, but it may be rowed as well if you have stout arms and enough need.'

'I think I would rather the wind did the work.'

'I will agree with that.'

MacDonald lit his pipe and puffed at it meditatively.

'Father used to give a hand in ferrying the sheep and I used to go out with him. You're a wee bit younger than me. Do you mind the time we did not come back?'

'I do, but not much; I must have been about seven years old and do not remember much from that age. You did come back though in the end.'

'Indeed; it all went wrong one day when a gale blew up on our way home, and we were swept out beyond the islands and into the Atlantic.'

'Now there you have the advantage of me Donald, for such a thing has never happened to me.'

'It happens sometimes. With Father it was the second time out on the wide ocean.'

'Well, I can see that you survived. But you and Father were ever a close mouthed pair and I never really knew what you did to get back. How was that?'

'I was gey afraid for the waves were high and the wind blew strong, but then I saw that Father was not afraid. He told me not to be ashamed of being afraid, because all around us was the majesty of God and we were in his hands. There was a reason for everything and we were meant to be here, so we must show our craft and work as men for our salvation.'

'Father was always strong in the Lord.'

'Oh yes!' said MacDonald with emotion, 'Father was a great one for accepting the will of Providence and so was Mother. I'm not sure that I take after him in that, or that I have his strength.'

'So what did you do?'

'We sailed before the wind and rode it out for two days and nights. We snatched some moments of sleep when we were ready to give up from fatigue, and we bailed, though that was not very necessary. Our boat was well made and sat on the wave-tops like a feather. We had water and oats on board so enough food to keep our energy going. Eventually the wind blew itself out and we made eastwards using the sun for direction. We made land on South Uist, and from there home.'

'I trust you gave thanks for your deliverance?'

'Of course; but I gave thanks for something else John, for what I had learned.'

'What is that?'

'That although you must respect the sea, there is no point in being afraid of it. If you get into danger on the sea, then whatever befalls you is going to happen, no matter what you do. If you are wrecked, or drowned, it is going to happen anyway. This being so, there is little point in being afraid and your mind is better given to using your skill to do all that you can to avoid it; the sea will respect your ability. Part of the reason I decided to make a living on big ships and leave the herring boats was that journey with Father. I am not afraid of the great waters or being out of sight of land, because what will be, will be. You know that Lattimore asked me to go and get help?'

'He didnae! That's one hell of a thing to ask a man if he was not prepared to do it himself.'

'Oh I agree. He should not have asked and I do confess that it has diminished him in my mind. It is one thing for him to ask, but quite another if I decide to do it.'

'You are not content to sit and wait for rescue? We can live here, if not very well.'

'Oh I know that, John. It is better not to tempt the sea and half my mind is to stay here sitting on the beach until some fine vessel comes close enough to see our smoke, but I do not think that I can.'

'Why not?'

'Because my mind tells me and Mr Wilson and Mr Morgan confirm it, that on what we are eating, we will not be as strong as we are for much longer. We can stay alive, but our strength and endurance comes from eating things other than grass and meat; we need bread or potatoes. If we are to attempt what I am minded to do, then we have to do it now while we have strength to even attempt it.'

'Are you going to do it?'

'It's quite a choice to think on and I am thinking on it John. I am thinking on it, but I would be lying to you if I did not say that my heart quails in me at the thought of the distance. I can give you no answer now. A lot will depend on whether or not we can find a better supply of food, though it seems unlikely. And then there are the bairns.'

'Aye. I take your meaning. They are at the age for growing, and they do not fare well on what we are eating.'

'That was my thought and I do hate to see weans suffer.'

'I am with you there, but it is, as you say, quite a choice. Well, if you decide for it then I am with you.'

'Why so?'

'Because if you do it, it's because you think it may be done.'

'Ach now John, that's another thing; it's not just myself is it? It would be other men, and the responsibility for their lives would be a heavy one. I'm not sure that I want that. And whatever happens you will not be coming.'

John MacDonald looked at his brother in surprise, 'Why not?'

'You know very well. The chances of such a thing succeeding are very small indeed; I would not expect to make it to Samoa. The boat with all in it would never be seen again. To place two members of one family in such a situation would be a foolish thing. And at any rate it would not be fair on Aunt Margaret to have both of us drowned now would it?'

'That's true enough; I did not think of that.'

'Aye well I did and I would not inflict such a loss upon her; I think it would be the death of her.'

'Obviously it would be a thing for volunteers; where would you head for?'

'Straight down the nor' east Trades back to Samoa, but perhaps it is not for volunteers. It would be better suited to right seamen and men of duty.'

'Why man that's 1,300 miles or more; why not somewhere closer like Napari or Kiribati?'

Donald looked at his brother and grinned. The matter was out now and things had been said.

'There's hardly anyone on Napari and Kiribati is a doubtful place to get help. Samoa is the place to go, for there will be ships and there is a British Consul. Besides which Kiribati is hundreds of miles south; the trades blow directly to Samoa and no beating into the wind.'

'And who would you be asking to go with you?'

'Well Ned Tumelty, because he's a fine seaman and he will wish to go. I should want three others.'

'All able seamen?'

'That goes without saying. They will all be good sailors.'

'Mr Ferguson then.'

'Yes. The Bosun is a fine seaman. He would be an asset.'

'Charlie Anderson and Bill Crosby.'

'That was my thinking too.'

'One from Denmark and the other from Nova Scotia; both hardy men on the water.'

'Aye. Do not be saying anything yet though, John. I have not quite set my mind to it and it is a thing I need to think more on.'

'I will not press the matter.'

'Please don't. It is something a man has to screw himself up to and I am not at the point of choosing yet.'

The communal pot that night had much of the sea about it. Thomas Morgan called it 'bouillabaisse' for it was full of shellfish from the rocks, a few clams, seaweed that looked like kelp and even a few fish. Some of the sailors had found forked branches from small trees and bushes further inland and carved them into two-pronged forks with which they had managed to spear some unwary but reasonably sized fish. It tasted better than the burgoo made with seabirds, but it was probably the change rather than the actual flavour; its main virtue was that it kept body and soul together. When the meal was finished the survivors were free to do as they wished until bed time. Most of the sailors set to work at various crafts and carved with their knives, whittling at platters, shaping coconut shells or making fish-spears to try. One man was trying to spin coconut fibre into thread with which to make a net, but Crone watched him dubiously, thinking that the sailor did not have the necessary skills and he probably would not succeed. Every man now had a spear with a point of some sort, but these were not being used in the normal run of things; simply propped up inside their sleeping huts in case there was a need to defend themselves.

The old tins had been chopped and hammered into rough shapes using the axe, then beaten over long sticks to form spearheads which had then been sharpened on the old grindstone. As there was not enough tin to make such spears for all, others simply had long sharp sticks, which had been charred at the end in the fire and hardened that way. Any attempt by outside aggressors to massacre this crew, would be met with force.

The fortnight since landing had been used in other ways too. Poles had been rammed in to the sand outside the huts and horizontals lashed between them. On top of this framework palm fronds had been laid to shield a patch of ground from the sun. This was very necessary because the heat of the sun during the day was terrific. The worst cases of sunburn had managed to recover somewhat from their initial exposure and most were able to move without pain. Five of them felt sufficiently recovered to join foraging groups on the shore in the early morning and as the sun went down, but still had deep weeping sores, crusted yellow and ringed with raised inflamed flesh, so spent most of their time under cover. Lattimore feared that some of them might succumb to some sort of infection, especially as they had become a target for the only pest on Palmyra, a persistent form of black fly. The positive side to this was that if the sunburn cases stayed in the huts they were not bothered so much because the flies appeared not to like shade, though on the sand there were, in places, swarms of them. All the sunburnt crew peeled horribly and the entire company was brown and getting darker; some of their backs were burned very dark, though deep red sun sores punctuated them. In the backs of two men flies had laid eggs into their sores and maggots had hatched, which at first caused horror in their minds, but Mrs Taylor told them not to be alarmed as the maggots would not eat any living tissue but only infected rotting matter. She had seen them used as a method of cleaning wounds in the war between the states. This had proven to be the case and when she eventually washed them away the wounds were clean and healing. Each man and woman now had a rough head covering of leaves and coconut fibre of their own manufacture and although they looked odd, they offered at least some protection. They also had a body covering of one sort or other, some being swathed in flag material or just large leaves. To describe them as a motley crew would be something of an understatement.

Not far from Lattimore, sitting round the fire in the early evening, not for warmth but for light, was Mrs Taylor, who opened a conversation on a topic she had evidently given some thought to.

'Captain, did you ever read The Swiss Family Robinson?'

'I can see why you ask that question ma'am. It is very appropriate under the circumstances, but I have to answer both yes and no.'

'How can you say both, Captain? Is that not rather a contradiction?'

'Not at all; I was given it to read by my father and mother who thought it held valuable Christian lessons which they wished to inculcate into me and indeed into my brother. I read about half of it then hurled it across my bedroom at the wall.'

'That's quite a reaction after only half the book. Why did you do such a thing?'

'It was the guns, ma'am. I did not mind so much that they seemed to have unlimited powder and shot, but that they blasted away at every living thing they came across.'

'But they had to eat, Captain.'

'That is undoubtedly true, but they were shooting far more than they could eat. Their instant reaction on meeting any living creature, be it on four legs or fowl with wings, was to kill it. Somehow that does not strike me as a good thing.'

'But were not beasts made to be used by men on this earth?'

'To some extent I will agree with that, but some they shot, then nursed back to health to keep. They were killing with an indiscriminate eye, Mrs Taylor, and I find it hard to reconcile Christian forbearance with that. Besides, the book is not realistic, as I think you will allow.'

'That depends in what way unrealistic.'

'Well, here you are on a desert island just like them. They had everything they wanted from their ship; very well I can accept that. There was much more time available to them to obtain all kinds of supplies from their ship, stranded as it was. We were not so fortunate.'

'You sound jealous, Captain.'

'Maybe I am. But it's not that which makes me jealous. I wish to God that we had had more time to remove goods from our ship, but it was their island that I objected to more. It was too idyllic.'

'I can see what you mean. They had everything they needed didn't they? Fruits, birds, animals and everything convenient of vegetable and animal to live off the fat of the land.'

'Indeed; I doubt there is an island in all the world where such abundant provision of the necessities of life may be found. They landed in Eden, Mrs Taylor. There are no snakes here, as the Reverend has pointed out, but this is no Eden. We scratch for our survival here and we hang on by our fingernails with just enough that can be described as food to sustain us.'

'The book then is a fantasy, Mr Lattimore?'

'Yes Reverend; it is. Here we are stranded on a desert shore, and who better than we to pronounce such a judgment? By and large I think the book to be full of pious and well meaning homilies, but as a guide to survival it is a nonsense.'

'I have always liked it, but I observe that you are not a family man. It is very instructive to children in the benefits of obedience to their parents. What of The Coral Island, Captain?'

'Mr Ballantyne? I have to say that as a lad it was one of my favourite books. But Reverend, here we are on a coral island. What do you say? Does it stand the test of reality?'

'I have to say that this particular island does not.'

'Yes, I think it more realistic than the Robinson book, but our three heroes had breadfruit, wild pigs and even fruit. We have none of those. I think we are worse off than they were.'

'I have to agree. I would swap their island for this one at any time!'

'Captain.'

'Yes Mr Crone'

'When we left the ship, sir, there was a large swell.'

'I have some recollection of that,' replied Lattimore wryly.

'But it does not follow that there is a swell there now.'

'That is true.'

'It might well be that parts of the ship which were inaccessible when we abandoned her, are accessible now.'

'Are you saying that you wish to go and look at it, Mr Crone?'

'I am, sir. I think it possible that we should be able to salvage some supplies from the parts left above water. There must be something of use and even if we only manage to obtain a few items of food it would at least provide some relief to the monotony.'

'It's thirty-five miles of open water to get back there, and the same to return.'

'Aye sir, but the sea is calm and there's not much of a breeze. It blows from the wreck to here too most of the time. I think our best oarsmen could get there easily enough and then come back with the wind.'

'How do the men feel about it? It's a hard thing to ask.'

There was a moment of hiatus, broken when John Campbell spoke up.

'Speaking for myself, sir, I'd like to do it. If there's a chance at getting some decent food to vary what we are eating then I'd like a bit of a row myself.'

There was a murmur of agreement among the crew members.

'You do realize that you might get nothing? That your efforts might all be in vain?'

'Aye sir, but we've been here for a fortnight and we're seamen. I'd feel better to get off this land and out to sea where we might do ourselves some good. After all, sir, if we just sit here it's going to be nowt but fishy burgoo day after day. I'd rather be doing summat.'

'Very well. Mr Crone, would you like to take this jaunt out to the wreck? Volunteers only though and not Mr MacDonald; I need another officer on the island.'

Crone grinned at the description of his proposal as a 'jaunt.'

'It would be my pleasure, sir. Hands up all men interested in crewing the launch.'

Every male adult hand save one shot up into the air, far too many volunteers, but Crone chose no passengers. The only person who really noticed the one who did not volunteer was Lattimore; he looked at Lancaster, but the stowaway's face remained without expression.

'Twelve prime seaman I need for the outward journey; three for each side and reliefs. We'll do it in no time!'

'I doubt that, Mr Crone,' replied Lattimore. 'If you row there at 2.5 knots it's fourteen hours.'

'Yes sir; I know it well. That way we should arrive after dark with all the hazards that implies. That's why we shall go faster. I aim for three knots.'

'Quite a target.'

'But very feasible, sir; the launch is built for more speed and with good men at the oars I think we can do it in just over eleven hours.'

'You'd stay there the night?'

'Aye sir; tie up to the ship, search her when it gets light enough then sail back by the afternoon of the following day.'

'When would you wish to do this?'

'First thing tomorrow morning Captain. If you can give us some of the hard tack for energy we can also take some coconuts and water. We'd leave at first light.'

'It's a fine enterprise, Mr Crone. You'd better start your preparations.'

'Aye sir,' said Crone and began to circulate among his chosen men who started to gather what they needed for their expedition; it was little enough.

Light was just tingeing the eastern sky the following morning when Lattimore shook Crone's hand.

'Good luck John. You're a fine seaman and I'll look to see you in the middle of tomorrow afternoon. Just be careful.'

'I will sir. We shall be perfectly safe, I'm sure of it.'

With calls of 'Good luck' and 'God speed' Crone and his men walked the launch out across the lagoon until the water was deep enough for some to get in and row. Eventually all were on board and the oars began to rise and dip in unison as they went out through the gap in the reef and headed nor' nor' west. On shore the watching eyes could not bear to stop following their progress until Lattimore gently reminded them that there was food to collect. Soberly the hunter-gatherers shuffled on their way to scrape for shellfish, clams, and anything else that may be put into a cooking pot.

At the back of Lattimore's mind was a worry that he knew was shared by the other people on the island. The men who had gone in the launch were their fittest and strongest, and in terms of defence, their best fighters. If people with hostile intentions came to the island then his group were exposed and weak and although the threat might be a mere chimera, it still made most of the castaways feel rather more vulnerable than they had. The only ones immune to the worry were the young girls, because they did not give such things a moment's thought and scampered in the carefree fashion of the young while looking for shellfish in the shallows near the rocks. Sleep that night would be fitful and interrupted by worrying thoughts of every noise in the dark.

Out on the sea Crone was taking his turn at an oar. He was a physical man of some strength, barrel chest with good biceps and had no intention of sitting at the tiller whilst others did all the work. He liked the regular exercise of rowing; the rhythm pleased him and he found it creative in that it produced tangible progress. His gusto was infectious and communicated itself to the boat crew.

'A song John; give us a song to carry us along.'

'Aye sir!'

Campbell, ever ready to sing, began with a favourite old rowing shanty, "Whisky Johnny":

"Whisky is the life of man
Always since the world began
Whisky-o, Johnny-o

John rise her up from down below
Whisky, whisky, whisky-o
Up aloft this yard must go
John rise her up from down below
Whisky here, whisky there
Whisky almost everywhere chorus &c."

Distance rowing, even for hardened seamen, is a fatiguing business. Crone changed the rowers every hour, but the men were very willing. The prospect of what they might be able to salvage from the wreck drove them on to greater efforts than they would normally have made. In their minds the *Henry*

James was a cornucopia of cans of meat, corn for bread, chocolate and all kinds of things that they had cravings for and best of all, for many - tobacco. In Wales there is a word to express what came over them. A great team spirit of *hwyl* possessed the crew as they rowed for all they were worth. The launch was twenty-seven feet long; a solidly built sea boat and she was never going to race to the shipwreck, but she moved as fast as a launch could reasonably go across a smiling sea. It is true that under a beating down sun the pace did slacken somewhat during the afternoon, but it was not quite dark when the expedition neared the ship. New energy came into the oarsmen's muscles as the wreck came into sight in the distance; soon they would be there. Flour, coffee, chocolate, tobacco, tins of meat, fruit in syrup, condensed milk, tea; every man had his own idea of the luxuries and necessities that might be salvaged from the *Henry James*. The last light of day was fading from the horizon as the launch nosed up to the stricken ship. They were able to tie up fore and aft alongside the poop rail, which was still above water, where she rode calmly as night fell. Crone's heart sank within him as the moon rose. He could see clearly that the waves were making a clean sweep of the ship, even in a relative calm. It did not bode well for what they might be able to do in the morning, but nobody gave voice to such a thought; hope, once kindled is slow to die. Conditions in the morning might be completely different. Having arrived at their destination, each man sat and crunched on a portion of hard tack and a measure of water. Leaving one on watch, the men stretched or sat as best they could and slept; not as hard as it might seem after a hard day at work on little food.

When morning came it became clear that their voyage had been in vain. The ship had evidently settled in two weeks and was sitting on the reef with the poop entirely under water; only the rail to which they were tied was above the surface. The deck cabin was a superstructure and not part of the skeleton of the ship; half of it had been washed away, and the interior of what was left had been scoured clean by the sea. The only part not entirely submerged was the forecastle which could be stood on, but the door was under water. Crone looked at it and his thoughts must have been transparent, for it was Thomas McClements who replied to what he was thinking.

'T'aint worth it, sir. There might be stuff in there and there might not; but whatever it is, there is no point in drowning to try to get it. We tried sir, but there's nowt here for us.'

'But I can swim. I can swim very well.'

'Aye sir; we know you can; but so can they.'

McClements nodded to the fins of sharks swimming round the ship.

'They're not very big, sir, but they're vicious enough, and if you met one of them in there…'

Crone was digesting this when he found himself faced with rebellion.

'Let's put it this way sir, and you can take this how you like. If you try to go in there we'll hold you down and row like hell away from this place.'

'You mean that Shearer?'

'I do, sir. There's nothing in there worth your life.'

Crone grinned ruefully, 'Is this mutiny then?'

'Aye sir; and we're all in it.'

He looked around and although some men in the crew were smiling, he knew they would not let him do it. If he had been a bad officer they might have let him, but he was popular and they would not permit it.

'Well if you put it that way, we'd better go back.'

It was evidently the general feeling that they should return to Palmyra Atoll, so Crone ordered that the sail be hoisted. There was relief that the journey back was not to be rowed, but a palpable air of disappointment fell over the group as they scudded towards their destination. As they dragged the launch back onto the beach below the huts and communicated the failure to the rest of the survivors, the same mood fell over the people who had stayed on the island. The children especially were disconsolate. For two days they had looked forward to the sailors coming back with decent food; now they had nothing, and their crying was bitter with dashed hopes. MacDonald looked at the tears running down Laura Hastings' face and he grew very thoughtful.

Later that evening it was time to eat and somebody had caught a large seagull. It had been determined that the meat should go to the children and the bird had not been put into the stewpot. One of the men had attempted to spit roast it, but it had not cooked very well and parts of it were almost raw. A chunk of the meat was given to Laura Mary Hastings and as the little girl tried to eat it, the taste of it revolted her system and she began to retch and she emptied the contents of her stomach. Dry retching continued until eventually she threw herself into MacDonald's lap, crying bitterly and went to sleep. John MacDonald came over to where his brother sat with his back to a tree nursing the small girl. Looking at Laura, John reached out and gently stroked her feet; then he too began to weep and said, 'She is not long for this world, poor child.'

The effect on Donald MacDonald was startling, as if he had received an electric shock and he looked at Laura in his lap with wide eyes, for without any thought, his mind had made a choice and all that remained was to put it into action. Some time later Laura woke up and she began to cry again telling MacDonald how very hungry she was. MacDonald looked at her strangely then spoke to her in words that to him seemed to come almost from somewhere outside of him.

'Do not cry now. It is of no use to cry because it does nothing.'

Then he took from off one of his fingers a small gold ring which he wore and put it onto one of hers.

'Don't cry. I am going away with the boat and I will get food for you to eat.'

Immediately Laura's face changed to one of great joy and she leaped up and went to tell her mother.

MacDonald had made his choice and he approached Lattimore.

'Captain. I have reached a decision and I would like to talk to you about it alone.'

Rather taken aback by the somber way in which MacDonald spoke, Lattimore took him along the beach to sit on a fallen tree trunk.

'Well Donald; what decision might that be?'

Chapter 7

The Choice

'I have decided that I am going to take the launch to Samoa.'

Lattimore said nothing, but just sat looking at MacDonald with an expression that could mean anything, though in reality he was so astonished that he did not know what to say. MacDonald took a breath and ploughed on. Lattimore noticed the absence of the word 'sir' and wondered what was coming next.

'I think it should take about nineteen or twenty days; I can speak to the British Consul in Apia and arrange a rescue. Depending on what ship is available and how the weather is, I think I could be back here within six weeks, all being well.'

Lattimore continued to look at him, and then he repeated MacDonald's last words, 'All being well?'

'Aye.'

'Of course, all may not be well Donald. You may never get there. May I ask what changed your mind?'

'The children,' said MacDonald laconically. 'If nothing is done then they will die. I will need the navigational instruments, the chart and the tables.'

'By your leave Donald, there are three officers on this island and I think we need all three here to speak of things such as this. If you do not mind, before we talk any further I should like to hear what John Crone says on this matter.'

'Aye.'

Lattimore stood up and bellowed across the gap between himself and the huts, 'Mr Crone!'

Crone appeared out of his hut and Lattimore motioned him over.

When he arrived Lattimore said, 'John, MacDonald wants to take the launch to Samoa.'

'That sounds like a good idea; I'd be happy to do it with him if he'll have me along.'

Lattimore was taken aback at Crone's ready enthusiasm, 'You think it's possible to do then?'

'I do, sir, and rather than sit here eating slop for the next however long it would be until a ship passes by, I'd rather go and get help myself.'

'But it's a dangerous thing to do is it not? A desperate venture indeed; you could easily die on such a voyage. It's about 1,300 miles, and in an open boat too.'

'Captain,' said MacDonald, 'It's really not your decision. I have made my choice; other men may make their own. Mr Crone is his own man.'

'I think that it may be done, sir,' said Crone eagerly. 'I should like to go in the launch.'

'Have you any experience in open boats out at sea, John?'

'I do sir, though not to the same degree as Mr MacDonald. I have to say that tempting the wrath of the Atlantic in a small boat is something I have never yet done, though I know he has. I have, however, been many times out into the Solway Firth and Irish sea; and in some quite rough weather too.'

'Ah yes; you're from Maryport. But I'm right in saying that most of your sailing experience has been on coal boats to Belfast and the Isle of Man? And that your small boat experiences were in fishing boats which came back into port at the end of the day?'

'Aye sir.'

'There's no need to look so crestfallen, John. I am not discounting your experiences, though you must admit that you are a very young man.'

'Aye, but believing that it can be done is half the battle, sir.'

'Well I'm not going to deny that.'

'If we want to go, sir, then the responsibility is our own; it is our choice and as it is our lives, I cannot think that you would deny us the opportunity to save ourselves. You could not blame yourself for any accident that may befall us, since the idea is ours and the decision to go would also be ours.'

'Again I do not deny that, but Donald knows what I'm talking about; don't you?'

'Aye.' Turning to Crone, MacDonald explained further, 'The captain means that there will have to be men other than us in the boat. Given the size of the launch and the distance to Samoa it would be sensible to have a five man crew.'

'So what you are saying is that we'd not only be risking our own lives, but those of others?'

'Yes John, and I'm not sure that I want that on my conscience. I will ask no man save Ned who is my friend. Any others must be volunteers.'

'One thing I am sure of, now that I have thought about it,' said Lattimore.

'What's that sir?'

'That you are not going, John. You stay here, even if Donald takes his chance, I need you here.'

'But why sir? I'd like to do it.'

'And I have heard you, and I say you do not go. Since I command here, that decision is final. As to why, it is simple. You know, and I know that sailing is a rough and ready sort of trade. You get all sorts of men taking ship and for many reasons. A few of this crew are unknown to me. Some of them signed on at Glasgow for this voyage. For all I know they could all be solid men, good honest and reliable. But on the other hand they could be thieves, liars and murderers; I simply do not know.'

'But why does that mean I cannot go to get help, sir?'

'Because a crew functions well if it is subject to authority; in this case my authority and that of my officers. If two of my officers go off to Samoa, the only commander here whose authority is clear would be me. I need you here, John, because we have women here; and girl children; and if authority and order break down at all, they must be protected. I trust that point is made?'

Crone looked at him, his mouth partly open; he had not considered this, though he was well aware that outrages at sea did happen, however infrequently.

'I can vouch for the Maryport lads sir; they are all good men.'

'I have no doubt of it; there are three others that came on at Maryport and if you say they are sound then I believe they are. I'm sorry if you feel disappointed, but I must have you here.'

'I won't deny some disappointment, sir, but if that's the case then I shall stay.'

'There will be other adventures in your life, John. I have one in mind for you anyway, but we shall speak of that later.'

'The men I want are good men all,' asserted MacDonald.

'Again, I do not doubt it,' said Lattimore, 'but that leads me to the question of volunteers. They cannot be volunteers, can they Donald? You know that as well as I do.'

MacDonald stroked his chin slowly, 'No. They cannot be volunteers.'

'But why not?' expostulated Crone. 'You said they had to be.'

'Because Mr Crone, the captain is correct. A well-meaning volunteer is one thing. An experienced seaman whom I trust, who knows the craft of small boats from infancy; now that is a different matter.'

'You are proposing to pick men to go?'

'No. Not in those words. What I propose to do is to ask particular men if they will do it.' He looked at Lattimore, 'I can do that because I am going myself.'

Lattimore flushed.

'Able seamen?'

'That seems right to me Mr Crone; their experiences will be similar to mine. They know well how to handle an open boat at sea, and with such a crew we would have the best chance of making a landfall at Samoa.'

'Who would you take?' asked Lattimore.

'To begin with I would ask the Bosun.'

'William Ferguson; he's a good seaman, and my own cousin.'

'Aye; and like me he learned the sea first in his father's boat fishing offshore. You do not mind him risking his life in this thing?'

'Willie's his own man and I would not try to stop him doing something he had set his mind on. Who else?'

'Anderson, Crosby and Tumelty; with such men I think our chances of success would be very high.'

'Ah now, that brings me to the most important question Donald. The chances of success - you seem to think that they are very good, but man it's a long long way to Apia from here. When I spoke to you before you thought it certain death. Our supplies are scanty at best and we have little to spare you and if you get caught in a storm you may sink and all drown. Why do you think now that you can do such a long and arduous thing? Your skills are one thing, but the sea is another and anything could happen.'

MacDonald looked at Lattimore for a long moment and replied in one word, 'Bligh.'

For a second the captain looked puzzled as his brain worked out what he had heard.

'Bligh? Bligh of the *Bounty* you mean?'

'Aye; you'll know the story.'

'Any sailor worth his salt does; an epic of the sea and a consummate display of seamanship. Perhaps the most remarkable open boat voyage in modern times. You seek to emulate him?'

Crone had blushed pink, 'I'm sorry, sir, but I don't know the story, at least not that part of it.'

'Well John I was not meaning to imply that you're not worth your salt! You are a young man, so I excuse you; it's time you did though. You know the tale of the mutiny on *HMS Bounty*?'

'I do know that bit, sir; everybody does.'

'What is not so well known and is too often underplayed is what happened to Captain Bligh after he was set adrift.'

'He made it home, sir.'

'Aye he did, but it's how he did it. He and his crew, in an overloaded boat sailed over 4,000 miles to a Dutch port in Timor from where they could get a ship home - 3,618 nautical miles. I do not think such a thing will ever be surpassed.'

'I'm not seeking to surpass it. The distance I propose is far less than that,' growled MacDonald.

'As I recall Bligh's boat was loaded so much that he only had six to eight inches of freeboard left. Some of the men who wished to go with him had to be left on *HMS Bounty* because even one more would have sunk the boat. They had to spend much of their time bailing out as it was.'

'Our launch is a good seaworthy boat, and with only five men we would not have that trouble. She's also part decked at the bows so we would not ship so much water.'

'That much at least is in your favour.'

'Aye, but there is more is there not? We can carry ample supplies, and not have to ration ourselves as he did. We also would not be passing any islands inhabited by bloodthirsty people trying to chase and kill us. And we would not be rowing; it's a good sail down the nor' east trades to where we know there is help.'

'Ample supplies?'

Such as we have. They were short on water and on food. We can collect enough water and take a large butt. There is little variety of food, but we can carry all the coconuts that could be wished for and although they are not a good food for energy, they will at least keep us going.'

'Coconuts! I think our burgoo, scant though it is, would be preferable to a diet of coconuts for three weeks.'

'I think we can stand it. It's not that long and the thought of what is at the other end will keep us going.'

'Oh Mister MacDonald,' said Lattimore, a hungry lean expression on his face, 'If you had not already convinced me, that last sentence would have removed all vestige of doubt. Heaven forfend that I should stand between a man and a three course dinner!'

'Steak and fried potatoes…'

'Thank you, John; I think we need not dwell on these matters. I take it that you are in favour of Mr MacDonald undertaking this venture?'

'I am, sir. I think it has a great chance of success and it is our best hope of rescue.'

'I agree. When do you propose to set off?'

'Tomorrow.'

'Tomorrow! I think you need two or three days of preparation; and you have to persuade men.'

'Are you going?' said MacDonald.

'No,' said Lattimore.

'In that case,' said MacDonald, 'Leave me alone.'

Seeing the shocked look on Crone's face at his speaking to the captain so, he relented a little.

'We have water; such of ship supplies as you can spare us, and the launch is ready. All we need to do is gather as many coconuts as we can. I shall speak to the men I want as soon as I can. There is no point in wasting a day because if this thing is to be done, then it is best done now. Besides…' Here

MacDonald paused and gave a rueful smile at John Crone. 'If we delay I might change my mind.'

Lattimore looked at him consideringly, trying to squeeze back a rudiment of their former regard back into the relationship. 'Somehow Donald, I cannot see that happening though it is always your choice. We shall feed you as best we can tonight and you may set off at first light. Will you travel at night also?'

'Aye; there is no land between here and Samoa, so I see no reason to heave to or use a sea anchor. We shall travel all the time. In this way I hope to make at least seventy miles or so each day, maybe better.'

'But how shall you see the compass in the dark?'

'I will take the oil lamp; it has not been used since we arrived, and there is a reasonable quantity of paraffin if we put it all into one tin.'

'But you will have no means of lighting it when darkness falls.'

'But I will. One of the advantages of being a smoker is that I have matches.'

'But why did you leave me to use the telescope to light a fire when we first landed here?'

'They were soaked, but now they are perfectly dry. We shall be able to light the lamp.'

'Well, all I can say Donald is that it's a good job that I am a creature of habit. I have been winding the chronometers at noon every day; you'd better have those.'

So saying, Lattimore felt in his pocket and handed over two small brass keys which MacDonald put into his tobacco pouch before stowing it away.

'Safest place to be,' he said, palpably softening his hauteur towards Lattimore, 'For I will never lose my pouch.'

The thought of MacDonald's attempt to reach Samoa caused Lattimore considerable inner turmoil and on several points. As captain, there was a sense that he himself should be the one to undertake the perilous journey in search of help. It did not sit well with him that his second in command was the man to lead such a desperate attempt; by rights, or so he thought, it should be him. That he did not have the same skills and experience in small boats that MacDonald possessed was something which his mind minimalised and it was completely overshadowed by the nagging thought that somehow he was shirking his duty. Rationally, he knew this was foolishness, but it did not stop him thinking it. Then there was the question of guilt. Like all captains who lose a ship Lattimore's mind was full of 'what ifs'. What if he had still been awake? Would he have sensed that something was wrong? Should the ship have been going slower at night, even if the waters ahead were clear of land for 2,000 miles? Might the steam pump have saved the ship if they had started it? Could he have towed her off with the boats? The sensible part of him knew the answers well enough, but he kept coming back to the main grinding thought. He was the captain, the man in charge. Responsibility lay with him and he had lost his ship; the beautiful vessel that had been his home for over four years was now a wreck; who else's fault was it? This thing in his head, for it seemed almost solid, though only thought, would not let go of him and much of the time his mood was down, morose, and not inclined to any cheer at all.

MacDonald took his chosen companions aside in order to find out if they were willing to go with him on his desperate journey. All of them accepted immediately, the only note of surprise coming from the bosun, William Ferguson.

'I confess, Mr MacDonald, that I have been wondering if an attempt should be made to reach Apia for these last two weeks, but did not think it my place to speak out in asking other men to risk their lives. May I ask why you took so long?'

'Because I was hoping Mr Ferguson, with God's help, that a ship might pass by and see our smoke, but it has not happened.'

'Your piety does you credit and I know what you mean, for the Reverend Taylor is a powerful preacher whose prayers are sure to be heard. Sometimes though I think the Lord sets us tests, and in these situations, he helps those who help themselves.'

'Aye well; then there's the bairns. I am distressed by the thought of their being stranded here.'

'Had you thought of taking everyone to Samoa?'

'The whole party? I think not Mr Ferguson. The boats would be crowded, as they were on the way here and the supplies would be limited. Also I think that the women and children would suffer much on a prolonged sea voyage in an open boat. No, the best thing to do is to go and find a ship to bring everyone off.'

'I think you are right. I will go with you; the venture appeals to me for it is a daring and audacious plan. I should much like to be part of it.'

'I am glad that you will be with us. May I ask you to see to extra stays for the mast, for there will have to be some hard sailing?'

'You can leave that to me Mr MacDonald. I will see to it.'

Anderson, Crosby and Tumelty were all in favour of sailing to Samoa as were many others of the crew who had to be declined, with regrets; and so it was that MacDonald informed the captain that they would proceed with their enterprise. Without further ado, Lattimore gathered all the survivors together and announced that MacDonald and some brave volunteers were resolved to set out to get help and would be leaving in the morning. The general reaction was gladness and when he asked them to scatter out with what was left of the day and bring back every coconut they could get their hands on, they set about the work with enthusiasm. As the nuts were harvested they were brought back to the launch and stowed in as balanced a fashion as possible. After stripping off the outside husks they found that 267 coconuts were stored in the launch which boat MacDonald had chosen for the trip. It was small enough for five men to handle, seaworthy and with ample room for supplies and men; she also rode the waves lightly and was easy to handle. Half the remaining supply of hard tack went onto the launch, fully seven pounds of it. More than half of the remaining tinned mutton, six pounds, was stowed carefully as was the ten-gallon keg of water. One pound of cheese was placed in the shade under the decked portion, and as a last benediction, two of the three remaining bottles of whisky that had comprised the emergency spirit supply for the boats. The final items on the boat were the chronometers, which Lattimore had saved from the *Henry James*, the compass, the book of navigational tables and John Crone's sextant. After a hard struggle with himself, Lattimore handed over his leather bound telescope. It had only been used once to start a fire when the survivors had landed and since the cooking fire and signal beacons were kept going constantly it may not be used again; it was more use to MacDonald than to him. Lastly a couple of lines with improvised hooks made from tin cans were stashed under the tiller seat.

That night, as may be imagined, the mood of the company gathered round the fire was ebullient, with one exception and that was MacDonald himself who had wandered off on his own. Dauntless men were about to set forth on a mission of rescue, and they carried with them the hopes of all. The remaining tins of mutton were opened and the boat's crew feasted on it as much as they could eat with hard tack. No man or woman who was to stay ate any, except for Mrs Hastings, though the children had some. MacDonald's view was that the food would have choked him had he been made to eat it in front of them and they not to have any. He and the entire company understood completely what they were doing. Their champions were setting forth to do battle against the sea for the salvation of them all. The least they could do was feed them up and give them as much strength and energy as they could before they set out on a journey that might lead them to their deaths. The food was washed down with half of the last bottle of whisky on the island thus giving the boat's crew a good send off and removing the bottle as a possible bone of contention in future; the remainder was for medical use only. More than anything else, hope soared eternal and bright over the encampment and when sleep came to the company, it came with a smile and the thought that they were finally doing something that might end their ordeal.

For MacDonald the evening was different. One of those black Celtic moods had descended on him and he was convinced that he was fated to die on the journey. This night was to be his last one on solid earth and he had warned men to stay away from him, saying he wanted to rest. Eventually he lay down under the launch which had been turned over and propped up on the beach, and the thought kept coming to him that this boat was to be his grave. He could not sleep and eventually got up and walked to the other side of the island which was only half a mile wide, and his mind was in turmoil. He thought of Job in the bible and like him, MacDonald cursed his days, asking why he had been delivered up to this fate.

'*C'ar son a ghabh na gluinean romham? Agus c'arson na ciochan g'un deothailinn?*'
(Why was I laid on my mother's lap? Why did she nurse me at her breasts?) Job 3:-12.

He then got down on his knees facing out to sea, with no one to observe him and he prayed to God for his help and his guidance. He quailed at the thought of what he was about to do and his mind raced with fear, uncertainty and doubts. There were a lot of tears and agonizing, asking questions about his life, what he was for, and why God was putting such a burden onto him. People who knew MacDonald professionally would not have recognized the dour and taciturn man they worked with as raw emotion poured out of him and into the night sky. Eventually he stretched out face down on the sand and some sleep overcame him. In the morning his brother John came to find him, having seen him leave the camp and knowing where he would have gone. As they walked back to camp, MacDonald told John of his plans and the course he intended; he was once more in control of his mind and steely determination was on him. One thing he was adamant about and that was that if John MacDonald attempted to get into the boat to go with him, then he would have him removed by force if necessary.

At the camp William Ferguson was already awake.

'I see that you are eager to be off Mr Ferguson.'

'Aye Mr MacDonald; I think that if we are to do this, then we had best be about it. However, there is one more thing I wish to say before we set off.'

'And what might that be?'

'There is no denying that it is a mighty perilous venture that we are undertaking. I should be easier in my mind if I faced it with men that felt able to call me by my given name.'

'I can see why that might be, Willie, and I agree.'

'Good Donald, now let us get Ned and Charlie and Billy and be away.'

The two men shook hands firmly and with a rueful grin at each other.

The entire group was up to see them off; there were many handshakes and wishes for good weather, but the one that counted most for MacDonald was that of Laura Hastings who stood looking at him whilst sucking her thumb, a habit she had not yet discarded.

'I'm sorry you have to go Mr Donald but I'll be happy if you do bring back some food.'

MacDonald knew she was far too young to have any idea of the dangers he was about to face.

'Well now, Miss Laura, I am fed up with eating the food on this island as I suppose that you are too?'

'It's horrid. I hate it.'

'Well so do I. I want to go and see if I can find a plate of decent brose and if I can I shall bring you some back.'

'What's brose?'

'Do you not know what brose is? Oh well now, it's the food they give to angels. Where I come from it is oatmeal soaked overnight in boiling water that is allowed to cool. In the morning you can add to it, honey, whisky and cream.'

'I'm not sure I'd like the whisky.'

'Believe me my child, even without the whisky it is a wonderful dish and fit even for you to eat.'

'Well you must be sure to bring some back for me.'

'You may be certain that if there is any to be had in Apia I shall return with some for you in about six weeks time.'

'You promise?'

'I do. I shall be back on this island with a ship and that is my promise to you.'

She nodded solemnly and went to hold her mother's hand to see him off.

The general expressions of goodwill and backslapping stopped when the Reverend Taylor stepped forward to ask for God's blessing on the crew of the boat. It was a powerful moment and when the Reverend knelt with his hands clasped, everyone sank to their knees as he prayed:

"Oh Eternal Lord God, who alone spreadest out the heavens, and rulest the raging of the sea; who hath encompassed the waters with bounds until day and night come

to an end; be pleased to receive into thy almighty and most gracious protection the persons of these thy servants. Preserve them from the dangers of the sea so that they may bring succour to us that we may return in safety to enjoy the blessings of our lands and the fruits of our labours with a thankful remembrance of thy mercies, to praise and glorify thy holy name; through Jesus Christ our Lord. Amen."

'Amen,' said the entire party with perhaps more feeling than they had ever done in their lives.

MacDonald walked towards the boat and found Mrs Hastings standing in his path, her face unreadable, a block of silence. She said nothing, but he knew why she was there; he kissed her cheek in farewell but as he passed she followed him to the boat, quiet tears flowing as rain. Then willing hands manned the sides of the launch and began to push it out from the sand and across the lagoon shallows towards deeper waters. As the depth increased, Ferguson climbed into the boat, followed by Tumelty and each took an oar, holding it aloft. Anderson and Crosby soon followed. When the water became deep enough to sustain all that it had to carry, Lattimore, panting as he pushed beside MacDonald turned his head and gasped, all formality forgotten, 'In you go Donald.'

To his astonishment MacDonald grinned in a manner not like him at all. It was the wide smile of a man without a care in the world, whose choice was made and who would abide by it, come what may. During the night he had forgiven Lattimore for his presumption, and had made his peace with what he had chosen to do. He would not carry hate or dislike on this voyage with him. Those things were of the earth and MacDonald was leaving it.

'Goodbye Ralph and God bless you.'

'Goodbye Donald, and may he bless you also and speed you on your way.'

MacDonald scrambled into the launch and took the tiller, looking at the four men who were his companions.

'Ready. Oars out. Give way together!'

Looking back at the beach on those left on the island, MacDonald saw an image that would be burned into his memory, unforgettable until the day he died. Somehow they looked forlorn, a strange group of figures clad in rags, many of them with sores and all of them deeply tanned from exposure to the sun. The men's hair and beards were getting long and they were all painfully thin. A wistful air hung over them, their eyes fixed on him and his boat, the repository of all their hopes, and he felt the weight of their desperation on him. Five men were leaving on a journey so much more like a desperate throw of dice than a reasoned and sensible thing. Many on the shore were on their knees praying and many were openly shedding tears; their voices came across the water calling out blessings and wishes of God speed and goodwill.

As the oars rose and fell in unison, the launch steered for the gap in the reef where the Pacific rollers flooded through in turbulence. The shore party, wary of sharks, made their way back into the shallows where the predators did not care to come, and turned to watch. MacDonald kept the bows straight onto the waves and the strong muscles of his crew propelled the launch through the rough waters and into the smooth swell outside in the deeper ocean. The wind blew fair from the north east under a sweltering tropical sun. MacDonald soon gave the order to ship two oars and set up the mast. He looked at Ned Tumelty and said, 'I maun get home safe to Aunty Margaret or she'll kill me.'

Tumelty looked at him, digested what he'd said, and replied laughing, 'Well Donald, we would not be wanting that to happen, so we shall do our best for you.'

Within a few minutes the sail was up and the remaining oars brought inboard. The launch gathered speed and headed away from Palmyra at around a brisk twenty-five knots as the wind filled her sail, singing in her rope work and raising their hopes high. On shore Lattimore watched as the white triangle of canvas got smaller and smaller until it neared the horizon and he could barely see it.

'Just get there, Donald. Just get there,' he whispered to himself. Then he turned to scan the group around him.

'Mr Crone.'

'Aye sir.'

'I mentioned that I had a task for you to carry out. If you will come with me please I wish to talk to you some more about it. It's an important job, Mr Crone, and I want us to think about it together. You are second in command now, and the duties will reflect in your pay from this moment. Come along please.'

Crone was well aware that the captain's remarks were aimed at preserving order, but he was very curious as to what this job might be that was so vital.

'Aye sir,' he said, and accompanied Lattimore down the beach to where they could talk privately.

Chapter 8

The Maryport Men

John Crone followed Lattimore down the beach, wondering if what the captain had to say would have anything to do with the 'adventure' that he had intimated previously; it did. Lattimore did not bother with a preamble, but straightaway set out what he wanted Crone to do.

'I want you to take the pinnace, John, and go round the island. Then I want you to go to the other islands.'

'Exploring, sir?'

'Exactly so; I need not tell you that we are in need of a permanent source of water. Frankly I have no idea if there is a rainy season and a dry season in this part of the world. So far we have been blessed with sufficient water for our needs, but if the rains do not come then we shall be in real trouble. Find us water if there is any to be had, John.'

'Aye sir, if it's to be had then I shall find it, never fear. I take it that you wish us to find other forms of food as well?'

'Of course; that goes without saying,' Lattimore gestured with his arm somewhat impatiently. 'Listen John; what I really want you to look for as well as the obvious is people.'

Crone had not thought of that, 'People sir?'

'Yes indeed; now look, I cannot remember exactly how many separate islands make up this atoll, but I do remember that it is in a horse-shoe and it must be at least eight or ten miles in length. We have not left this one island since we arrived here; that's my fault, because we should have.'

'Why do you say that, sir?'

'Because I'm sometimes slow to think, John; we've been taking it for granted that this place is uninhabited, but we don't actually know because we haven't looked.'

'But surely we would have seen signs of life by now, sir? Smoke? Canoes? Something like that.'

'It's not likely I admit, but eight miles is quite a long way if you're on an island. These trees are tall and you cannot see through the jungle. We need to know, because if there are people here, or signs that they call, even occasionally, then they may be of help to us.'

John Crone's imagination was much taken by this thought and he grew quite animated.

'Well Captain, I do not think you have anything to criticize yourself for; I have not thought of that and neither has anyone else. There are places that ships do call for fresh fruit or water and this might be one of them. That makes sense and I'd like to go and find out. It would be champion if it turned out that there were people on the other side, or signs that they were calling here.'

'Ah now John, I'm glad to find you so keen,' said Lattimore dryly. 'However, I'll sound a note of caution here; if there are people they might not be friendly.'

'Savages you mean, sir?'

'Now that is a line straight out of The Coral Island, John. It is true though that there are many places that the missionaries have not penetrated to where tribes make war on each other and yes, some do practice cannibalism. Frankly though, I do not know. What I do know is that there has been a massacre on this island and that we have buried a man with an axe in his head and other people who have obviously been murdered. We do not know who did that, so until we do I'm inclined to treat any people we find with a degree of caution.'

'We'd best take our pikes then, sir.'

'I agree. The party should be armed. Pikes, harpoon, clubs, and of course the knives that we have.'

'And who should the party consist of, sir?'

'I thought four of you. You are, after all, only poking around inside the reef and will not be going to sea. Oh, and take the boy with you. He's been very quiet and he needs something to do.'

'Alex will go sir. Who else?'

'I think since you will be leading the expedition you should choose your own men.'

'Very well, sir; I'll take Thomas Morgan, James Wilson and Samuel Young.'

'The cook, my steward and an ordinary seaman; that's a curious choice. May I ask why those three?'

'Because I know them, sir; they're all from Maryport.'

'I know that John, but why not three prime seamen instead?'

'Oh they can handle boats. Just because they take on a job as a cook or a steward doesn't mean they can't pull an oar, but it's not that. They're marras, sir.'

'Marras?'

'Aye sir; marras is mates in Cumberland. What it means is that if we run into any bother I know they'll back me up. Other men might run away, but these three will be there if I need them. Thomas is very tall sir and can be rather intimidating when he has a wish to.'

'So you can rely on them?'

'That's it, sir. I can trust them with my life and in any situation we find we'd help each other.'

'Then it's a good choice, Mr Crone. Get them together and tell them what you want to do. It might take you several days to explore the whole place satisfactorily, but the distances involved are not great. I suggest you take some water with you and I can allow some hard tack and of course there are coconuts everywhere. I'd like you back each evening for the main meal. One more thing though.'

'Sir?'

145

'Keep the bit about searching for other people among yourselves. I don't want to give anyone false hope. On the other hand, the fact that there is a mission gone to find rescue and you are going in search of food and water will be very good for morale if nothing else.'

Crone got his companions together quietly and told them of the captain's instructions, along with his caution to not speak of finding other people except among themselves. Thomas Morgan was joyful at the news.

'All I seem to have done since I got onto this island is chop things up to make stew. It'll be good to go and see what's round the other side. Someone else can make the stew instead.'

'And if there's trouble?'

'To be honest, a bit of trouble might be welcome. There's a head of steam in me that I would not mind letting out and if that means punching the head of someone who deserves it, then so much the better.'

Crone laughed. Many stewards he had come across at sea were meek and mild men, but Thomas was well set up, above average height and muscular; he could well imagine that he chafed at inactivity.

There was little point in delay, so Lattimore handed over a small amount of hard tack and Crone filled some of the bottles found in the huts with water and soon the pinnace floated in the lagoon. The party that had launched the boat was animated by the sight of some triangular fins, cruising round in the deeper water, but fortunately they did not have to venture further than knee height before the oarsmen could take over.

'I'll not deny that they are a sobering sight,' ventured Mr Hastings, 'but are they dangerous to humans?'

'I think not,' puffed Reverend Taylor who had been putting his shoulder to the work of launching the boat. 'Their natural food is fish, which they chase and eat.'

'But I thought that sharks attacked humans?'

'Not at all; I had a discussion much like this with some parishioners in Samoa and they pointed out that if sharks ate humans normally, they would not eat very often.'

'So you think they will not attack us?'

'I think if excited by the presence of food or prey they might bite, but not from malice; rather cautiously like a dog testing something to see if he could eat it or not.'

'I do not much care about their motives; I just do not wish to be bitten at all.'

'Why then Frederick, it is probably best to stay out of the water.'

This caused a general laugh at Mr Hastings' expense, but the company was uniformly in high spirits, as indeed they should be. They had sent forth an expedition in search of rescue and now another was setting out to search for food and water. All was positive save the monotony of the food and the merciless nature of the sun, whose relentless beating down still had the power to burn even their tanned skins.

Out on the boat John Crone smiled; he was happy sitting at the tiller, his head shaded by a broad hat woven from palm leaf strips, glad to be doing something. In front of him Morgan, Wilson and Young rowed gently along, the fourth oar in the hands of Alex Sutherland, the ship's boy. He was a well set up lad of fourteen and strong for his age, as he had to be in his job. Regarded as little more than a trainee, the life of the ship's boy depended very much on the disposition of the captain, whose servant he was. The captain thought him a promising lad and had employed him because he knew his family back in his own home port of Larne. Alex's prime duty was to act as Lattimore's messenger, but also to carry out errands for the officers and the passengers. If he was bright enough he might, eventually, aspire to learn the arts of seamanship and climb the ladder towards becoming an officer himself; if not then he might end up as an ordinary Jack Tar. Alex was bright enough, but he had not been particularly happy this last couple of weeks for there was nothing much for him to do save gather food. He was now off on an adventure and he smiled at the thought. He was a good match at the oars because although he was not used to it, neither were the men; ordinarily it would be the ABs who rowed the pinnace.

They were armed as well. Thomas Morgan had appropriated the old harpoon that had been found in one of the huts and put an edge on it before setting off. In bloodcurdling tones he had announced that if they met anything with hostile intent then it would be damned sorry. Young and Wilson both had pikes with tin tips, quite sharp, and Alex had a jackknife on a lanyard round his neck. Crone himself favoured a large wooden club, not unlike an Irish shillelagh, which he fancied would allow him to put up a good defence if anyone attacked him. He noted with some amusement that Thomas Morgan had attached the boat's painter to his harpoon.

'Expecting to catch a whale Thomas?'

'No sir, but you never know; might get a turtle or something good to make soup from.'

Crone grinned; Morgan was ever the optimist. His confident and warlike crew now sculled slowly up the placid waters of the lagoon, heading east along the south side of the island, and soon were out of sight of the camp as they turned a corner. The water they glided across was rippled with small wavelets stirred up by a gentle and cooling breeze and underneath them was as clear and pellucid as Venetian glass. It also teemed with fish and corals of all colours ranging from vermillion red to vivid green. At one point a large ray, like an underwater kite swam under their fascinated gaze causing Sam Young to exclaim, 'Devil fish!'

'Can you eat them?' asked Alex.

'Probably,' replied Crone, 'But you have to catch them first. I think I'd prefer to eat fish that actually looked more like fish.'

Away from the boat the white sand under them reflected back shades of aquamarine, turquoise, bright blues and emerald, all bounded on the shore side by a dazzling white strand overhung with palm trees leaning at almost horizontal angles. Further behind them the stands of *Pisonia* were backed by the tallest coconut palms festooned in an inexhaustible supply of nuts. Out to sea behind them, their boundary was defined by a white line that marked where the ocean rollers broke against the reef, sheltering them from its swell. In front of them was the inner lagoon of the atoll, stretching round in a horseshoe whose inside they must crawl along. In appearance it was Paradise on earth, but with no apples or fruit of any other description. It might, thought Crone, be possible to enjoy the place a lot more if the food available were more varied. Still there was no doubt in his mind that the survivors had not been exploiting the lagoon enough; more energy must be spent on fishing. As a sailor on commercial vessels he could not repress the thought that there was enough free copra to be found here to fill quite a few cargoes for an enterprising merchant to enrich himself. But of course to gather the nuts and dry the flesh sufficiently would need a workforce and there was none.

Soon the pinnace came to the limits of where the foraging parties had gone, about a mile and a half down the shore from the camp. Close to shore as they were, the boat party could not help but wonder at the abundant bird life that was loudly present, rising and squawking on every corner; perhaps the captain's concerns that they would run out of bird's eggs was misplaced. As it transpired, there was not much more of the island to go. Another half mile brought the pinnace to a place that appeared to be a bay, but as they drew level to it they could see through to open water where, in the distance, they could see the line of the outer reef.

'Very well; let us go through there and see what we shall see,' said Crone.

It was not much of a gap, only about fifty yards wide and very shallow with a sandy bottom. They had got most of the way through it when the boat stuck on a sand bar.

'Ah we must lighten her,' said Crone. 'Thomas and Sam, see if you can help push her off with oars. The rest of us into the water and heave.'

It was a few minutes of puffing, but soon the boat was floating on the other side of the submerged bar and the channel ahead looked clear. The water was warm and pleasant to the skin and the exertion enjoyable.

The men now scrambled back into the pinnace, but the boy Alex was more reluctant to re-embark, liking the feeling of the water on his skin.

'A bit nicer than sea-bathing at Allonby, eh Thomas?'

'I wouldn't know Jim. I never had a mind to get frozen to death, so I've never done it. Alex - what have you done?'

'I've cut my foot, Mr Morgan, on a sharp rock.'

'Ah well, get yourself back in quick and let's get it bound up.'

'Quick about it too!' snapped Crone. 'There's a damned shark coming.'

Alex was back in the boat almost on the word 'shark' as Crone added, 'It must have smelled the blood or something. Thomas; what the hell are you doing?'

Morgan did not reply immediately, for as the black tipped reef shark approached the boat and cruised alongside, he stood up and speared it through with the harpoon. It immediately began to thresh about and rock the boat, slamming into its side and causing a great flurry of water and shouting of profanity from the men in the boat. A five-foot long shark can cause quite a disturbance. Morgan was not abashed at all, but began hauling on the rope with all his strength, 'Quick marras! Give us a hand. It's shark steaks all round!'

It was undoubtedly the word 'steaks' that made the difference. From a mad inconvenience and alarm, the shark suddenly became dinner; it was after all just a big fish. They hauled on the rope and heaved it snapping and wriggling into the boat. Crone fetched it several wallops on the head with his club and it stopped threshing and lay quite dead.

'You're a mad fool, Thomas,' he said to Morgan, 'But I want a good cut of this for the fright you've given us all.'

'Eh it's just like fishing for mackerel off Maryport pier, but bigger.'

'Aye well that's as may be, but yes it's bigger. Now shove it under the deck and cover it with a sail or the sun will soon turn it bad. That'll feed everyone tonight.'

'Not tonight, sir; shark has to be prepared and I'll have to cut it up and soak it overnight.'

'Why so?'

'Cos if you don't soak it well and wash and squeeze it, sir, it doesn't taste good. But if I soak it overnight and give it a good rinse it'll be fine.'

'Have you eaten it before?'

'I have, sir, and cooked it too, in Samoa. Food is an abiding interest of mine, wherever I go and I like to try new things. It tastes a bit like chicken.'

Crone tried to fight down a sudden tendency to drool, but could not.

'Chicken you say?'

'Aye sir; quite mild and nice; very meaty.'

'Meaty!'

'Oh aye.'

'If it isn't, Thomas Morgan, I'm as like to roast and eat thee!'

'No need Sam; I'll roast and eat myself!'

Laughing over this the crew of the launch headed back west, following the north coast of the island. To their great disappointment, no stream revealed itself running down from the island to the sea. There was compensation though in that they did not have to row and the sail was stepped up so that they were able to scud easily along. At several points they landed and waded ashore to look in the jungle to see if they could find a pool, but they found nothing. At last they came to a place about a mile and a half along the coast where Alex and Sam Young had moved into the jungle about a quarter of a mile, when they became aware that something big was moving through the undergrowth towards them. They could hear footsteps as twigs and ferns broke underneath it; what could it be?

'An animal!' breathed Alex.

'Perhaps it's a wild pig. They often have wild pigs on desert islands,' whispered Sam. 'Let's rush it. I'll spear it and you grab it. Roast pork!'

With a wild yell intended to paralyze their prey with fear, they jumped up and ran forward only to be frozen in horror when the object of their rush gave a piercing scream that stopped them in their tracks. There followed a group of men led by Mr Carter with spears raised, which they lowered when they saw that Mrs Taylor was not under attack.

The boat party had not realized that in their circumnavigation of the island, they had arrived diametrically opposite their huts, which were on the south coast whilst they had landed on the north. Their base was only about half a mile in a straight line through the trees and Mrs Taylor's group had been allocated the area to forage that day.

'Lord save us, but I nearly died of fright. What on earth are you boys playing at?'

By this time Crone had come up and the sheepish Alex and Sam had to explain their actions.

'Do I look like a wild pig?'

They avowed that she did not, but they had mistaken her for one; which did not help much for she was determined to play them out for the fright they had given her.

'So I do not look like a pig, but you mistook me for one anyway. That's not the most flattering thing you could say to a lady of my years.'

They were bright pink and completely at her mercy by now. Crone, who had intended to haul them over the coals saw their shuffles and confusion and knew that he did not have to lift a finger in castigation.

'Well now for this insult, which no lady should have to bear from anyone calling himself a gentleman, there is but one penalty that will satisfy me. I want a ride home.'

So it was that the pinnace completed its circumnavigation of the island and as it turned the point to move eastwards back towards the huts, Mrs Taylor sat in regal state in the bows allowing the offshore breeze to cool her brow and calm her senses after her shock.

Lattimore was pleased at the shark and even more at the prospect of a steak in the morning, but disappointed that no water had been found. Crone was sanguine about it.

'It's not that much of a problem sir; we shall set off again in the morning and work our way around the rest of the islands. From what I have seen most of them are not very wide. We won't have to go all the way around most of them; we just have to land and walk a couple of hundred yards and that will take us clear across them.'

Morgan and Wilson had a lot of help with butchering the shark and they slowly carved it into steaks and chunks, which were taken away and placed into a range of containers and soaked in seawater. In the morning Morgan intended to wash them in fresh water before roasting them on skewers by the fire. They had to be cooked for breakfast because in the tropical heat there was no guarantee that the meat would not rot before it could be eaten. It proved to be as he had said and the breakfast enjoyed by all the survivors was the best they had so far on the island. The water the meat had been soaked in smelled repulsive, but once washed it appeared to be wholesome flesh. When roasted by the fire it was savoury and Morgan's promise made good; it did taste like a meaty chicken. It was the general verdict that shark should be on the menu again, but that it would be best caught in the morning so that it could be cut up and soaked in the afternoon to be eaten at night. Lattimore agreed with Crone's view that they should use the pinnace for fishing in the lagoon and it was agreed that this be done when he had completed his exploration.

The following day Crone set off once more on his examination of the islands of the atoll; this time they went straight past the gap where they had caught the shark and continued round the chain. Each island they came to, they landed on and as they moved eastwards it became apparent that they were fairly identical. By and large they were thin spits of land that could be walked across in a few minutes, though some parts were broader than others. Everywhere there were land crabs of various types and especially hermit crabs, which Crone found amusing. He had not known that this species lived on land before he had come to Palmyra and their propensity to use coconut shells as their home, scuttling around with them on their backs, made him laugh. A few of them had found their way into the stewpot, but they were so small that it was hardly worthwhile catching them compared to the larger species of red land crabs, or the huge coconut crabs that would feed half the party. As elsewhere, there were no quadruped animals of any description, just the omnipresent birds and more crabs. Methodically, Crone worked his way around the atoll, landing, searching for water and finding none. He had high hopes of one of the larger islands in the lagoon that was almost circular, but once again the search was futile. Each night the crew of the pinnace rowed back across the lagoon to the camp for their burgoo, but with nothing useful to report. Crone had found that the atoll consisted of sixteen separate islands, larger and smaller, thirteen of them strung together like beads on a string with little channels between each of them. The other three lay within the lagoon; offshore were smaller islets that were too numerous to count, but he had his eye on one, which lay to the side of the gap in the lagoon and away from the rest. Lattimore was half inclined to stop the exploration as unproductive and use the boat for fishing, but Crone persuaded him that having started the process of exploration, it might as well be finished. So it was that the Maryport men rowed one more time across the lagoon to land on the last island. The sea here was rougher as it edged the gap in the reef where the swell came through, so they rowed the boat up as far as they could then hauled her up onto the sand. Crone distrusted the waves so he left Alex to watch the boat while he and the men pressed inland.

It was not a large island, perhaps four hundred yards long and two hundred wide, but the moment he entered the jungle line Crone felt a change of atmosphere. He attempted to shrug the feeling off, but this place was oppressive with a brooding creepy feel to it. It was absurd, he told himself, and he should not allow his imagination to run away with him, but then he turned to look at Thomas Morgan. The Steward's face was set, and he held the harpoon in front of him as if ready for action. He looked at Crone.

'Ah'll tell thee what, marra. I'd just as soon not be here.'

The abandonment of rank betrayed the depth of his concern. Jim Wilson and Sam Young had the same expression.

'Why's that Tom?'

'It's like there's summat bad here.'

'How do you mean?'

'Have you ever been up to Hermitage?'

'The castle?'

'Aye.'

'A grim sort of place that is. More like a blockhouse than any castle I ever saw. Yes I went there a few years back. Why?'

'Did you feel a funny sort of air to the place?'

'I think most people do considering what happened in those walls, torture, killings and general nasty stuff.'

'Well, that's what it feels like here.'

'Aye,' said Jim. 'Like boggles; it feels bad; as if something has happened here.'

'Or is going to,' said Crone tightening his grip on his club. 'Keep your eyes skinned.'

With great caution they moved towards the centre of the island, yet all the way finding nothing to distinguish it from the others they had already examined. That changed when they came into a clearing where they found ferns growing around tree stumps. Men had been here before, but why had they cleared the space?

'Look at that!' said Jim Wilson. 'That's not natural for sure.'

He was right. The sandy soil and coral had been dug up and piled to one side. The hole thus formed was perfectly square, about ten feet either way, and it was full of water.

'Now why would anyone do something like that?' asked Morgan.

Crone said nothing but moved forward. The water was clear and clean and he could see right down to the bottom; round the edge ferns grew and the water level was a foot below the ground level. Strangely there were horizontal marks around the rim such as one might see in a tidal estuary. He cupped his hands and lifted the water to his mouth to taste it.

'It's fresh!'

'Really?'

Morgan, Wilson and Young were down on their knees drinking also.

Crone stood up and considered the pool, staring at it in a concentration almost profound as the wheels of his brain whirled.

As he turned he caught sight of something half hidden in a clump of ferns and went over to see what it was, and found the half rotted remains of what had been a stout wooden box, its lid lying off to one side. It looked like something that had been buried for a long time then dug up. He bent down to look at it and his mind whirred with possibilities.

'Not a coffin or owt like that is it?' asked Morgan nervously.

Crone laughed a small grim laugh, 'I can see why you might think that in this spot, but no, it's not. It's been in the ground, but it's been dug up.'

'What do you think was in it?'

'Your guess is as good as mine, but if it was what I think then it was stuff that men are prepared to kill and even massacre for.'

'Oh. I see!'

'Well it's a possibility, wouldn't you say?'

Crone stood up, 'Right Thomas; I want you to go with Alex and Sam across the lagoon. Bring the captain back here with the water butts and any containers you can get. Tell him we've found water.'

'Why don't you come, sir? I don't like leaving you here in this place.'

'I appreciate that Tom, but we shall be fine, Jim and I. There's no danger here.'

'But how do you know that? You're only guessing that they came back for treasure and took it.'

'Aye, it's a guess, but if I were a betting man and could find out what did happen here, then I'd put money on my version.

Now be off and don't fret. For now I want to observe this pool. I think it's a bit special.'

With a puzzled look and some reluctance Morgan set off back to the boat to carry out his orders. Crone sat down by the pool, watching it as James Wilson kept careful lookout.

It was nearly two hours before Lattimore arrived with a party of men and water butts.

'Well done John. I cannot tell you what a weight this takes from my mind and so close to the huts too; an assured water supply just across the lagoon. I'm a happy man this afternoon and glad that you insisted on this last island. But why did you not come back and tell us yourself?'

'Because I wanted to watch the pool sir.'

'But why? It's not going anywhere.'

'Oh I know that, but it's a most particular pool.'

'In what sense?'

'The level of the water is rising. You will observe that there are horizontal water marks up the side.'

'What do you think that means?'

'Well I've had time to sit and think about it and I think this pool rises and falls with the tide.'

'You think this is water from the sea?'

'I did wonder that at first; if it was seawater filtering through the sand and leaving the salt behind, but I don't think so now.'

'Then what?'

'I think it is rainwater, but that it collects in this pond and that the sand underneath is soaked with seawater. The fresh water floats on top of the salt water which rises and falls with the tide.'

'Then we must be careful to take only from the top?'

'I don't think so. I think the salt water is beneath the surface of the sand and does not come above it. At any rate, with such a reservoir of fresh water we will never be short of it. But, sir, I think this is a happy accident of an evil thing.'

'What do you mean John?'

'I mean that I think this hole was dug for a purpose and not for water. I may be wrong of course, but it is the work of man I think you'll agree?'

'I have no doubt of it - it is quite regular.'

'You'll remember the story you told the passengers?'

'I do, but I had no idea that you knew the story.'

Crone laughed, 'On board ship, sir, there are few secrets. Since we landed, Mrs Hastings in particular has repeated that story several times. Most of us think there is, or was, treasure buried somewhere on Palmyra.'

'Was?'

'Oh yes. I think it was buried here, but now it's gone. Look at this box.'

'It's hardly conclusive evidence.'

'I agree, but it's as good a theory as any I think. What else would a wooden box being doing here and especially one that has so obviously been in the ground?'

'But if that is the case, who took it? And how did they know it was there?'

'In your story, sir, there was a second raft of pirates who escaped from this island and were never heard of again.'

'You think they made it to civilization and came back?'

'I think they made it sir, but the story dates back over sixty years. If they came back they would be very old indeed. No. I think someone came who knew the secret and where the treasure was buried; they came here and took it. If that is the case then we are in no danger of being attacked.'

'But the massacre was real. Who carried out the killings?'

'I think it likely that someone came back for the treasure and found castaways on the island. They killed them because they wanted no witnesses. There is no treasure on Palmyra sir. There was, but it's gone.'

'And we are in no danger of attack from murderous villains.'

'Exactly sir; we must exercise caution if anyone comes of course, but I think we are safe.'

'You've a good head on your shoulders, John Crone.'

'I hope so sir, or I'll never make captain; but somehow I think I will.'

'I think you will too, John. I have to say though that this place gives me the shivers.'

'Me too. I think the memory of what was done here lingers. It is not a pleasant spot.'

'No. But it gives us water John.'

'All we need until Donald brings help.'

'Let's hope that hour will not be long in coming. In the meantime I will send watering parties of men with less…imagination, if we need water.'

'I'm grateful sir. Thank you.'

Both men's thoughts flew out across the waves and the miles to a small boat bound for Samoa and to those in it, wondering how they fared and what they were doing.

Chapter Nine

Leviathan

Far out across the ocean miles MacDonald peered ahead into the heat and haze of midday and the unending blue of the water. The launch was making good time and he had just taken his noon sightings. He worked out his calculations and announced that by his reckoning they had made seventy-one miles since the previous midday.

'That is pretty good going Donald, if you are correct, and as you are a right good seaman, I take it that it is so.'

'Well, I should hope so Willie. I have been doing it for a number of years now and, if I could not, then my hopes of gaining my Master's ticket would be very slim indeed.'

'So we have made seventy-one miles today. Remind me - how many did we make yesterday?'

'Sixty-eight by my reckoning, but it is not very precise.'

'So how many miles do you think we have covered altogether?'

'In the five days since we left Palmyra I think we have journeyed 348 nautical miles.'

'And the nearest land to us if we should meet with an accident?'

'That would be Palmyra.'

'Suddenly this wee barky seems very small.'

'That's because it is, Willie. We are no more than a cockleshell on the ocean, but keep your spirits up man. It is a well-found cockleshell; a good and seaworthy boat.'

'I looked at the charts. It's my hope that we shall reach Samoa and not go sailing past.'

'Aye well I'll not deny that there is a chance of that. You know it as well as I do. At any rate if we can steer a good course we should get there, no matter the size of our vessel; and there is no land between where we are and Samoa, so it will be plain when we reach our goal.'

''I seem to recall that we thought something like that before the ship was wrecked.'

MacDonald thought for a moment, 'Well now, did we hit anything after leaving Samoa and before we reached Palmyra?'

Ferguson ruminated on this, 'Well... no.'

'Well there you are. We shall not hit anything on the way back to Samoa, because there is nothing to hit. You may be quiet in your mind.'

Ferguson made a wry face, but made no answer save to chuckle to himself.

'On the other hand,' said Charles Anderson, 'We'd better look sharp now; there's a squall heading right at us.'

MacDonald looked up quickly. Anderson was right; a dark line was heading across the sea towards them to starboard with an almost unbelievable rapidity.

'My God! We must turn into it; do it now.'

His voice was almost a scream but it was too late. The squall hit them as the boat began to turn and she broached, a huge amount of water coming into her as her side was swamped.

'Bail for your bloody lives!' yelled Willie Ferguson as men grabbed at anything that would hold water and frantically scooped it over the side. 'Bring her round into the wind for God's sake.'

MacDonald strained at the tiller and thrilled with a sudden horror as he felt a ripping vibration through his hand. The rudder had been taken for granted when preparing the boat, because from the outside it looked like a sound piece of timber. Now it showed that it was indeed sound, but the pintles that held it in place were not, being rusted partway through. They snapped and to his despair MacDonald was left holding the tiller which was suddenly useless and he was powerless to do a thing as the force of the water carried the rudder away and it disappeared into the raging waters never to be seen again.

It was fortunate for them that this squall, like so many of its ilk was of short duration, a sneeze rather than a storm, and within a few minutes it passed over leaving them rudderless but sailing fast with what Willie Ferguson called a 'slashing breeze' full behind them. They could not be without a rudder, but sailors are nothing if not inventive. There were two spare oars in the launch and they contrived to lash one to the tiller handle with ropes and tight knots where it formed a kind of steering oar which was primitive but effective. Thus they were able to maintain a steady course before the wind and make the most of it. Indeed, at noon the next day when MacDonald took a sighting they found that they had covered 132 miles since the previous day's reckoning. As if losing the rudder was not enough, the Fates had another trial in store for them as Tumelty was the first to realize.

'Donald, I think we have a problem here.'

'What is it Ned?'

'This coconut is bad.'

'A bad coconut? Then open another one.'

'That's just it Donald. I have. This is the sixth coconut I have opened and they have all been bad.'

'Now that is a puzzle. It's too many for coincidence. We are nearly at the lunch hour so each man take a coconut and let us try them.'

With worried expressions on their faces each man on the launch took a nut and cracked it open. In each case the inside was turning yellow and green and the oily milk had curdled into a sour liquid smelling vaguely alcoholic. In some of the nuts was only foul green slime.

'Well, this is a bit of a disaster,' said Ferguson.

'A bit!' said Crosby sharply. 'That's most of our food supply. If they're all like that then what the hell are we going to eat over the next two weeks or more?'

'What has happened to them?' asked Charles Anderson.

'I'm not sure,' replied MacDonald. 'Perhaps it has something to do with the sun?'

'Aye that might be it,' mused Willie Ferguson. 'They have been lying there exposed to the sun ever since Palmyra. Perhaps we should have covered them up. The heat has caused the insides to ferment.'

'Ach, we did not think of it because we saw nuts lying on the ground in Palmyra and they were in the shade. How were we to know that the natural covering would not protect the insides from the sun?'

'That may well be, Willie,' replied MacDonald, 'but they do not have their natural covering. We stripped the husks off to take up less space in the boat; the nutshells themselves are obviously no protection.'

'We should not have done it then.'

'We know that now, but being wise after the events does not help us in this predicament. These nuts are most of our food supply as Willie said and we are in a mess, there's no denying it.'

'What can we do about it?'

'One thing I do know is that we do not panic. Willie said that it's a bit of a disaster, but it is considerably more than that; it is very serious for us, but panic will get us nowhere. The first thing to do is to see if any of the nuts can be saved. We must take it nut by nut, so let us place the nuts on the bottom layers under the shelter of the decking. It may be that we can save a few of them.'

'And if we cannot?'

'Then indeed we have a first class problem, but I will have no despondency about it. Each man in this boat was a fisherman and we float upon an ocean. There is food here, if we can catch it.'

MacDonald stopped talking, interrupted by Anderson who had begun to bang his fist up and down on the wooden seat beside him whilst giving out short sharp cries that sounded like rage and distress at the same time. Four of the men in the boat were, like many sailors, very phlegmatic individuals and with the fatalism of their kind it was in their natures to deal with the vicissitudes of life as they came. Anderson's behaviour was perhaps more human as he ceased to bang his fist and his face contorted as he yelled out across the sea in a pronounced Danish accent, 'God Damn! God Damn! God Damn!'

'Aye, well I cannot see that shouting is going to do a lot of good with the situation Charlie, and especially if you take the name of God in vain.'

'Are you made of wood, Willie? That's most of our bloody food. We are going to bloody starve.'

'Well that might be, and it might not be, but I'll tell you one thing; blaspheming and swearing about it is not going to provide any answer to your problem.'

'We should have known. We should have thought about it. Of course all fruit goes rotten in the sun.'

'Hindsight is a wonderful thing Charlie. If only we'd known so many things in our lives, what better men we would all be for it. Well the fact is that we did not know; we do now, but a fat lot of good it will do us. What's done is done; now for the sake of my ears will you stop making that din?'

'But what are we going to do about this?'

'What we can, and we can start by staying calm and talking about it.'

Anderson subsided, his outburst crushed by the obvious disapproval of his undemonstrative shipmates, but his unhappiness continued, registered in his sullen face and occasional discontented muttering to himself.

They passed coconuts along and stowed them under the covered part of the deck, which was about seven feet long from the bows. Finally they had about seventy nuts under there and Ned Tumelty declared that the work had given him an appetite. He took one of the remaining nuts and cracked it open. Like the rest it was yellow-brown or green inside and the milk was sour with an alcoholic smell, symptomatic of fermentation. He poured it away and washed the kernel in the sea. Then he smashed it into pieces and began to chew. As he did so, his face took on a disgusted expression but with great determination he chewed on and swallowed a mouthful; then he took another bite. After he had eaten about two thirds of the nut he gagged and looked at his crew mates.

'I cannot eat any more of this, but I shall eat the rest later. This is food and it will keep us alive. There is nothing that I know of that says food must taste good; if it nourishes then I give thanks for it.'

'I am not so sure of that,' said MacDonald. 'It would be like eating the fermenting mash in a distillery. I am fairly sure that if we eat it we will get bad guts. If that happens then the bad effects of eating that rotten stuff will outweigh any good we get from it.'

The taste of the coconuts was truly disgusting, but Anderson and Crosby both decided to share in Tumelty's bravado. They shut off their disgust reflexes as best they could and chewed rancid coconut. The results were predictable. Within a few hours the three coconut eaters had swollen bellies and were in considerable discomfort; their guts gurgled and they had a constant feeling of nausea. MacDonald and Ferguson had contented themselves with a tot of water and a nibble on some hard tack so were unaffected, but three of the crew were effectively out of action for the time being. All they could do was lie groaning in pain on the floor of the boat, complaining of burning feelings and that their bellies were swelled until they could not expand any further. The reactions really began when they began to vomit often and copiously over the side of the boat. Eventually they stopped being sick only because they were exhausted and had nothing left to be sick with, and lay moaning in the bottom of the launch. As far as sailing her was concerned they were completely out of action and useless. Soon after that there was an explosion of chronic flatulence and then the diarrhea began.

For men, the act of urination in an open boat at sea has never been a problem, merely a simple question of point and let fly into the waves. Defecation is a different matter, for it has to be done over the side of the boat, an awkward manoeuvre at the best of times, and the person doing it has to hold on securely. When that night came, it was one that MacDonald and indeed all of the men involved, would never forget. Crosby it was who had been due to take the tiller for the first part of the night, but he was clearly quite incapacitated so MacDonald himself took first watch. Ferguson had to tend to the sick. The First Officer sat hunched, looking at the compass by the dim yellow light of the oil lamp that he lit each night from one of his jealously guarded matches kept in his tobacco pouch and now inside his shirt. He did smoke from his dwindling supply of tobacco, but lit his pipe from the chimney of the lamp, allowing himself one pipe each night. He looked forward to it and he thought it helped to keep hunger at bay. Selfishness was not a vice from which he suffered and although he smoked most of the tobacco, he did pass it round for his companions to puff as well, which they appreciated, since they were all smokers. Tonight though he had his pipe to himself for Ferguson was kept busy holding on to weakened men with no dignity left who had to continually perch on the side of the boat to rid their protesting and painful bellies of the poisonous rot passing through them. The one saving grace of the whole thing was that it was not cold, being the tropics. It also helped that there were no women around so the sufferers abandoned their trousers as the frequency of their visits to the gunwale was quite high. Before he would let them fully back into the boat Ferguson insisted that a bailing pan full of seawater be sloshed down their backsides to clean them off as, 'I'm not sharing a boat with that!'

The compass needle pointed resolutely to the north as MacDonald kept the launch firmly on the bearing it was set to; he had estimated 1,300 nautical miles to Samoa, but it was a very small target. He was quite confident that his noon calculations were sufficient to set his course for Apia, so although it was a clear moonlit night, he did not bother trying to find the horizon with the sextant. He knew the stars well enough and could see Polaris, which was a friendly and familiar sight, but he did not need it. This was just as well, because it would no longer be visible by the time they approached Samoa, which was on the other side of the Equator. Apart from the fact that three of his crew were sick, and the coconuts might all be spoiled, the voyage had gone remarkably well thus far, and until now his spirits had been high. The food situation worried him, because there was a long way to go. The use of the nuts would have to be decided in the morning. Shortly after midnight the frantic dives for the gunwale had more or less subsided and MacDonald called over to the Bosun.

'Willie, get one of the bottles of whisky and give each of them a good measure and mind, make it a very good one.'

Ferguson did not argue for he knew the reason. Whisky has many good properties, but as is well known, it has a very calming effect on the stomach; it would relax his patients, help clean them out and best of all, a large enough dose would give them hours of restful sleep. There is also no need to persuade a sick sailor to drink, and they did so willingly. It was not too long before the invalids were stretched out and snoring.

'Now have a dram yourself, Willie, and give me one as well, because it will do us both a power of good. I'm minded to have a sleep and you too. We have been awake for far too long and we both need to rest if we are the only two able to work this boat.'

'All of us to sleep? How will we stay on course?'

'I'll lash the tiller so that it cannot move. The wind is gentle enough and we are making a good speed and the water is calm. There is little enough to do and no reason to get over tired since there is no land to bump into. Providence has been very good to us up until now.'

'Aye, up until now, but I cannot think that this situation is entirely good, Donald.'

'No. It is not. But however much we complain about it all our lamenting will not alter what has happened; bide it we must and will.'

Ferguson settled down in the bottom of the boat and MacDonald sat for a while longer finishing off his pipe and watching the trail of phosphorescence in the boat's wake. He had seen it many times before on numerous voyages, but had never been so close to it. Someone had told him that the phenomenon was caused by minute sea creatures, like so many fireflies, that could be observed in a microscope. He had never seen that, but he was mildly interested enough to put his hand over and cup some water up in it; drips of shining light fell from his fingers, but when he drew it up into the dim light of the lamp he could see nothing in his hand but clear water. Nodding, though not quite sure at what, he turned to the tiller and tied it firmly into position before curling up beside it. In the warmth of the tropical night, under millions of stars glittering above him, and lulled by the steady glide of the boat across a calm sea, he soon fell asleep.

It was some hours before he woke but it was still dark. For a few minutes he wondered why he had woken up, for nothing appeared to have changed; the boat still made steady pace across a smooth sea, the stars had moved round, the lamp still glowed on its hook, but something had roused him. Then he realized that he was not alone in being awake; everyone was.

'What was that?' asked Charlie Anderson in a low whisper as if not wishing to be overheard.

'I have heard nothing,' said MacDonald. 'What have you heard?'

'It was a sort of moaning noise, but very long and loud.'

'I see,' said MacDonald. 'Tell me now, you are some years younger than me; have all your voyages been on steamships up until the time you joined the *Henry James*?'

'Well yes, but how did you know that?'

'I have heard such a sound many times before, but it is I think because I have not served on a steam ship. The noise of the engines probably scares them away or masks the sound.'

'Scares who away?' asked Anderson, not without a certain trepidation.

'You mean what, Charlie. I suspect that you are hearing whales singing. I am surprised you have not heard whale song in the northern seas, but perhaps you have not been so fortunate.'

'You mean that noise was whales?'

'I do not know since I was asleep, but from your description, yes it was. Certainly something woke me up.'

Just then a fresh outbreak of moaning noises came from somewhere; the sound seemed to be all around them and no-one could tell where it came from.

'It sounds like lost souls or the ghosts of the dead moaning in the deep,' muttered William Crosby with a look of concern all across his face.

'Well I am sure that there are many who might think that; indeed I have heard it said before, but such pronunciations are the product of an over active imagination. Those are whales singing to each other and they are not too far away.'

MacDonald's reply indicated a man who had seen something of the world, who was inclined to be skeptical of such superstition and had no patience with it in these circumstances; anything that generated fear was not welcome.

Anderson's curiosity was now roused, 'Why can we not tell the direction of them?'

'I think the noises they make are underwater; we hear them when the noise comes to the surface muffled by the depths; and it also comes up through the timbers of the boat.'

'If we hear them, can they hear us?'

'Now there is a good question, but I do not know the answer.'

Ferguson said slowly, 'Perhaps if we do not wish to attract their attention we should not make too much noise?'

'That's a good point,' said MacDonald. 'We have a very small craft and do not wish to be bumping into a whale. Let us speak in whispers for now, until we know that we are clear of them. The great question in my mind at the moment is not to do with whales, but whether you men are fit for duty. How are you all feeling? You had quite a night of it.'

'Please do not remind us,' said Ned Tumelty. 'I wish I had not eaten the foul stuff and I am sorry for the trouble it has caused. Thank you, Willie, for all that you did for me last night.'

'I've seen you in more dignified situations, Ned. You have paid for what you did I think, but I would not advise eating any more of those nuts.'

William Crosby now interjected, 'It's clear that we must not eat the nuts, but what are we going to eat?'

'For the moment,' replied MacDonald, 'I think you should not eat a thing. Your guts must still be churning.'

The three sick men all agreed that they were; not only that, but they felt weak and ill. MacDonald went on, 'Now Willie and I have no problem with our bellies and are both hungry. If you do not mind we are going to crack open some of these nuts to see if we can find any that are fit to eat.'

So saying, he moved forward and pulled a coconut from under the planked over deck and cracked it against the base of the mast. When he pulled it open, the inside was foul; he threw it overboard. The next one was the same, and the next. Willie Ferguson looked at MacDonald and pursed his lips.

'That's not good Donald.'

'No, it is not.'

'What are we going to eat?'

'We must catch some fish. There's enough fishermen in this boat!'

'Aye, that's true enough. And the nuts?'

'Crack them Willie; every one of them. If there's any good then we can eat it, but if there is none then they go over the side. Apart from anything else they weigh quite a bit and throwing them over will help our speed.'

Methodically the men cracked every coconut on the boat and each was found to be rotten; over the side they went. When the last bits of rancid coconut were bobbing in the wake of the launch William Crosby asked the inevitable question.

'So what food do we have left?'

'Five pounds of hard tack, four one pound tins of mutton. Half a pound of cheese and one and a half bottles of whisky.'

'It's not enough to carry us another 1,000 miles, Donald.'

'No it is not, but for the life of me I cannot see any alternative; can you?'

'Well, it's less than four hundred miles back to Palmyra.'

'Against the wind, tacking all the time? Or perhaps rowing? The food would run out long before we got there. We have a better chance sailing as fast as we can before the wind and trying for Samoa.'

'What about water?'

'Water will not be a problem I think. The barrel is full. Our rain harvesting has worked well.'

In the tropics it rains a lot. MacDonald had rigged up a small triangle of sailcloth to channel water down into the top of the barrel when the showers came.

'You say that it is not enough, but I mind that Captain Bligh had less than we have on his great journey.'

'Oh aye; how are we better off than him?'

'The ration on board his boat was one ounce of bread per man and one quarter pint of water a day. If we served each man with an ounce a day we have enough for fourteen more days at sea. As to water, if rains come, we have more. But we also have meat and cheese.'

'That's a very positive view of things. An ounce a day you say. We shall be rather peckish I'm thinking.'

'That is an understatement, but I propose to have my ounce now and I advise you to do the same. As to William, Ned and Charlie, you may do as you wish, but until your bellies settle you'd probably best stick with water and some whisky.'

'Will we still get the bread we miss?'

'Aye Charlie; you will. You will need the strength it gives you, so if you eat tomorrow you shall have two ounces. At any rate I'm thinking that tomorrow we shall have a feast.'

'A feast you say! How will you manage that?'

'Once a tin of meat is opened then it must be eaten completely or it will rot. I propose that we open a tin of meat every three days and that should give us just under three ounces a man each time. Bligh did not have that.'

'We have the cheese too!'

'Yes William, but that is weeping and I think will go rancid before too long. It should be eaten no later than tomorrow.

Now then, your griping guts will not prevent you dangling hooks and lines over the side, so two of you can get on with fishing.'

'But what will we use for bait Donald.'

'A very good question; try some of those shreds of coconut on the deck there. All we need is one fish and after that we can use pieces of that.'

With optimistic hooks dangling shreds of rotten coconut over the side, the launch swept on, pushed by a moderate breeze steady on a course SSW towards Samoa. The sun came up onto another scene of endless blue water and yet another brazen hot day.

They had not gone more than a mile with the fishing lines out before the water about twenty feet off their port bow was disturbed by a spout erupting out of the sea with a great hollow hiss of air and a huge shape surmounted by a fluke arched up above the surface. The consternation in the boat was considerable.

'That is a big whale!'

'One smack from that tail would sink this boat and kill us all.'

MacDonald contented himself with saying, 'Take in sail. I do not want to bump into it.'

The sail was lowered and the boat slowed down until it came to a stop.

'It's coming nearer!'

'O, God help us all.'

'Do not fear it; it is only wanting to have a look at us.'

'Do you think so, Willie?'

'I do. I have heard of such things before and I do not think it will attack us, and especially if we do not attack it.'

The whale showed no sign of hostile intent and came right alongside the launch until they could have stepped out onto the great blue hump of its back. Charlie Anderson stared at it with undisguised awe and not a small amount of fear.

'Just look at the size of it! I knew they were big, but I have never seen one as close as this before.'

'Aye; it's a great fish, such as that which swallowed Jonah.'

'Do you think that story is true?'

'I do Charlie. It's in the Bible and that is good enough for me.'

'I did not know you were so religious, Donald.'

'That's because I'm not; I have never been a great one for attendance at kirk. I am a Christian though, and I believe in the Bible.'

'Are you not afraid?'

'No, because I think Willie is right; he just wants to look at us: there! See?'

As Anderson watched in disbelief a huge eye came level with him and looked right at him and he at it. For a moment he held its gaze then hesitatingly reached far out over the gunwale and put his hand on the enormous head as the men behind him gasped and stayed still, watching and saying nothing. For long seconds Anderson kept his hand touching the whale, until it slipped down below the surface and vanished for a few minutes. The men in the boat sat wondering what to do next when after about four minutes had passed the whale surfaced again some distance away and began to swim north. As the gap between them increased MacDonald instructed that the sail be hoisted again and soon the launch was heading back on course for Samoa in a wind which was increasing.

Anderson sat for a long while and there was silence in the boat. He kept on looking at his hand, still feeling the touch of the whale and occasionally he shook his head. It was Ferguson who broke the silence:

"Canst thou draw out Leviathan with a fishhook?

Or press down his tongue with a cord?
Canst thou put a rope into his nose
Or pierce his jaw through with a hook?"

Anderson looked at him and asked softly, 'What is that from?'

'The book of Job, Charlie; you have laid your hand on Leviathan and "he is king over the sons of pride".'

'Is it blasphemous to think that I feel like I touched God?'

'Not so I think, for it is one of his greatest works of creation. You have done what few men have done and I think you have had a blessing. I felt it enough to just witness it, but you touched him.'

'That's all well,' growled MacDonald, 'but I do not expect you to catch anything as big as that. Get those lines out again and get me some fish. The wind is freshening and I think we are in for a blow. There will be no fishing if that happens, but it will set us well on our way to Samoa.'

On a breeze that stiffened quickly to a brisk wind, the launch forged ahead, ever south south west, heading for Apia and civilization.

Chapter 10

Utopia

'William, I am worried about Dottie.'

To the Reverend Taylor this pronouncement by his wife was something to be taken seriously, as Isabelle was not a woman who worried readily. It was a luxury she could not afford in her position as a missionary's wife. The first part of her married life had been spent in what many westerners would have regarded as outlandish parts of the world and she had been expected to deal with all kinds of problems associated with having a popular and proselytizing preacher for a husband. Taylor sometimes admitted to himself that he had not left it entirely to his sense of romance when he had begun courting her. He knew that in his life's work he would need a woman who was practical and strong; there had been a few ladies who had pulled at his heart strings, but he had married the sturdy daughter of a fellow preacher, handsome rather than beautiful, and he had never regretted his choice. Love had grown in this match, as it does in many, and although it had never been volcanic in its passion, it burned with a steady and sure flame. Isabelle was his friend and partner, and often his foil, for she did not allow him to rule her, so if she worried it was a sign to him that she meant it.

'What are you worried about? The new baby?'

This euphemism served well enough; Dorothea Hastings was, he knew, twelve weeks pregnant and her situation on this island was not ideal.

'In a word, William, yes. This is no place for a woman in her condition.'

'I will agree, and would go further; this is no place for anyone without better food, but as to her condition, she has had four other children without any difficulty whatsoever. Why are you worried that this one will be any different?'

'You mention the food; that is one reason, but she is displaying signs now that to me indicate that she should not go foraging.'

'The problem with that, Isa, is that if she does not gather food, someone else will have to get food for her.'

'Well I know that, and I agree that in this predicament it is best that everyone hunts for what they eat for a communal pot. That does not seem too much to ask. Ordinarily we do not gather our own food save in the sense that we go down to the store and buy it or send the maid. I do think that if she continues to go out foraging, then she will get tired and the bending and exertion may eventually bring on a miscarriage.'

'You think the food to be a problem too? Because it is monotonous?'

'No. Because it is what it is. There is no bread or corn or starchy food of any kind. We are all losing weight William and we have all had bouts of dysentery; if you had a mirror I think you would soon see that you are not the man you were a few short weeks ago.'

'I could observe that there is not any great objection to that, my dear. I have become a rather portly gentleman in recent years and losing some embonpoint at my age is surely no bad thing.'

'That may be, but it is involuntary and if it were for a short time would do you no harm, but we are getting thin; Dottie does not need that. She is eating for two now and needs to keep up her strength and her weight to help the baby grow.'

'You say there are signs that she is being affected. What are they?'

'She is getting very bad headaches.'

'But that is normal is it not? I recall that you had headaches.'

'These are bad ones, William. As you said, she has had children before, but these are the worst headaches she has experienced.'

'I am sorry to hear it, but that is not all, I think?'

'No. If you want the rest of it, she is exhausted to the point of distress much of the time, but attempts to hide it. She feels dizzy or light headed a lot; she should drink more than she does. There are a few other things that it would be indelicate to discuss but believe me, they are not as I would wish.'

'Well as to the last item, we have a ready supply of water now. She should drink what she needs to.'

'I think she has in mind that the water is collected by people taking pains; either to catch the rain or to row across the lagoon.'

'Ah, she's your daughter; that instinct not to put other people to inconvenience or to put them out is pure Isabelle.'

'Oh, so I'm to blame?'

Taylor laughed loudly, 'No, but you have to allow that self abnegation is a trait not unknown to you; I should expect it in a child of yours, and of mine.'

'That's true enough, I suppose,' replied his wife, 'But William, what can we do to help her?'

'I cannot think that there is a great deal that may be done in our current situation.'

'Why whatever do you mean? Of course there is something that may be done.'

'Very well Isabelle, tell me what more may be done.'

'For one thing, a woman in her condition should not have to be wandering around in the heat of the day gathering food.'

'You are suggesting that she be excused foraging?'

'I am suggesting just that.'

'But if she does not gather food then someone else will have to gather it for her. I cannot ask the men to take on an extra burden like that.'

'True enough William; I guess that would be us taking it on. We shall simply have to gather a bit more.'

'Quite an undertaking I think. It's hard enough scraping enough sustenance round here without feeding someone unable to forage. We shall need help.'

'Well quite; we shall need the cooperation of the other people here.'

'I shall speak to Captain Lattimore and see what can be done; it may well be that some amelioration of her circumstances may be effected; we can only ask.'

His wife knew that Taylor would find it difficult to ask anyone for help; it was not in his nature to do so, preferring to give help than to receive it, but she was appreciative of his recognition that it had to be done.

'Thank you, William; I think that would be the right thing to do.'

Isabelle Taylor knew that her husband would not linger in his intention to seek an interview with Lattimore, so went happily back to where Dorothea was lying in her hut. The Taylors had not even considered the fact that neither of them had a weak voice. The Reverend had a bass baritone rumble and a habit of projecting to a congregation; Isabelle, in over thirty years of marriage had developed a high voice with an edge that could cut through her husband's verbiage and make him listen. Outside their hut, lying in the shade and taking his ease from the midday sun, was Hugh Shearer, a native of Thurso in Caithness, and he had, quite involuntarily, heard every word that the Taylors had spoken. Now he waited until they left, got up with a very thoughtful look on his face and made his way across the clearing in front of the huts to join his fellows under a tree where he commenced a low voiced and very animated conversation, unobserved by Lattimore, which involved quite a lot of consternation. The words 'bairn' and 'eating for two,' were heard more than once and the main thrust of the majority argument was that it was an unmanly thing not to help a woman with an unborn and innocent wean. It appeared that there was some dissension in their talk, but that it was limited to one man who kept on repeating that 'It's not fair; it should be shared out equally.' A closer inspection would have revealed that the speaker was William Lancaster and that his opinion was not shared by the men round him. Thomas McClements and Charles Dordey were getting quite red in the face as the argument grew heated. Morgan in particular was quite vehement,

'Look you, I've no time for stowaways mister, but you take the biscuit. When I left Maryport my wife was about to give birth with our first and if she were in this situation and some louse had tried to deny her what she needed to keep our bairn healthy and safe, I'd knock his head off his bloody shoulders.'

His face was scarlet with anger, and Patrick Burns asked him gently, 'What's her name Tom? You've not been married long have you?'

'We married January last year and I had to leave when the ship sailed. The nipper was due a week later. Mary Agnes is my wife's name.'

'A sailor man's life is not always convenient for family,' said Burns shaking his head and glad that the anger was going from Morgan's face, deflected by thoughts of home. He thought too soon.

'You married in January and left England in August; and you say your wife was due to give birth? Tasted the goods before you bought did you?'

Lancaster might have been trying to make a joke, but his manner did not suggest it and Morgan looked as if he was about to explode, but he was beaten to it. McClements, who had been kneeling, suddenly leaned forward and slapped Lancaster hard on his face, declaring vehemently, 'You're no a man; ye're a selfish canting ferlie and gin ye carry on you're gonna get dunted hard.' Then he spat full in the stowaway's face. Lancaster, not the bravest of men, though certainly an opinioned one, turned red, gulped, then got up and walked away to avoid further trouble accompanied by jeers from the men he left.

'Ye're a bloody coward too; a man wi nae baws,' McClements called after him. 'Stay out of my way ye hackit Jessie.'

Ralph Lattimore listened to what Reverend Taylor had to say. He had no experience of wives or daughters being pregnant and thus far in his life, outside of his own mother, had few dealings with women. He did know that ladies who were expecting children required a basic minimum in their food and that the amount of effort they could make was restricted, so he looked Taylor straight and level in the eye and gave him a response as soon as he had finished speaking.

'The answer is a simple one, sir. The lady must not do any more foraging and must take all the ease she needs. She must eat and drink all she needs too. I think it will not throw any great strain on our resources. Our problem is not the amount of food that we may obtain, but the type. She must eat more than anyone else and for obvious reasons.'

'You do not think the men will object to having someone eat who does not gather or contribute in any way?'

'They are men, sir, and should have a natural regard to ladies in her situation. At any rate I am not inclined to make it a matter for discussion, because this is not a democracy. I command here and if I say that it will be done, then it will be so. I shall tell the company tonight that Mrs Hastings is excused foraging.'

Having gained the concession he most wished for, Taylor decided to chance his luck and go further.

'I know that there is some tinned mutton left and some hard tack, Captain.'

'I see what is in your mind Reverend. The lady and her child need extra nourishment. I shall give some thought to the matter. I have been letting the cook thicken the burgoo with a modicum of powdered hard tack but the meat may be a bone of contention.'

'I understand. If it comes to survival then men can become selfish.'

'Indeed, sir. I would not wish to provoke any outbreak of difference among the crew.'

'No more would I. You know Captain, it may be necessity that drives it, but as a minister I observe that if it were not for the question of food, we almost inhabit a Utopia.'

'How do you mean, sir?'

'I mean that since we landed on this island we have worked together in mutual cooperation for the good of all. The rank hardly matters in the gathering of food and no-one has any advantages conferred by station in life or fortune. In the face of a common adversity we work together in harmony. It is a Utopia.'

Lattimore thought for a moment or two before replying.

'No sir, I do not think it is. We are surviving here because we are working together and there is order to things. If we ever stop working together then I think our situation would be far worse.'

'Why would we stop working together?'

'Humans are selfish things, Reverend. They do not always do what is good for them.'

'That is true enough; I have seen it often in my ministry.'

'The problem here is that we have agreed to cooperate. With my crew that should be beyond question, because I command their cooperation; they obey my will.'

'Does that not mean that you are some sort of dictator or tyrant?'

'I'm not one for going into such fine detail, Reverend. As far as I am concerned they will do as they are told and it is necessary that they do. And for that I need to command. I'm not out to set up any ideal society or system here; I am trying to make sure we all survive. So to my mind it's not Utopia; it's a dangerous and very precarious situation we find ourselves in and we are doing what we can in the best way we can. Will that do?'

'I guess it will have to Captain. You're the boss; at least over your men.'

Lattimore knew the word, though it was not in common use in British ships. He smiled.

'Yes. I'm the boss.'

Lattimore's background had made him a suspicious man, but as he had grown older, he had become more self-aware and he knew himself to be such. He was a Protestant from the Belfast hinterland and although he himself was not a particularly observant man religiously, he had been brought up in a very strong atmosphere where on one side were 'Us' and on the other side were 'Them'. The out and out sectarianism of the working class streets was something he did not share and the riots of 1886 which had killed dozens of people, both Protestant and Catholic, in Belfast had inspired a certain disgust in him rather than anything else. He had travelled the world before the mast, then as a Second mate, then as Master, and his crews had been made up of men from many races and religions. Not a few of them had been Catholics, as were several of the castaways with him presently, but he had grown tolerant with maturity. So long as a man did his job fairly and squarely and did right by him, then Lattimore did the same in return and had no time for bigotry. That said, with such an upbringing, he could not shake his view that the world was a place of good and evil with no shades in between; and he feared evil, so guarded his mind against it. In the back of his mind this applied to his crew because in this situation they were 'other' and held in check because he had been set in command over them. But they were men with minds and muscles and they had the potential to rebel. This was the evil that he feared, though to any balanced consideration he had no reason to. Nuances are things that often come to human beings as they get older; they might eventually tinge Lattimore's fears with shades of grey, but until he learned to trust men he did not know, his world was not a particularly fluid one.

Now that he had decided to issue a command that Dorothea Taylor would be excused work and would eat food gathered by others, he could not avoid thinking how the news would be received. He now trusted the Maryport men; John Crone was obviously their leader and they would obey. The Taylors and Mr and Mrs Hastings could be relied on, and the boy Alex too. His mind ran through the other men; John Campbell the sail maker and John MacDonald the carpenter had both sailed with him before and were solid men. There would be no trouble from that quarter. Patrick Burns was an older seaman who appeared steady and reliable, but what of the rest? Samuel Donnell, Thomas McClements, Hugh Shearer, Charles Dordey, William Lancaster the stowaway, Mr Carter and Mr James the steerage passengers made the rest of the tally apart from the four little girls. That was seven men whom he did not know. Then again, most of them had not known each other previously. Lattimore's mind relaxed at the thought that even if there were a troublemaker among the unknowns, he would not command enough support to do anything stupid. Still he wished that he knew them better, trust had the power to make a man sleep well at night. Lancaster in particular troubled him, because there was an air to him that spelled a dislike of authority. Of course, it might be that he was misjudging the man; he had done nothing to merit distrust, but Lattimore could not shake a feeling of unease about him.

Four girls ran past him chasing each other and heading into the jungle. No-one made any attempt to stop them because it had become obvious over the past few weeks that Palmyra was, apart from food, rather a paradise for children. There were no snakes, no mosquitoes and no dangerous animals; it had even been discovered that in the clear waters of the shallows near the beach it was safe to splash and bathe because no sharks came in close. If you wished to encounter them you had to take the boat further out. Estella, Nancy, Laura and Ada, were in their element. There were no lianas on Palmyra and no rope with which to make a swing but there were plenty of trees, some almost recumbent, to run up. Ada had read *What Katy Did,* and made the heroine her role model in that she scrupulously did as she was told by her elders. The original Katy had to spend four years in bed by going on a swing that she had been told not to; the penalties of disobedience were quite clear and Ada had no intention of ending up like that. Like Katy, she wanted to do something with her life such as painting or rescuing people. She was quite an accomplished artist for her age as the rocks along the beach could testify where she made her sisters sit for her to draw their portraits on flat surfaces with pieces of charcoal. That the next rain washed them off did not bother her as it gave her fresh surfaces to draw on when she next felt like it. A large amount of diversion could be found from skimming stones across the smooth water of the lagoon, and more from drawing with sticks in the wet sand by the edge of the sea, but their favourite pastime was undoubtedly telling stories, though make-believe tea parties with shells for plates and coconut shells for cups were also popular. They did collect food too, though it has to be said that their main contribution was coconuts. This was a welcome thing, because if the girls collected coconuts it left their elders free to go after other things such as fish or crabs. The girls might have an aversion to killing for their dinner, but no aversion to eating it. The sloppy burgoo that remained their staple was now more of an accompaniment to the main dish of the day that was fish. Using a variety of techniques the castaways contrived to catch more fish from the lagoon by using the pinnace to go out into the deeper water. Thomas Morgan and James Wilson would gut them and spit them to cook by the fire and they provided a delicious variant to the contents of the cauldron, which were not always appetizing.

It was at the evening meal that Lattimore announced that Mrs Hastings would not be expected to collect for the pot any more and would have to rest a lot because she was expecting her fifth child. Of course the announcement was taken without demur, but he was surprised when Patrick Burns spoke up as he did. Burns, as an elder top-man and respected among the crew was evidently feeling a sense of some responsibility when he asked permission to bring up a matter that had been troubling the men.

'If it please you, sir, some of us had noticed that Mrs Hastings had been showing this last week or so and it's right that she should not be foraging in her condition, but there's something else that ain't right, Captain.'

'What is that Burns?'

'It's the meat, sir. A lady who is expecting a child sir, she needs nourishing and this burgoo is not enough. We've been talking about it, sir, and we think that she should have the meat and what's left of the hard tack. And if she can't eat it all, then we think the rest should go to the children. They're growing, sir, and they need it more than we do.'

Lattimore was taken aback by Burn's statement; it was what he had been thinking, but had not quite seen how to broach it to the crew.

'Is this what you all think? The remaining two tins should go to Mrs Hastings and the children.'

Burns hesitated before he replied and his eyes flicked back to where his crewmates were sitting. Apart from them by a good few yards, sat William Lancaster who was glowering, but not far from him sat Thomas McClements, breathing hard with a look as hard as nails.

'Aye sir; we are in agreement, but Mrs Hastings first. Some of us are married, and we have children. It's what we'd want if it was our wives or bairns. Women and children first is the rule isn't it, sir?'

'That's right, sir,' asserted Hugh Shearer. 'Weans must come first, Captain. The innocent unborn should be the care of us all.'

'That is so isn't it, Captain?' asked Burns again.

A murmur of agreement welled up all from the men on the other side of the fire, save one, but Lattimore failed to notice that exception.

Lattimore's emotions rose up and removed the gap between Burns and himself; these were good men and all his thoughts of mutiny or dissent were nothing but his own fevered imagination.

'Yes, Mr Burns. That is the rule. I thank you for reminding me of it and it shall be done as you and the crew wish it. Are you all of the same mind?'

There was a slight hesitation before Burns answered, but it was so quick that Lattimore did not see it.

'Aye sir; thank you, sir.' Burns was evidently quite struck by the 'Mr' afforded to him and sat down back among his fellows and soon general conversation returned to normal.

The Reverend Taylor could not resist a return to the previous conversation.

'Utopia Captain?'

Lattimore grimaced; he was pleasantly surprised at the crew's suggestion, but was not about to concede Taylor's idea that anything about their current predicament was Utopian in the least.

'No sir; I think not. Being men they have acted with a natural concern, which I am gratified at because it is right and proper, but if I had ordered it then they would have obeyed, and that is also right and proper. I command here.'

Taylor looked at him for a moment, and paused on the point of telling Lattimore that he did not command the passengers again, but decided against it and changed the subject.

'For now, however, we have far more practical matters to attend to. One of your men has the most appalling toothache.'

'Really? Who is that?'

'Charles Dordey.'

'Well why has he said nothing?'

Taylor laughed, 'It's fairly obvious Captain. He's very young and he's scared out of his wits of having it pulled.'

'If he's got a bad tooth then pulled it must be. Dordey!'

'Aye sir.'

'Come over here. Now show me your mouth.'

'It's nothing, sir.'

'If it's nothing, then you won't mind me seeing it will you? This is an order Dordey; show me your mouth.'

Reluctantly and with a background of his crewmates smiling at his expression, Dordey opened his mouth.

'I can't see Dordey. Bend your face towards the fire so there's light.'

When the seaman bent towards the flames Lattimore peered in and could see that one of his lower left molars was virtually black and that the whole area around it was swollen.

'How long has it been like this?'

'Weeks sir,' called out Thomas McClements.

'You mean it was bad even back on the ship?'

'Aye sir, but it flares up now and then. This is the worst turn he's had, sir.'

'Well there's no question of it, Dordey; that tooth must come out. You should have spoken before.'

'Please sir, no sir. I'll be fine, sir.'

'Not with that in your mouth it won't. It has to go and somehow it has to go in the morning. There's not enough light to do it now. Can you sleep with that?'

'Yes sir.'

'Spoken like a true son of Ulster!' said Lattimore patting him on the shoulder.

'He's fibbing sir,' called out McClements. 'He moans half the night with the pain of it.'

'I see. Get what rest you can Dordey, but we shall have to see to that, make no mistake.'

When Dordey had returned to his place, Lattimore spoke to John Crone and Reverend Taylor.

'Upon my word gentleman, I say that tooth has to come out, but I have no idea how to do it. On board ship I was expected to be my own surgeon in such cases and I had a pair of dental pincers for the purpose, but here I have nothing. I'd be glad of your ideas.'

'I beg your pardon, Captain, but I think I may be able to help,' came a voice, and Patrick Burns moved to sit down beside Lattimore.

'Have you pulled teeth before?'

'I have Captain.'

'You seem to have accomplished quite a lot in your life, Burns. How do you come to have such knowledge?'

'I've been knocking about the seven seas for a number of years now, sir, and one of the people I travelled with for some of the time on one of my ships was a kind of medicine man. Before he returned to seafaring he sold his patent draughts and oils in sailing taverns, but among the services he provided, was pulling teeth. I assisted him a few times on our ship, and on occasion, when he had imbibed too much of his own confections I did the pulling.'

'I have to say Mr Burns you're a handy fellow to have around.'

'Why thank you Mr Hastings sir. I appreciate the compliment.'

'The problem is that we have nothing to pull the tooth with.'

'Now there, Captain, you are wrong.'

'Oh; what do you propose to use?'

'You'll recall, sir, that there were a few old tools that we found in the hut when we arrived.'

'I do, but I saw no pliers.'

'Nonetheless, sir, there was a pair.'

'Why do I not know about them?'

'Well there's not been much use for a pair of pliers. They were found after we moved in and there has been no use for them in what we do; they are small and very rusty.'

'I think they must be cleaned and boiled before you use them,' said Reverend Taylor. 'I am a firm believer in the teachings of Dr Pasteur and you must be quite certain that any germs are completely destroyed.'

'I will sir; you may depend on it,' replied Burns.

In the morning the stage was set for what appeared to be a drama, because all of Dordey's mates wanted to see his treatment, though his apprehension was plain to see. As the time came for the operation he was shaking visibly, but there was no choice but to do it, and he had screwed up his courage to face the inevitable. Lattimore produced the final half bottle of whisky and poured a quarter of a pint into a coconut shell, which Dordey downed at one go. They then left him for a while until the alcohol had its effect. The patient was made to lie down with his head on a log whilst two men held down his legs. Another two held his arms.

'Now Dordey,' said Lattimore, 'I'm going to give you another tot. When you've swallowed it I want you to be a man and open your mouth open as wide as you can, understand? There will be a lot of noise, but whatever you do keep your head straight and your mouth open.'

Dordey nodded, gulped the whisky down and gaped wide. Burns nodded to Thomas Morgan behind the sufferer's head, and he immediately began to bang an old tin can right beside the patient's ear whilst shouting loudly into it. Burns bent over Dordey's chest, braced himself with one hand against it, and quickly he reached into the sailor's mouth with the pliers. He gripped, wiggled the tooth back and forward and pulled with a twist. Dordey screamed blue murder, but kept his mouth open all the time; it was all over in seconds and very slick. As the patient was released Burns stood up and displayed the rotten molar to the assembled audience who gave him a round of applause to which he replied,

'I thank you, I thank you. I'm here all week and my fees are light.'

Dordey was led away to lie down and recover from the trauma he had just gone through and to doze off the effects of the whisky. He did not say anything, his mouth being firmly clamped down on a wad of cotton torn from the tail of his shirt to staunch the blood. He was excused duties for the day, but was being pounded on the back, grinning as his mates told him that he had acted in true sailor fashion. In some odd way the pulling of the tooth once again pulled the group together. It was the nearest thing that they had approached to any kind of medical emergency on the island and together they had found the skills and the means to surmount it. Unconscious though it might be, the experience of watching the extraction, of participating in it and solving the problem helped foster the feeling of community and mutual assistance.

It was Reverend Taylor who asked the obvious question to the amateur dentist.

'Why the noise Mr Burns? Why not just pull the tooth?'

'I have been told, sir, that the noise stuns the patient and takes the edge off the pain. It's been my observation that it seems to work. Dordey might be able to give you a better idea of whether it does or not.'

'I shall be sure to ask him; it may come in useful in missionary work. Believe me we have rather more to do in that line than just preaching the word of the Lord.'

Lattimore felt strangely lifted by the success of the tooth pulling. He had been in low spirits initially because of the thought that the survivors were having difficulty with something that any competent dentist could do in a minute or so. Now that the tooth was gone he felt differently; it seemed that they could surmount problems if they drew on the skills available in the group. Somehow it assuaged some of his guilt that he was responsible for their being there in the first place.

'Well Reverend, I hope that we shall not have any more such incidents to attend to on this island for there is not much whisky left. The next patient will not have much to numb the pain.'

'Let us hope then that there will not be a next patient and that Mr MacDonald will be able to effect our rescue soon and ferry us to where more civilized methods of medical and dental care may be found.'

'To that, sir, I can only say "Amen" and pray for his safe arrival at Samoa.'

'Be sure that I do so, several times a day. I do not wish my grandchildren to fret away their lives here any longer than they have to.'

Lattimore smiled faintly, and the two men set off to forage in the rock pools along the shore in comradely fashion; they were developing quite a taste for shellfish, little enough of a bond, but good enough to work together with.

Chapter 11

Willie Ferguson's Taste in Shoes

MacDonald woke to a scene utterly changed from when he had gone to sleep. He looked up at Willie Ferguson who was now holding the tiller and the bosun grunted at him.

'I think we are in for a bit of a blow, Donald, unless I am much mistaken.'

Looking out across the boat and back towards the north east, MacDonald had to agree, for the sky was the colour of lead, as indeed was the sea. Its perfect blue had been replaced by a dull hue with white wave crests chopping into large and swelling masses of water. It looked for all the world like the beginnings of a North Atlantic gale, save in one respect; the wind was warm, indeed almost hot.

'You are right and it looks as if it will be severe.'

'We shall ride it I think.'

'I think so too, but that sail is the only one we have got. If it carries away or shreds then we shall be in trouble.'

'Shorten sail, Donald?'

'I think it is all we can do. Enough to keep her going forward, but not enough to allow the wind to tear the mast out of her with the extra stays we have on.'

Anderson and Crosby moved to grab the sail, lowering it a good half of its height and folding the lower half into its reef points where they tied them firmly. If the remaining portion were damaged they would at least have the lower part to rig up.

'I did think of setting up some sort of sea anchor Donald. What do you think?'

MacDonald thought about this idea, which entailed the streaming out of a form of drogue that would drag in the water behind the boat to slow her progress.

'You were thinking of using the union flag in the locker?'

'It would put it to practical purposes.'

'Aye, it's a good idea Willie, but I think we shall not. We are nowhere near any land and the wind seems to be set from the nor' east. If we run before it we shall make good headway and no need to slow her save by shortening sail.'

'That's fair enough. Everything else we'd better tie down.'

'Oh aye; I expect we shall be thrown about a bit.'

MacDonald's talent for understatement was never more forcefully demonstrated, for as the hours went by the wind became stronger and stronger and the waves grew higher than houses. At first the boat rode the crests like a duck and their progress was quite exhilarating. Battered by the great force of the wind which grew to a shriek so that they could not converse save by bellowing at each other, they kept the stern of the launch to the wind and thanked Providence for their good fortune and such a speed. This phase soon passed, however, because the waves grew higher yet and danger presented itself. As the launch plunged down into the great gulfs between the waves, it also passed out of the wind, which meant that she slowed at the bottom and began to yaw to one side, slewing around in danger of presenting her side to the oncoming wind. Crosby yelled in alarm as he saw the wave behind him tower over his head in grave danger of crashing down on him.

'You can haud your wheesht right now!' MacDonald was not a man to bellow often, but he would not be allowing any panic on his boat. The launch rose up out of the trough, but of course there was another trough to come.

'Take hold of those oars you, Crosby and Anderson. If that happens again then you may break your backs or yell as much as you like, but keep her stern into the swell or it'll be me you'll have to deal with, never mind a wee bit water. It wilnae skelp your lugs, but I will and worse than your Mammy ever did! You're seamen! Now act like it.'

MacDonald's sudden return to the use of surnames brought back the habit of obedience to orders and the two ABs took their oars, not without difficulty and set them into the rowlocks.

'I'm on the tiller, Willie and Ned you are on the bailers. I want any water out of her before it comes in!'

It was a sad attempt at humour, but it at least brought a ghost of a smile to their faces. As it proved, they did not have too much to do. The boat plummeted down into the next trough, and as before, she lost way and began to turn to one side. Down in the trough though, the water was smooth and there was no wind at all. A couple of strokes on the port oars pulled the boat's head round to the south west again and she rose. No water came in and she lifted well. MacDonald found time to thank God that the storm was taking place during the daylight hours so that they could see clearly enough which way the correction should go. The conditions grew worse as hours went by and they were deluged with rain as thunder crashed around them and lightning split the sky above their heads. Great sheets and bolts crashed across the sky and hit the sea with a ripping and crackling sound that terrified most of the poor mortals under it except those who had resigned themselves already to their fate.

"The Heavens declare the Glory of God;
And the firmament sheweth his handiwork."

'Psalm number nineteen. You know your bible Willie.'

'So do you, to know where it came from, but it is nonetheless true.'

'It certainly is. It makes me feel small and insignificant.'

'That is what we are, Donald. That is exactly what we are, and yet if he wishes, we will come through this.'

'Then I hope he is looking down on us in a kindly mood this day for if ever we needed his help, that time is now.'

'Are you not afraid now Donald?'

'No Ned; I am not afraid. Fear is what would kill us and there is no point to it. We are in this boat and in it we will either live or die; it is one or the other. One thing I know is that as far as my part in it is concerned, I will work with all of my craft to make sure this boat and all in it reach Samoa.'

'And if we do not?'

'Well then we shall have tried and will no longer have to worry about it. In the meantime that rain has given us quite a bit of water we do not need. I'd be glad if you removed it.'

With a smile Tumelty set to baling. Soon the wind was screaming with such force that they could not make themselves heard. No midday sighting was taken, as the sun could not be seen through the furious downpour that assaulted them. If the truth were told, thought MacDonald to himself, he was afraid, but he knew that he must not appear so. Someone had to appear unafraid, because if his crew felt fear then their wills would sap and ebb. He must be strong and thereby keep them strong because they believed in him, and so also in the success of their voyage.

It seemed that fortune began to smile on the crew of the little boat, because as the hours went by the fury of the wind lessened and the troughs began to calm. By the time night came the storm had abated, so that the waves once more were merely the height of houses. The oars could be shipped for there was now no point where the sails would lose the wind. As darkness fell, MacDonald issued each man with a dram of whisky to fortify him for the night ahead, because he knew there would be no sleep. They also each chewed on an ounce of the hard tack, but it in no way satisfied their hunger. What followed was an awful night of wind and wave, made worse by the fact that flying spume and rain made it impossible to light the lamp. The only saving grace of their situation was that somewhere up in the sky, though they could not see it, was the moon and they did have some dim vision inside the boat. Occasional gusts from the nor' west caused the tops of some waves to come over the stern, but the rain once again became torrential. That there was no shelter from it, save for two men who could crawl wet under the decked area, did not matter for it was not cold. No one did seek that refuge though because there was no possibility of sleep. The problem was that the rain was so copious that it was almost as if some angry god above the clouds was spraying a hosepipe into the boat. They had to bail constantly and if anyone lay down on the duckboards water would have simply soaked them as thoroughly as if they were in a bath. When morning came it found them red eyed and worn out, but with one overarching mercy. The worst of the storm had passed and it was becoming unmistakably calmer with each passing hour. Soon the rain stopped, the wind moderated and the sun came out.

To the surprise of the rest of the crew, MacDonald stripped off his wet shirt and trousers when the waters grew calm enough whilst remarking to his surprised companions, 'You'll be wondering what on earth I am doing.'

'If you think that then you would be right,' said Ned Tumelty, a wondering look on his face.

'It's a good job there are no lassies about,' stated Charlie Anderson, 'But I have seen worse in the forecastle.'

'All the same Donald, to stand naked in a boat is a situation that would normally not pass without remark,' asserted Willie Ferguson. 'What are you doing?'

'I have had the fortune, or maybe misfortune to have read Captain Bligh's book on his voyage. I do not remember it all by any means and wish I had taken more notice of details, but I do remember that after every rainstorm he ordered his men to take off their wet clothes and wash them in seawater before wringing them out and putting them back on.'

'An excellent seaman, that Captain Bligh, though I fear somewhat cruel to his men when in command of a ship. I take it that he had good reason for this odd practice?'

'He did. Salt water evaporates quicker than fresh and he did not wish his men to sit round in damp clothes any longer than they had to, thinking it would be bad for them. Their clothes dried quicker if they did this and I intend to follow his example.'

'You expect us to do this as well?'

'You may do exactly as you wish in this regard Willie; it is your choice, though I do observe that a couple of you are beginning to reek in a manner not too salubrious.'

'Are you implying that I smell?'

'I'm implying nothing but I do tell you straight that there's a rare old stink to you and especially about your oxters. You smell like a midden.'

This judgment brought a wave of hilarity from the other crew members, but MacDonald turned a gimlet eye on them as well.

'Oh you may laugh my wee laddies, but there's a fine stench emanating from your direction too and I'm only glad that I spend most of my time upwind of you. The cheapest hoor down the Govan Road would run a mile from you even if you waved a sovereign at her.'

Ferguson sat stunned for a moment and then smelled his armpits.

'I suppose it is a while since I had a wash. That's some straight talking there Donald, but you are right. Cleanliness is next to godliness. I shall bathe.'

So saying he stood up, grasped the tiller rope and jumped over the side to the surprise of his shipmates. For a moment he disappeared under the water then reappeared, hauling himself back to the side of the boat using the rope where he scrubbed under his arms and in his nether regions vigorously. Climbing back into the boat he removed his clothes, wrung them out and put them back on.

'Very refreshing; now Donald I shall smell sweeter than you for you have only washed your clothes.'

'That's soon remedied my man, for I shall follow your example.'

So saying, MacDonald seized the rope and did just that. With broad grins the others followed suit, one after the other, the only mishap being with Tumelty who foolishly let go of the rope and found himself in danger of being left behind as the boat sailed past him. MacDonald reached down and grabbed his arm to pull him back to the gunwale.

'It's not a good moment to go for a swim Ned.'

'I cannae swim.'

'Then it's a glaikit wee loon you are to be letting go of the rope.'

'It was not my intention.'

'That is as may be. The result would have been the same, intentional or not; a drowned sailor would be no use to anyone except to the fish. Be more careful.'

With a clean crew and clothes that rapidly dried in the sun, the launch sailed on as the sea took on its former blue and benign appearance. The weather cleared quickly, so that MacDonald was able to take the midday sighting and when he did his eyebrows lifted in surprise.

'What is it Donald?'

'Well Willie, if my reckoning is correct we have made two hundred nautical miles since midday, the day before yesterday.'

'Well that's very good going Donald; it seems to me that if it gets us so far on our way perhaps another storm or two might be welcome.'

Ned Tumelty, his eyes wide in horror, protested.

'Mr Ferguson, please do not say that! It's a great temptation to Mother Nature and you might get what you wish for.'

'Ah that's superstitious nonsense, Ned Tumelty; I cannot be doing with it; I never did. Such things as whistling up a wind or blaming Jonahs for ill luck; it is all so much mince. At any rate, we have things on our mind which are rather more urgent than being afraid of shadows.'

'That is true enough Willie; what do you think is the worst of our problems?'

'Right now, Donald, it is fairly obviously food. In the last three days I have eaten three ounces of hard tack biscuit and frankly it's not enough. My stomach thinks that my throat has been cut and I swear it's flapping against my backbone.'

'As I recall, we were trying to catch some fish just before the storm came. We can try again.'

'You can try all you like, but I doubt you will get any.'

'Why?'

'I think you know full well, Donald. This is the deep ocean. You do not find fish in the deep ocean. You have been a fisherman; you know it as well as I. It's a kindly thought, but we know better I think you'll find.'

MacDonald smiled ruefully. He was well aware that his intended deception, designed to encourage, was as thin as tissue.

'I do know it. You are right; fish prefer shallower waters, weed, rocks and cover. But it is better to fish in hope than not to fish. We may catch something.'

'Aye; we may and we may not. We are by your reckoning either halfway or just under that on our way to Samoa. There are at least six hundred miles further to go, all open water and that on an ounce a day of hard tack and water, with a few ounces of meat every few days. We are going to get thinner and weaker Donald and we need to preserve some strength to make land at the end of our journey.'

For MacDonald's patience this flat statement made out aloud in front of the three Able Seamen was enough, but it was not in his nature to snap. Instead, he looked bleakly at Willie Ferguson and asked him in dry arid tones, 'Well Willie, what do you propose that we do about it? Eat someone is it?'

Ferguson looked shocked.

'I am surprised, Donald, that such a suggestion should even pass your lips in reference to me. Eating someone would not be the Christian thing to do.'

'Oh yes, we are all Christians so we will be decent, though I will observe that Dansker has some tempting hams…'

Anderson went pale under his tan, for tales of sailors in their situation turning to cannibalism were common currency in forecastle yarns, but before he opened his mouth MacDonald laughed. More than this he laughed loud and long, which as far as they were concerned, was unheard of.

'Dinnae fash yourself, Charlie; I am not about to take a bite out of your leg; you may relax. There will be no eating of people on this boat.'

The look of palpable relief on Anderson's face set them all to laughing again, but when the fit was over MacDonald turned an enquiring look at Willie Ferguson.

'So what do you suggest?'

'Well Donald, I might just invite you to join in my repast if you will return the favour from your own resources.'

'What in the name of God are you bumping your gums about Willie Ferguson? I jalouse that you're pulling my leg, for you are a pawky chiel, but I have nothing about my person to eat and neither have you.'

'You're wrong Donald. Give me my ration and I'll prove it to you.'

Intrigued, MacDonald reached under the tiller seat and pulled out the wooden box containing the hard tack. Carefully he broke pieces off the slabs until each was approximately the same size and weight, which he judged to be an ounce. Each man took his portion and a coconut shell of water from the ten-gallon butt, which was brimming because of the rain. With an arch expression and a ceremonial air, Ferguson took off his shoe and held it over the side, washing it. Then reaching into his pocket he pulled out his clasp-knife, opened it, and said, 'I may come from the other side of the North Channel but I still know my Burns.' Then he declaimed loudly,

"Fair fa' your honest sonsie face
Great Chieftain o' the broguish race
Aboon them a' ye tak your place,
Painch, tripe or thairm;
Weel are ye wordy of a grace
As lang's my arm..."

'Aye. You've been a good and faithful shoe, but your time has come. You may go to the great cobblers in the sky for your master has other need of you.'

So saying he brought the knife down and stabbed the shoe and looked up at the others, who had those expressions that told of wondering if he had gone mad. He smiled then placed the shoe in front of him and cut off a thin strip off it. As they watched he chopped the leather fine, shredding what he could, until he had a little heap of desiccated hide. Then he bit his hard tack, chewed it and took a good pinch of shoe leather at the same time.

'What's it like?' ventured William Crosby.

'Well, it's not so bad. Then again it's not so good either. It tastes like eating a shoe.'

'But why are you eating your shoe?'

'Well, I do not need shoes on the boat and if we reach land I can get others. But I need to eat something to help fill my belly. Hide comes off meat; there may be some nourishment to it, but even if not it helps fill me. Would you like some?'

'But will it not give you a bad belly? Like the coconut?'

'That is not likely,' said MacDonald. 'The leather has been through a process and although it may not taste very good I do not think it will do any harm. I accept your invitation Willie and I shall return the favour in due course.'

Ferguson waved expansively.

'Help yourself Donald, and eat hearty.'

'I shall have a strip, the same as you, but I think we should ration it. As you say, we have a long way to go. Do you think we can get two meals worth for five men out of each shoe?'

'Pushing it I should think, but we can try.'

'I did not think of eating the shoes. What made you think of it?'

'Ah well now, it was your mentioning of biting Charlie on the leg; it put me in mind of the Donner Party. You'll remember them?'

'I do not, so you will have to enlighten me.'

'It was a thing that happened forty years ago in the great American gold rush of 1848. A large party of people heading to the goldfields got cut off by heavy snow and they ran out of food. One of the families was called Donner, hence the name. They ended by eating people, but first they ate leather. That is how I knew that it might be done.'

'I see. That was well remembered. I do not know if it will actually do us any good, but it will at least provide something to pad out the little we have. We shall eat all our shoes if we have to. It will at least keep the saliva going.'

'My father was an erudite man and he read it in the newspaper; I mind him telling stories to us that he had seen; that was one of them.'

****

For the next ten days the weather stayed good and the trade winds stayed steady. MacDonald managed to take his midday sighting every day without difficulty. Gradually they worked their way through the bread until there was hardly any left. The eating of the shoes did help bring saliva, but there was a price to be paid as everyone in the launch developed a low level kind of dysentery, not as severe as had been experienced with the coconuts, but debilitating nonetheless. They had caught no fish and the meat was all done. The cheese was long finished and all their shoes had been shredded and eaten, even the leather soles; the whisky had been finished two days previously. All they had was a meagre mouthful of hard tack once a day, and the leather on the captain's telescope. Since there was nothing to eat and the air was hot, their saliva more or less ceased to flow so their tongues swelled up and their lips cracked and throbbed. Every man was weak and the least effort exhausted them; there was no fat on their bones at all and their cheeks had fallen in so that they looked hollow and gaunt. The matter of food had become urgent, because it was plain that they did not have many days left in them and that death had become a companion, a presence in the boat. If death came to them then it would be in one of its worst forms for adults in full possession of their faculties, for it would be through starvation. It was sometimes easy for MacDonald to see why the old horror tales told in so many forecastles might be true, where castaways killed and ate their own kind to stay alive. Although his personal taboos were too great against such a thing, he could see why men did it. His own hunger gnawed at him with a real pain and his protesting guts demanded food though he had nothing to give it. His companions, he knew, were just as desperate and men in such a case are often driven to desperate measures in their fight to stay alive.

Sixteen days into the voyage MacDonald was astonished to see Charles Anderson pull his knife from his pocket and hold the open blade to his wrist. Since the Dane's emotional display when the coconuts went rotten, MacDonald had been rather wary of his moods and feared he was about to witness something rash. Anderson saw his look and smiled faintly.

'Do not worry Donald; I'm not about to end it. I have an idea that's all.'

'What idea is that?' demanded Willie Ferguson. 'What sort of idea is it that makes a man hold an open knife to his wrist?'

'This sort of idea,' said Anderson screwing up his face and deliberately cutting his wrist with a quick downward slash.'

'What in the name of God are you doing?'

'Staying alive Donald,' said Anderson, putting his streaming wrist to his mouth and sucking hard.'

'You're drinking your own blood?'

MacDonald's face was a mixture of consternation and disgust, mingled with an unwanted curiosity.

'It will do you no good. It will make you weaker.'

'I don't think it will. I heard of some soldiers in America during their civil war. They were taken prisoner and marched a very long way without food to a camp. They drank their own blood to satisfy both hunger and thirst. They survived.'

'They survived, but it might have been simply because they still had sufficient fat and energy to survive. You cannot say that it was because of their drinking blood.'

'Blood is nourishing Donald. Just think of black pudding.'

'I'll not dispute it, but your body will have to make more to replace what you drink. That will not keep you alive, for I think you will lose strength. Anyway it's too much like cannibalism for my liking.'

'I am not drinking anyone else's blood, so how is it cannibalism?'

'It's a kind of self-cannibalism then.'

'I do not agree.' Anderson sucked some more at his arm. 'At any rate it is my business and I will do it if I wish.'

'It is your business,' said MacDonald. 'But I think it unwise and have said so. If you continue to do it then be it on your own head.'

'I will take the risk,' replied Anderson binding up his wrist with a strip torn from his shirt.

'So will I,' said Crosby, and copied Anderson in every particular.

From this time on these two men opened their wrists every day and drank their own blood to the fascination and mesmerization of the other three.

On the seventeenth day outward from Palmyra MacDonald, with a pang of guilt, took his knife and cut the leather binding off Lattimore's prized telescope, telling himself that if he ever saw the Captain again he would have it rebound. They ate it that evening with the last of the hard tack and they did so in silence; they knew very well that according to MacDonald they had travelled 1,300 nautical miles. They also knew that they had tempted fate greatly in making it so far, but they were not at Samoa and had sighted no land or craft of any kind since leaving the atoll. Sitting so long in the boat had resulted in three of them, Ferguson, Crosby and MacDonald himself getting swollen legs, despite having stood up at regular intervals to try to exercise them. MacDonald was not sure if he could walk, but was grateful that he could think. Looking at the others he wondered if they were past that for Anderson and Crosby sat staring into space, their eyes apparently empty, chewing what might be their last meal automatically; they had drunk their own blood that afternoon as was now their habit. They were all very weak now and moving was an effort, something to be thought about and done with reluctance. Their faces had all fallen in and cheeks one padded and well fed were now hollow. Speaking was difficult because they were so dry, with thickened tongues and their lips throbbed painfully. MacDonald knew that he had a face like a skull, though he could not see himself in any mirror; his companions were so emaciated that they looked like a collection of skeletons with brown skins stretched over them, and his own appearance must be much the same. Their reserves of energy and fat, already depleted by their stay on the island, were now utterly exhausted and they barely clung to life, spending much of their days asleep save for the man steering; the body's way of conserving what life remained.

Privately MacDonald wondered if he had made a mistake in choosing to make this attempt, for they should be at Samoa by now and he dreaded finding that they had sailed right past it, because in the vastness of the ocean it was a very small target and he was doubting his own navigational skills more and more.

'Are we done for Donald?'

Ferguson's voice, like those of all the men in the boat, was weak and hard to use.

'I don't know Willie. We should be there by now, but we are not.'

'You are thinking we have gone past?'

'I fear we might have. I'm sorry for it, because if we have then we are dead men.'

'Do not be sorry Donald. You forced no one to come. We are all free men.'

'I know that, but it was my idea. I am responsible.'

'Not for me you are not. I am my own man and if I had not wanted to come then I should have said so. If I die here then it is the will of God and no doing of yours.'

'It's not a good way to go, Willie.'

'Why, Donald, I know that, but I doubt we shall know much about it at the end. From what I know of these things we shall be quite unconscious and the sun will finish us off all unknowing. There is nothing we can do now except light the lamp and go to sleep. If you don't mind I shall say a wee prayer tonight though.'

MacDonald knew Ferguson's reason for praying, something he did not usually do; he thought he might not live through the night. Indeed he felt his own life force to be flickering so low that he thought he himself might not. There are many people who go through their lives with an unspoken assumption at the back of their minds that the ordinary rules of mortality do not apply to them. MacDonald was not such, and perhaps it was his upbringing, so close to the sea, and so often on it that made him aware and accepting of the idea that he too would one day die. He answered Ferguson gently,

'Of course I don't mind. If ever we needed God's help it is now.'

He bowed his head as Ferguson prayed in a voice faint and weak:

"Lord, be merciful to us sinners for thy mercy's sake.
Thou art the great God, that hast made and rulest all things;
O deliver us for thy name's sake.
Thou art the great God to be feared above all.
O save us that we may praise thee.
Amen."

'Amen,' repeated MacDonald as he lashed the tiller and lay down to rest, perhaps never to get up again. He wondered if they would be found by a ship eventually, to the horror of those on it, dried out and mummified or pecked by seabirds. Perhaps they would never be found and their boat would wreck or sink in some far off place and they would have no decent burial.

Privately he prayed that the end would come without his knowing, perhaps this very night, so that his death would not be prolonged. All of them settled down to go to sleep; you were not hungry when you slept. He was the last to drift off and when he had done so the boat resembled a group of blackened and desiccated corpses, skin barely clinging to skeletons. Death came and sat beside Donald at the tiller of the boat, and though Donald did not see him, he grinned in the Scotsman's face. As he lay trying to sleep his aunt's face came into his mind as clear as a bell and he spoke to her faintly.

'I'm sorry Aunty Margaret; I tried my best, but I do not think I shall be coming home this time.'

At his last flicker of consciousness he knew that all hope had fled from their minds; his last thought was a line of an old Breton prayer:

"O God thy sea is so great, and I am so small."

Chapter 12

The Great Game

The sun came up the following morning on a perfect morning such as the Pacific gives in fine weather. It was their eighteenth day at sea. The turquoise sea was virtually mirror smooth and the wind had almost ceased, turning into small zephyrs barely enough to stir a sail. The far horizon was barely discernible as the bright blue of the sky merged into ocean and the light twinkled off the water. On this painted scene, rapidly being warmed by the heat of the day, a battered looking launch could be seen bobbing, ripples around it, with sail hanging more or less limply and barely moving. A birds-eye view inside this vessel would have revealed five forms stretched out uncomfortably and so emaciated that they looked as if the sea and the sun had combined to mummify them into cracked parodies of what may be found in Egyptian sarcophagi. At first glance they looked dead, and only the closest examination could reveal that each still breathed, though almost imperceptibly. It was MacDonald who woke up first, though at first he did not know why; something appeared to have sounded in his head and woke him up. Weakly he pulled himself into an upright position and his bleary eyes stared round at the sea. Ahead he could see what looked like a black cloud low on the horizon. Almost too afraid to think what he was seeing, he kept quiet; he had to be certain before he said anything to the others.

Willie Ferguson crawled aft to where MacDonald sat and whispered to him, 'There's an island on our beam.'

Coolly MacDonald replied to him,

'That island is Manua.'

Then he pointed ahead, 'And that is Upolu. Hold the tiller please Willie while I take the bearing.'

Ferguson did so and tears poured down his cheeks; by now the other three were aware that land was in sight and they also wept. Anderson and Crosby were completely incapable of moving from where they were and not one of the men could say a word. Nonetheless they smiled and the air of happiness in the boat was palpable. Steadily and in a light breeze the launch headed towards Upolu, the main island of Samoa; when MacDonald took a noon sighting he found it to be fifty-four miles off. By midnight they were within a few short miles of the Samoan coast, but a storm with thunder and lightning blew up in a final display of their fragility, and they had to stand off the coast until daylight; there was not much sleep for anyone. When dawn came, the sea was calm and flat, and they had furled the sail, being content to drift until the sun came up. MacDonald lay in a state between waking and sleep, one arm crooked over the steering oar and he became dimly aware that he could hear voices. Human beings were talking in what sounded like an animated conversation; as quickly as he could drag his dehydrated frame, MacDonald turned towards the voices.

Two men were sitting in what MacDonald knew to be a va'a a aluatu canoe because he had seen them in the harbour at Apia just a few weeks before, though it seemed like a lifetime ago; they had been heading for the boat anyway, but they stopped rowing when he appeared above the gunwale and their faces wore expressions of astonishment and consternation. They looked like Samoans to him, with well-muscled torsos and their lower parts clothed in the garment they called a lava-lava, though at the moment they looked as if their jaws were going to stay open permanently in surprise. By now Anderson, Crosby and Tumelty were all awake and calling out as loud as they could, waving their arms, tears weeping and smiling at the same time; there was a feeling, almost an excess of joy in their faces. Willie Ferguson had been deeper into sleep than the others and sat up slowly in response to MacDonald's croaked, 'Wake up! Wake up!'

'Are they Christian men or savages? Not that it makes any difference, for I am near enough dead anyway.'

'Have some water Willie; it will help.'

'With difficulty MacDonald helped Ferguson to sit up and drink some water they had gathered during the previous night's storm. When they looked out towards the approaching men they also realized that in the near distance was a line in the morning haze that indicated the presence of land. About a mile away was a schooner that had clearly seen what was happening and had hove to. Round the boat a school of dolphins played, the friendly dogs of the sea, a sure sign that they were now in an area of ocean where fish could be found.

The canoe came close to the launch and one of the men called out to them in Polynesian. In dumb reply MacDonald held out his hands indicating that he did not understand, and then he called out one word, 'English.'

This caused some surprise with the occupants of the canoe and of several others which were now approaching the scene.

'Are you Europeans?' shouted one of the men with a distinct accent.

'Yes; we are shipwrecked sailors and in great need of help. Please help us.'

There was a moment of conferring among the canoes and then they approached the launch.

'We are going to take you to the schooner. There is a British man who is captain and he will help you.'

'How is it that you speak such good English?'

'Because I went to the mission school in Apia sir; most Samoans speak our own language and English.'

By now the other men in the launch were sitting up and they lost themselves for a full minute of laughing, crying, pounding each other weakly on the back and loud incoherent shouts of joy in both English and Danish.

'We made it, Donald. We have made it.'

'Yes we have, Willie.'

'You have made it,' said one of the fishermen, 'but where from?'

'We've come from Palmyra Atoll,' said MacDonald. 'There are men, women and children stranded there. We need to get help.'

'Palmyra! God must have been with you to get you so far.'

'We must get help to the people on Palmyra.'

'First of all you need to get some help yourself by the look of you. When did you last eat?'

'A proper meal? I can't remember.'

'We are going to tow you to the schooner; Captain Bissett will know what to do with you. My name is Iosefa by the way and this is Manaia. Are you English?'

'I am Scottish.'

Two of the canoes attached ropes to the front of the launch and each lifted a single triangular sail.

MacDonald looked a mile or so across the water and the schooner was heading towards them, attracted by the numbers of men in the canoes standing and waving their arms. Within a very short time MacDonald and his men, incapable of walking, were being hauled up the side of the *Vindex* schooner to meet Captain David Bissett, who looked at them uncertainly. The launch was tied to the rear of the schooner to be towed.

'Don't mind me asking, but are you Europeans?'

'Of course we're European; what do you think we look like?'

'I'm not sure; I thought you were aborigines when I first saw you. You're burned with the sun I presume. Who are you?'

MacDonald was weary and his head ached, so he passed his hand in front of his eyes. He knew the schooner's captain meant well, and that he had a Scottish accent, but he was in no frame of mind for interrogations. He responded faintly, his voice a croak.

'There are twenty-five people cast away on Palmyra Atoll. We must get help to them.'

The schooner captain's eyes widened, but he now realized how weak MacDonald was.

'I'm sorry. You are obviously not in a good way. Let us get some food and water inside you. The questions can wait until later; we must get you to a place where there is help. We can also set about getting aid to Palmyra. If you've come from there, then you've had a long journey in that boat.'

It was not more than an hour when MacDonald looked about him and realized that they were entering the wide mouth of a semi-circular bay through a gap in a reef, and that he knew it as Apia Harbour. He had been given water, then a mug of tea and a plate of tatties and mince, so new life was slowly returning to him, although he did not have sufficient strength to stand from the seat he had been placed on.'

'Donald.'

A hand pummeled him on the shoulder and he looked round to see Willie Ferguson grinning at him in the next chair.

'Donald, that is some navigation that you have just pulled off. You'll know me for a man not given to hyperbole, but I have to own that it is impressive. Palmyra to Samoa in nineteen days and bang on for Apia. Well done my friend; when we get back I'll have a few drams with you for this.'

A chorus of agreement came from the others with smiles that were full of gladness, as indeed they should have been, because death should by all rights have carried them all off. As the schooner entered the harbour Captain Bissett shouted down at the canoes that populated it. One of the va'a a aluatu craft raced ahead into the harbour, faster than the schooner could go and a man jumped from it and headed straight for the English mission, a short distance along the seafront. When the schooner came up to the small quayside willing hands reached down and tied her fast; MacDonald looked up at the crowd which gathered and realized that most of them were white; they had been taken straight to the settlement area where there was a mostly German colonial town. Waiting for them was a man dressed in the white of a Methodist pastor who looked slightly out of breath as he had been running.

'Are you British?'

'Yes sir; we are; two of us are Scots, one from Ulster, one Dane and one from Nova Scotia.'

'I understand that you have been shipwrecked.'

'That is true. We have and there are twenty-five men women and children in need of help on Palmyra Atoll.'

'You have come from there in that boat?'

'Yes sir.'

The man looked completely shocked.

'Great Heavens! Well we must do something about effecting their rescue, but first of all I think we must see to you. Come ashore now with your crew. What is your name?'

'I'm Donald MacDonald, sir, First Mate of the barque *Henry James.*'

'You were here only a few weeks ago. I met Captain Lattimore at a reception at the Consulate. My name is Samuel Davies. I am a member of the London Missionary Society and we run the English Mission here in Apia.'

'I was probably minding the ship then, sir, but Captain Lattimore is still on Palmyra.'

'Let us get you to a place where we can look after you; up you come.'

'I'm sorry sir, but I fear none of us can walk.'

MacDonald tried gamely to stand, but he had not the strength and neither had any of the others.

'Great Heavens,' he exclaimed again. 'But you must have been through quite an ordeal. Hold on a moment.'

Davies turned to speak to one of the men at his side.

'Fetu, I think we will need a cart or two; can you find us a couple of wagons please?'

The man nodded and ran off to intercede with some of the wagon drivers round the port.

'Rangi; can you and some of your friends lift them out please?'

'Yes Reverend Davies; I think we can do that.'

A group of men came down into the boat and lifted the five passengers up onto the quayside.

'They weigh next to nothing Reverend; I think they need to see the doctor.'

'I agree Rangi. Here's Fetu with some carts; let's get them to the hostel now.'

'Can we please convey our thanks to these men first, sir? The men out there who found us.'

'The fishermen? Yes indeed, but from what I gather they are all coming in and want to shake your hands.'

'Do they? What for? I cannot understand what they are saying.'

'That's easy enough to explain,' said Iosefa, coming forward. 'Word is spreading that you have sailed that boat across the open ocean from Palmyra. That is an astonishing thing; everyone wants to shake hands because of it, simply to say that they have.'

'I'll try, but there's a lot of hands. We were lucky and are so grateful that you were out there and found us.'

'We fish for bonito and would have been out there anyway; every one of us is happy that we were able to help. You are great sailors!'

'That's all one to me,' replied MacDonald, grasping his hand as firmly as he could. 'Thank you for bringing us in; from the bottom of my heart.'

The prostrate men were loaded onto carts and trundled down the road towards the English Mission, a large white wooden building with smaller ones clustered round it. As they moved down the road, the carts were surrounded by men and women, shaking each man's hand saying, 'Well done!' Word had spread like wildfire.

The missionary turned to MacDonald with a smile and explained what was going to happen.

'We have a small hospital where we shall lodge you at first until you can walk, but then you shall be in our hostel. There is a college attached to the Mission where we teach Samoan missionaries who go out among the other islands to do good works.'

'We shall have beds? With sheets?'

'With sheets Mr MacDonald; nice clean and white sheets.'

'Have I died and gone to Heaven?'

'I cannot make such a claim, but I sense your pleasure in the idea.'

'I can only thank God for such a deliverance and for the sheets.'

'You thank God for the clean sheets?'

'I do sir, with all my heart.'

'Why then Mr MacDonald I am sure that he accepts your thanks. Here we are now. There are nurses here who will see to you; and I shall speak with you later.'

'But sir, I have to see to the rescue of the people on Palmyra.'

Samuel Davies looked at him kindly.

'It gives me pleasure to see a man so devoted to his duty and to his fellow man, but my dear sir, your job is done. I shall leave you now and go to see the British Consul, Mr Wilson. Do not concern yourself with this any longer; the rescue will be organized you may rest assured. May I ask if the people on the island have food and water?'

'There is sufficient to sustain life, sir, but in the absence of potatoes or bread of any kind all are growing thin and will weaken in time.'

'But apart from growing thin they can live perhaps indefinitely by using the island's resources?'

'I believe so sir though with the children it may be a different matter.'

'That is a great relief to me though I am concerned to hear about the children and I am sure that it will be an urgent matter to the Consul. He is a man with much on his mind. He is also the local Anglican vicar you see. The former British Consul Mr Powell was transferred to Stettin; I believe that he wanted to live in a cooler climate. The Reverend Wilson volunteered to fill in until the arrival of his successor, probably in August. He will be a Mr DeCoetlogen. Are you and your men in need of anything else Mr MacDonald?'

'We have no money sir.'

'My dear Mr MacDonald, if our mission did not extend Christian charity to help our own countrymen in distress then you may be quite certain in your mind that I would not be working for it. Between the London Missionary Society and the British Consul we shall see you right and on your way. Please give no more thought to money. You shall have all your material wants supplied.'

MacDonald and his companions were taken into a low building with a thatched roof near to the mission and found that it contained eight beds; this was the hospital Davies had referred to. They were too weak to even remove their own clothes so a small squad of male orderlies attended to this, then sponged them down and into a semblance of cleanliness. When this was done finally they were put into beds and left in the charge of two local women trained as nurses. Davies had explained that they had been instructed by a pair of Nightingale nurses that the Society had sent out from England, and that in his view their practice was as good as in any London hospital. Each man was given a large bowl of taro and chicken porridge but it was very thin, so as not to overload their stomachs. Their consolation was that if they had no difficulty in keeping it down they would be allowed solid food next day. When this meal was eaten every man of the crew fell fast asleep and stayed in that state for the rest of the day when they were roused and fed more porridge, this time taro with fish.

When MacDonald woke up the following morning he found the call of nature upon him so gingerly slid his legs out of bed and onto the floor. To his pleasure he found that he could stand. To be sure he felt weak and wobbly, but he called out to the nurse who was in an anteroom, asking where he could find a lavatory. It was not too long before the rest of the crew was on their feet too. The mission had no resident doctor and apparently the only trained doctors in Apia were attached to the German company, but for reasons that were not explained to MacDonald, these were not sent for. There was an English tourist staying in Apia at this time, and among the close knit Anglo-American community he was known to have a good knowledge of surgery, having been a medical student, though not completing his studies. So it was that Mr Smith, at the request of Reverend Davies, came to look over the launch crew and after examining each of them pronounced that although they were all emaciated, there was nothing that he could see very much wrong with them that a few days of rest and food would not put right. That was good enough for MacDonald and he asked Davies if he could go now and speak to the British Consul.

'Yes I think so. He thought you might want to see him, so I will take you along there as soon as you are dressed. Don't worry though; he's a good man, our Reverend Wilson with a subtle mind, and very efficient. I am sure that plans for the rescue will be well advanced.'

Dressed in a new white cotton shirt and a pair of duck trousers in the same colour with a palmetto hat on his head against the sun, MacDonald, accompanied by Davies, strolled from the mission heading round the bay a short walk to the British consulate. The missionary was pleased to act as a guide, pointing out the sights to be seen.

'If you look over there across the water, you see that village on the low sand promontory? That's Mulinuu. It doesn't look much I know, but that is traditionally the seat of power in Samoa and where the King lives.'

'There seem to be a lot of people over there.'

'Yes there are. Those are soldiers in the army of King Tamasese.'

Davies looked at MacDonald closely, but his tone now took on a certain diffidence, even awkwardness.

'I do not want to spell out any details of local politics if you don't mind. Some of it affects you, and in ways you probably will not like, so I'll leave explanations to the Consul. I don't want to get it wrong you see.'

Mystified but willing to wait, MacDonald merely nodded. In the harbour he could plainly see two ships that were admirably equipped to go to Palmyra, both being steam powered warships. One flew the American flag and the other the British. On enquiry Davies identified them as *HMS Calliope* and the *USS Mohican*.

'There is a third warship on station here, the *SMS Adler*, but she is currently steaming round the island.'

MacDonald grew enthusiastic.

'Now that is what I call the working of Providence. One of those ships can rescue all the people on Palmyra within a few days!'

'I fear Mr MacDonald, I really fear that it may not be as simple a matter as we would wish.'

MacDonald looked at him in astonishment.

'But it is simple. There are people in need of help and those ships can provide it very quickly and with ease.'

Once again, Davies was not forthcoming, but his expression showed that there was more to be said about this matter.

'I am sure that the Consul will explain the situation to you in as much detail as you could wish.' He continued, 'Over there, further round the bay, everything you see is German. They have turned 10,000 acres of that land over to copra production for the oil and they are clearing more for cattle, and it's all done by a company that is based in Hamburg. Those buildings are all their stores, barracks for their workers and guards and their manufactories. Think of our East India Company in former days and you have the idea of the sort of thing they do.'

'But Samoa is not a German possession; how do they own so much?'

'In this world Mr MacDonald I fear that might is all too often right. They have concessions because they are strong. Now we are entering Matafele; Apia is really a long string of villages joined together, but this part as you may see could justifiably lay claim to being the main section.'

MacDonald looked about him and could see why; this central part of the settlement had neat western colonial style buildings, some of them with two storeys and a few of them quite large. Most were in wood and painted white though towards the Eastern part were houses and shops in different subdued colours. Davies nodded towards the neat painted houses.

'That's where most of the German residents live and where their consulate is. You'll find they have German shops, bars, all kinds of stores and that's where the Catholic Cathedral is too.'

'That huge white church with the two towers?'

'That's the one; it quite puts our church to shame but there you are. It was built some years ago by Monsieur Bataillion, on the instructions of his brother, who was the Catholic bishop here. A trifle ostentatious I think. Now if we cross here, the Mulivai Bridge, we are into the Anglo-American part of town. There you see Mr Moor's stores; he is American and right across the street is the establishment of Messrs. McArthur who are English. They are rivals, but friendly; I wish the same could be said for all of the expatriate community.'

Before long they came to the British consulate and were shown into the office of the Reverend William Wilson who welcomed them cordially.

'Sit down Gentlemen, sit down and have a cup of tea; it's too early in the day for anything else I think.'

It was a pleasant room shaded by a verandah outside and cooled by the thick bougainvillea that draped magenta from above. Outside could be seen the brilliant blue of the bay and the white line of the reef far out.

'First of all Mr MacDonald, let me congratulate you on one of the most remarkable things I have ever come across in my career. It rivals that of Captain Bligh, and I am deeply astonished by the whole thing; 1,300 miles across the open Pacific in a launch; quite amazing.'

'Thank you, sir; I am glad to be here though very conscious of the fact that we nearly did not make it.'

'But you did and that is the main thing is it not? Now, as to the rescue of your ship's company, I have chartered a schooner to go and get them.'

'A schooner, sir? One of the steam ships would be a lot faster and the people on the island are much in need of help.'

'I know they are Mr MacDonald, but there is no steamship available.'

MacDonald looked puzzled and was about to query this, but Wilson waved a hand and continued.

'I know what you are thinking, but it is useless. It is quite true that the corvette is a British ship and that Captain Kane could sail to Palmyra much faster than a schooner. The American ship could do it as well and I am sure that Commander Day would like nothing better, but the irony of the situation is that I cannot ask them; I simply cannot put them in that position. It would be impossible for them.'

'I'm sorry sir, but I do not see the problem. You are not a seaman and I am. If a proper seaman hears of others in distress then he helps. I am sure that if you asked the captains of those vessels then they would speed quickly to help my unfortunate shipmates.'

'I'm afraid that they might Mr MacDonald and if they did then it would end their careers which is too much to ask. Their orders are to stay here and I will not ask them to move; it would set up an awful conflict for them, so they will not be asked for assistance. You will not ask them either.'

'I may do just that; I can think of no reason why I should not,' exclaimed MacDonald indignantly and standing up. 'A schooner would have to tack into the winds for weeks to get to Palmyra when a steamship could be there in a few days. If this Captain Kane is a seaman then he will help my captain and his company.'

Wilson looked at him with a weary eye.

'Please sit down Mr MacDonald. There are things you do not know so I shall explain. I owe you that much.'

MacDonald sat down and Wilson began by asking him a question.

'Do you know what the Great Game is, Mr MacDonald?'

'I fear I do not sir; I am only a sailor and know nothing of games.'

'Very well; the Great Game is like a huge game of chess that is played between the powers of the world. They play for position, for territory, for status, for resources and for empire. For example, we play a lot against Russia on our border with India and at stake is our influence along the North West frontier and in Afghanistan. Foreign powers are our opposition and of course we wish to win advantages over them. Understand?'

'I do sir, but what has this to do with Palmyra?'

'This Mr MacDonald; Samoa is a board on which the game is played right now. The board moves you see and the game is played out all over the world, but at this moment the attention of three powers is right here in Apia.'

'The British, the Americans and the Germans?'

'Exactly so; we have been here a long time and so have the Americans and our commercial interests have entailed a certain rivalry, but it has always been a friendly sort. The United States probably wish to establish some sort of protectorate here, but our government has been content to leave Samoa as an independent nation, a status they are well equipped to sustain, being thoroughly Christian with a developing economy and good education. But then the Germans came along.'

'The German company?'

'Exactly. Now their Emperor is a very ambitious man and it is plain that he wishes to take Samoa as his own possession. To that end they landed troops from five warships last year and used force to set up one of the Samoan chiefs, Tamasese, as King of Samoa. He is a puppet of course and he is King because he will do exactly as the Germans tell him.'

'Does this mean that Samoa is German then?'

'Well it was a coup and the way they act you would think so. I never met such an arrogant and aggressive set of men in my life. Their Consul Becker is…'

Here the British Consul stopped and passed a hand over his brow.

'Well never mind that; the fact is that they have not taken over and the reason is because the Samoans have never had that sort of 'King' that we conceive of in Europe. Most of them do not wish the Germans to take over and they have found a leader in the person of another chief called Mataafa, a Malietoa or Great Warrior. Samoa is in the midst of a civil war Mr MacDonald.'

'A war! I had not noticed anything.'

'No. You probably will not. Here inside the municipality is regarded as a neutral area, though I fear it will not remain so. Outside here, in Samoa proper there are battles between the two sides which are bloody and ruthless.'

'Is it safe here sir? Is that why the warships are here? You need their protection?'

'No Mr MacDonald; we are quite safe. The Samoans have no axe to grind with the British or Americans. They are also a very civilized and mostly gentle people and they have been driven to this by the pretensions of the German Emperor.'

'Gentle? I heard on my last visit that if they take enemies prisoner in battle they cut off their heads.'

'Ah, now that is a misunderstanding.'

This interposition from Mr Davies broke the conversation for a minute or two.

'I cannot see that cutting someone's head off is a misunderstanding,' said MacDonald.

'Oh yes, I see. Yes they did cut off heads, but they did it because of a misunderstanding you see.'

'No I do not see. You are going to have to explain that I'm afraid, sir.'

'Well,' said Davies, looking embarrassed. 'It is true that Samoans used to cut peoples' heads off if taken prisoner and some still do, but it is the fault of the Church that they did so.'

'The Church?'

'I'm afraid so; we are to blame - *mea culpa*. You see some of the early missionaries were very strong preachers and the stories they told conjured up very vivid images in the minds of their congregations. One of their favourites was that of David slaying Goliath and cutting off his head. Another was the death of Saul when the Philistines cut off his head with shouts of wild rejoicing. Taking the Bible literally many Samoans thought that this was Christian practice in battle.'

'You mean that they did not do it before the missionaries came? That is extraordinary.'

'Yes indeed; there are many beheadings in the Bible. The Samoan warriors began to cut off heads and display them to their chiefs who would utter quite artificial but very loud shouts of joy as they thought the Bible instructed them to. The Samoan chiefs were very puzzled over the practice, for it was not one of their customs before we arrived here. We instructed our pastors to explain the error and this has been done so the practice is dying out, but it has not completely disappeared.'

'No it has not,' said Wilson. 'The rebels took some Germans prisoners last year and they were beheaded. The trouble is that such incidents give the Germans excuses to act punitively; and that is what they do.'

'The warships are here to counter the Germans then?'

'Exactly so Mr MacDonald. Last year they brought in five warships and landed a considerable force. They could do so again, but an armed presence from our side holds them in check. Make no mistake, the situation here is very volatile and there is no love lost between the Germans and ourselves. The Americans have established a strong presence in the southernmost island of Samoa and I do not think they will be challenged there, but the Kaiser's men could move to take over here at any time. *HMS Calliope* is here to dissuade them from being foolish, as is the *USS Mohican*. If *Calliope* leaves then it might decide the Germans to make their move.'

'And that is why she cannot go to Palmyra.'

'Indeed. The situation is very critical and I report directly by regular letter to Lord Salisbury himself.'

'The Prime Minister!'

'In person; so you see that in sending a schooner to Palmyra instead of the only available warship, we are serving the higher interests of our Queen and country and defeating the ambitions of a dangerous rival.'

'But the people I left on Palmyra are on a diet that is barely able to sustain them. They will get progressively weaker and their systems will become prey to all sorts of ills. Is there really no way that they can be relieved more rapidly? I really fear for their welfare.'

'I do understand Mr MacDonald; I really do, but my hands are tied and there is nothing more than I can do. Believe me, since I heard the news that you brought, I have been working long hours to prepare a relief for Palmyra with the resources that are available. I realize that the rescue might not be as expeditious as we would all wish, but there is nothing else I can do with what I have. If there were a steamship free then I should send it, but there is not.'

The weariness and determination in the Consul's voice were obvious; he looked tired and his sincerity and openness convinced MacDonald that continued insistence would do no good and would even look churlish. He swallowed an urge to press for more urgency and decided to take a mollifying approach.

'I understand sir. Thank you for explaining; I think I was hasty in my judgment.'

'Not at all, my dear sir; not at all. On the face of it you are quite correct. Those poor people need to be rescued from their predicament as soon as possible; that is what I am doing. However, I have something else to say on this matter.'

'What is that?'

'Let me speak frankly Mr MacDonald. After what you have done, you are in a position that many men would envy.'

'How do you mean?'

'I mean that you have done something incredible; something that is hardly surpassed in the annals of the sea. My admiration knows no bounds and you are in a position to be a very famous man; a national hero.'

'Heaven forfend!' MacDonald was horrified.

'So you are not tempted to be famous Mr MacDonald, to write a book and to be the lion of the year in all the newspapers at home?'

'I am not! That would be an awful thing. Besides, I was only doing my job.'

'I think it was rather more than that, but I am glad that you take that attitude. You see I have a favour to ask.'

'What is that sir?'

'I'd like you to stick to what you think. I'd like you not to speak to the papers and to continue to downplay what you did. You see if a story like this gets onto the front pages all across the world, then the attention of everyone will be on Samoa. If that happens, then it will become a great stage and people will watch what is going on here with keen and eager eyes. It will heat the situation up, for there is nothing more that Emperors like than to strut on the world stage. At this moment Samoa is a small part of the great game. Thrust us centre stage and anything could happen.'

'War, sir?'

'Indeed, war.'

'Be assured Mr Wilson that I shall keep quiet and I will tell my crew-mates that they must do so too. They are close mouthed men; may I explain the circumstances to them?'

'By all means, but also tell them not to bruit it about. This is a great service to your country and an act of self-abnegation that few men would be capable of. In exchange, Mr MacDonald, I shall charge all your comforts to government expense while you are here and do my best to ensure you swift passage home.'

'Speaking for myself, sir, I do not wish to go home: not yet anyway. I want to go with the schooner.'

'Back to Palmyra? But two days ago you could not walk. I think that very unwise.'

'That was lack of food. I'm eating now and getting stronger every hour. I have to go back sir. Please.'

'Really Mr MacDonald, I have to advise very much against it.'

MacDonald decided that a stand was necessary.

'Sir, though I appreciate everything you are doing and I understand why the steamships cannot be asked, I have to insist that I be allowed to go back to Palmyra on the schooner. I gave an undertaking to return to that island with help and I will not break that promise.'

His eyes blazed with fervour and his sincerity and strength of will were apparent. He did not elaborate on the statement; the Consul might not have taken his promise to bring a small girl a dish of brose as seriously as he did. Wilson looked at the intensity of his determination, and conceded the point.

'You have to see this through?'

'Yes sir; I think at least one of my men might wish to go back as well.'

'Very well; I understand. I'll arrange it.'

'Thank you sir.'

'If you go down to the quayside, you will find the schooner *Vindex*, which you are already familiar with; that is the vessel which I have chartered. She actually belongs to one of the Samoan chiefs but he employs a Scot to command her. Captain Bissett, whom you have met, will be on board preparing to sail in two days on 13 May. If you wish to make contact with him, tell him that I have assented to your wish to go to Palmyra with a companion and that I will honour any financial adjustment to our arrangement. He's a reasonable man whom I have dealt with before so he'll be fair. In fact, he is held in much esteem in these parts, Samoans and Europeans alike, for he is a most obliging fellow who will go out of his way to help. Now let me shake your hand Mr MacDonald. No, no; the honour is all mine. I wish you all good fortune and if we do not meet again, then a safe journey home.'

MacDonald was in a much more positive mood when he left the Consul's office in company with Reverend Davies. On the way to the waterfront he said in a neutral tone, 'You were right. I do not like the way the politics affect what I am able to do.'

Davies pursed his lips.

'I don't blame you, but his hands are tied you know. If there were any way to do it quicker then he would do it. I know him well and say that without any hesitation. Please do not think badly of him.'

MacDonald looked at him bleakly.

'I do not. I can see that he has no other choice. I just wish...' and his voice tailed off.

'I know; I do know,' said Davies, patting his arm.

Down at the quay he found the *Vindex*, and now that he was not tired out, and fogged by weakness, found her a tidy little vessel and said so to Captain Bissett when he went on board.

'Yes, she was the pilot schooner for the Auckland Harbour Trust until last year. They decided they wanted a steam craft so sold her off. My owner has a trading company with the islands and is a very big noise around these parts, so here I am.'

'I hear that New Zealand is like Scotland Captain. Is it so?'

'I can understand why you are asking Mr MacDonald. You are from the West I think.' said Bissett, smiling.

'Aye, Lewis; you're a Dundonian from your speech.'

'That's bang on the money; I emigrated down here more than twenty years ago.'

'That old Scottish yearning for foreign parts and new lands to see.'

'You have me right enough.'

'We're a long way from old Scotland now,' said MacDonald.

'True; well in answer to your question, New Zealand is very like Scotland in places but with one vast improvement.'

'An improvement over Scotland? I have a mind to see it.'

'Aye Mr MacDonald; there are no damned midges.'

MacDonald laughed, 'You have a good point there. Now I suggest we turn to more serious matters. Is it not possible to sail sooner Captain?'

'I fear not. I am to take twenty-five people off Palmyra Atoll; as I'm sure you realize, that needs a lot of food, water and bedding. It also calls for supplies of clothes and all sorts of necessities for which the Consul is paying. Frankly, Mr MacDonald, I am amazed at the efficiency that can gather such things together in such a short time. I understand that Mr Wilson has called on the resources of both the US and Royal Navies to get the stuff together so quickly. Believe me, we are doing our best.'

'I know you are and I am ashamed I asked. I'll be here later to take up my berth if you do not mind.'

Back at the mission MacDonald found that his companions had been moved into the hostel and each had a small cabin like room with a bed and a writing desk. He briefed them fully on his conversation with the Consul and explained about the *Vindex*. Then he asked them what they wished to do. For a short while there was silence, then Ned Tumelty spoke.

'If you don't mind, Donald, I think I'll go home. I have no wish to set eyes on Palmyra again and as long as I know the rescue is proceeding I'd like to make my way back home.'

Charlie Anderson and William Crosby were of the same mind. As MacDonald had already figured, Willie Ferguson preferred to see the thing through to the end and go back to Palmyra. After all, his cousin was still on the island and blood is thicker than water.

The following day, 12 May, MacDonald and Ferguson took leave of their erstwhile companions and with small bags containing changes of linen supplied by the mission, they made their way down to where the *Vindex* was still being loaded with supplies and were shown where they would sleep. This voyage was going to be Spartan and rest was to be taken in hammocks; it did not matter. The ship was being laden with all kinds of things in sacks and tins that the people on Palmyra Atoll would be overjoyed to see; portable soup, tinned meat, vegetables, potatoes, tea, chocolate and tinned cake for the children. As dawn came on Sunday 13 May 1888 *Vindex* loosed her moorings, raised sail and began to move seawards towards the mouth of the lagoon. A considerable number of the expatriate community and many Samoans as well, had made their way down to the tiny wharf, for Apia was not yet a very developed harbour, to cheer her on her mission of mercy. The heroism of the venture had caught the imagination of the entire population and there were many shouts of 'good luck' and 'bring them back safely'. The schooner scudded across the calm water inside the reef and the crews on the two warships, who evidently knew their mission, lined the rail of their vessels and as they passed each one they took off their hats and waved them in the air under the eye of their officers. 'Huzzah! Huzzah! Huzzah!'

Vindex made her way out of Apia harbour and began the first of many tacks towards the north east. The rescue was on the way to Palmyra.

Chapter 13

A Captain's Resolution

Ned Tumelty stretched himself luxuriously as he lay in bed four days after MacDonald had sailed in the *Vindex*. He was content with life all things considered, and he had reflected to himself several times that he was a lucky man, for you had to be thankful for blessings received. He had in the space of just over a month, survived a shipwreck, scraped a living on a desert island and made an almost impossible voyage across the Pacific, the like of which would make many seasoned sailors blench. Now that help was on the way to Palmyra he had no worries about the people on the island. He was in a nice hotel room at the expense of the British consulate, as were his companions and it was comfortable with a good bed, painted wooden walls and bamboo blinds keeping out the fierce rays of the tropical sun. It is true that they were not the finest rooms that could be offered by the Tivoli Hotel, but to Ned it was luxurious beyond compare when he thought of his hut on Palmyra Atoll. The sailors' initial stay at the hostel belonging to the English mission had ended after a week when it became obvious that they had recovered their strength sufficiently to allow their rooms to revert to their usual purpose for student missionaries. The Consul had waved away their thanks by deprecating what he was doing, ostensibly in the name of Her Majesty's government.

'You need not worry Mr Tumelty. Your expenses will not be borne by the British taxpayer ultimately. It is my business to look after the interests of British citizens in these islands; *Civis Romanus Sum* and all that, but the Colonial Office is niggardly and cheeseparing in these matters. They will recoup whatever is spent here from your company's insurance you may be sure.'

Ned, like many Scots of his generation, had strong elements of classical Latin beaten into him at an early age with a tawse, so he understood the implications of Reverend Wilson's Latin tag fully. Like all ship-owners, the North British Shipping Company paid a fee to their insurance company, and in return for that any survivors of their crews who fell victim to marine disaster would be returned home as efficiently and cheaply as possible with different rates of assistance according to rank. Tumelty, Crosby and Anderson could not live the life of luxury but they could be expected to subsist to a reasonable standard and get themselves home quickly and economically. The best way to do that was for them to find passage in some ship on a similar circumnavigatory voyage to the *Henry James,* which would not be too difficult for sailors prepared to work their way home.

Walking to his window, Ned opened the blind and looked out across the sweep of the bay. For perhaps two miles along the coastal strip he could see European style buildings in various colours. In and round as well as behind them were luxuriant growths of palm trees, breadfruit, guavas and lush Samoan rainforest. Inland were fertile valleys where grew nutmeg, pineapples, ginger and banyan trees with numerous taro plantations. Tumelty had thought he was dreaming when he saw a pigeon on the street that appeared to have teeth in its bill, but he was assured that he had not been seeing things. After seeing several, he was still fascinated by the sight of what he thought was a kind of squirrel that spread its arms and glided from tree to tree, and he wondered how these flying foxes would be received in Scotland. The air was warm and humid, but tempered by a cooling breeze from the ocean. Above the port a mountain raised its head, covered in trees and overlain with thin patches of rising vapour, which the breeze scarcely appeared to affect. The reef out to sea had a wide gap in it and since the prevailing wind was from the north east, the ocean swell came through it uninterrupted. The harbour was primitive and the quayside small, so most visiting ships moored in the bay where the waves made them roll uncomfortably and the noise of the surf breaking on the beach was constant. For some reason Ned could not account for, when he closed his eyes his mind flew to the shore at Mallaig when he heard the waves crash on the beach, but here there were no midges, just pesky mosquitoes, for which reason you had to sleep with a net over the bed. As far as he could make out this was the only great inconvenience to life in this town.

It was strange to him, but most of the faces he could see on the street were white. There was nothing to hinder Samoans from coming into the municipal area, but most did not unless they had business there, or employment. This might have been because the vicious civil war had entered a lull for the moment, but Ned and his companions had seen no evidence of it. Rumour said that the rebel King Malietoa was amassing large forces for an attack on King Tamasese's army, but things moved at a slow pace and no-one had any idea of when the offensive was to occur. Nonetheless, Ned had been assured repeatedly that the municipal area was safe, whatever happened.

The street running along the shore, which linked all the parts of the town was busy for much of the day. There were sailors, merchants, clerks, priests, ladies looking to shop, strollers and Samoan labourers down by the quay. Out in the bay the harbour was surprisingly busy for the two warships were not its only occupants. They each sat, double-masted with a single funnel and painted black, low, swift, and designed for war; though not large they did have a sinister and dangerous look to them. Ned could see three trading schooners, German cargo ships, a tramp steamer, three barques and a score of Samoan fishing boats. It became easier to understand why it was so bustling when he realized that Apia, though not a good natural harbour, was the only coaling station for steamships for thousands of miles; they had to come here on their journeys across the Pacific and so it became realized that Samoa was of strategic value in the centre of the region. Inside the Eleele sa, the boundary of the neutral zone, he could have been in almost any tropical town in a possession of any of the great empires.

Ned walked downstairs with the idea of asking on the waterfront if any ships were due that might want three experienced seamen. He only got as far as the sidewalk, because all the people who had been wandering the street suddenly crowded onto the sides as a column of Samoan rebels came marching down the street, four abreast and in step. Their upper bodies were bare, well muscled, and many had rubbed themselves over with perfumed oil. Their lower quarters were clothed with the ubiquitous lava-lava, but all were tattooed from the hips to the knees so much that it looked like clothing. Ned had learned that tattoos were necessary for respect. Many of the marching regiment had bleached their hair with lime made from coral, so that it took on a reddish appearance, and each man carried a well cared for rifle. They looked extremely formidable as they marched in silence along the road to where it skirted the shore, and across the water was the fortified area where King Tamasese's men were. They were in plain sight and they knew it, well within gunshot, and near enough to launch a sudden attack if they wished.

'What are they doing? Will there be trouble?' asked Ned of a man standing beside him who was evidently a European resident.

'No, there will be no trouble. They are doing it because they can. It is, if you like, a show of strength and defiance. But there will be no trouble.'

'But how can you be sure, sir? Just one shot would set off a bloodbath here.'

The stranger regarded him with curiosity.

'You evidently have not been in town very long. This is the Eelele sa. Any Samoan who broke the neutrality of this zone would be an outcast from family, from clan and worst of all, from church. This is a demonstration of power. They have a perfect right to march here. It is after all Samoa and their own country.'

'Well notwithstanding that, I have to say my heart is in my mouth.'

'Understandable, but needless I assure you. In a day or so Tamasese's men will hold a similar parade for the same purpose, but nothing will happen.'

'Will this ever be resolved, sir?'

The stranger looked serious.

'I think it will. Germany is determined to possess these islands; Britain and the United States are united in their determination that she will not. It will be resolved, but I think it will require a resort to arms. It will happen sooner or later, I do not know when, but it will only be done through an effusion of blood.'

'That's a great shame, sir.'

'Yes it is. If the great powers would only leave Samoa alone then she'd be just fine. They are a grand people, gentle, kind and civilized. They'd be a good friend and trading partner, but we live in bad times.'

The entire European population of the town consisted of between three and four hundred people, but the place was thriving because they were all in Apia to work, so there was a buzz of activity by day and by night. The place was full of rumours and gossip and people were always looking for something new to talk about. The great exploit that the three seamen had participated in had seized the collective imagination of the entire expatriate community and they had taken Ned and his companions to their hearts. They had not yet had to buy a drink in any of the crowded bars and had to tell the tale of their voyage over and over again, answering a dozen questions from all sides. A generous subscription had been raised so that the survivors had money in their pockets. They had been given donations of clothes, tobacco, drink, shoes, belts and all that they required. The dinner invitations had flooded in and they dined at a different house each night, all social class put aside in the fascination of being in the presence of men who had done something completely heroic. The community in turn found the sailors to have the natural courtesy and diffidence of deep sea mariners and loved them for it. Charlie Anderson, the Dane, was more reserved in company and less willing to talk, whilst Crosby, from Halifax, Nova Scotia was quite ebullient, especially when given a drink. The Europeans usually partied a lot and the current craze was for dancing, the most fashionable of all being for Scottish reels. Dances were held in an assembly room or in the larger houses and were attended by perhaps twenty ladies and thirty or so gentlemen. The dancing itself was conducted with great energy and spirit and dress was kept as tropical and cool as possible with all the windows wide open. The temperature always hovered around eighty degrees Fahrenheit and did not vary much throughout the year. Tumelty and his companions were lucky in that they had not arrived in the wet season that runs from September to March.

Tumelty had been amused to meet a Frenchman at one of these gatherings who seemed at first not to know the difference between him and an Englishman.

'You English wherever you go, always carry your games with you and I feel certain that when I pass to another world, if it should be my bad fortune to be cast into the bottomless pit, I shall find a Scotsman dancing the Highland Fling, and an Englishman a country dance.'

Ned had pondered on this for a moment and replied, 'Ah well now, if that happens it will be because as a nation we

Scots have developed the habit of making the best of a bad thing. In such a way we may often turn it to a good thing. The Englishman is merely copying that habit. At any rate I should hope that you would not be a misery and would join the party.'

The Frenchman laughed and replied, 'Well perhaps I would teach you a farandole, but you might all fall over.'

'Ah well now, that would depend on how much whisky was available.'

'Or absinthe!'

'Aye? I cannot abide it, but each to his own; slainthe!'

'A votre santé.'

Not all of the inhabitants of this far-flung corner of the world were quite as friendly. This is not to say that they were unfriendly, but British society was riven by class divisions. Bill and his two companions may have been part of a story so intrepid that most men could not begin to imagine what they had been through, but Tumelty, Crosby and Anderson were still Able Seamen. Captain Kane of *HMS Calliope* was clearly a fine seaman, but his elevated station and his cut glass accent kept a distance between the sailors and himself. He was keen to hear what they had to say, listened with interest, and asked some very pertinent questions that showed he was a master of his craft, but they did not warm to him. His habit of interpolating their story with, 'Well done my man!' or 'Jolly good show,' brought out a certain hauteur in them as well and they were glad when he made his excuses and went off to talk to someone else. Commander Day of the *USS Mohican* was different. He may have been a graduate of the Annapolis Naval Academy, but he treated Tumelty, Crosby and Anderson as grown-ups and with no hint of condescension. It appeared that he saw not his inferiors in rank, but civilians, citizens of a foreign country and he was polite to them. They in turn warmed to him. Day did more than listen and ask a few sailing points. He was most particular and wanted proper answers to his questions.

'So there are American citizens on the island you say. Four adults and four children?'

'That is correct sir; Reverend and Mrs Taylor with Mr and Mrs Hastings and their four little girls. There's another gentleman in steerage who is American too.'

Day looked shocked.

'But I know them! I had the pleasure of making their acquaintance here just a few short weeks ago.'

'Aye sir; the Reverend has been inspecting missions and schools across the region for some months now.'

'And what is the general condition of their health?'

'When we set out they were in reasonably good health, but the whole party were becoming excessively thin.'

'I gather that the supply of food on the island is not of the best?'

'There is enough to sustain life, sir, but there are no sources of starchy food; there are no fruits or berries of any kind save coconuts and for antiscorbutics they are using pepper grass.'

Commander Day looked very troubled at this and asked a few more questions before making a confession.

'I am very sorry Mr Tumelty that I cannot immediately proceed to Palmyra, but I am expressly commanded to remain on station here.'

'We know that sir, and we understand your reasons.'

'You do?'

'Oh yes, sir. We're not daft though and we are close tongued on some things. Suffice it to say that you are doing your duty and following your orders. We do not think badly of you because of that.'

'I am glad to hear it, because I could be at Palmyra in something like eight days if I could proceed. I wish to help, but may not.'

'Well they are safe enough sir, and the schooner will get there sooner or later.'

'Against the trade winds, Mr Tumelty? At this time of year that could take a month or even more.'

'I do not think the wait will harm them, though it is to be regretted that the rescue could not take place sooner.'

Day looked even more troubled.

'I am in complete agreement with you on that score; if ever I was tempted to disobey my orders I have to say that it is now.'

'Don't do that, sir,' replied Ned cheerfully. 'It isn't worth it. Donald will see them right in the end, just you wait and see.'

Towards the end of Tumelty's twelfth day in Apia a very large four masted barque rode gracefully into the harbour and he exclaimed to his companions,

'If that's no Glasgow built then I'm a Dutchman!'

She proved to be the *Armadale* and she was indeed owned by J & A Roxburgh of Glasgow. Carrying a mixed cargo from the Clyde to New South Wales, just as the *Henry James* had been, she was bound for Portland, Oregon with a cargo of coal. From there she would proceed home via Cape Horn with whatever her agents would supply. Needless to say, three prime seamen, with a story such as they had to tell, had no difficulty whatever in gaining berths, especially as there were two illnesses and one injury among the regular crew. It was not long before Ned Tumelty, Charlie Anderson and Bill Crosby left Samoa and were heading home to Glasgow.

****

Captain Henry Hayward of the *Mariposa* was not shy in announcing his arrival at Pago-Pago, the main town of Tutuila, American Samoa. The *Mariposa's* siren saluted the hills three times, the echoes bouncing round the superb natural harbour which made the town a very welcoming haven for ships of all nations. She was a beautiful iron ship, only a few years old, low lying and sleek, with a clipper stern, and well-named, being "butterfly" in the Spanish language. A single tall funnel soared up perpendicular amidships whilst fore and aft were tall masts with furled sails just in case they needed a more traditional mode of propulsion. The lower part of her hull was black, but the upper strakes and superstructure were all pristine white and pierced with numerous portholes, indicating the presence of dozens of cabins. Her rail was lined with men and women excitedly chattering and pointing at the shore, their voices rippling across the water, laughing and merry. Soon the steamer turned her nose towards the waves and dropped anchor; before too long her shore boats were ferrying the first of many passengers ashore; some because they had reached their final destination and others to see the sights, to shop or just to look around. It was an hour or so before activity around the *Mariposa* became quiet enough for tactful observers to think that those on the ship might have some time to do other things than look after their customers.

It was not too long before a hired boat came out from the shore and a smart young lieutenant ran up the companionway and asked to see Captain Hayward. On being shown to the bridge, he was ushered into the presence of a neat and trim figure in a captain's frock coat and a cheese-cutter hat. The captain had dark hair cut short, and a fine moustache with an air of much strength of character. This was Hayward; the lieutenant handed the captain a letter from Commander Day of the *USS Mohican* then waited whilst he read it. As he did so, his brow furrowed and his concentration became intense.

'Do you know what is in this letter?'

'I think so sir, if it pertains to Palmyra Atoll, but of course I do not know it in full.'

'Indeed. Your commander is of opinion that these people must be taken off that island as soon as possible.'

'Yes sir.'

Hayward's face betrayed furious thought, then after a pause he spoke,

'Thank you Lieutenant Cressop. Commander Day is quite correct and I must do something about this situation, especially as you have come so far to give me this letter. I should be pleased to dine with you on board this ship at 7.00pm this evening if it is convenient to you. There will just be the two of us to start with, but we will be joined by a third.'

Just before seven o'clock that evening a shore boat carried Lieutenant Cressop across to the steamer where he was shown to the captain's cabin.

'Good evening Lieutenant. May I get you a drink? Bourbon perhaps?'

'Thank you sir.'

'Have a seat Lieutenant. I think I may promise you a fine meal shortly.'

'I would much appreciate that sir. Thank you for your invitation. It will be a nice change from the usual navy fare.'

'Now on that I may not comment, never having been in the service, but I hope that our food will be to your liking. We are having a particularly fine ragout, which is a specialty of our chef. I usually dine with the First Class passengers, but this evening I think there are some questions of national security concerning the United States which may come into our discussion so initially we shall dine alone.'

'Initially sir?'

'Yes. Initially. I have on board a very influential passenger, His Grace the Archbishop of Wellington, Doctor Redwood. I have invited him to join us just after eight for brandy and cigars, so I suggest we talk as we eat.'

'You think the Archbishop should be consulted in this?'

'Only in some of it Lieutenant, or he would be here now.'

Hayward pressed a bell and his Steward appeared wheeling a trolley with a savoury smelling collection of dishes; he swiftly served their food and left them to their discussions.

'It's my understanding that there are American civilians as well as other nationalities stranded on that desert island, Mr Cressop.'

'That is correct, sir.'

'An island schooner has gone to take them off along with the other people?'

'The *Vindex*; yes, she sailed twelve days ago with two of the men who made the voyage from Palmyra to here.'

'But that's the point isn't it? She sailed. She's going to have to tack all the way against contrary winds at this time of year. It could take her a month of hard work to get there.'

'I thought it might be nearer to six weeks.'

'Yes; that would not be unrealistic.'

Captain Hayward paced up and down the deck of his cabin, his face working furiously.

'Hell, I could be there in six days, maybe five and a half.'

'Yes sir; I am aware of that.'

'Commander Day stated in his letter that you were unable to go to their assistance owing to matters of national importance. They must be of great consequence if you find yourself forced to ignore the unwritten laws of the sea.'

'Our orders are clear, sir, and we may not leave harbour at Apia until we are relieved.'

'Your ship is only a sloop of war Mr Cressop. Common sense tells me that if these islands are of such importance then your relief will be something of rather larger force.'

'Your inference is correct, sir, and I may tell you I think, for it is common knowledge. The *USS Trenton* and several other units of the Pacific Squadron will be based here for the foreseeable future. She is on the way to Apia right now, having left New York in January, and we anticipate her arrival early next year.'

'The *Trenton*! Now that is a ship of force. Eleven eight-inch guns if I recall, and auxiliary armament in addition; Washington must deem this a very important place.'

'Indeed so Captain Hayward, and a complement of nearly five hundred men, but for the moment *USS Mohican* is the US Navy in these waters and here we must stay.'

'I guess that this is our response to events last year?'

'I believe it is, sir.'

'Then Washington is responding well. Five German warships landing troops and throwing their weight about is a clear declaration of intent. The Kaiser is evidently not shy of thrashing about him with a big stick; he wants his place in the sun.'

'We have a stick too sir.'

'Yes Mr Cressop, and so do the British, hence the presence of the *Calliope*. This little scene has the potential for disaster; war on a world-wide scale.'

'That is my perception also; an unpleasant thought, quite unlike the food. This ragout is delicious.'

'I am glad that you like it; the chef is actually French. Nothing but the best on board the *Mariposa* Mr Cressop; we carry some celebrated people and they expect luxury.'

He paused a moment, collecting his thoughts.

' I can well see why you have to remain in Apia and why the same applies to the British. I take it that the *Adler* is still on station there?'

'She is, sir, though not in harbour.'

'Well of course she does not have to be; the Germans are the proactive ones here; we are merely reacting to what they do.'

'I have no doubt that she is showing force in support of their puppet King somewhere along the coast. The Germans operate in his name you see.'

'I do see,' said Hayward slowly, 'and I also see why it is imperative that you do not leave Apia at least until the *Trenton* gets here. That being so, I have no choice.'

'No choice in what, sir?'

'Your commander cannot leave Apia and neither can the British. Apart from my ship, you are the only powered ships currently anywhere in Samoa at this time. I must take the *Mariposa* to Palmyra Atoll, Mr Cressop. There is no other ethical thing to do.'

'You may get there and find that they have been rescued already.'

'I know that. But I could not sleep if I passed the island knowing that they might still be there. My course runs some thirty miles to the south of Palmyra.'

Hayward mused for a moment, 'That was a hell of a thing; those men did; quite admirable. Just think of it Mr Cressop! 1,300 miles in a launch across the open Pacific; that's seamanship.'

'I agree sir. I have never heard the like of it. Will your owners mind a deviation from your course though? You have a contract to carry the British Royal Mail. I thought they stipulated that passage of mails must be as quickly as possible and without detour?'

'They do Mr Cressop and there are financial penalties attendant on those who default in that respect, up to and including loss of a very lucrative contract, but there is another factor to consider.'

'What is that, sir?'

'Mr John D Spreckels of San Diego, President of the Oceanic Steamship Company and thus owner of this vessel, is an American, and there are Americans in need of help on Palmyra. If I do not take this ship there I think he'd tan my hide and hang it on the wall of his office.'

'You know him well?'

'Yes I do, or at least enough to know that if he did not have my back on this then he would not be a man I would wish to work for. But he is and so I do.'

'When will you sail, sir?'

'I have to keep to my schedules, Mr Cressop. Timetables are important to passengers who might rightly complain if their business was upset by my sailing sooner. There are four passengers to take on here and then I sail at ten o'clock in the morning, the day after tomorrow.'

'I trust your passengers will not mind the variation in route.'

'Ah now, that is where His Grace comes in.'

'The Archbishop of Wellington?'

'The very man, and a very popular fellow aboard this ship, for he is as sociable and as decent a person as you could possibly meet. He also has the finest beard I have ever seen in my life.'

'You are enlisting his aid?'

'I certainly am. If anyone can convince the passengers that it is worth adding a possible day to their journey in order to rescue some castaways, then it will be him.'

'I am certain they will need no convincing, sir.'

'I do not share that certainty Mr Cressop. In many regards the *Mariposa* is very much removed from being a normal passenger ship.'

In response to a querying eye from Cressop, Hayward continued,

'You see, although we do carry a number of second class and steerage passengers we deal mainly with what you might call the luxury end of the passenger market. We carry some very rich people indeed, those who want to travel in style. We also carry important men in the worlds of business and commerce. Some of them are on schedules and they have affairs to conduct which rely on the departure and arrival dates of this ship. It is no exaggeration to say that a delay in the arrival of the *Mariposa* at Honolulu or San Francisco could cost fortunes. I have to bear that in mind Mr Cressop, because if my company got a name for unreliability, then it could prove disastrous.'

A soft tap on the door was unheard by Hayward who continued his discourse, unaware that Archbishop Redwood had entered the cabin behind him.

'You get all sorts on a passenger carrying vessel at sea and some of them are not as accommodating as I might wish. I am reasonably certain that I can deviate from my course enough to pick these people up and still meet my scheduled arrival time in Honolulu, but some folks can be mighty irascible about such unplanned events and I do not want some touchy millionaire complaining about deviations from advertised itineraries. You think that it might not happen, but I assure you that it can, and the consequences may not be thought on. I do not wish my owners to be sued for loss of contracts or business. I suspect you'd be surprised by the sort of thing that can happen on board the *Mariposa*, but diplomatic handling and a little foresight can head off potential problems before they arise.'

'That sounds fascinating Captain Hayward; I do hope that you will elaborate on that for me.'

'But of course, Your Grace,' replied Hayward, not put out at all, swinging round to shake his visitor's hand. 'I am always ready to talk about my ship and I did not want this young man thinking that life on board a civilian vessel was uninteresting. Allow me to introduce Lieutenant Cressop of the US Navy.'

The newcomer, a man in his late forties with dark hair and a large and very impressive square-cut beard, beamed and held out his hand to the firm shake of the Lieutenant. Once the introductions were made, the Bishop continued in the line of conversation that had already started.

'So tell me, Captain, of some moments which have enlivened the routine of life on board your ship. I have to say from what I have seen that all runs very smoothly, whereas Lieutenant Cressop serves on a ship of war, which by her existence means that she is exposed to death and disaster all the time.'

'Now there I have to differ Your Grace. I regret to say that death and disaster are no strangers to the *Mariposa* though I could wish otherwise.'

'Indeed? Please tell us what happened.'

'Less than two years ago one of the boiler tubes was displaced and blew the fire out of the furnace. Five men were scalded and two of them died. There was no confusion or excitement among the passengers or crew, but I have to say that we are, civilian ship or not, subject to the same vagaries of life and death as is the lot of any vessel at sea.'

'Ah yes; we are all subject to the accidents of life.'

'Yes Your Grace; such things can happen on any steamship at sea, but when they do it is not pleasant.'

'To say the least; I cannot think that there would be too many fatalities though. Have you any other anecdotes of a less deadly nature to relate?'

'I have Your Grace, but first I would like to let you in on some details of a problem facing us at this very moment?'

'I am all ears, Captain,' said the gratified prelate.

Carefully leaving out all details of power politics and international relations, Hayward made the Bishop aware that a group of people had been shipwrecked and were in need of succour and that he wished to make a detour from course to do so.

'Let me guess, Captain' said the delighted Archbishop, 'You wish me to speak with our fellow passengers and, as you Americans say so figuratively "square" it with them?'

'That's about it sir. I wish them to know what is going on and that we shall be about a life saving mission.'

'This is utterly unexpected and quite thrilling. I little thought that my journey to San Francisco would lead to such an adventure. Of course my dear Captain Hayward, you may depend on me to use all my influence, such as it is, to persuade my fellow passengers to accept the lengthening of their journey without demur. But I am sure that the thrill of it would be enough; there will be no dissent and they will all be delighted!'

'I do hope so Your Grace; there are businessmen among our guests to whom time is money. I hope that they may be brought to an understanding of the necessity of this.'

'Leave it to me Captain. They shall be like lambs believe me. You say that the Reverend Taylor is on the island with his family. They are well-known and I had the pleasure of meeting them at the hot baths in New Zealand some months ago where they took the waters. Of course we must go to their rescue; it is quite out of the question that we would not.'

Shortly afterwards Cressop took his leave of Hayward and the Archbishop, well satisfied that Commander Day back at Apia on the *USS Mohican* need no longer worry about the people stranded on Palmyra. Punctually, at 10.00am on Wednesday 23 May 1888, the *Mariposa* hauled up her anchor and headed out into the open sea. Captain Hayward let it be known that his aim was to reach Palmyra Atoll in the morning of 29 May if at all possible. The entire ship buzzed with excitement. Hour by hour the beautiful steamer cut through the water at twelve knots, eating up the miles, many on board quite shamelessly wishing that they would get there before the schooner they knew had mounted a rescue. The big question eating at all their minds was what would they find when they got there.

Chapter 14

Dissent

Three weeks after MacDonald's departure, Lattimore woke one morning and began what was now his routine task. It is in the nature of human beings to appreciate variety in what they do and Lattimore knew well the consequences of monotony; he did not wish people to become bored and to lose hope, perhaps succumbing in the end, not to hunger but to lethargy. He had divided the company into work groups for the purposes of foraging, but he had also divided Palmyra into zones or beats for them to operate in. It was his custom to change the beats each day so that ennui did not set in, variety being the spice of life. Breakfast consisted of what was left in the pot from the previous evening, and consequently was a very light meal. Leaving the hut he shared with Crone, Campbell the sail-maker and MacDonald the carpenter, he found his crew and passengers gathering outside. Looking them over he was heartily sorry what they had come to but there was no help for it. Every one of them was showing the signs of the diet they were eating and were painfully thin. The sun had burned them all a deep brown, flecked with chronic peeling and some of them had open red sores caused by blisters and sun damage, against which they had no protection save the crude palmetto hats they had woven. Sunburn had caused agony for many in the first few days after the shipwreck. Some of their feet were in a woeful state because the rags and leaves which they had bound them with on their first arrival on the island easily fell to pieces and were not much protection against the sharp rocks of the coral they had to clamber over in their search for food. What was left of their clothing was disintegrating in the humidity of the climate. The person that Lattimore had most unease about was Mrs Hastings. Although she was excused foraging, her diet had been more or less the same as that of the rest of the castaways, though she had been given meat, and the great fear that hovered over all was that she might lose her baby. Her abdomen was distended in the way that a woman seven months pregnant should be, but the rest of her body was in sharp contrast as her face had grown sharp, her ribs could be discerned plainly and her arms were as thin as sticks. The tinned meat was now all gone, and there was nothing else that she could be given to sustain the new life growing inside her. How much longer she would be able to last was anybody's guess, but although it was unspoken everyone expected her to miscarry at any time. The future of her unborn child, and perhaps of herself, depended on rescue as soon as possible.

Lattimore did not want to admit to himself that he worried for the safety of all the people on the island in the way that they might not survive. There was a fear in his mind that the whole party might die, their bones to be found bleached and dry by some crew of a passing ship. Nonetheless, his mind had acknowledged it to a degree and manifested it in his wishing to manufacture a memorial so that those who found them would know who they were. As with all island Palmyra had flotsam and jetsam washed up on the beach and among the detritus of the sea one day was a small plank of wood, probably a relic of some wrecked vessel. The captain knew something of carving from his youth, helping in the stone masons' yard; it was easy for him to use his sheath knife to cut into the timber the following inscription in fine Roman letters:

R LATTIMORE. Barque. Henry James. Glasgow.
Newcatle. To. Frisco. Wrecked on . Reef
NW 35. Miles. 20. Crew. 10 Passengers
Ap.16/88.   Landed. Ap. 17.
Left. Here.

His distraction of mind may be gauged by his omission of the s from Newcastle, and no sooner had he done it than he saw it and cursed softly under his breath. Figuring that whoever found the inscription would know what he meant, he decided to leave it as it was. The end he left blank and wondered if he would ever fill it out. Reverend Taylor saw the plank but said nothing, contenting himself with a wry smile and a grunt as he patted Lattimore's shoulder. The captain stored it out of sight in his hut.

Most of the survivors now complained of headaches and constipation; some had the opposite and suffered diarrhea. Not one man or woman among them was as strong as they had been and yet Lattimore knew that they had to go out again and not come back until each of them had something to put into the pot. Whilst they ate then they would maintain a certain level of strength that they should not fall below. The only way that they were going to get off the island alive was to work together and there could be no passengers in that endeavour, except Mrs Hastings by virtue of her condition. On the positive side, no-one had any serious illnesses, they looked very bad superficially, but on the whole they were in surprisingly good shape.

'Good morning Shearer.'

'And to you Captain,' responded the Able Seaman.

'I think today you and your group will have the rocks on the western part of this island.'

'Aye sir; thank you.'

Hugh Shearer accompanied by McClements, Burns and Donnell began to walk out of the area by the huts when Lattimore stopped them.

'Hold up a moment. Where is Lancaster? He's in your team.'

Shearer hesitated then replied, 'Aye he is, just as you told him, but if it's all the same to you, sir, we can do without him.'

'What do you mean?'

Shearer looked at the other men and Burns nodded at him.

'Best tell the Captain, Hugh.'

Reverend Taylor, who had been hovering waiting to speak to Lattimore, came closer so that he could hear better, sensing trouble.

'Fact is, sir, that we don't want him. He's a lazy bugger and he don't pull his weight.'

'In what way does he not pull his weight?'

Patrick Burns interpolated, 'When we gather food, sir, and bring it back, the fact is that he's hardly looking and some days he gets nowt.'

'Well, what on earth is he doing if he's not looking for food?'

'To be frank, sir, he's malingering. We think he doesn't like being out in the sun and he stays as far as he can in the forest shade.'

'But you can't do that if you are supposed to be scouring the rocks. I thought he was going to be invaluable after he caught those birds on our first day here.'

'So did we sir, but the birds are a lot more wary than they were. I think they see us as hunters now and if we try to go near them these days they fly away squawking.'

'It's true,' said Lattimore. 'I've noticed that myself. We are having to go further and further to find birds we can get near now. There have been very few in the pot for this last week. So what has he brought back in the last few days?'

'A couple of red land crabs sir; that's it.'

'That is all Shearer? But they are everywhere; it's hardly a day's work to catch so little.'

'No sir.'

'So in reality, when you bring back what you have found and give it to Thomas Morgan, sometimes he has not contributed to your finds at all?'

'That's right sir.'

'And that's why you'd rather not have him in your team? He's been eating what other people have found and putting little back?'

'That's about it sir. He's a wrong'un and we can do without him. Summat else sir; if he's not contributing he should not be eating. It ain't right what he's doing.'

'I see. Well thank you for your frankness. I can see that I shall have to tackle him about it.'

'Aye sir.'

Shearer's group once again made to walk off, but Burns stopped and turned round to add something else to the information already given.

'Best to let you know, sir, that he's gotten really thick with Michael O'Flaherty.'

'Best to let me know? Why?'

Burns pursed his lips, 'Maybe nothing sir, but O'Flaherty has always had a mind of his own so to speak, and views sir.'

'Views?'

'Aye sir; I'd rather not say more. Nowt may come of it.'

'I see. Well thank you for telling me. Where is he now?'

'Lying in the hut, sir. He won't get up.'

'Will he not?' asked Reverend Taylor.

'No, Reverend, he will not. He says he's too tired to go foraging today.'

'Too tired?'

'Yes Reverend.'

'Well hang it all, but we are all tired.'

'I know sir. But that's what he said.'

Burns moved off and the other foraging parties dispersed as Lattimore directed them to various places for that day.

'Well Ralph,' said Taylor. 'What are you going to do? You can't let it go. Our little society functions only because of mutual cooperation and if that breaks down…'

'Anarchy,' said Lattimore grimly.

'Indeed, and anarchy is something we cannot afford.'

'Well William, I'd be glad of any suggestions you may have.'

'Short of going in there and kicking his ass out of bed?'

'It crossed my mind.'

'I'll talk to him,' said Taylor firmly. 'Order must be preserved and I think some reminding him of his sense of duty is necessary.'

'I'd be glad if you did. He's a strange man and I think that in his case persuasion may have more effect than ordering him.'

Taylor looked at him wisely, 'You must be head honcho, Ralph. Someone has to be, for all of our sakes. There has to be order because without it we could all starve.' Then he went off to find Lancaster.

Lattimore followed him with his eyes and reflected that the Reverend had changed his position slightly in a few weeks and was no longer so insistent on his own independence of action. The virtues of cooperation had evidently impressed themselves on his mind.

Entering one of the low huts Reverend Taylor adjusted his eyes to the gloom out of the bright sun, and found William Lancaster lying on a sort of palliasse made of palm fronds piled together.

'Good morning Reverend. Have you come for a pastoral chat? It's the first time I've seen you in here.'

'I have had no reason to enter your hut before, Mr Lancaster. It's a private space belonging to you and your messmates so I have respected that.'

'Oh very obliged I'm sure, but they are not my messmates you know. I was never crew on the ship; you may have heard that I was a stowaway.'

'Yet you worked your way to Australia and then on to here. You have a capacity for hard work it seems.'

'When I have a mind to Padre, but sometimes I don't feel like it, so I don't bother.'

'Like today?'

'Oh, you mean I have not gone out foraging. That's right. I don't feel like it.'

'May I ask why?'

'You may; and I may answer, and in fact I will. It's hot out in that sun and I am most fearfully burnt and have no desire to get even more burnt. I also have a headache and may go out later to find something, but right now I am more inclined to stay right here in the shade. Why are you not out foraging Reverend?'

'Because I am here talking to you; when I'm done I shall go.'

'Then perhaps you do not need to talk to me. Maybe you should be off about your hunting for a morsel to eat.'

'To be truthful, I heard that you were not going out and I wondered why.'

'Well now you know, though it is my business and nobody else's.'

'I never said that it was, Mr Lancaster, but I now think that it is.'

'And how is that?'

'You say that you may go out to forage later and yet you may not. What do you eat tonight if you do not?'

'I daresay that there will be enough in the pot for all.'

'You would eat food that other people gathered and yet not put in anything yourself?'

'Sure, why not? We all do it all of the time.'

'How do you mean?'

'Oh come on Reverend. That's the way the world works. There are rich people all over the globe who do not a stroke, yet are quite happy to eat the food and spend the money which is generated by other people. If there's enough in the pot for all, then what does it matter where it came from or who gathered it?'

'It matters to me. If I go out in the sun and gather food then why should you, an able bodied man quite capable of fending for himself, enjoy the fruits of my labours?'

'Are you arguing that a boss should not enjoy the fruits of the workers in his factory? Or that the landowner should not enjoy the fruits of his tenants' labours?'

'No, of course not.'

'Indeed you are not. That would be upsetting the natural order of the world. If men are not allowed to get away with no effort all their lives and to live off the work of others, then it would be a scandalous thing would it not?'

'You are turning my words around.'

'No I'm not, Reverend. The world works in exactly that way. I read a book not long ago called Capital by a man called Karl Marx. The whole system of the world works on people exploiting other people. Well I don't buy it. If they are happy to live off the work of others then so am I.'

'But that's just laziness and hypocrisy.'

'Good gracious Reverend, you sound like a revolutionary.'

'But can't you see man that if everyone acted as you do, there would be no food in the pot at all?'

'Of course I see that, but the fact is that they don't. And until they do, I see no point in exerting myself. If I feel like gathering food later then I shall do so. If I do not then I won't.'

'And you'll still line up for your food tonight? What if the others don't want you to eat what they have brought?'

'Then I suppose I will have to appeal to their Christian charity.'

'Christian charity? How does that work?'

'You're asking me Reverend? My, my. Are you telling me that you'd see a man starve or go hungry in front of your eyes? I shall plead incapacity through lethargy brought on by bad diet, and to their pity.'

'You'd use their religion and their pity to take from them what they have garnered and do nothing for them in return?'

'Of course. We all have to eat, Reverend Taylor.'

'We'll see about that you lazy bastard!'

Thomas Morgan had been just outside the door and had heard every word. Now he swept into the hut and in Cumbrian style, spoke his mind.

'Them as doesn't work and is able to, doesn't eat. I would not mind if you were ill or injured or crippled. It's a poor society that can't look after its weakest, but you're just an idle bugger and if you come near the pot tonight without putting summat in then just watch out. I'll chop your bloody fingers off. You wait and see.'

After Thomas had left, fuming with indignation, Taylor continued,

'You have to see his point. You've been rumbled by the people whose work you propose to exploit. What are you going to do now, if you don't gather for the pot?'

'I may have to make my own arrangements, a contingency I have been giving some thought to.'

'Declare independence from the rest of us?'

'Why not? You Americans did it not so long ago. I think I'd be able to shift for myself quite well.'

'Is that not rather selfish?'

'We are all selfish Reverend. Every human being is a selfish creature and we all do what we do for our own interest.'

'Nonsense. What about love, altruism, the desire to serve mankind?'

'All done for our own convenience, Reverend.'

'And what about God? Do you think he sees and hears you now and approves of what you are saying and doing?'

Lancaster smiled blandly at him.

'Happily Reverend I am not troubled by belief in any deity, so your God need not trouble himself with my concerns.'

Taylor got to his feet in high indignation, 'An atheist!'

'At your service, Padre.'

'You damned well ain't. Now I know why I have not seen you pray.'

'Nor will you. Your God is a fairy tale conjured up to scare the credulous and dun them into compliance with fears of hell and devils.'

'Just who the hell are you? You ain't no ordinary working man.'

'I never claimed to be, Reverend Taylor. You may have taken it for granted that everyone on this island was of your congregation, but we are not. And I am no ordinary working man, I agree, because I work when I have to in order to live.'

'I meant in your education.'

'Now that's a compliment; thank you. Yes, I went to a good school. They threw me out at age sixteen when they found me with my hand up the skirts of the headmaster's daughter. He told me that I would never amount to much. I fear he may be right.'

'I know he was!' bellowed Taylor and stormed out.

On the edge of the clearing Lattimore was waiting and saw the Reverend come out in a state of anger.

'At a guess I would say that you have not succeeded.'

'I have not! The man is an atheist and a thoroughly selfish individualist. Damned son of a bitch! He is as completely self regarding as the most dyed in the wool Republican I have ever met!'

'The last I will take your word for Reverend, for I have no experience at all of American political ideology, but I think I probably have to go and talk to him.'

'I think you must. But Captain, reasoning will not work.'

Taylor briefly outlined Lancaster's views on the world and work and when he had done Lattimore made a wry face.

'The direct approach it is then.'

Without waiting for a reply he got up, walked into Lancaster's hut, accompanied by Bruno and stood by where Lancaster was lying, the dog panting beside him.

'Get up now and go join the rest of your party foraging.'

'I don't think I will, Mr Lattimore.'

'I am giving you an order, and it's Captain Lattimore to you.'

'You can't give me orders, Captain, as I think you know. We are not onboard ship and I am not a member of your ship's company.'

For a moment Lattimore was nonplussed.

'I command here and you worked on my ship.'

'The last part is correct, but I was not of your company. You logged me as "stowaway" did you not? I signed no contract to obey you, though I was prepared to work my passage. You had a right to command my work and obedience on board ship, but not here Mr Lattimore. Captain you may be to others, but not to me.'

So here it was, the challenge to his authority that he had feared. Lattimore swallowed and asked hoarsely, 'Are you going to obey my orders or not?'

'I am not. I am under no compulsion to do so, and you know something else Captain? I don't believe that any of the other people here are bound to do so either. Legally, I wonder how it would stand in a court of law. I don't know. Do you?'

Lattimore could not answer him directly, because he did not know either.

'But hang it man, can you not see that we are better together in the face of this? That we live by our communal efforts? If this group falls apart then there may be insufficient food and people may die. We have to act and work together.'

Lancaster smiled.

'Well, I know that's what you think, but I do not agree.'

'We have women and children to provide for.'

'They are not my responsibility, Mr Lattimore. On this island as anywhere else the only person I am responsible for is me and those I choose to take responsibility for.'

'But you'll eat food that others gather.'

'Indeed. But I do not ask them to. They are not responsible for me either.'

'And Mrs Hastings? And the children?'

'Are their own responsibility or those of her husband; certainly not mine.'

'It is possible,' mused Lattimore, 'That you may be the most selfish man I have ever met.'

'I doubt that Mr Lattimore. Tell me, have you ever read any Jeremy Bentham?'

'The philosopher? I have heard of the man but not read him.'

'He wrote that any community is a fictitious entity. All it is, is the sum of the interests of the people in it. In other words, the only reason individuals group together is for mutual advantage. He also thought that any human action is made for selfish means and that what governs what we do is not love of God or families or relations, but pain and pleasure.'

'Pleasure?'

'That which gives us advantages he called "pleasure". If it disadvantages us then it is "pain". This is the underpinning philosophy of some of our great political organizations; the

Conservative Party in Britain and the Republican Party in the United States.'

'So to you there is no community; only individuals who come together to help themselves.'

'That is correct.'

'But that is exactly what we are doing here.'

'Indeed it is.'

'Then why will you not forage?'

'Because I choose not to. I do not march to your drum Mr Lattimore. I never have marched to that drum. I march to my own. Since I see no gain from going out into the blazing sun to bake and cut my feet on the coral, I shall not do so. I shall wait here and take my ease.'

'And eat from the pot?'

'Maybe.'

'That would be contemptible.'

Lancaster looked at Lattimore, smiled faintly and shrugged.

'Would it be as contemptible as a captain who was asleep in bed when his ship ran onto the rocks? Or as a man who was responsible for my being on this godforsaken place but still thought that he had the power and the moral right to order me around?'

His words hit Lattimore like a punch to his gut, pouring petrol onto the flames of his own guilt in losing his ship. Lancaster looked at him with a faint sneer, then he lay back on his bed and closed his eyes. Lattimore stared at him; rationally he knew that there was nothing he could have done to save his ship, but the words had been targeted to hurt, and they twisted in his head like a knife. There was nothing he could say that he trusted himself with so he looked at Lancaster with a final glance of disgust then walked out to where Reverend Taylor waited.

'Any luck?'

'No. He's staying in there and it seems there's nothing I can do about it.'

'What happens if everyone here takes his attitude?'

Lattimore grimaced, 'Then I think people will start to die of hunger. Let's go and hunt for food.'

The only hut that did not have any permanent occupants sleeping in it was the fire hut, where a small blaze was kept going all the time. When Lattimore came back to camp that evening with two fish that he had succeeded in spearing, he found that Lancaster had moved his palliasse out of the hut he had been sharing and placed it along the inside of the fire hut. When he queried this arrangement Lancaster pointed out that the huts had already been there when the survivors landed and they did not belong to anyone. Lancaster did not feel like sharing a hut with men who did not like him, so had moved out of there and into this one, as he had a perfect right to do. Lattimore did not press the point.

The first crisis came at mealtime just after six in the evening. Lancaster walked towards the communal pot holding a stick. Thomas Morgan and a group of other men saw him coming and stood in front of him with faces like stone.

'You don't put in Lancaster, then you don't take out. Simple as that.'

'Are you offering me violence, Thomas?' asked Lancaster.

'If he ain't, then I am,' said Thomas McClements.

'No need,' answered the stowaway. 'Fire, I take it, being an element, is free?'

Morgan looked at him and nodded. Lancaster held his stick in to the fire until it was well ablaze and walked away down the beach.

'What's he up to?' asked Reverend Taylor to Lattimore. 'He could have lit that in the hut.'

'I think he was making a point.'

'What point?

'Just watch.'

As they watched, further along the beach Lancaster held the blazing brand he carried to a heap of wood that he had evidently piled up before; he had been out that day. His fire shone out in the gathering gloom as he walked out onto the rocks jutting into the sea. The fish came closer into the shore towards evening and from somewhere that he had previously placed it, he took out a long forked branch whose two points he had sharpened. Within a few minutes he had speared two fish that were soon cut open, gutted, and roasting on sticks beside the fire.

'Well he's done it. He's declared independence. He does not have to speak to us or contribute or work in any way.'

'Yes William,' breathed Lattimore quietly, 'and if any of the others decide to follow suit then we may be in serious trouble.'

The following morning Michael O'Flaherty, one of Lattimore's crew, refused to forage and moved his palliasse into the fire hut to keep Lancaster company. Lattimore was furious and ordered O'Flaherty to get out and hunt for food. The reply he got made it clear that O'Flaherty had been well schooled. Lancaster lay on the other side of the hut, listening and expressionless.

'I will not go out Captain Lattimore. We are not on board ship now. I have no more to obey your orders than I would if you met me walking down Sauchiehall Street.'

'Damn it man, you signed on for the duration of the voyage.'

'Sure Captain, I did that right enough, but you see the voyage is over. The ship is sunk.'

'You are being paid to follow my commands.'

'I was paid up until the moment the ship sank. Are you telling me, on the Bible Captain, that my time will be paid for by the company now?'

'I can't tell you that; I will press for it though, I assure you.'

'But you cannot warrant it. I will be content with what is due to me up to the time of sinking Captain, but I will not follow your orders now.'

Lattimore tried the same arguments he had with Lancaster, but to no avail. O'Flaherty went further than the stowaway had though.

'You're from Carrickfergus and then Larne aren't you, Captain?'

Lattimore allowed that he was.

'Proddy country that, Captain; now me, I was born in Dungarven. That's not Proddy country; it's not far from Mitchelstown. Did you hear what happened there last year?'

'Vaguely, but nothing of detail.'

'Well, there was a rent strike going on there and a protest meeting was held. Some friends of mine were there to hear what was said. The Police wanted to take notes and tried to force their way through the crowd by beating people with truncheons. When sticks and stones were thrown at them they opened fire and killed two men.'

'What's this got to do with you not foraging?'

'Everything; you're a fine seaman and a good captain, I'll give you that. But I give you just one example of what Protestant domination has done to my own people to show you that it does not sit easy with me to take orders from Protestants.'

'Then why did you ship with me?'

'For the same reason as everyone else, Captain, and it was not for love or respect for your person. I needed to earn money. Well here we are on dry land, I have pay coming to me when we get home for the work I did and I'll take no more orders. Out of respect to your fairness to me personally I am willing to entertain requests in future, but not today. Today I do not feel like foraging. A good day to you now, sir.'

Lattimore walked out and back to Taylor and told him what had happened. Then he gathered together John Crone, John Campbell, John MacDonald and Mr Hastings for a discussion with himself and Taylor. Quickly he set out what was happening with the two men who were refusing to forage; then he asked for their thoughts on the matter. No-one replied instantly, but eventually John Crone broke the silence.

'I think, sir, that we may be in danger of making too much of this.'

'In what way?'

'I mean that we outnumber them, sir. There are enough of us to forage and to keep the pot going to provide for those that contribute.'

'But Lancaster stated that he would happily eat food gathered by others.'

'Aye sir,' growled John MacDonald. 'But in order to do that we have to let him and frankly if he tries then there will be trouble.'

'Violence you mean?'

'Oh yes Captain,' said John Campbell. 'We are not stupid men and have been talking about this among ourselves. We are united in our thought that if any able bodied man contribute to the pot then he shall eat, but if he does not contribute then he shall not eat; not at our expense. We won't stand for that.'

'The choice is his, sir,' said John MacDonald. 'If he tries to take what others have gathered, then I for one shall knock his block off.'

'And you will not be alone in that,' said Campbell.

'I cannot condone violence,' said Reverend Taylor.

MacDonald looked at him with a twinkle, 'Aye well you don't have to condone it Reverend; but whether you do or not it may happen.'

Lattimore had to be sure, 'And you say most of the crew feel this way?'

'Oh yes, Captain,' replied Campbell. 'Be in no doubt, sir. We are alive and likely to stay that way and we know it is because we work together. That's what a good crew needs to do, and with a good captain to order things. That's the way we like it sir. Shipshape. Besides, there is another thing to consider.'

'What is that?'

'Custom and practice of the sea, sir; I don't want to sound like a sea-lawyer, Captain, but I would think it normal and usual for a crew to continue to obey lawful commands in situations such as we find ourselves in. The other way leads to chaos and we don't want that.'

'And the steerage passengers?'

'The Americans? Very much into team work, sir; they'll be fine.'

'So you see,' said John Crone, 'I think we can just ignore those two. We don't actually need them, and I assure you that if either of them gets into trouble and needs help then they will pretty soon come crawling back. That's when all their individualism flies out of the window and they start whining. You see they want to do things all their own way - until they need you.'

The short meeting broke up and Lattimore strolled away in company with Taylor.

'Do you feel better now Ralph?'

'I do, I confess that I do. For the moment at least.'

'I think what John said was much to the point. We can last indefinitely here so long as a group of us hold together.'

'Yes,' Lattimore replied, turning to face him. 'But the cracks in our little community are all too evident.'

Turning to face the sea he continued, 'Much depends on Donald. I wonder if he made it. Where is he now?'

'Your guess is as good as mine, but it is the main question in all our minds. Indeed, where is MacDonald?'

Looking out towards the night horizon they saw the lights of no ships and so both men turned and walked back slowly to the huts, deep in their own thoughts.

Chapter 15

Full Steam Ahead!

'She sails well today David.'

'She does Donald. I find it hard to think that you have never shipped on board a schooner before now.'

'I never have. Coal boats, coasting vessels, brigs and barques but not a schooner. This one is big for the name.'

'Two hundred and eighty tons, ninety feet long and a total crew of fifteen for this trip; I usually only have ten, but there's a bit more work this time.'

'You can say that again. I did not imagine having to go back to Palmyra close-hauled and tacking all the way. We cannot be making more than about forty miles a day at the most.'

'Thirty-three and nine tenths by my reckoning; that's pretty good going, Donald.'

'Aye. I ken weel that it is for any sailing vessel, but I cannot help thinking that a steamboat would be there by now. We are nine days out of Apia and we have done about three hundred and sixty miles. There's a mighty long way to go David, and no guarantee that we can keep up this rate.'

'I'll not dispute that, but there was no steamship able to do it, so this is what you get.'

'Oh I'm not complaining. I know very well that this is a pretty good rate of progress; I'm a sailing man myself remember. I'd wager though that you were not prepared to make a voyage like this at this time of year.'

'You'd win the bet. I would not go out of my way to sail into the teeth of the nor' easterlies at this time of year. I was expecting to ship a hold full of copra and have a fast run down to Wellington.'

'And from there?'

'Oh, I was going to have a couple of weeks off, Donald. I have a wife and daughter there and I do not see as much of them as I would wish.'

'Well that's the curse of a sailing man's life, I fear.'

'Have you anybody waiting Donald?'

'I do. It's my Aunty Margaret who is a very strict woman. She always makes me swear to get home safe and I'm quite afeared of what she might do if I do not obey her. She's a very willful sort of wifie.'

Bissett laughed.

'That's good advice; get home safe. You're a prudent man then? Given what you did in getting to Samoa, I find that hard to believe.'

'I think I am. I try to be at any rate. Perhaps I do not always succeed.' MacDonald stopped for a moment and sniffed. 'You'll pardon my ignorance I hope, but why is dried coconut so important round here?'

'Bissett smiled. 'The copra is used in Wellington for a number of things. I think a lot of what I take goes to make soap, but it's also pressed for oil for cooking and all sorts of things. Chemists use it too, I gather.'

'It's valuable then?'

'No, not really; it's of low value in itself, but in bulk it fetches a good price. That's why the Germans cultivate thousands of acres of it on Samoa.'

'I gather they'd like to take the place over.'

'They would Donald but I hope they do not succeed. I think they'd be bad masters if they had the run of the place.'

'Would we be better?'

'I doubt it. Samoa is a place best left to its own devices. We don't need them and they don't need us. I have always found them a delightful people.'

'Even when they are killing each other in a civil war.'

'Aye, well now Donald, I think there is a very good chance that war would not be going on if it were not for outside interference.'

'How do you mean?'

'The Samoan idea of "King" has never meant what it means to people in the European world. Our King was the boss, the ruler, the maker of laws. In Samoa there have always been chiefs in different areas and a very complicated system of clan loyalties. If you were a chief then you might collect names that signify that you have the loyalty of an area. Get enough names and you can call yourself "King." Malietoa's given name for example is Mataasa. "Malietoa" means "Great Warrior" and only one chief can hold that name. His rival is Tamasese and he would love to have that name.'

'It all sounds rather complex.'

'It is; and the Germans, Americans and British putting their oars in, training and arming the factions is no help at all. Left to their own devices it would probably have all been sorted out years ago, because Samoans are strong Christians and prefer peace.'

'You know the place well.'

'I do. I'm not sure which I prefer; here or Fiji, where I worked for a number of years bringing in indentured labour to work on the cotton plantations.'

'That's why there are so many hammock hooks below.'

'Correct.'

'Where did you get them from?'

'India; contracted for five years.'

'A lucrative trade?'

Bissett shrugged, 'A living Donald, and that's about it. It pays my wages and keeps my owner happy.'

'And you?'

'I'd rather carry timber. A lot less trouble than human beings, I assure you.'

'I can believe it.'

'Right; if you'll excuse me, it's time to change tack.'

'Something he doesn't have to worry about!'

'Who? Oh I see. You've good eyes.'

Far far to the south Bissett and MacDonald saw a column of smoke reaching up from under the horizon. The ship making the plume was not visible and they watched it for a few minutes as the schooner's crew altered the angle of her sails and she heeled over onto her new course, zig-zagging ever north north eastward on her way to Palmyra.

'That's the future.'

'You think so, Donald?'

'I'm much afraid that I do, though Willie might not agree with me.'

He nodded forward to where Willie Ferguson perched on a hatch cover chatting to some of the schooner's crew.

'You would not wish to work on one?'

'I'm realistic, David. If I need work and I am offered a position on one then I shall take it; but I have to say that my heart belongs to sail.'

The two men watched and eventually turned to their own affairs. After an hour or so the smoke had disappeared and the unknown steamship was gone on its own course.

****

Nearly a thousand miles away from *Vindex*, Lattimore was well aware that he was facing a growing potential for violence to break out on Palmyra. Lancaster and O'Flaherty were not popular and although he could understand that, it was what went with the unpopularity that caused him to be apprehensive of what might develop. He knew very well that most of the men in the crew had not taken the refusal to forage save for themselves by the two 'rebels' in a very favourable light. At first this had manifested itself in long stares at them as they went about their business, but James Wilson the cook had taken it a step further. As Lancaster had walked out one evening with O'Flaherty to go and catch his evening meal, Wilson had ostentatiously cleared his throat and spat copiously and accurately just in front of Lancaster's feet. The stowaway had stopped, smiled in the infuriatingly smug way he had, stepped over the spittle and gone on his way. O'Flaherty perhaps had it worse because he was a member of the ship's company and was obviously seen by his former messmates as a traitor. Thomas McClements, a very aggressive Glaswegian, had to be spoken to by Lattimore after he observed him deliberately barge into the Irishman so hard that he knocked him over onto the sand. When a furious O'Flaherty had picked himself up, McClements snarled at him.

'D'ye want to make something of it wee man?'

Lattimore had stepped in and ordered the Scot to back away and go to his hut to cool off, but he did so with a bad grace; the captain knew that he could not be everywhere and if the bad feeling continued then sooner or later there was going to be trouble when he was not present to stop it.

Dorothea Hastings was a strong woman and chafed at being kept idle whilst others went out to look for her food. Her bump was by now very obvious though, and she recognized the wisdom of doing as little as possible on the diet she was forced to live on, for she did not wish to lose her baby. Sensible of the need to be relatively inactive, she nonetheless exercised her authority as a mother and every morning told her daughters to do their best to bring back something to add to the pot. When they went away foraging she was left to her own thoughts, wishing above all for something to read, but there was nothing. All she could do to relieve the tedium was to take herself for a short walk occasionally along the shore, dabbling her toes in the water and holding aloft a palm frond to keep the worst of the sun off. It was well for William Lancaster that she was awake and in her hut when Thomas McClements sprang the trap he had been planning. The crisis arrived by design when Lattimore was foraging, and it came over, of all things, the latrines, which were at the end of the huts and down wind of them. McClements came back from hunting for food with several fish and he came back early in company with Samuel Donnell, Hugh Shearer, Charles Dordey and the boy Alex Sutherland. They deposited what they had brought under palm leaves near to the cooking pot to await the return of Morgan and Wilson, then lay down under the shade of the trees; it transpired later that they had positioned themselves strategically and deliberately. They had not long to wait until Lancaster felt the need to relieve himself and came out of his hut to visit the latrines. He walked across the sand, but as he was about to reach the hole that had been dug with a tree trunk across it and a screen of leaves around it, McClements moved to place himself between Lancaster and the latrines.

'Where do you think you're going?'

'For a piss,' replied Lancaster nonchalantly.

'Oh aye? And where are you going to do this pish?' demanded McClements.

'In the latrine trench, of course.'

'Oh, I don't think so,' said McClements, with a smooth menace to his tone.

'Look, all I want is a piss alright?'

'Not in my trench you don't.'

'Your trench?'

'Aye that's right; the trench that I dug with some of my pals.'

'As the common latrine.'

'As the latrine for a group of shipmates who help each other out; I dinnae recall you digging any of it.'

'I wasn't asked to.'

'That's beside the point. You didnae dig any of it, so you don't get to use it.'

'That's absurd.'

'Ye calling me absurd?'

'No McClements; I'm not calling you absurd. It's the situation that is absurd.'

'Same thing as far as I'm concerned pal. This started with you wanting a pish and now you've affronted me.'

'Affronted you?'

'Aye, that you have and in front of my pals too; I'm going to have to cut you for that, you bastard.'

'Cut me?' Lancaster's habitual insouciance was forgotten as McClements drew from a pocket his clasp knife, already open and held it in his hand, thumb and finger at the base of the blade in the hold of a man accustomed to slash, not stab.

'Now just hold on a minute...'

'Haud on is it? Oh I don't think so.' Here McClements made a slash towards Lancaster's face. 'I'll not be told what to do by no work-shy scrounging Sassenach bastard.'

Just then Thomas Morgan returned to the clearing with his own catch and saw what was going on; he stood and watched. Lancaster, aware that Morgan had seniority among the crew, appealed to him,

'Thomas; are you going to let this man cut me?'

'Me? I'm not responsible for what he does. That's your way of thinking isn't it? What's it got to do with me?'

'But you're the captain's steward!'

'I have that honour. But you say you have no responsibility to anyone else and that's a blade that cuts both ways.'

'Help me man! He's going to cut me and he means it.'

'I know he does, but it's not my business. I think nowt of you mister, and as far as I'm concerned you sort your own problems. That's your creed isn't it? You're on your own.'

Lancaster looked sick and faced McClements who smiled at him.

'Don't need anyone else do you pal? Dog eat dog world isn't it? I think you need a mark to remind you of that.'

He moved towards Lancaster, his hand held out to slash at his face, when a high voice called out 'Stop!'

There is something compelling in the female imperative voice and McClements stopped immediately, stood up from his aggressive posture and acknowledged the presence of Dorothea Hastings.

'Yes ma'am.'

'Mr McClements I am surprised at you. I thought you such a responsible man.'

'I am so, ma'am, but this man boils ma…. I mean he drives me to anger ma'am.'

'Yes, I think I have understood that. However, Mr McClements I would far rather that he used the latrine than that he did not if you follow my reasoning.'

'Ma'am?'

'Well consider the alternative Mr McClements. I have no shoes and if he did not use the latrine then unless he dug another I would have to watch where I was stepping all the time, so that I did not put my foot into what he had done. Did you think of that?'

McClements was embarrassed, 'No ma'am, I did not.'

'Indeed. I would be most grateful if you would allow Mr Lancaster to set about his natural functions unhindered and even more grateful if you will allow me the pleasure of a few minute's private conversation with you.'

'Yes ma'am; I'd be honoured ma'am.'

Lancaster was allowed to proceed about his business as McClements's friends dispersed. He returned to Dorothea's hut and sat down with her in the shade. She thought for a minute before asking him a question.

'Tell me Mr McClements, do you believe in good and evil?'

'I do Mrs Hastings. They are as real as the sand and the waves out there. I have seen them many times in my life at sea.'

'Quite so; do you think that threatening William Lancaster with a knife was good or evil?'

If McClements had been standing he would have shuffled his feet.

'Well ma'am, I guess it was somewhere in between; he needs a lesson.'

'That may be so, but you have not answered my question. I gave no grades in between good and evil. I asked if threatening someone, in this case William Lancaster, with a knife was good or evil.'

'Put that way ma'am, it's evil.'

'I do not see you as an evil man, Thomas.'

The use of his first name blew away his defences like smoke on the wind.

'I'm not ma'am. It's just that what he's doing is not right. It angers me beyond reason and I think he should be taught a lesson.'

'What lesson is that?

'That we should be helping each other.'

'Indeed I agree with that lesson and with you, but how does cutting him with a knife teach that lesson?'

McClements thought for a moment, his face red, his anger gone and his thinking stripped bare.

'It doesn't, ma'am.'

'No Thomas; it doesn't. All it would do would be to make you a criminal and set the law against you. So please do not cut him and indeed please give up all thought of violence against him.'

'I will ma'am, since you have asked me, but there are others who feel stronger than I do and I do not think any good will come of it.'

'That I am sure of, but I will alert the captain that perhaps he needs to be on his guard.'

'Need he know of this?'

'I think he must, but I think you should tell him.'

'Me? Why me ma'am?'

'Because then you will be back to your open, honest, and normal self, Thomas; the evil impulse to do harm will be lanced like a boil.'

McClements winced, but agreed to tell Lattimore when he returned to camp.

'Now as a matter of fact, Thomas, I agree with you. I do not like Mr Lancaster's view of the world. I think it lacks all charity and is unchristian. I think that if everyone in this world held his opinions then this earth would be a savage and uncivilized place where the weak suffer and the strong rule the roost.'

'But still you spoke up for him.'

'That's because, although I do not agree with him Thomas, I must hear him out. We have to listen to all views even if we disagree with them, however profoundly or violently. My world is one where people help each other and so build it into a better place; one fit for beings with the spark of God in each of them, and that includes listening to each other, particularly and especially if we do not like what they say.'

'You make it sound like the Kingdom of God on earth ma'am.'

'I'm the wife of a missionary; I'm allowed to hope for such things.'

She put her hand on his arm, 'Thank you for listening to me; I would hate my girls to see this island refuge become a place of angry and violent men. In some ways it is an Eden for them and you men have helped with that. The serpent that has appeared in the shape of selfishness and individualism does not help; but it is not in the majority of us. Let us not allow it to be.'

McClements stood up to go.

'I won't allow it, ma'am. You are right. I dislike the man more than I can say, but I'll let him alone. I cannot answer for the others, but I will speak to them. I may have influence.'

'Thank you; I am sure you have.'

She smiled her thanks and he left. True to his word, he did tell Lattimore when the captain returned with his haul of shellfish. McClements was brief, apologetic and transparently repentant, so Lattimore nodded and thanked him for telling him, and clapped him sympathetically on the shoulder. Then he called a meeting that consisted of John Crone, Reverend Taylor, Frederick Hastings, John Campbell and John MacDonald; the men who held some kind of authority in the hierarchy of the island. Describing to them what had happened in their absence, he regretted the necessity, but something would have to be done concerning Lancaster and O'Flaherty, not for fear of what they might do, but for their own safety. It was plain that there were people who wished them ill and it was unfair to expect Mrs Hastings to hold the line between angry men, however justified their rage might be. She had shown her strength in dealing with the situation when it arose, but it was not right to expect a lady in her condition to do so again.

'I think that what you are saying,' ruminated Reverend Taylor, 'is that we cannot expect all the men to follow the rule of law that normally holds. They seem to be applying a sort of natural justice that springs from their own views.'

'I think that's right Reverend. We are over a thousand miles away from the nearest law of any kind and it may be that we are stuck here for a very long time.'

'So,' said Frederick Hastings, 'the only law we have here is that which we ourselves impose.'

'Correct Mr Hastings,' replied Lattimore.

'But the men who wish to "punish" Lancaster and O'Flaherty as they see it, have they no fear of what penalties they might face when we return to civilization?'

'With respect Frederick,' said Taylor, 'I think you are begging the obvious question.'

'Which is?'

'Will we ever return to civilization?'

'You think we might not be rescued? Captain Lattimore, what do you think?'

Lattimore was reluctant to answer this question, even to himself, but now it had been asked, he had no choice but to respond.

'I think sir, that how the company behave depends very much on the hope of rescue. If our men knew there was a ship on the way to us right now, I have no doubt that the usual rules of civilization and law would apply for fear of the penalties they would incur if they harmed Lancaster and O'Flaherty. But if the idea spreads that we are here for good then the fear of law will gradually vanish. They will apply their own rules. Men who refuse to work for the common good may be seen as intolerable and insupportable.'

'So they may serve their own notions of justice on dissidents?'

'Yes Reverend; I think they might.'

'Then I hope and pray, Ralph, that MacDonald made it to Samoa, not just for our own lives, but for his; and that a rescue ship is on the way.'

'I hope for that too because in the face of indignation and outrage, the idea of that ship may soon be the only thing stopping Lancaster and O'Flaherty from being harmed. It may soon also be the only reason why my commands are followed.'

John Crone spoke up now with a possible solution to their problem.

'We must be the police. It's the only way to stop trouble.'

'Explain please.'

'If there is trouble at home sir, people send for the police. If our presence is the only way of keeping order in this situation, then we must carry out that function; at least one of us must be present around Lancaster and O'Flaherty at all times.'

Crone's suggestion was taken up and discussed, but the common sense of it was plain enough for all to see. They had no way of knowing that there were in fact two ships on the way to rescue them. From now on there would have to be at least one of this group in or around the huts at any time, day or night to stop any trouble. It was convenient that Lancaster and O'Flaherty did not move much away from the area of the clearing until the evenings when all had returned, but from now on the senior men had to take turns to be on duty at the huts. The general consensus was that this was a wise precaution and John Crone was detailed to inform Lancaster and O'Flaherty of it, along with the advice that they would be wise to stay near to the 'duty officer.' A brooding tension settled over the camp that night born of suppressed resentment, anger, fear and the potential for violence, and once there the feeling did not go away. That night Taylor prayed long and fervently for a ship to come while he and his fellows still had the authority to protect Lancaster and O'Flaherty from the indignation of the rest of the crew.

****

On the *Mariposa*, Quartermaster William Chambliss had taken the helm for his watch and was keeping a close eye on the compass so as to stay exactly on course. Captain Hayward was anxious that there should be as little deviation as possible from a straight-line route to Palmyra.

At some quiet moment Hayward went over to his chart table and bent over it, looking very closely. After a few minutes he opened one of the large drawers underneath the table and drew out another chart. Spreading it out he examined it minutely and compared the two charts. As he did so, his eyebrows rose and he nodded and gave a low whistle; then he nodded to himself and put the second chart away. Leaving his cabin he made his way towards the stern of the ship and looked at her wake. She was making her way at her usual cruising speed of twelve knots. The *Mariposa* left a broad and foaming track of pulverized water behind her as she ploughed through the waves. Her Chief Engineer, Henry Wilson, was worried at sustaining the demands on his engine any faster than this. "Handsome Harry" as he was known on board, a nomenclature which most of the lady passengers would have supported, had been quite vehement on the matter of speed on previous occasions, the incident of the boiler pipe accident and the dead men being much in his mind. Hayward knew this very well, but he pursed his lips and then he took a walk down into the engine room where the Chief Engineer sat in his cubbyhole.

'Speed her up, Harry. I want every ounce of steam and every mile you can give me.'

'Full speed Captain?'

'Full speed.'

'You know my reservations about pushing the engines so hard.'

'I do and I take full responsibility for it. I will enter it so in the log, Harry, if it makes you easier.'

'It doesn't. It's the danger to the men I fear.'

'We have to reach those people. We have to get them off that island as soon as possible. From what I understand they are subsisting on a diet that is barely enough to sustain life. I have thought about it a lot and it seems to me that leaving them there is giving too many hostages to fortune. Illness, storms, or an insufficiency of food gathered and they will be in serious trouble and danger of death. Therefore maximum speed please; now. That is an order.'

'Yes sir.'

Although Wilson agreed reluctantly to the extra speed, he stated that he would post a man to keep an eye on the shaft bearings and if they began to overheat then the ship would have to slow down willy-nilly. Hayward nodded in acknowledgement, but the deed was done. The whole ship now throbbed as the engines worked to their maximum sixteen-knot speed, and the energy was mirrored among the passengers and a great excitement took hold with a nervous energy urging the ship forward on its mission of mercy. Everyone felt a surge of adrenaline at the thought that they were participating now in an epic race to save lives, a rescue mission, for like all good stories the plight of the castaways had grown in the retelling. The upper deck was lined with First Class passengers, the men wearing boating jackets and yachting caps, the women in white dresses with straw hats, all making great play with binoculars, even opera glasses as they scanned the ocean ahead for anything of any interest at all, even though they knew they were hundred of miles from their destination. Particularly close attention was paid to the idea of sighting a sail that might be the schooner *Vindex*, which they knew had set out before them; nothing was seen however. Deck quoits and cards were abandoned for a much more interesting pastime; namely a matter of life and death. One of the ladies was brave enough to ask the captain a question as to what might happen if the ship hit something at this speed.

'You mean hit a rock, ma'am? There are no rocks on our course; these waters are well charted.'

'No Captain; I know that I can rely on you for that. I meant something like a whale. Would the *Mariposa* be sunk by a whale?'

Hayward looked at her then replied, 'She has never been so sunk, ma'am.'

'Oh Captain, so if she did hit a whale she would not sink?'

'No ma'am.'

'But sailors are notorious for their inveracity are they not?'

'Worst liars I ever saw, ma'am. Do you know, after forty years at sea I would not believe myself under oath.'

'Oh Captain!'

That night, 24 May 1888, Captain Hayward put on a special British themed dinner with flags and bunting for the occasion of Queen Victoria's birthday. The British citizens who made up about half of the passengers were much gratified at this and gave the loyal toast with three times three and patriotic speeches were made of a suitable nature. The toasts included the United States, the health of President Grover Cleveland and the excellent captain of their wonderful ship. During the day all that anyone wished to do was scan the horizon.

The boat deck was similarly lined with people from the second class cabins whilst the third class, usually expected to stay in their cabins or their small social saloon, had been allowed the area above the stern for outdoors, suitably roped off from the area forward. The Archbishop of Wellington had done his work well and not a single person onboard had made any demur at the possibility that they might be delayed in getting to their destination. Talk was that there might need to be a committee of relief set up to look after the needs of the poor souls to be rescued. Above all was the electric awareness that they were on an adventure that would furnish them with the subject matter of dinner party stories and anecdotes in boardrooms and clubs for years to come. The ship itself seemed to feel the spirit of the people on board and to catch some of the atmosphere and she surged through the water like a maritime greyhound, a bone in her teeth, and at night a long shining trail of phosphorescence behind her under a large tropical moon that lit her path.

Chapter 16

A Nautical Omission

On Palmyra Atoll feelings among the crew had risen to a head of steam where an explosion was inevitable and which, when it happened, might not be controllable. The defection of O'Flaherty to join Lancaster in his refusal to work for the common good was seen by most of the men to be scrimshanking, malingering and beneath contempt. If it had been restricted to just that, then it is possible that the captain's rule of law might have prevailed; the Reverend Taylor, once so dead-set on maintaining his rights to do exactly as he wished, appeared to have modified his views and had become noticeably friendlier and much more cooperative. Perhaps Lancaster's brand of rugged individualism had demonstrated to him the grave disadvantages to be had in their situation if their efforts were divided. Lately he had begun to call the captain by his first name, and Lattimore reciprocated. Unfortunately, the peace imposed by having an authority figure always present at the camp was short-lived. Lattimore was an Ulster Protestant, and O'Flaherty was a Catholic; this in itself had not presented the captain with any particular problem until O'Flaherty had revealed that he had always felt uneasy taking orders from a 'Proddy'. Although taken aback, Lattimore was not enough of a religious man to feel it deeply, and what rankled with him was that a crewman was refusing orders; his chief regret was that he did not know enough law to be sure if O'Flaherty was bound to obey him or not. There was some comfort to be derived from the knowledge that O'Flaherty did not know either, and ultimately if they were rescued Lattimore had determined that he would take him at his word. O'Flaherty would be paid his wages up to the moment of the wreck and not a minute beyond, even if the other men were paid full time. He was, for the moment, content with that. It was unfortunate that there was one man in the crew who was not.

Charles Dordey was from Ravenhill in Belfast, a Protestant and very young; at eighteen years he was inclined to be hotheaded and intolerant of other points of view. Two years previously he had been present at, and indeed had taken part in, the violent riots between Protestant and Catholic that had shaken the city. The popular Protestant preacher Hugh Hanna had been persuaded that his annual children's outing to the countryside should not be accompanied by drumming and marching so disappointed local Protestants held their own marches into Catholic areas; sixteen year old Dordey was among them with his drum. The result was bloody street fighting that went on for days in which fifty people died. O'Flaherty was not from Belfast, but in the current climate on Palmyra that did not matter to Dordey. He had worked with O'Flaherty amiably enough onboard ship but, as far as he was concerned, the Catholic had overstepped the mark in his refusal to forage and the matter had been bubbling in his head for a few days; now it had reached boiling point. Normally he was a well-muscled and even stocky figure, but as he stood outside O'Flaherty's hut he looked thin and emaciated. Six weeks on the island had removed all the meat from his bones and his ribs stuck out in sharp relief. It was almost two o'clock in the afternoon and Dordey had been foraging along the coral to the west of the beach; he had cut his feet, he was hot and had just deposited some seaweed, a couple of crabs and a coconut by the cooking pot. James Wilson was already at work gutting and skinning, throwing whatever had been garnered into the stew that was simmering nicely. Any new finds would be thrown into the mix as they arrived. This was not something that gave Dordey any joy, for his head ached, he was tired and full of frustration at being stuck on the island. As he turned from what he had laid under the palm leaves by the pot, his eyes rested on a hut where lay two men who had done nothing all day save lie in the shade. His eyes turned to gimlets and a boiling noise came to his head as he strode determinedly over to the fire-hut.

'Hey you in there. O'Flaherty, you Taig bastard; come out of there and face me if you dare.'

There was no prevarication on O'Flaherty's part. He came straight out of the hut and faced up to Dordey; he was two inches taller than the Belfaster and looked down at him.

'What do you want Proddy-whoddie?'

'This, you Fenian scum.'

Dordey swung his fist at O'Flaherty's head, took him completely by surprise and knocked him down. The Catholic was up right away and launched himself at Dordey, butting him in the midriff and knocking him against a tree whilst Dordey fought to fend him off. At this point Frederick Hastings, the duty officer, arrived shouting at them to stop; he grabbed O'Flaherty round the waist and wrestled him off Dordey who took advantage of this by punching O'Flaherty on the side of the face.

'You stop that now!'

'Don't get in the way Mr Hastings. I'm going to do for that Fenian bugger and he's got it coming.'

'If you don't stop Dordey, I shall hit you myself.'

'Will you now, Yank? Well do your damnedest, for I am laying that one out.'

Dordey made to punch O'Flaherty again, so Frederick Hastings hit him in the face.

'Well now,' said Dordey, 'If it's two of yez I'll even things up, and he picked up a thick billet of wood lying near the fire.

'Put that down Charlie.'

Dordey looked round and saw that Thomas McClements had come back to the camp.

'I will not Tommy. This man's a Fenian and I'm going to kick the lights out of him.'

'That's not a good idea and you should stop now.'

'I'm surprised at you taking that attitude, Tommy, after what they did in your own town in 1883.'

Dordey was referring to a terrorist dynamite campaign carried out by US based Irish Republicans. In January 1883 they had exploded bombs in Glasgow at Tradeston Gasworks, Possil Street Bridge and Buchanan Street Station; a dozen people had been injured although no-one died. Considerable anti-Catholic feeling had been stirred.

'O'Flaherty.'

'Yes Tommy.'

'Were you involved in any way in the Glasgow bombings?'

'I was not!'

'Do you have any sympathy whatsoever with the men who carried out the Glasgow bombings?'

'I do not. I understand why they did it, but I do not agree that what they did is the way to go. I am for Parnell, reform and home rule.'

'Parnell! There you see Tommy; that trouble-maker.'

'That trouble making Protestant, Charlie.'

'He's a traitor to his religion.'

'I don't think he is, Charlie. He just has a political point of view. Charles Stewart Parnell just wants to see a united Ireland where a man's religion is not relevant to the way he's treated.'

'Now you sound like a traitor to your religion, Thomas McClements.'

'And what religion might that be? Christianity you mean?'

'I mean Protestantism!'

'Ah well now, I cannot be a traitor to that for I am not and never have been a Protestant.'

'Of course you are. What else would you be?'

'You have taken me for a Protestant all these months Charlie, but I'm a Catholic.'

'But you're from Glasgow.'

'Aye, I'm a Weegie right enough and from an old Scottish Catholic family.'

'You're a Left-Footer!'

'That's quite enough of that thank you,' said McClements, bridling at the insult. 'You call me that again and I'll knock your neb down your throat.'

'That's not very helpful, McClements,' said Frederick Hastings, still in position to separate Dordey and O'Flaherty.

'That's "Mr McClements" if you please Yank. I'm as good a man as any and I'll have some respect or I'll know the reason why.'

'I did not mean any disrespect of course.'

'Then don't talk to me like a servant.'

'Oh to Hell with this!' shouted Dordey and flung himself at O'Flaherty, fists whirling.

The Irishman was nothing loath and punched him back with tremendous blows to his body. Hastings yelled and attempted to part them again, but O'Flaherty caught him on the face with an elbow and knocked him back.

'Stay out of this; it's private.'

McClements had been spoiling for a fight for a long time and now he saw red. He grabbed hold of Dordey's shoulder and spun him round planting a straight right onto the Ulsterman's jaw. He went down and out for the count.

'Right you bastard,' said McClements to O'Flaherty. 'Ye'll be joining him.'

Several of the crew lined up beside McClements shouting at the Irishman, calling him a traitor, a man who betrayed his pals, and O'Flaherty began to panic, seeing that he was about to be attacked by three or four men. He called out to Lancaster to help him, but the stowaway stayed out of sight in the hut.

The little girls had now appeared from the jungle and had stood for a few minutes watching the scene, but had begun to scream when the fight broke out, and between this and the shouts of the men, the din was tremendous.

The situation was out of hand. Frederick Hastings realized that in this position he had no authority at all, and he saw with great relief that Lattimore and Taylor were running up the beach towards what they could see as trouble kicking off. Lattimore was not quite sure how to deal with what he saw unfolding in front of him as he and Reverend Taylor panted into the clearing so his first move was to grab hold of McClements and pin his arms down while shouting, 'Stop it McClements! You stop this right now!'

McClements was not inclined to obey, especially as O'Flaherty, seeing his main opponent helpless, threw a punch straight on to McClement's head. This provoked the Glaswegian to a fury and he broke free from Lattimore and grappled with O'Flaherty and they fell on the floor together in a flurry of tremendous punches, not caring where any of them landed. John Crone was tearing up the beach now with a couple of his Maryport men; perhaps they might make a difference. Lattimore's brain whirled, looking for a way to stop this riot, but luckily the noise had subsided somewhat and all except the two combatants were able to hear a sharp voice from above that had in it a rising note, almost of hysteria.

'Ship! Ship!'

High up in the lookout tree Patrick Burns's voice rose in screaming joy, but no-one minded at all. For a second everyone froze where they were, except for the two men knocking Hell out of each other on the floor. Non-combatants, men, women and children; even Bruno the dog looked wonderingly upwards with an expression of mystification. McClements and O'Flaherty noticed the sudden silence and rolled apart looking to see what was happening. Lattimore's brain was quicker than anyone else's.

'Where away?'

'Out past the gap in the reef sir; Look, Look! It's a ship!'

Over towards the south west was a single plume of smoke from a steamer.

'Ramiel help us!' said Taylor.

'You know your Bible better than I do, William,' said Lattimore, in no doubt that Taylor's exclamation was religious. 'Who in the name of God is Ramiel?'

'Ramiel, my dear Ralph, is the Archangel of Hope. He is here right now and if you'll excuse me I have work to do.'

Taylor knelt on the sand and began to pray silently, his lips moving; several of the crew joined him.

'Get some damp palm leaves on that fire, Donnell and Shearer,' ordered Lattimore, more concerned with practical matters of the world. 'I want to see a smoke a mile high.'

All strife forgotten and irrelevant, they scrambled to obey.

He looked at the column of smoke on the horizon that stretched lazily upwards and saw as surely as Moses in the wilderness that it represented law, order and authority, restored all to their duty, their places in the scheme of things and that the crisis was almost over. The others just had to realize it too.

'A pillar of smoke by day, and a column of fire by night,' breathed Reverend Taylor. Authority, law and civilization were approaching the island.

For the next few minutes the tension among the people on the beach was almost unbearable; by now they had all returned to the huts, where smoke poured into the blue above and the Union flag fluttered bright against the dark green of the forest canopy.

'What do you see Burns?'

'It's a big steamship Captain and she's heading right for us; no mistake. Her course is square towards us.'

'Donald must have made it to Samoa,' said Lattimore, almost to himself, but his words were taken up by the people around him as some of the men, their recent discords forgotten, elated beyond bearing, danced in joy.

'Three cheers for Mr MacDonald; Huzza! Huzza! Huzza!'

On board the *Mariposa* the excitement was scarcely less than on the island. From the moment that the lookout had called "Land ahead!" from the masthead, all available glasses were trained on the dark blob in the ocean, fast approaching. As the ship neared Palmyra at a speed of fifteen knots the white line of a beach could be seen and on it were figures, smaller than ants at first, dragging a boat towards the reef. Before long the big steamship came to a distance of some two miles offshore and swung round, broadside on to the land. Hayward now gave his orders.

'Mr Chambliss, drop anchor if you please.'

'Aye sir.'

'Mr Hart, as First Officer I think this duty falls on you.'

'With great pleasure, Captain.'

'Four good men Frank; off you go.'

'Aye sir.'

First Officer Hart ran down the companionway from the bridge and onto the boat deck where a group of crewmen looked at him expectantly and all wanting to serve.

'Barpark, Erving, Allan and Driscoll; man the boat.'

There were some disappointed looks among the men left, but Hart took no notice of that; he was not a man to be argued with. Clambering into the boat as the oarsmen stripped away the cover, he commanded the men on deck 'Lower away,' and the derricks let the lifeboat smoothly down into the water. Pushing the boat away from the side of the ship with a bargepole, Hart ordered his crew, 'Give way together,' and they began to row towards the reef. Looking at where he was going, Hart was the only man on the boat who could see what lay ahead and he did not like it one little bit. The swell was heavy and the surf was breaking over the top of the reef with a roar. It was also low water and the tide had just turned, so was surging in through the gap in the barrier and into the lagoon beyond. As far as Hart could see the deep part of the lagoon only extended about half a mile inside the reef. The rest of the way, about a mile, was very shallow, barely covered by the water and to his amazement he could see a party of men pushing a boat through water barely enough to float it.

Lattimore knew very well that the crew of the approaching lifeboat would view the entrance to the lagoon with some trepidation and had decided that his men were fit enough to go at least part of the way. Joy, relief and adrenaline lent wings to their efforts and ten of them heaved the pinnace through the shallows, cutting their feet to ribbons on the sharp corals but they barely felt it. When the water was deep enough to float her they climbed in and headed for the gap leading to the sea, hoisting their sail as they crossed the lagoon. The pinnace breasted the swell and her sail was assisted by determined arms on the oars right through the waves and into the calmer water beyond where it headed for the *Mariposa*'s boat. As they drew closer Lattimore looked at the men in the boat to which he was heading and his eyes pricked. He could see an officer in a smart dark blue frock coat with two gold bands round his arm and a crew of men in the uniform of their company, well fed and muscled, rowing towards him. Hart looked across and saw a man whose hair had grown almost to his shoulders and a bushy beard. He was burned dark brown by the sun, and naked save for a sort of ragged kilt from his middle to his knees, with a sheath-knife stuck in the waist. The rest of the men in his boat were similarly burned, some with sores on their backs and emaciated. Nonetheless, they seemed to be pulling their boat well.

'Hart, First Officer of the *Mariposa*.'

'Lattimore, Captain of the *Henry James*.'

'Shall you transfer to this boat, sir?'

'No. I think not,' said Lattimore. 'I do not wish to have any mishaps at this stage and my men know the area inside that reef better than you Mr Hart. I suggest that we transfer some of my men to you to take back to your ship and that I meet you back here with some more of my people from the island.'

'Are you sufficiently strong and in health to do that, sir? You'll have to row against the wind.'

Lattimore grinned, 'All day long if we have to Mr Hart. You are well-named for you have put fresh heart into us.'

'It shall be as you wish sir.'

The palpable relief on Hart's face could not be hidden; he was not a small-boat man.

As the first of the men in the pinnace began to scramble over onto the *Mariposa*'s boat Lattimore asked the obvious question.

'Did you know we were here?'

'We did, sir. Your First Officer made it to Samoa with all his men.'

'Where is MacDonald himself?'

'I am told that he and another man are on their way here to rescue you by schooner. We seem to have overtaken them. The other three are on their way home.'

Lattimore thought for a moment, 'By schooner. I see. Tell me Mr Hart, would you have a pencil and paper about your person please?'

'I know of no First Officer that would not, Captain,' said Hart, feeling in his pocket for the required articles, and tearing a couple of sheets out of his notebook.'

'Of course; thank you. I shall return your pencil on board your ship. Now I shall go back and send my Second Officer off with the ladies.'

'We had heard there were ladies, sir. How many?

'There are two, and four girls; they will be on the next boat. I shall leave the island last Mr Hart, and bring up the rear.'

'That is as it should be, sir,' said Hart, a note of respect in his voice. 'Have there been any deaths since you landed on the island?'

'Not one; and no serious illnesses either.'

Many men would have been loath to go back to the island with such a prospect as *Mariposa* offered just in front of them. Five men from Lattimore's boat had by now clambered over onto Hart's vessel; so burned and thin were they that the American crew were visibly moved and put their backs to their oars with a will so that their passengers could receive help as quickly as possible. As the boat approached the *Mariposa,* the occupants could see dozens of men and women lining the sides. Three cheers rang out, to be followed by exclamations of both pity and horror as the survivors drew closer and their sunburn and sores and emaciation could be made out. A companionway had been lowered to water level so the men were able to walk up onto the ship's deck, which they did rather unsteadily. Doctor Giberson the surgeon was on hand to examine them, and insisted on each man being taken away to the crew's washroom where they could clean themselves up whilst he examined them with salves and swabs. Mr Smith, the Purser, organized a team of seamen to have this done as quickly as possible because there would be more people coming soon. The Archbishop of Wellington, his eyes full of concern, was seen circulating among passengers of all classes, his most repeated phrase in each conversation being, 'They must be decently clothed.' Within a few minutes the Purser was being inundated by items of clothing donated by the passengers. Word rapidly circulated that there had been no deaths and no serious illness on the island and this good news added to the general air of gladness on board the steamship.

Lattimore and his four men rowed back to the shallows and waded ashore to where John Crone was waiting with the rest of the survivors. Mercifully the tide had risen and the pinnace floated most of the way.

'Change the men at the oars, John, and take the ladies, the children, Mr Taylor, Mr Hastings, Mr Carter, and Mr James, out to the ship's boat. Then return for me and the rest if you please.'

'Aye sir; I will.'

For a moment Lancaster seemed as if he was about to demur and go in the second boat, but Lattimore gave him a withering glance, and he looked away. Mrs Hastings and Mrs Taylor climbed aboard the boat followed by the four girls and the new crew pushed it out through the shallows until it floated deep enough for them all to board. Lattimore waited until they had hoisted the sail to head for the gap in the reef, then he turned towards the huts. Entering the fire hut, he took a container of water and doused the flames, making quite sure that they were extinguished. Then he sat down, pulled out the two pieces of paper that Hart had given him from his pocket, along with the pencil, and wrote:

"Dear Donald,

There are no words that can express the gratitude that I feel towards you for our deliverance from our present troubles. I understand that you succeeded in making Apia through what trials I can barely imagine, and alerting the authorities to our plight. Today is Tuesday 29 May and the great steamer Mariposa has just arrived to end our sufferings, bringing word that you also are on your way with aid. I hope that you understand Donald that we have gone on board the steamer and are on our way to Honolulu and San Francisco; I could not ask people to await your arrival.

When you do arrive, you will find that we have gone and I hope that the disappointment of it will be tempered by the fact that our salvation has been brought about through your actions and that you have the eternal gratitude of every man, woman and child on this island. I can hardly believe the feat that you have pulled off and I hope from my heart that you understand why I made my initial request for you to try it. I hope to see you one day before too long to shake your hand and thank you in person for my life and those of all of us.
Your friend
Ralph Lattimore."

When he had finished he folded the paper and placed it on the floor of the hut halfway between the door and where the fire had been. On top of it he placed the plank on which he had, just a few short weeks before, inscribed his name. Looking at it thoughtfully he pulled out his knife and began to carve what he had feared he might never be able to put; the date of his leaving the island, 29/5/88. He did not take such care over the carving of these characters and when it was done he made sure that the note, held down by the plank, was just peeping out from under the wood. When he was done he stuck his knife into his waistband and picked up the bottle containing all the whisky that was left on Palmyra; about a tumbler full. Then he returned to the beach with Bruno and stood watching as over a mile away Crone transferred his load to Hart's boat, then began the pull back to the island. To himself he muttered, 'He's a good seaman, John Crone. He'll be a fine captain one day.'

Out beyond the reef Mr Hart's face worked with emotion as he assisted Mrs Taylor and Mrs Hastings to cross into the *Mariposa*'s boat. To his eyes they were an extraordinary sight, their faces burned, their arms and legs bare and the remains of their nightdresses forming ragged tunics down to their knees. They said nothing, but huddled in the boat as their husbands followed them. Reverend Taylor introduced himself and his son-in-law to Hart.

'You are Americans, sir.'

'We are, and never was I so glad to see a fellow countryman as I am now.'

'Where are you from?'

'San Francisco.'

'That is our destination sir. May I ask your name?'

'I am the Reverend William Taylor and this is my wife and daughter, my granddaughters and my son-in-law.'

Hart stared at him.

'You are the missionary?'

'I am.'

'I have heard of you, sir, and am sorry to see you in this condition.'

'No matter; The Lord has delivered us from our time of trial and we give thanks for it.'

'We have every form of modern convenience on board the *Mariposa* sir and it will all be at your disposal soon.'

'Excuse me.'

'Yes Miss; what is your name and what can I do for you?'

'My name is Laura Mary Hastings. Did Donald send you.'

'Was he the man who sailed from here to Samoa and told people that you were here?'

'Yes; that is him.'

'He's not here Miss. He's on his way back here with another boat, but we were faster. I guess he'd rather you came with us, than waited any longer on the island.'

'He kept his promise.'

'He did Miss. He certainly did.'

Before long the lifeboat was at the ship and as before the passengers gave three cheers as they came alongside. This time Hart bounded up the ladder to where Hayward stood waiting and announced the arrival onboard of a distinguished missionary. A buzz of excitement went through the watching crowd as this piece of information flew from mouth to mouth. One of the sailors came up to the deck and noises of pity were heard at the sight of his back, covered in open sores caused by sun and salt water; he was taken straight to sick bay though he proved to be remarkably well, his lesions being superficial. Then Isabelle Taylor and Dorothea Hastings came up the ladder in their rags with their four little girls and looked around them at the wide eyes and curiosity. On the island they had been strong and had stood the deprivation as well as any of the men, but now they felt naked in front of the staring and superior beings in front of them. Both women began to cry and slumped on their knees weeping from sorrow and relief all combined with shame at appearing so in front of such people. This did not last long for within seconds there were cries of sympathy from the women surrounding them and the ladies were led away quickly, to be washed, clothed, and fed. Hayward stepped forward and took Taylor's hand gently.

'Captain Henry Hayward, sir; I am glad to see you. More glad than I can say.'

Taylor looked at him.

'Captain Hayward; I do not think it blasphemous to say that for me I could not be gladder to see you than if you were an angel of the Lord in person.'

'I may be that one day sir, who knows, but not yet. At any rate, I can offer you the services of my ship and the good wishes of everyone on board; let us tend to you now. Please go with Mr Smith, our purser, and he will see you washed, clothed and fed.'

As the Reverend was led away, Hayward returned to the bridge and scanned Palmyra through his binoculars.

On the island Lattimore walked over to Thomas Morgan where the steward stood by the cooking pot; it was simmering gently.

'Seems a shame to waste it sir,' said Morgan, with a twinkle in his eye.

'I'll tell you what Thomas,' replied Lattimore. 'If that's really what you think then it's all yours my lad! Fill your boots.'

Morgan looked at him and laughed; before long both men were laughing until the tears ran down their cheeks.

'Proper food tonight, sir.'

'Oh I think so, Thomas. I should damned well think so. Bruno; you shall have proper meat tonight. Maybe even a bone.'

He uncorked the whisky bottle he carried and passed it to Morgan.

'Have a drink, Thomas; there's no point in wasting it.'

'After you, sir.'

Lattimore smiled, then nodded and took a sip.

Morgan also took a sip and passed it round to the other men, all save one.

William Lancaster looked at them laughing together; did his eye betray envy at their camaraderie? He had now not a friend on the island. In the wait for the boats O'Flaherty had called him some very nasty names for not backing him up when he was in trouble; he had finished up by spitting out the words 'piosa cac' at him. Lancaster did not know what that meant, but he thought he probably did not wish to. Soon Crone arrived back in the shallows and the remaining men pushed the boat back out to float in the lagoon with Bruno already onboard wagging his tail. The last man to board her was Lattimore who sat at the tiller, facing forward.

'Do you not want to look back, sir?' asked Crone. 'We spent time there that we will not forget all of our lives.'

'No John, thank you,' replied Lattimore with a smile. 'I do not care if I never set eyes on that cursed place again. That's where I want to look.' He nodded at the *Mariposa*. 'That is one of the most beautiful sights I have ever seen in my entire life.'

The boat sailed out through the gap in the reef and met with Hart's boat.

'Thank you Mr Hart; you need not have troubled yourself this time; we shall sail to the ship.'

'Yes sir.' Hart stood up, balancing in his boat and saluted Lattimore who was touched by the gesture and returned the courtesy. As the pinnace approached the *Mariposa* this time the passengers roared their approval completely ignoring the conventional notion of three cheers. The pinnace was tied up at the bottom of the ladder and the last of the survivors climbed up to receive the attentions of the onlookers. As they did so most of the steamer passengers were overcome by the sight of them and began openly to weep. The last to board was Ralph Lattimore.

'Up you go boy,' he told the dog and Bruno ran up towards the people waiting above. Then he himself climbed upwards as the people on the steamship cheered as if their throats would split. He stood at the top of the ladder, a strip of cloth about ten inches wide wrapped round his lower body and a sheath knife shoved into the waist. That was all he wore but his gold ring; with him was Bruno the Newfoundland dog. Almost he seemed to stagger as he stood on the deck and Purser Smith and Doctor Giberson stepped forward to support him, one on either side. They assisted him up a further ladder and onto the bridge, which Hayward had asseverated was the proper place for a captain to receive a brother captain. Here they presented him to Captain Lattimore with all the courtesy and formality of the sea. Lattimore was not without a sense of the theatrical and when Hayward held out his hand the Ulsterman took his sheath knife out of his waistband and gave it to the captain of the *Mariposa*. Then he took his hand saying,

'Captain Hayward, allow me to surrender to you my command, and all that I possess in the world.'

Quite astonishingly, Bruno, who had been watching and seemed to understand what was going on, held his paw up for Hayward to shake. This was too much for Frank Hart who immediately began to weep and had to retreat from the scene frantically dabbing at his eyes. Hayward was visibly moved, but tried to smile. He reached into his pocket for his handkerchief as his own eyes welled up and then after wiping them took Lattimore's hand firmly.

'My dear Captain Lattimore; that is not all you possess, for everything on this ship that is in my power to give is yours. Now come with me, sir, into my private cabin. You shall have a bath, see the surgeon and take some refreshment and then we will talk. Bring your dog with you.'

'My crew? My passengers?'

'Are being taken care of. I have relieved you sir, and they are now in my charge as are you. Now let us see to your needs.'

Later, when Lattimore had bathed in Hayward's private washroom, had been examined by the doctor and was sitting, once more clad in a borrowed captain's uniform, for he and Hayward were much of a size, Hayward sat down opposite him.

'There is much to talk about Captain Lattimore, but I decided a few days ago that I wished to have a private word with you before allowing you to associate with anyone else.'

'May I ask why?'

'You may. It is because you lost your ship Captain, and that is one hell of a thing for any captain. I know as one to another, that you will be blaming yourself.'

'That's true enough. I think I will blame myself all the days of my life. I should have kept a sharper watch.'

'There was no reef marked on your chart?'

'True also.'

'Any ship under way at black of night is in danger of hitting rocks Captain Lattimore, but I think you took all the precautions you needed to considering that what you hit was not on your chart - or so I have been told.'

'That is correct. There was nothing on my chart save open water.'

'Indeed. There is just one thing I wish to ask you more; were you using Admiralty charts?'

'I was. I understand they are the best.'

'Then all is explained sir. Look at this.'

Hayward went over to his chart table and put two charts together.

'These, Captain Lattimore, are British Admiralty charts; some of these have not been altered since they were first drawn by Captain James Cook, over a century ago. As you may see, to the nor' nor' west of Palmyra Atoll is nothing but clear water.'

'As I said.'

'Now these are charts prepared by the US Navy in recent years showing the same area. What do you see?'

'I regret that I will not be able to see the writing Captain Hayward. My spectacles were lost in the wreck.'

'Ah then you must use this. In fact you had better keep it, for I have several and it will be some time before you can replace your glasses.'

Hayward handed over his magnifying glass.

Lattimore thanked him, then studied the new charts and looked up astonished, 'Kingman's Reef.'

'May I ask if your charts were supplied by your company?'

'They were.'

'Then they should have invested a little more money in a more modern set, Captain. You stand absolved of all blame in the loss of your ship for you had no way of knowing that reef was there.'

Lattimore's face cleared, 'You mean…'

'That in my eyes, Captain, and in the eyes of all right thinking men you have been the blameless victim of a nautical omission.'

Hayward did not realize it, or maybe he did, but to Lattimore his words were an absolution, almost a benediction. The guilt that he had been feeling ever since the wreck, the mist at the back of his mind that he could not clear, now disappeared. Ever since the *Henry James* had hit the reef, all had been chaos and turmoil, but now order was returning to the captain's universe; it felt liberating, and good.

Chapter 17

The Kindness of Strangers

By six o'clock in the evening Mr Hart and his team of seamen had hauled their lifeboat back onboard the *Mariposa,* and next to it, sitting on the deck, was the pinnace from the *Henry James*. The whole rescue had taken three and a half hours from start to finish. Lattimore's emotions had run the gamut of extremes in that time, and now that Hayward had absolved him from blame in the matter of losing his ship, he began to feel more like his old self. He was aware of a vague feeling of disbelief in his head; part of his psyche felt stunned at the suddenness of the change. Human beings can display almost infinite adaptability to circumstances, but adjustment to rapidly changing conditions does not always follow immediately and culture shock lent an unreality to what he was experiencing. Hayward had given specific orders to the kitchen staff following advice from Dr Gilberson, who knew that malnourished people who were suddenly given large amounts of food could be very badly affected by it, becoming ill, and in some cases even dying. There was to be a grand meal in the saloon, but the portions were to be modest; the survivors could be fed up over a period of days. When the *Mariposa*'s steward, William Barfoot, came and announced that the captain's table was ready, Lattimore allowed himself to be led through to where all the survivors and a large gathering of First and Second Class passengers was waiting for him. Bruno was left in the captain's cabin with a plate of meat from the galley, but not, as yet, too much. As Lattimore entered the saloon they gave him a round of applause and banged on the table.

'Upon my word, Captain,' said the Archbishop, welcoming him to his seat, 'A remarkable thing. Most remarkable; to suffer through a shipwreck and six weeks on a desert island and to lose not a single life nor to have any suffer serious illness. It speaks volumes of a commander who can accomplish that; a triumph, sir.'

'I think Your Grace, that we have been very lucky and that we had some help from above.'

'God you mean? Of course Captain; I have no doubt that he has smiled on you and given his aid.'

'Well we had a powerful advocate to do our praying, Your Grace.'

'You hear that William?' The Archbishop looked across to where Taylor smiled in modest agreement.

'It's a pity he's not a Catholic,' continued the Archbishop, 'But he's a good man to have on your side in a fix like yours has been.'

'I could not agree more, Your Grace, at least with the second part of your sentiment.'

'And then there was you, Captain. You organized and commanded and ensured that all were fed.'

'We did what we had to, sir.'

'So I gather; but towards the end, I hear from the Reverend that some were inclined to make difficulties?'

'That is behind us, Your Grace.'

The Archbishop looked at him, his eyes boring right into Lattimore's own.

'So you say Captain and I see that you are a good and Christian man in your forgiveness. I shall think on this with my committee, because although you may not wish to visit consequences on anybody, not all of us might agree with that.'

Lattimore involuntarily looked down the table to where William Lancaster sat and found the stowaway's eyes fixed on him. Deliberately, he looked away, grateful that at that moment a waiter poured a glass of champagne beside him and another placed a plate in front of him on which nestled a steak of moderate size.

'I did think of a fish course Ralph,' said Hayward, 'But then I recalled that you might have had enough of fish for a while.'

Lattimore smiled his agreement, but did not speak.

In front of them appeared dishes filled with steaming vegetables and Lattimore shook his head in disbelief as Hayward helped him to potatoes, but not too many.

'How do you feel, Captain Lattimore?' asked Mrs Grayson, one of the First Class passengers.

For a moment he weighed his words, then replied, 'This is a wonderful metamorphosis. Two hours ago I was cooking a pot of crabs, eels and grass, and now I am dining sumptuously and drinking champagne. I guess the pot is still boiling, as the fire was going when we left; but thank God we don't have to eat its contents now.'

A roar of laughter came from the Reverend Taylor and he cried 'Amen to that!' Looking down the room to the other tables, Lattimore saw that the laugh was general and that his crew probably thought he had made the best joke ever. They had looked very strange when they had arrived on the *Mariposa*, but he did a double take when he saw them now. The donations to the clothing bank set up by the Steward had been generous and comprehensive. He was used to seeing his men in their working clothes; mostly pale duck trousers with a shirt and belt. The clothing they were wearing now had come from some very well to do people, for in some ways the *Mariposa* was a floating luxury hotel for the rich. His rough sailors sat transformed, all of the men in jackets and ties but most of them were in tails and dinner dress, boiled shirts, black bows at their necks and patent leather shoes. There had not been time for any of them to have the attentions of the ship's barber and above the ultra-civilised garb they were hirsuit and unkempt like a bunch of elderly tramps, though clean and smelling of carbolic soap. Across the table sat Mrs Hastings and Mrs Taylor now looking more like they had before the wreck, their tunics gone to be replaced by decent blouses and skirts. The four girls were similarly lucky, as there were a few passengers of similar age to them who had willingly handed over clothing to the castaways.

'I have to congratulate you Captain, although the Archbishop has already mentioned it.'

'For what, Doctor?'

'Well,' said the ship's surgeon, 'I have conducted brief examinations of everyone who was on the island and I find that you are all in remarkably good health. I had feared from first sight that you might all be suffering from malnutrition. Apart from the fact that your comrades are very thin, there is nothing I can discern in anyone's constitution that causes me any concern. I see no reason why you should not resume normal eating habits gradually over the next two days if this meal causes no ill effects.'

'Oh Doctor, I cannot see it doing that. No, not at all,' said Lattimore, savouring the taste of potato and gravy in his mouth.

'As for alcohol…'

'It will help us to a sound sleep Doctor, but I shall be moderate; as will we all.'

Lattimore looked round the company with a meaningful expression, but it was needless.

'Do not worry about that Captain Lattimore,' said Hayward. 'I have already taken the precaution of instructing the staff not to allow anyone to over-imbibe or indeed to overeat.'

When the meal was over the survivors were treated most humanely, because although the crew and passengers of the *Mariposa* were brimming with questions, they allowed them to retire, for in all their cases, whether of sunburn or lack of energy, it was agreed that sleep was the best healer. Lattimore had been given Captain Hayward's sleeping cabin. The captain of the *Mariposa* had instructed that a cot bed be made up in his day cabin for his own use and when he had bid Lattimore goodnight the Ulsterman had gratefully closed the door and surveyed the perfectly made bed in front of him with disbelief. The bath he had taken earlier in the evening had been an experience he would never forget; he had not washed in warm water for six weeks and the sheer sensual experience of it on his skin had taken him unawares. He climbed into bed and pulled the sheet over himself, crisp, ironed, smelling faintly of soap and thought he had never felt anything so good in his life. His brain was working so hard that he feared that he might never get to sleep, but exhaustion and relief from the stress of being marooned did their work and he was soon dead to the world, in which state he stayed for a full thirteen hours. Hayward had instructed that none of the survivors should be woken and everyone on the *Mariposa* spoke in whispers and went as far as possible on tiptoe past where the sleepers had been quartered.

When the last of the *Henry James* people had departed to their various cabins, the Archbishop of Wellington called a meeting in the corner of the saloon of what he had christened his Committee of Investigation and Distribution. They settled into comfortable green and upholstered leather armchairs. He was, naturally enough, the Chairman; a Mr Nisbet acted as secretary and made notes of what they decided. The first matter was simple enough.

'As you saw ladies and gentlemen,' said the Archbishop, 'the generous efforts of our fellow passengers collected a great quantity of clothing which was placed into the hands of Mr Smith who has distributed a good deal of it amongst our unfortunate fellows. He has undertaken that the rest of it will be similarly given out. The distribution of this is of course governed greatly by both size and gender. I take it that we are all quite happy to allow Mr Smith to continue with what he is doing and entirely at his own discretion?'

The eight other men and women around the circle signified that they were content with this course and there were nods among the spectators clustered round the meeting.

'Now to the most important function of this committee; our new shipmates if I may call them that, are in want of money. It is all very well to clothe and feed them, but eventually they would go ashore without a penny to their name. This is a world that runs on money and of course, as I intimated to many of you before we reached Palmyra, I was going to start up a subscription list to raise a fund to help the survivors. I am happy to say that since they came onboard the money in its entirety has been handed over to Mr Smith and it amounts to some $578 US dollars. This is a considerable amount.

Round the saloon went a murmur of approbation and a couple of low whistles.

'I am deeply gratified and moved at this display of generosity and Christian charity to our fellow creatures in need and it puts me in mind of the Good Samaritan. They are not here of course, but on behalf of the survivors I thank you very much indeed.'

This time a small and gratified ripple of applause sounded out.

'Mr Powell, as many of you know, is a banker and it is in that capacity that I asked him to make a list suggesting how that money might be divided which is concomitant with how wages are paid on a ship. It is in the natural order of things that officers receive more than enlisted sailors who work for a lower wage. In a few minutes I shall ask him to read out the suggested amounts for each grade, but before I do that, there is the matter of the man Lancaster and his associate O'Flaherty to consider.'

The Archbishop paused as all eyes were on him.

'I believe I see that you are all familiar with what happened as regards these men on Palmyra. Is anyone not aware of their actions?'

Everyone was aware; Reverend Taylor had not been slow in telling people of the last and potentially greatest trial that Lattimore had to face on the island.

'I am going to reserve to myself the right of Chairman in using a casting vote in the event of a tied decision, but I think I shall remain silent while that decision is discussed. There are elements to it of governance and charity that make me think that laymen might see things more objectively than I. If a majority emerges then I am happy to acquiesce in their decision. The question is, given what we know, is the committee happy for these two men to receive a gift of money from this fund?'

The members of the committee looked at each other, but the first to speak was Mr William Sutherland of Carnoustie, Scotland, who was most determined and emphatic in a good brogue.

'I have to say that I'd rather throw the money overboard than have either of those men get a red cent of it. I think the way they behaved was morally reprehensible and destructive of good order. I have no time for them at all!'

'I quite agree,' said Mrs Elliott, a well to do lady from San Diego, 'If every man on that island had followed their example then I think it likely that none of them would have survived. In such a situation the labour of every man, woman and child is essential and for them to refuse was odious and selfish.'

These two comments caused nodding and agreement in the committee although there appeared to be some dissent among the spectators. The next to comment was Frank Hart, who represented the crew of the *Mariposa* on the committee.

'I'm First Officer on this ship and one day hope to be a captain, so I have something of a dog in this race. If I speak my mind, I have to say that what those men did represents a breakdown of authority, which, if it happened on board a ship, would be mutiny. In a life or death situation where you have to scrape for every mouthful you can get, I consider that they put everybody on that island in jeopardy. I'd give them nothing.'

Mr O'Higgins, a cattleman from Laramie, was in some doubt at first.

'The Archbishop mentioned the Good Samaritan a while back and that hit me where it counts. I go to church and I say my prayers and I do study my Bible as well.' Here he looked around quizzically, 'I have to say that I do not recall the Good Samaritan asking the man he helped about his record of helping people before he gave aid. It was unconditional.'

'That is true enough,' said Mr Sutherland. 'However, I also read my Bible and I have in mind the words of the Sermon on the Mount, "All things whatsoever ye would that men should do to you, do ye even so to them." It seems to me that these men refused their help and have no right to expect it from others now.'

The Archbishop looked pained and as if about to speak, but recollected that he had said he would not.

'Yes,' said O'Higgins. 'But by that rule, if we do not help those two men then we have no right to expect it from others.'

'That's a bit of a clove hitch,' said Hart. 'If we help them we'd be both right and wrong.'

Mrs Grayson had not spoken yet, but now found a balance in what she thought.

'I can see that in Christian charity we should help them. I can also see that if what they did was reflected in others' behaviour, then what happened on Palmyra might have ended tragically. It was also a breakdown in authority and I agree that it was morally reprehensible.'

'Contemptible even!' snorted Hart.

'Well yes, I can see that Mr Hart, but there is something else. I used to be a schoolteacher once you know, before my marriage, and this makes me think of lessons.'

'Lessons?'

'Yes Mr O'Higgins. Lessons. We have raised a large amount of money and we could distribute it regardless of conduct, but think of the effect.'

'The effect, ma'am?'

'Yes sir; do you imagine that what has happened here today is going to escape the notice of newspapers and the public?'

A murmur swept across the saloon.

'This will be in the newspapers. The whole of America, even the world will talk of it; it will spread like wildfire. And what lesson do you think will be drawn from our distributing money to men who refused duty and aid?'

'Ah!'

'Exactly sir; "Ah". So the real question here as far as I can see is, do we, the members of this committee, give our consent to a lesson going out across the world that no matter what you do, how you defy authority, refuse your comradeship and help and lie idle all day, you will still, in the end, be rewarded by the charity of others? That there are in fact no lines in the sand, no rules, no conditions?'

There was silence.

When no-one spoke, the Archbishop leaned forward and said, 'It seems to me that we might now well be in a position to make a decision as to whether or not these two men receive any of the funds raised. If you are for them receiving money please show.'

Not a hand went up.

'Those against them receiving any money?'

Every hand went up.

'That is unanimous then,' said the Archbishop. 'I did not feel in all conscience that I could sway this decision, but it does seem to me that a society where people are seen purely as selfish individuals who do nothing except for personal gain would be abhorrent. I favour the idea of Christian community and that people should help one another. The motion is carried.'

'Not by me,' came a voice among the spectators.

'Mr Evans?'

'I do not agree with your decision Your Grace, and I wish to say so.'

'Very well sir, you have done so. However, the decision has been taken by the committee and the funds will be distributed accordingly.'

'I contributed to those funds and I wish to see those men relieved.'

'You contributed to a fund that I made clear was to be administered by a committee whose participation I sought. That committee has decided.'

'I do not agree with the decision and wish to see those men receive help. They merely pointed out what I see to be a truth; that the world is made up of individuals who are fundamentally selfish and act for their own ends. Human cooperation is based solely in that, Your Grace, and I have heard politicians say similar; and have read philosophers who say the same. Why punish them for that? Of course they should be helped.'

'Ach haud your wheesht!' muttered Mr Sutherland darkly, looking as if he wished to visit violence on the speaker, who thankfully did not understand him.

'Then of course, Mr Evans,' said the Archbishop smoothly and quickly, 'You are quite at liberty to help them. However, this committee is another matter.'

Evans, a timber merchant from Seattle, did not pursue the matter further, but withdrew into another corner of the saloon where he and a small knot of other men held their own discussion.

'Damn Republicans!' muttered Frank Hart.

'Mr Hart!'

'Oh I do apologize, ma'am. I forgot where I was momentarily.'

'Now now, let us keep politics out of this matter if you please ladies and gentlemen. Let us proceed to Mr Powell's list for distributions and see if it meets with our approval.'

'I have it here, Your Grace,' said the banker, pushing a piece of paper forward.

'Oh, do read it to us Mr Powell. Sometimes I get tired of the sound of my own voice.'

'But you have such a fine baritone voice, sir.'

'Too kind Madam, too kind, but Mr Powell…'

'Very good, Your Grace; I thought it a good thing to remember in my calculations the five men who brought the news of the shipwreck to Samoa in such an heroic fashion.'

'Yes, I would think that most appropriate. Such a valorous thing merits some reward such as we are able to give.'

'Very well sir, I propose to divide as follows: Captain Lattimore $75, the brave MacDonald $60, Mr Crone $25, the Carpenter and the Sail-maker $30 each. The Bosun, Mr Ferguson $26.25 and the Cook and the Steward $17.50 each. The brave fellows who accompanied Mr MacDonald in the launch shall receive $18.75 apiece whilst all the ordinary seamen will receive $12.50.'

'They should be happy with that I think Mr Powell. That's the best part of a month's wages for a seaman.'

'I think they should, Mrs Grayson. As to the rest I think $50 to Mr and Mrs Taylor and $60 to Mrs and Mrs Hastings, the last taking into account their children.'

'That would seem a fair and equitable distribution to me,' said the Archbishop, ' And those persons who are deemed by the committee to have proven unworthy of any share by reason of their gross insubordination to Captain Lattimore, receive nothing.'

Mr Evans called over the saloon.

'Had you already decided Mr Powell? You had those figures prepared knowing that the committee would not award money to those men?'

'Not at all sir,' replied Powell, pulling a paper from an inside pocket. 'I prepared two sets of figures, one with the malcontents and one without. The allocation was always to be as the committee decided.'

'My group has decided that Lancaster and O'Flaherty will each receive $18.50 subscribed among ourselves.'

'That is most generous of you Mr Evans,' replied the Archbishop. 'Doubtless they will be duly grateful.'

For the committee, this was the end of the matter. Each castaway had clothes on their back and money in their pockets. When they landed at Honolulu the British Consul would be able to take care of them. The crew would have wages coming from their company up to the time of the wreck and would be sent home by the Consul on what ships he could arrange. The stowaway could go and do as he liked, though Mr Hart was heard to say that he wished him to the Devil. O'Flaherty was left to the mercy of Lattimore, though the captain was determined that he should have no more than his due. All that remained to be done now was to get to Hawaii where Hayward could hand his charges over and be about his own business. In his mind, however, was a matter that he wished to settle between himself and Lattimore; he did so privately over breakfast the very next morning.

'I hate wearing a ring Ralph. It always seemed to me like strangling a finger and it always felt that way too.'

'I don't follow,' said Lattimore, puzzled.

'Just because I do not like wearing a ring does not mean that I do not have a ring.'

'A wedding ring Henry?'

'Indeed - I wear two rings on a chain around my neck; one is my wedding band. As to the other…'

Hayward reached to his second shirt button and drew out two rings on a chain. One was a plain gold wedding band and the other was a gold signet, not unlike Lattimore's own, with a compass and square engraved on it.'

'We are brothers of the same order it seems.'

'Indeed it does, Ralph, and I am bound by oath to give you help to the utmost of my ability.'

'I think you have already done that well enough,' said Lattimore with a smile.

'Well that may be, but I am minded to do more. It seems to me that there are two options that I can offer you and both have advantages to you.'

'What might those be?'

'Firstly, I have to say that my employer, Mr John D Spreckels is a man for who I have the highest regard. His business interests range far and wide and in California, particularly in San Diego, he is a power in the land. The mercantile arm of his business is large and the *Mariposa* is but one of many vessels that he owns. I am quite certain that he would have a good berth for a captain such as yourself.'

'A captain who had lost his ship,' said Lattimore in a subdued voice.

'That is neither here nor there to me, Ralph. I have formed an opinion and I know very well that the loss of your vessel was not down to any shortcomings in your conduct or character. If I recommend you to Mr Spreckels as a man worthy of his attention then I am certain he would find you a command or at least a position as a First Officer.'

'That's very good of you, Henry, and I am most touched and flattered by what you say. Thank you. It bears thinking on, though if I accepted I should probably have to move out to

California with my wife. She must be consulted before I could accept anything.'

'I understand that Ralph. The second offer is that if you are not inclined to stay in California, then you continue on this ship to San Francisco as my guest anyway. You can stay for a few days at my house before taking the overland train to New York on your way home. I guess you will need to think about what I have said, but there is no hurry; you've had a lot to take in over a very short time.'

'It's true; I have that. Indeed, I should like to think it over, but I like the sound of what you say and I shall carefully consider both options. Here's my hand on it.'

The two men shook hands firmly.

'Good, then that is settled,' said Hayward. 'We reach Honolulu soon and you can see to the safe discharge of your people into the hands of the British Consul. My wife and daughter will be very pleased to see you when we reach my house, for I have no doubt that you shall be quite the lion of the town when the newspapers get hold of this story.'

'Newspapers! I am not sure I like the sound of that. Could it not be kept quiet?'

'You are a modest fellow,' laughed Hayward, 'But these things will out. We have a ship full of your admirers, Ralph, and as soon as we are ashore I have no doubt the telegraph and telephone wires will hum. I assure you that Mrs Hayward and Cassie are quite able to protect you. If any reporter sets foot through our picket fence then my daughter is fully capable of whupping them with a broom. We have a fine guest room with a large bed.'

'I should like that of all things.'

'Then it's settled.'

'But my crew?'

'Are no longer your concern, Ralph. They will be in the care of the British Consul so in good hands. They are not children, but grown-ups, and they may go their ways with tickets home, money in their pockets and the rest of their lives to live, as indeed may you. I imagine they may even be paid through your company's agent in the port, as may you. The *Mariposa* will be in Honolulu for two days; quite enough time to settle all affairs I think and that means that you have done your duty well by them. Whatever happens then, your destiny is yours once again to do as you please.'

The only being at all discontented on the *Mariposa* was Bruno who was found to have a very large leech attached to his stomach the day after the rescue. Dr Giberson deemed it as part of his duties to see to it, so he detached it safely and carried it without ceremony to the ship's rail and threw it into the sea. The dog showed no sign of appreciation whatsoever. When the ship reached Honolulu she moored at Spreckels' dock and the shipwrecked victims took leave of their saviours. Their thanks were profuse and the crewmen, led by Lattimore, met Mr Wodehouse, the British Consul, who saw to their accommodation in a seaman's hostel close by. There were passports and tickets to arrange; but this would take a few days. In the case of Lattimore, who was aware of what he wished to do, the process was expedited. A passport was written for him while he waited, and he returned to the *Mariposa* in company with Hayward. Reverend Taylor and his wife, Mr and Mrs Hastings and their children had declared their intention to stay in Honolulu for a few weeks where there was a branch of their church and friends with whom they could recuperate. It was then their intention to rent a house where Mrs Hastings could spend the remainder of her pregnancy and her confinement. Their parting with Lattimore was warm and grateful, expressing the hope that he would call on them if he returned to California; he assured them that he would. By contrast, William Lancaster left the ship without a word. He merely looked at Lattimore and left; his former captain never heard nor saw anything of him again. With O'Flaherty Lattimore was as good as his word. He found the agents of the North British Shipping Company and with advances from them, paid off his crew right up to the day they landed in Honolulu, telling all save one that he would always be ready to provide them with an excellent character. From the moment they were paid they were once again free agents, released from their contracts and able to ship out, or apply to the British Consul for repatriation as British citizens in distress. O'Flaherty was paid until the very moment of the wreck and not a minute after. The man took the money, but could not look Lattimore in the eye.

'May I ask if you'd give me a character too, sir?'

'You may. I'd give you a character as an excellent seaman O'Flaherty, which you are, but I would feel duty bound to add a sentence at the end.'

'What might that be, sir?'

'That you would not be a man I would recommend to be shipwrecked on a desert island with.'

The justice of it hit O'Flaherty square in the teeth and he flushed, nodded and walked out.

With John Crone, Lattimore found the farewell more difficult. He took his hand and said bluntly, 'You saved my life, John. Without you pulling me out of the sea that day I would not be standing here now. I will be seeking another command when I get home to Belfast. I'd be glad to have you as my First Officer. I imagine you'll be after your ticket now.

Crone flushed pink in appreciation of Lattimore's gratitude and wrung his hand in return.

'Thank you sir; it's a kind offer and I may well take you up on it. For now, I have family back in Maryport and I wish to see them soon. There's nothing like a shipwreck to make you appreciate home. James Wilson is of the same mind so I think we will be speedy on our way back, though now we are here in

Hawaii we are of a mind to spend a few days looking round before we ship out.'

'All of your Maryport men?'

'No sir: Thomas Morgan and Samuel Young will also stay here a while, then ship out for home, but they want to go via Australia, although I have told them I think going through the United States would be quicker. I want to get home as soon as possible and back on a ship, sir; I want to work my way up to captain as soon as I may.'

'You will do it, John; you are a right seaman and a good fellow; now good luck to you, for I must be on my way.'

'Good luck to you, sir, and all success in your new ship, whatever she may be.'

On 2 June 1888, with Lattimore and Bruno on board, the *Mariposa* turned her prow towards San Francisco and began the 2,400 mile trip towards her home port.

Chapter 18

A Chinese Puzzle

The schooner *Vindex* approached Palmyra Atoll from the west, nine days after the *Mariposa* had rescued the crew and passengers of the *Henry James*. Donald MacDonald strained his eyes towards the entrance of the lagoon, and to the white strand of beach a mile or so beyond it, but he could see nothing at distance. Captain Bissett was surveying the island through a brass telescope and passed it after a minute or so to Donald with a single word, 'Nothing.' Willie Ferguson also stared intently at the dark green of the tree-line beyond the shore.

'I think the flag's still flying Donald. Is that no a speck of colour I can see?'

MacDonald studied the scene carefully, trying to hold the telescope steady against the rolling of the boat, and finally discerned the Union flag flapping in the breeze above the huts.

'You are right Willie; the flag is there, but I cannot see a soul. Nor can I see any smoke.'

Bissett looked at him meaningfully.

'Why do you think that might be, Donald?'

'Well they could be foraging, though it is unlikely that the camp would be deserted or that no-one would have seen us by now. Or it is possible that they are no longer there and have been rescued by another ship.'

'Aye, both of those are possible. There are two other possibilities though. The first is that they might be laid low by disease. It's been over a month since you were here, Donald. Did they all seem healthy when you left? No signs of epidemic or fevers?'

'None that I know of; they were all healthy, so I doubt that it is disease. What is the other possibility you have in mind David?'

'Funny business.'

'Whatever do you mean?'

'I mean that this is the Pacific and there are plenty of nasty characters doing all sorts of things around the islands who should not be doing them. If we do not see signs of life on the island as we approach then we would be wise to be very careful. You'll bear in mind that Palmyra has not got a good reputation and that there has been at least one massacre here and not so many years ago.'

The schooner neared the entrance to the lagoon and dropped anchor just three hundred yards short of the reef; still there was no sign of life onshore.

'Aye well, that settles it,' said Captain Bissett, reaching into his pocket and pulling out a key.

'Mr Briggs?'

'Aye sir.'

'As my First Officer, I am handing over command to you until and if I return from that island. If you see or suspect any trouble when I am ashore you are to ditch the anchor and make all sail to Samoa. There you will advise the authorities that an armed party will be necessary. Understand?'

'Aye sir; You expect trouble?'

'I don't know, Mr Briggs, but we must be prepared for it. Mr MacDonald, Mr Ferguson, myself and four good men are going ashore now, so please have the boat lowered.'

Bissett called his crew together and explained his worry on the lack of life ashore and soon had four volunteers. The shore party followed him to the door of his cabin where he used his key to unlock the arms cupboard; inside were six rifles, which he handed out, along with ammunition. His own weapon was a sinister looking Colt revolver that came with a bandolier holster which he put over his head and under one arm. Propelled by four strongly pulled oars the ship's boat was soon through the lagoon entrance and, it being high water, they were able to approach most of the way to the beach before she grounded. There was still no movement in the huts.

'Now then men,' said David Bissett. 'I see no sense in delay and I will not make a target of us by hanging about on the waterline. I intend to trot to the huts, so quick about it and be ready in case of attack. Do not enter them for fear of disease; we must be cautious.'

Fanning out across the sand, the party ran towards the huts and soon reached the first one on the left. Two loaded rifles were pointed through the door by men on either side and Bissett carefully looked inside, his pistol cocked and ready.'

'Nothing. Try the other ones.'

All of the huts were empty. Bissett was puzzled.

'Unless they are all away hunting for food, they are not on the island.'

'They are not,' said Donald. 'The fire is out and Captain Lattimore would not allow that to happen. And look in the pot.'

Bissett looked and there was a rotting burnt mess covered in flies and maggots.

'They did not eat that meal,' said MacDonald, 'and I think that means that they have gone. Let me look around awhile.'

'But there is no-one here.'

'Aye David; I know that, but I'm not looking for people and I know Ralph Lattimore. Just haud on.'

MacDonald thought for a moment, then he went unhesitatingly into the fire-hut. His eyes adjusted to the gloom and he saw an inscribed wooden plank with a small sheet of paper poking out from under it. He read the inscription on the plank and then Lattimore's letter. When he had finished the letter he went outside and gave it to Bissett, who visibly relaxed and called out to his men, 'They've been rescued by a steamer and gone to Honolulu.' Smiles of relief broke out and men eased cartridges out from the breeches of their rifles.

'The *Mariposa* was due into Tuitila a few days after we left, Donald. It looks as if they have overtaken us and taken your people off. It might even have been that steamer we saw a week or so back, to judge by the date on that letter.'

'They're on their way home, David. That's all that matters.'

'Are you not disappointed, Donald? All your effort and all this way?'

'Oh, not at all. The *Mariposa* came here because her captain knew there were people to be rescued. He got here before us, and that is all to the good. It has saved those poor people many days on this island that they did not need to endure. No, I am not disappointed at all. Are you?'

'Oh no, I don't believe so; I'm being paid by the Consul, so I lose nothing. I'll have to run back to Apia of course and return these stores, but that's a minor matter. It was, for me, a business transaction; I am paid and so are my crew.'

'But did you not want to rescue them after all your trouble beating against the wind for a month?'

'Well I'll allow that it would have been a grand thing to have done, but if it is not to be then I shall shrug my shoulders and get on with life.'

'You're something of a fatalist I find.'

'I'm a realist, Donald. We are here; they have gone. Now we shall return to Samoa.'

'And I can go home.'

'That's what you want most?'

'Right now, more than anything in the world.'

Bissett looked at him speculatively.

'So you'd be glad of a steamship to carry you off as soon as possible.'

'No offence, David; you're good enough company and I am grateful for all you've done, but I'd love to see Glasgow again as soon as I can.'

'Well we'd best get you set out on that journey as soon as we can then.'

'I can't set out now though can I, David? I'm stuck on a schooner that's heading for Apia for the best part of the next three weeks. Then I can start thinking about getting home.'

Bissett clapped him on the shoulder.

'I know how it is for a man to wish to get home to see his family and friends. We should have a pretty fast run back to Samoa and the sooner we start the sooner you'll be there.'

'Haud on. Afore we go I have something to do.'

MacDonald crossed over to the flagpole and hauled down the Union flag. Folding it he put it inside his shirt and then with a sheepish grin he headed for the ship's boat.

'Now that was a good thought,' said Bissett.

'I'll not leave it there, and I may hang it on my wall as a reminder when I'm old and grey.'

Willie Ferguson also took an object from the site of the castaways' ordeal, and that was the plank that Ralph Lattimore had carved.

'The plank goes back to the man who carved it. He's my own cousin and he can hang that on his wall.'

'If he wants it,' said David Bissett. 'I doubt that I would want such a reminder, but I guess he might if it's worth your trouble to carry it home.'

'Well if he does not want it, then I shall keep it.' was the pithy reply.

As the schooner turned her stern to Palmyra Atoll and began to fly down the Trade winds back towards Samoa, MacDonald stared at the beach, the reef and the huts where his crew-mates and passengers had taken refuge after the shipwreck. Turning away finally, he gave vent to an involuntary 'Hmmph!'

'Penny for them, Donald.'

'Och well Willie, I was thinking that I am glad to have no more to do with that place. When I get back to Glasgow I think I'll head up to Lewis for a while and stay with my Aunty.'

'Where it's nice and cold.'

'Oh no. It's summer there now and beautiful.'

'Apart from the midges I imagine.'

'Now you've spoiled my reverie. But yes; it will be nice to be home.'

With a cracking wind behind her *Vindex* was back in Samoa in ten days. Donald MacDonald and William Ferguson had no difficulty at all securing places before the mast on the fast clipper *Samuel Plimsoll*. After a fast passage round Cape Horn following the classic clipper route, they arrived in London, her home port, by the end of August 1888. MacDonald took train to Glasgow and thence to Lewis, having kept his promise to his Aunt Margaret.

****

On the *Mariposa*, Ralph Lattimore's apprehension was growing as the days passed. He voiced his worry to Captain Hayward sotto voce at dinner one evening.

'I am really not looking forward to the publicity which you think is going to attend our arrival in San Francisco.'

'Now why would you not be? Have you an aversion to fame Ralph?'

'I have to be honest. I'm alright as the captain of a ship Henry, but if it comes to facing reporters and giving statements and speaking to them, I'm not happy about it.'

'Do I detect a trace of shyness?'

'You do. I am not one of those people who likes standing up in front of an audience, though I have seen that you revel in it.'

'Oh, I admit it. I am well aware that it is not to many men's tastes to be the centre of attention, but I love it.'

'You do seem to be rather more outgoing in that line than I.'

'Well I am afraid, Ralph, that you are just going to have to put up with it. If it's any comfort though, fame is a fickle mistress. It does not last long unless you work at it. You'll be the talk of the town for a day or so and then it will fade. Fear not my friend, you are not going to be a man of lasting notoriety.'

'You are speaking as if you have considerable experience in dealing with public attention, Henry. Have you?'

Hayward laughed loudly and forgot that the conversation was *a deux*, 'I admit that I have, though in my case I was not an active protagonist in the drama, but was pulled into it as an involuntary participant.'

'Your case?'

'Oh yes Ralph; there is a tale hanging here which I shall tell momentarily if you wish to hear it and have the patience to bear with my relating it, for I am not a natural teller of yarns.'

'Very well, you'd better tell me your tale I think; I am all ears.'

'Yes Captain Hayward; please do and tell us all if you will, for I am sure it will be diverting.'

Hayward looked at the Archbishop of Wellington and smiled as he looked round his table at his guests, who were now all listening to the conversation between the two men and looking at him in anticipation.

'Very well, Your Grace; the story is well known throughout the US and I suspect that it will be taught in law schools, from what I've been told, for many years to come, but it is entertaining enough. I'll start by saying that there is a great number of Chinese people working in San Francisco and that the US government was becoming alarmed by the numbers of them entering the country. So in 1881 a Treaty was set in place with China which prohibited further Chinese coming into the country for the next ten years.'

'For what reason were so many entering the United States, Captain?'

'To work, Your Grace.'

'Are they good workers?'

'I agree with one of our greatest literary men, Mark Twain. He finds them to be industrious, free from drunkenness, quiet and peaceable. As I recall he said that a disorderly Chinaman is rare and a lazy one does not exist. In California they are valued greatly and without them many of our public works would not exist, particularly the railways, the roads and large city buildings.'

'Then why did your government exclude more of such valuable labourers from entering your country?'

Hayward did not hesitate.

'Reasons of race, sir. I have no doubt of it. You will find some that avow that such an influx of cheap labour was depressing the wages of white workers, but to my mind it was a fear that they would turn California into a kind of Chinese enclave.'

'Was their fear justified?'

'Not to me; they make, for the most part, excellent citizens. I exclude the gang violence which has been imported from China; we could do without the Tongs, but your ordinary decent Chinese person makes a very good American if you give him a chance, though many do not.'

'Forgive me, Captain; please continue with your story.'

'Well it was in 1881 that a man called Chew Heong from San Francisco journeyed to Hawaii to visit relatives and work there for a couple of years. He had been working and living in the US as a resident for over a year. While he was away the US government passed the Chinese Exclusion Act, putting the 1881 treaty into US law. It prohibited all Chinese immigration and excluded them from US citizenship. Chew Heong was not troubled by it, because he was not an immigrant, but had a job, friends, family and a home in San Francisco. It was this that gave me one of the greatest headaches in my thirty years at sea.'

'Oh, how was that Captain?' asked Mrs Grayson.

'What Chew Heong did not know was that the act also stated that any Chinese who had settled in the US and left to go elsewhere, had to obtain certification permits for re-entry. Fact is that I did not know it either. Chew Heong boarded the *Mariposa* at Honolulu in September 1884 and we proceeded to San Francisco where the collector came aboard to examine the passenger manifest.'

'Collector, Captain Hayward?'

'Yes Mr Powell. Every US port has a collector whose task it is to examine who has a right to enter the US and who does not. He found Chew Heong's name on the list, interviewed him briefly and denied him entrance to the US.'

'What happened to him then?'

'I was obliged to detain him on the ship sir.'

'Did you have to throw him in the brig Captain?'

Hayward laughed pleasantly, 'No Mrs Grayson. We do have a brig and you are welcome to inspect it any time you wish, but I did not have to use it on this occasion.'

'So what did happen?'

'I took his word that he would not attempt to leave the ship and he stayed in his cabin. However, I did allow him to contact his friends ashore and they got him a lawyer. The result was that he sued for a writ of *habeas corpus* stating that the US was depriving him of his liberty by holding him a prisoner in a steamship in San Francisco Harbour.'

'That makes you sound like a real monster, Captain!'

'Oh, I did not take it so, ma'am. He was kept on the ship at the behest of the US government. I did not ask to be made his jailer, but I guess that's how it ended up.'

'Well not really; how did the matter end?'

'The local courts were divided on the issue and it was sent to the Supreme Court of the United States to decide.'

'But did the *Mariposa* not have to sail with him on board.'

'No, Ralph; my owner Mr Spreckels, as I have intimated previously, is a patriotic American. One of his vessels was involved in a very important law case so he took the *Mariposa* out of service. She stayed idle in San Francisco harbour until the Supreme Court made its decision.'

'You must have been kicking your heels Captain. Were you frightfully bored?'

'No, Your Grace. It was a make do and mend period. I had the ship cleaned, inspected everything, painted everything and made everything as it was when the ship was first launched. Besides, I was in my home port; my wife and daughter saw a lot of me and were pleased.'

'How long did they take? I imagine a very long time.'

'Not so; Mr Spreckels applied some pressure; he could not be expected to keep such a vital part of his business out of employ for an extended period so the case was expedited. The decision came in the early part of December '84 and it was in Chew Heong's favour.'

'You don't say!'

'I do Mr Powell. The Supreme Court of the United States ruled that he had the right to re-enter. It was just over two months in deciding which I understand is quick.'

'I should say so. What did you do when you heard the news?'

'I shook his hand, saw him onto the shore boat and wished him good luck. He was most cordial in his farewell and thanked me for looking after him.'

'You have not seen him since?'

'No Ralph; I have not. I understand though from legal people who have shipped with me, that the case is something of a cause célèbre and now features in the teaching of courses in law across the whole country. The *Mariposa* has a small claim to fame in the legal world. And of course it was in the newspapers, as this escapade of yours will be. It will not be her first time in the headlines; but I can, for the most part walk around town unrecognized. I am therefore in a very good position to inform you that the attention you will receive, unwelcome though it may be to you, will be fleeting and transitory.'

'You say so, and I pray you are right,' said Lattimore.

'Never mind Ralph,' said Hayward, clapping him on the shoulder. 'Newspapers and the public are fickle. I'm sure they will soon forget, but for the moment I recommend you revel in being the hero of the moment, and enjoy it.'

The Archbishop interjected, 'Captain Lattimore, I have had many dealings with the gentlemen of the press over many years and I offer a word of advice if I may.'

'Your advice would be very welcome Your Grace.'

'I recommend you to write out a short statement for the reporters in which you give a brief account of what happened to your ship, your crew and passengers, and yourself. It does not have to be very long, just enough to satisfy them so they can write their piece. You can hand them out when you land and that will minimize their unwelcome attentions.

'That would mean an awful lot of writing, Your Grace.'

'Not at all Ralph,' smiled Hayward. 'I'll get my clerk to type it out and print copies on the ship's press. We have time to do that.'

'You have a printing press?'

'We do; to print out the ship's newspaper. We must keep our guests informed and amused on their voyages with us, you know.'

Lattimore smiled, 'That is an excellent idea, Your Grace, and I thank you for it. I shall write the statement after dinner.'

Now that he had decided what to do, Lattimore diverted the conversation from himself by asking the Archbishop where he was heading. This proved to have just the effect he desired for the Archbishop smiled across his whole face in a great grin that lit up the room and his enormous beard wagged with laughter.

'I'm going to Rome!'

'You look as if it is something you are going to enjoy.'

'Yes, Captain Lattimore, it is. I love Rome. I have been before you see, but that was more than twenty years ago when I was sent there to rest. I was rather ill at the time, suffering with severe bronchial trouble and it was thought that the hot summer at the Holy See would help me. It did, but for much of the time I was feeling very fragile and did not see much of the country. This time I shall, because I feel as fit as a flea and I'm going on church business. But on the way, there it is that I shall have my real treat.'

'What might that be, Your Grace?'

'I'm going from New York to Queenstown for a short visit to a place that is dear to me.'

'You've lived in Ireland?'

'I had that joy, Captain Lattimore. A great blessing I think, for I fully enjoyed my time there when I taught Greek and Latin at the Marist College in Dundalk. There were young men preparing for the priesthood and for our New Zealand mission. I have been in New Zealand a long time, but I do admit that it will be wonderful to visit Dundalk again. I have happy memories of it and the friends I made there.'

The conversation around Captain Hayward's table drifted to the beauties of Ireland, skirting the problems of that troubled land, and on to Italy and the wonders of Florence, Assisi and of course Rome. Lattimore was thankful not to be the centre of it all. He wrote his statement and the ship's clerk obligingly printed off fifty copies. Hayward did not expect there to be reporters waiting when the *Mariposa* docked; there was, as yet, no telegraph cable between Hawaii and the US, but the news would spread like wildfire soon after they had landed. Lattimore was prepared.

Seven and a half days after leaving Honolulu, on 10 June 1888, the *Mariposa* entered the strait called the Golden Gate and sailed into San Francisco harbour, berthing at the Spreckels wharf in Potrero, where her passengers disembarked and went their ways with much well wishing, shaking of hands, and promises to meet again soon. Nothing throws people together so closely as a sea voyage. Hayward took Ralph Lattimore a short walk up into Potrero Hill, where a neat looking house behind a white fence was waiting for them. It was on this walk that Lattimore told Hayward that he had decided he wished to go home to Larne.

'Don't misunderstand me, Henry. I have appreciated your offer more than I can say and I see it as a great opportunity, but it's not for me. I have realized that however much I sail the world I do have a place that I call home and it's Ulster. Agnes will not wish to leave there either. I want to go back. I'm sorry if that disappoints you.'

Hayward smiled, 'It's your life Ralph and I have no axe to grind. I thought you might want to go home and I understand that. It's what I do every voyage. Now come in and meet my family and see what a good San Francisco welcome feels like.'

It did not take long for Hayward to explain to his wife and daughter the circumstances that had led him to bring a stranger home, though the questions and exclamations of wonder and admiration continued for hours, as he had to tell his tale in great detail. When he woke up the following morning there was a crowd of people outside the house, mostly very loud men, pushing and shoving each other. They were reporters, though thankfully a couple of local policemen had arrived and were keeping them in order and away from the door. Steeling himself, Lattimore went outside and answered a few questions before informing them that he had written a statement giving full particulars, and handed out the printed sheets he had prepared on the *Mariposa*. Within a few minutes the men had all gone, running excitedly down the road. By lunchtime his story was in the city newspapers; by evening throughout California and the west and by the following morning the whole United States. Over the next few days the story of the *Henry James* was syndicated throughout the Pacific area, Australia, New Zealand and even got a very small mention in some British papers. Several of the erstwhile passengers on the *Mariposa* were gratified to be quoted in some of these articles, and one of them, Mr William Sutherland, of Carnoustie, even had his whole account of the rescue published, though without his name being appended. On the first day though, when the reporters had gone, it was safe for Hayward to take his guest down to the office of the British Consul who supplied him with sufficient funds to buy a ticket on the Overland Flyer train two days hence. He also visited the telegraph office and was able to send a telegram reporting the loss of the *Henry James* to Gavin Cowper, the general manager of the North British Shipping Company in Glasgow. After two pleasant days closeted in the Hayward household, the captain of the *Mariposa* took Lattimore across to the Oakland Wharf where was a mile-long railway platform. This was the western terminus of the Pacific Railroad. With much shaking of hands and expressions of gratitude from Lattimore, he and Hayward parted, promising to meet again (which they eventually did) and Lattimore was on his way east. He did not have a first class ticket which would have given him a bed and a cabin to himself, but he did not have the cheapest either. He did not mind as he found himself in a cabin with four bunks in second class on the overland express; his companions were civilized men and thankfully none of them snored. Eighty-eight hours later he was in New York where he did not bother with the British consul. He headed straight for the Thomson Hotel which was owned and managed by a relative of his brother in law, where he was welcomed joyfully, and enabled to send a telegraph to Agnes at home telling her that he was safe and on his way home. After a day of rest he set out to find a means of putting the thought into action. Walking the docks until he found a steamship heading for Glasgow, he boarded and introduced himself to the captain; a week later he was home reporting to his employers and rejoicing that he was once more anonymous and able to spend some time with his wife in Larne.

Chapter 19

Rewards and Medals

'Come in!'

The Prime Minister was feeling fraught on this particular morning and in need of a cup of hot coffee. His head was aching and he felt rather irascible, a trait which he often feigned for use as a political tool, but which at the moment, was quite genuine. He knew very well that part of the reason for his feeling overworked was his own fault. A Prime Minister really had very little to do on a day-to-day basis because of the way the British Government worked. It would have been perfectly feasible to place a trusted confederate at the Foreign Office, but he wished to handle foreign affairs himself. They were so involved and delicate at times, such an intricate web of alliances, pushing, pulling, moving and shaking that he did not trust anyone else to oversee them. He liked being at the centre of a web of foreign relations that spanned the entire world. It also provided a certain variety to life, for it meant that he spent much of his working life not in the cavernous Cabinet Office, but in the rather more attractive office of the Foreign Secretary down the road; the staff made better coffee here too. The door opened and his secretary came in.

'Yes Wishaw?'

'The Chancellor of the Duchy of Lancaster, my lord.'

'My nephew; good. Send him in directly, if you will, and please fetch some coffee.'

The door opened again and the elegant etiolated form of Arthur Balfour entered.

'You wanted to see me, my lord.'

'Yes Arthur; I want you to arrange for something to be done to reward the Americans.'

'The Americans, my lord?'

'Yes; the ones that rescued the people off that island; the officers of that ship; oh yes, the *Mariposa*. Some sort of recognition for what they did.'

'But my understanding is that all they did was go to the island and ferry the people off. They did not even land, but transferred them from the boat that the survivors brought off themselves. Surely a cordial thank you would be sufficient?'

'Yes. I am aware of this, but I think it would foster an atmosphere of goodwill in their state department if we made some larger gesture in that direction. I do not wish to form an alliance with the Americans any more than with anyone else, but kindly feelings towards us in Washington are bought cheaply by such means.'

'Would it not be better coming from the Foreign Office, my lord?'

'Undoubtedly it would. But then of course it would have my hand all over it as from the British Prime Minister.'

'You want it done at a lower level.'

'You understand me perfectly. A muted but elegant recognition that will strike the right note; you have my permission to communicate with the relevant Consuls to make the arrangements. Just send me a copy of what you say.'

'Very well my lord; will that be all?'

'Not quite Arthur.' The Prime Minster peered at Balfour over his glasses. 'I want you to understand that I asked you in here because I wish this to be sorted out by you personally, and not some clerk or office boy. It must be done discreetly and if possible with barely a mention in the British Press. Let the Americans make of it what they will, but I want no fuss on this side of the water. Do you understand me?'

'Perfectly, my lord,' replied Balfour. 'It shall be as you wish. You may rely on me.'

'Oh I know I can Arthur, and even more on your ambitions. Let it be done smoothly.'

'As silk, my lord.'

So it was that Mr Charles Mason, Her Britannic Majesty's Vice Consul in San Francisco, intimated to Mr John D Spreckels, owner of the Oceanic Steamship Company, that the British government were highly appreciative of his conduct in the affair of the *Henry James* and were very complimentary in their remarks about Captain Hayward. Her Majesty's government would very much appreciate an opportunity at Mr Spreckels' earliest convenience of making a presentation to the gallant Captain Hayward and his crew for their heroic efforts in rescuing the crew and passengers of the *Henry James* from Palmyra Atoll. Mr Spreckels was delighted; invitations were issued far and wide for a dinner to be held on the *SS Mariposa* in San Francisco harbour on the evening of 15 December 1888. The company that attended the dinner and presentation was very distinguished, a gathering of the great, the good and the extremely rich; the very cream of Californian society. Press coverage was lavish; readers were reminded of the arduous feat of Chief Officer Hart and his men, who dragged a heavy boat miles across coral shoals in the course of rescuing the shipwrecked survivors of the *Henry James*. Mr Spreckels presided over a magnificently sumptuous meal with champagne and fine wine that would have done credit to the best hotel in San Francisco.

When the repast was at an end Mr EB Jerome, the Deputy Collector of Customs for the Port of San Francisco was invited to make the presentation with some appropriate words. His words were economical and to the point. The presentation of a handsome piece of plate for Captain Hayward had been made through the State Department by the British Government, which added great dignity and prestige to the occasion. He trusted that Captain Hayward would live long in the consciousness of having done a good and noble act, which had been signally recognized by the two greatest and most enlightened nations on earth, the United States and Great Britain. The presentation was an honour conferred on the entire American mercantile marine and he hoped that all saw it in this light. The captain had obeyed the higher laws of humanity and rescued one score and five of human beings who would otherwise have perished miserably. The risk, which Captain Hayward had taken in changing his course, had shown him to be a man of the greatest moral courage and the strongest human sympathies. Amidst loud applause Mr Jerome then presented Captain Hayward with a richly chased silver punch bowl, twelve inches in diameter; upon it was an oval space, which bore the following words:

"Presented by the British Government to Capt. HM Hayward, Master of the American ship Mariposa, of San Francisco, in acknowledgment of his humanity and kindness to the shipwrecked crew of the barque Henry James, of Glasgow, which was wrecked off Palmyra Island on the 10th of April 1888."

Mr James then presented a valuable gold medal to Chief Officer Hart that had a suitable inscription and silver medals with £2 each to the crew of his boat. Each gift was accompanied with appropriate words of praise. The presentation ended with the toasting of Captain Hayward's health.

In rising to reply, Captain Hayward disclaimed any special merit in the rescue and stated that the prime factor in such a case was that a captain should know his employers. When he received Commander Day's letter from Lieutenant Cressop about the plight of the castaways, his immediate reaction had been to ask himself what Mr Spreckels would say if he were present. He knew at once that Mr Spreckels would say 'go and rescue those people.' This modest speech brought further enthusiastic applause.

Mr Charles Mason, Her Brittanic Majesty's Vice Consul in San Francisco, paid several compliments to Captain Hayward and said that the conduct of Mr Spreckels had been highly appreciated by the British Government. The policy of the Oceanic Steamship Company was fine and manly and he trusted that it helped towards strengthening bonds of friendship that would help the development of several British colonies in the Pacific to the advantage of both parties. Mr Spreckels was much pleased with these remarks and said so.

First Officer Hart made a short speech in acknowledgement of the toasts made for him, but he was perhaps allowed to be slightly blasé, for in the course of his career at sea this was the third medal awarded to him by the British Government for saving life at sea. There followed a further round of toasts and after a most enjoyable evening the guests departed, as Captain Hayward shook hands with them at the top of the gangplank. All agreed that they were impressed with the hospitality of the President and Directors of the Oceanic Steamship Company and that the evening was a fitting kind of Roman triumph.

This might well have been the end of the matter as far as the British Government was concerned. Good feelings had been fostered between Britain and the United States, another brick in the building of a firm friendship between two great nations. There remained, however, one inconvenient fact; a humble Scottish seaman had accomplished something so remarkable and so brave that it is hardly surprising that The North British Shipping Company expected to hear that their employee was going to be honoured in his turn. When nothing was heard from the British Government the directors of the company decided to take matters into their own hands and in early 1889, forwarded the name of Donald MacDonald to the Board of

Trade, reiterating the heroism of what he had done. They reminded the President of the Board of Trade of the events surrounding the shipwreck of the *Henry James* and expressed the hope that MacDonald would receive the Board's medal for bravery at sea. This is the ultimate accolade to which a merchant seaman may aspire; an official record and recognition of the most exalted heroism; a seaman's version of the Victoria Cross. The recipient of such an award would expect to be feted and honoured. It was the prospect of this that forced the Prime Minister's hand into a second intervention in a matter that he might otherwise have considered to be closed. Reading in a Cabinet memorandum that MacDonald's name was about to be confirmed as a recipient of the medal for bravery at sea, The Prime Minster sent for the President of the Board of Trade.

'Sir Michael Hicks-Beach, my lord.'

'Good morning Michael; thank you for sparing me a few minutes this morning; I shall not detain you long. Do sit down.'

'Thank you, my lord. How may I be of service?'

The Prime Minister looked at him shrewdly and narrowed his eyes in what might have been a smile. It was difficult to tell; he was a heavy man with a large white beard, a bald head and a forbidding brow.

'I have a crisis brewing, Michael, that needs some very careful handling. Part of it is a minor matter with which I would appreciate your help.'

'Of course my lord; consider it already given.'

'Well I knew you'd say that, but I have to tell you in advance that I do not like asking you this favour; it means robbing a noble fellow of what is due to him. I really do not see any help for it though.'

'Sometimes politics makes us ruthless, but what needs to be done has to be done.'

'True enough.' The Prime Minister sighed and Hicks-Beach waited for him to set out what he wanted. 'It's about Samoa.'

'Yes, I saw the memorandum but it does not really concern the Board of Trade I think.'

'Ah well, yes it does in a small way. I shall explain. In a moment though; here is Wishaw with some tea.'

When the secretary had departed, the Prime Minister took a sip of his cup, and then began to set out his immediate concern.

'You will have heard that there has been a catastrophic disaster in Apia. What you may not have realized, because I have been keeping it rather sub fusc, is that nature averted something that might well have been rather more shattering.'

Hicks-Beach nodded. There had been a most enormous Pacific storm of gigantic strength in Samoa on 15 and 16 March 1889 which had blown in straight off the sea and wrecked almost every ship in the harbour at Apia. The United States had stationed the *USS Trenton,* the *USS Nipsic* and the *USS Vandalia* in that place to put in check the German warships *Adler, Eber and Olga.* Watching them had been the British corvette *HMS Calliope.* All save one had been driven onshore and utterly destroyed by the fury of the sea and wind; the loss of life had been very heavy.

'I understand that Captain Kane behaved in a very laudable way.'

'Oh yes, indeed. Every other ship dragged its anchor and could not make any headway against the force of the gale. *Calliope* had already been bumped you know by one ship. The *Vandalia* was heading straight for him completely helpless, but he slipped his anchor and avoided her. He managed to take the *Calliope* in the gap between her and the *Trenton*, which was sinking by then. There was nothing he could do in such a sea; the crew of the *Trenton*, poor fellows, cheered his seamanship as he took *Calliope* past and out to sea. I have in mind to do something for him, and I will. Such good thinking should be applauded in the service I think.'

'So what do you wish me to do, my lord?'

'Ah well; it's this chap MacDonald.'

'MacDonald, my lord?'

"Yes.' The Prime Minister waved a piece of paper at Hicks-Beach. 'Have you not seen this?'

'Oh, that MacDonald. Yes I have; a very valiant man; he's been put forward by his company for a Board of Trade medal. If it were not for his actions, I fancy that all those people who were stranded on Palmyra would be dead. He fills all the criteria perfectly and it will be a wave through I think.'

'Indeed. He is a noble fellow. I want you to reject his medal application.'

'Reject it my lord?'

'Yes Michael; it is regrettable, but I'm afraid it must be so.'

'Might I ask why, my lord?'

'You may, and I shall tell you, *entre-nous*. If you give MacDonald a Board of Trade medal for bravery at sea then you will make national heroes of him and his crew.'

'Would that be a bad thing, my lord? It seems to me that the country could use a few heroes right now.'

'Yes, it would be a bad thing. It would be all over the front pages of every newspaper in the land. There would be dinners in their honour, parades to welcome them home, receptions at the Palace and so on. It must not happen.'

Hicks-Beach did not answer, but lifted an eyebrow, knowing that the Prime Minister was going to continue.

'Don't you see Michael? That storm has created a power vacuum down there. The Germans will send some more warships and so will the Americans. I shall order *Calliope* to remain down there to keep an eye on things, but I do not want the great British public getting itself worked up about Samoa. If they do then every jingo in the land will be demanding that I send a battleship at least; maybe a squadron to throw our hat in the ring. You know my policy.'

'Splendid isolation, my lord.'

'Indeed. If we avoid alliances and entanglements, then this country will prosper. We do not align ourselves in the quarrels of others or wind ourselves about with expensive alliances with even more expensive obligations.'

'Yes, my lord.'

'Very well; given the strategic position of Samoa and my own wish not to over-extend our empire's resources in that region, it's been my policy to play umpire rather than become an active participant. The United States is a power friendly to us and has been signaling for some time that they wish to absorb the Samoan Islands into their own sphere of influence. I have no objection to that, and would far rather they had it than Her Majesty's blustering nincompoop grandson. Any notion entering the heads of some of our jingoes that we should have Samoa can only cause trouble and certainly no good. It was bad enough in September when that Scottish captain was killed in Apia.'

'I do not recall the incident, my lord.'

'No. You would not, because it was not in our newspapers; I made sure of that because I want no scallywags making hay with it. It was the poor chap that took MacDonald to Palmyra, David Bissett. It seems that he was hit in the head by a stray bullet as he left the British Consulate. So for that, among other reasons, I do not want the attention of our newspapers on events in Samoa. It might embroil us ultimately in a war down there.'

'With the Germans, my lord?'

'Yes, of course with the Germans. Bismarck is having his work cut out to contain Wilhelm at the moment and I would not be in the least surprised if the Chancellor was sacked before too long. If that young man takes matters into his own hands then we shall be in for a lot of trouble, believe me. Samoa is a possible flashpoint. I want this matter buried as far as possible and muted so that it is barely noticed. No medal.'

'No medal, my lord.'

'I've already had a word with some of the editors; the Press will bury it. That should have the effect I want.'

'I will do as you wish my lord. But what of MacDonald? The man is a hero. He should have something.'

The Prime Minster made a moue.

'I know you are right. He was very gallant, but I have made enquiries. He is a very modest and self-effacing man. If we do not make a fuss, then neither will he.'

'It does seem unjust that he should have nothing when he was the instrument of saving so many lives. The exploit that he pulled off is thoroughly admirable. As a man, I admire it myself.'

The Prime Minster sighed.

'It can't be anything official, Michael, I mean not from the government; if you must then have a word with Lloyds. They might feel inclined to do something for him. So long as it is not from the government, it can't do a lot of harm and will not attract much attention; please ensure that it does not.'

Donald MacDonald had been employed as First Mate on a regular steamer running freight from Glasgow to Belfast and back since his return from New York. He was puzzled on his return from the latest of these at the beginning of April 1889 to be met with a note requesting him to report at the office of Gavin Cowper, his company's General Manager as soon as possible. It was not long before he found himself in the company offices on the Govan Road and facing the manager.

'Sit down, MacDonald. You'll have a dram, I think.'

MacDonald was bemused enough at being called in to Head Office, but the offer of a whisky from a man in such an exalted position nonplussed him. Cowper detected his bewilderment.

'Aye, it's not every man I'd offer my best malt to, but the news I have to give you merits a drink in my opinion. You're not to be given a medal from the Board of Trade.'

'I'm not bothered about that, sir. I need no medals to do my job and that's all I was doing.'

'I thought you'd say that. It's well known that you are not a man for blowing his own trumpet, but the board of directors of the company you work for have different thoughts. Man, you and your crew did something straight out of a storybook for boys. It was heroic and I have to say that I think it's the single bravest thing I have ever come across in my life. Now I can see that I'm embarrassing you, but it's out of your hands. The government may not know its back from its front, but we do. Some idiot behind a desk in Whitehall decided to give a presentation, and much of the credit, to the Americans who reached Palmyra before you.'

'Well they did take the captain and survivors to safety. That was not done by me.'

'That's beside the point. They would not have known those people were there unless you had made that incredible journey. Anyway, you sound like the Board of Trade clerk who wrote to me telling me that they would not award you a medal because it was not you that carried out the rescue.'

'It's true enough.'

'Truth it might be MacDonald, but sometimes truth is not justice, so I come to the second part of what I wish to say to you. After strenuous representations by this company, and others amongst the Glasgow shipping community, Lloyds of London have been pleased to award you their medal for saving life at sea. As far as we are concerned, the government may take a long walk off a short pier. We are quite determined to honour you and I must ask you to accept the admiration and thanks of the mercantile fraternity of this city. No, it's no good protesting; this will be done. It's the highest accolade we can give you and we are sensible of the dignity of the proceedings. There will be a ceremony on Friday 26 April, but it will not be held here. Dunlop and Sons have a fine palatial building at 70

Wellington Street and they have offered the use of their grand hall for the presentation. I am to instruct you to be there. What's the matter? You're not looking very happy.'

'I am not over fond of large gatherings at the best of times, let alone one with me as the centre of attention. Would I be expected to speak, because I swear to God that it would be beyond me to do such a thing?'

'I would not have taken you for shy, MacDonald.'

'Nonetheless, I do not wish to speak to an audience, sir. Could I not just be given the medal by you privately?'

'Not a hope my friend; if you do not wish to speak then I understand why; it is not all men that like to address a crowd, but we have several people in our association that do. In fact many of them too much, for they do love the sound of their own voices. Fear not, I shall represent your worries to the Board and someone will be nominated to speak on your behalf on account of modesty. It will be fine.'

'Will the other men be there? My boat crew?'

'No. They have each received letters commending their actions from the company and have been rewarded with gifts of money. At any rate, each of them is on a different ship and on different oceans. This medal is for you, MacDonald; you led this thing. Have you seen Captain Lattimore since you got back?'

'Yes sir; he gave me a braw dinner and a few drams when I saw him back in February. I was able to return his telescope to him.'

'Oh yes; I recall that you ate the leather off the telescope.'

'We did, but I had it rebound, which pleased him. Will he be at this presentation?'

'No. As you are aware he was given the *Carnmoney* and she is halfway to Australia at this moment.'

'She's a fine barque; I am glad he was given a new command so quickly. He's a good captain.'

'So he is. We could not have a man of his abilities staying idle on the shore; we know very well that the loss of the *Henry James* was not down to any fault on his part. And we have no fears for the *Carnmoney*. Captain Lattimore was most particular in the purchase of a complete set of the most up to date Pacific charts.'

'It's a pity he cannot speak for me.'

'Well there it is; but never fear. The man we choose will do you full justice. Now lastly, we forwarded a letter to you from Reverend Taylor. He said some very handsome things about you and much to your credit. There was a private insert in a second envelope; I trust that it was as complimentary.'

'It was, sir, and very good of him, but I was only doing what had to be done.'

'He said his girls were writing to you.'

'Aye they did; each of them wrote me a wee note thanking me; it was braw.'

'Mr MacDonald; you have nothing to fear from having dinner with a few folk and accepting a medal. You are a very popular man with a lot of people.'

'I do know it sir, but I have to admit that the thought of speaking in public fair makes me think to boak.'

'Well you won't have to, so put it out of your mind.'

Watching MacDonald walk down the street after he had left the offices, Cowper shook his head, marveling at the human condition which could make a man brave enough to dare the Pacific Ocean in an open boat, yet feel sick at the thought of addressing a few Glasgow businessmen.

'It takes all sorts to make a world; one of the bravest men I have ever met, and yet…'

He shook his head and went back to his desk.

Whether or not MacDonald's fears were allayed, and whatever the attitude of the Board of Trade, it did not matter. The desire to show esteem, and determination to recognize merit in one of their own, could not be extinguished among the Glasgow shipping merchants. Those who gathered to do honour to MacDonald and his crew were the leading lights in a very select brotherhood and this was plain in the selection of the presiding chairman. It was Mr Nathaniel Dunlop, owner of the Allan Line. He related the tale of the *Henry James* presenting the facts of the matter in fulsome and heroic terms before likening MacDonald's actions to those of a winner of the Victoria Cross. Some of what he said was not quite accurate, for he stated that the captain had asked for volunteers to take a boat to Samoa, but then he described the voyage itself.

'…It was an enterprise of danger and privation, but yourself and others volunteered for it, even more in number than were needed, for happily there is no shortage of courage in the British sailor in time of peril.'

Here Mr Dunlop had to pause as the applause of the audience was deafening.

He continued in like vein.

'I do not know of anything in the annals of navigation more daring than that done by those men in that boat. (Applause) The privation, suffering and dangers of that dreadful journey are too harrowing to be narrated.'

Finishing his retelling of the tale, Mr Dunlop continued; '…you were enabled to return to Great Britain with the consciousness of having done, along with your comrades who I have named, one of the noblest deeds that the annals of merchant shipping record.' (Applause)

Now Mr Dunlop grew indignant and his peroration trenchant.

'I am glad to say that when our Government, which should be foremost in such things, are insensible, as they seem to have been in your case, to your claims to their recognition, that Lloyds have stepped in with this testimonial. Intrinsically it is of little value, but in reality it is no mean prize. It is the token that your countrymen have heard of your praiseworthy deeds, have appreciated and rewarded them, and desire that you should have them in remembrance. I hope you will keep this medal, which it gives me great pleasure to hand to you, as a testimony of how your countrymen regard the enterprise that you led with such courage, humanity and skill to such a successful end (Applause). I congratulate you on being the recipient of such an honour.'

As Mr Dunlop finished, there was a murmur of agreement that turned to cheers that threatened to raise the roof. MacDonald turned pink with emotion as he shook hands, then sat down as Mr Lyle from his own company rose to respond for him. He acknowledged the presentation and reminded the assembly that it was MacDonald's fears for some little girls and their mother that induced him to undertake such a hazardous enterprise. Mr Lyle was pleased to record the gratification of his firm that Lloyds Committee had stepped in and awarded this medal. The shareholders of the company had presented each man with a generous cheque, but this medal was of more value inasmuch that it was a public recognition of a noble deed, done in a brave and noble manner, one of the noblest in the merchant shipping records. This last brought the house down with tumultuous applause and Donald left the ceremony feeling both gratified and abashed, with many slaps on the back to a roaring chorus of 'For he's a jolly good fellow' and three loud cheers.

The refusal of his own government to recognize what he had done did not trouble Donald MacDonald one little bit. In his mind he had been doing his job and the course he had taken was one in which he had no option, for being the man he was, the choice to sail to Samoa was the only one he felt he should have taken. The difficulties he had faced were to do with the sea and he was a man of the sea; it was his chosen and only vocation. As a man he could not stand while women and children suffered hunger and danger of starvation; he answered the need in the only way that he could. As the meeting broke up, his medal snug in a presentation box in his pocket, he shook hands with Mr Lyle who asked him to come and see him in the morning. The company valued men like him and would do things for his career; he could sleep well at home knowing that he had good prospects. He still did not wish to be a captain, though it was good to know that his constant employment was assured. Smiling at the thought, Donald MacDonald went out into Wellington Street and, like the modest man he was, stepped calmly out of history and went home to Lewis and to Aunt Margaret's cooking. Of the award, the medal and the praise, and even the voyage he had told her nothing and never would; she would only worry.

Gracenote

Donald MacDonald had made up his mind that he would not attempt to become captain of his own ship; his thinking never changed and he did not wish to have the responsibility. When he had rested long enough at home in Lewis, he once again took to the sea to earn his living, but always as a first officer. He liked the circumnavigational trade, for the journey to Australia, to the west coast of the United States and back home round Cape Horn was a thing that challenged his seamanship and appealed to the sense of the professional. Such a voyage also paid better than the shorter journeys that he might have had in coasting round Europe, or in the transatlantic routes. So it was that in 1896, eight years after the wreck of the *Henry James,* MacDonald found himself at Portland, Oregon. He was first officer on the *Auldgirth,* a fine barque only four years old, and his mind was at peace with the world. He leaned on the taffrail of the ship which was moored close up against the public quay; he puffed on his pipe, for there were two more days until he sailed and he had a few slack hours. He watched the busy life of the port in front of him with dozens of people going to and fro about their business.

Suddenly he realized that there were two young women standing at the bottom of the gangplank and one of them was calling up to him.

'Excuse me sir, but were you ever the mate on board the *Henry James?'*

Somewhat startled by this reminder from the past, MacDonald moved down towards them and replied,

'Well ladies, I saw the last of that ship.'

To his complete astonishment the young woman who had asked the question walked up towards him tearfully and pulled one of her gloves off. On her finger was a gold ring which she took off and gave to him. He recognized it at once as his own. With much emotion he put his hands on her shoulders and with some difficulty spoke to her.

'Then you are Laura Mary Hastings.'

'I am sir,' she replied. smiling and sobbing at the same time. 'And this is my sister Ada.'

Printed in Great Britain
by Amazon